A Book Of

FINANCIAL SERVICES

For

B.B.A. Semester - VI

As Per New Syllabus w.e.f. 2015

Dr. Nachiket M. Vechalekar
Associate Dean - Post Graduate Programmes
IndSearch

Mrs. Rekha V. Kankariya
M. Com., D.T.L., MBA (Finance), NET
Assistant Professor,
St. Mira's College for Girls,
Pune.

NIRALI PRAKASHAN
ADVANCEMENT OF KNOWLEDGE

N3466

Financial Services - BBA (Semester - VI) ISBN 978-93-5164-840-6

First Edition : December 2015
© : Authors

Published By :
NIRALI PRAKASHAN
Abhyudaya Pragati, 1312, Shivaji Nagar,
Off J.M. Road, PUNE – 411005
Tel - (020) 25512336/37/39, Fax - (020) 25511379
Email : niralipune@pragationline.com

☞ **DISTRIBUTION CENTRES**

PUNE
Nirali Prakashan : 119, Budhwar Peth, Jogeshwari Mandir Lane, Pune 411002, Maharashtra
Tel : (020) 2445 2044, 66022708, Fax : (020) 2445 1538
Email : bookorder@pragationline.com, niralilocal@pragationline.com
Nirali Prakashan : S. No. 28/27, Dhyari, Near Pari Company, Pune 411041
Tel : (020) 24690204 Fax : (020) 24690316
Email : dhyari@pragationline.com, bookorder@pragationline.com

MUMBAI
Nirali Prakashan : 385, S.V.P. Road, Rasdhara Co-op. Hsg. Society Ltd.,
Girgaum, Mumbai 400004, Maharashtra
Tel : (022) 2385 6339 / 2386 9976, Fax : (022) 2386 9976
Email : niralimumbai@pragationline.com

☞ **DISTRIBUTION BRANCHES**

JALGAON
Nirali Prakashan : 34, V. V. Golani Market, Navi Peth, Jalgaon 425001,
Maharashtra, Tel : (0257) 222 0395, Mob : 94234 91860

KOLHAPUR
Nirali Prakashan : New Mahadvar Road, Kedar Plaza, 1st Floor Opp. IDBI Bank
Kolhapur 416 012, Maharashtra. Mob : 9850046155

NAGPUR
Pratibha Book Distributors : Above Maratha Mandir, Shop No. 3, First Floor,
Rani Jhanshi Square, Sitabuldi, Nagpur 440012, Maharashtra
Tel : (0712) 254 7129

DELHI
Nirali Prakashan : 4593/21, Basement, Aggarwal Lane 15, Ansari Road, Daryaganj
Near Times of India Building, New Delhi 110002
Mob : 08505972553

BENGALURU
Pragati Book House : House No. 1, Sanjeevappa Lane, Avenue Road Cross,
Opp. Rice Church, Bengaluru – 560002.
Tel : (080) 64513344, 64513355,Mob : 9880582331, 9845021552
Email:bharatsavla@yahoo.com

CHENNAI
Pragati Books : 9/1, Montieth Road, Behind Taas Mahal, Egmore,
Chennai 600008 Tamil Nadu, Tel : (044) 6518 3535,
Mob : 94440 01782 / 98450 21552 / 98805 82331,
Email : bharatsavla@yahoo.com

niralipune@pragationline.com | www.pragationline.com

Also find us on ⓕ www.facebook.com/niralibooks

Preface ...

With a gross domestic product that is growing by more than 7 percent a year, India has made remarkable progress ever since opening its economy, in 1991. The country has accomplished this feat despite the substantial handicap of an underdeveloped financial sector.

India's financial system holds one of the keys, to the country's future growth trajectory. A growing, increasingly complex market-oriented economy and its rising integration with global trade and finance, India requires deeper, more efficient and well-regulated financial markets. It's a well-known fact that finance is the lifeline for any business enterprise. Therefore a nation's economy must be based on a sound financial system.

The financial services industry is one of the largest industries in the world today and has transformed markets and national economies bringing in its wake progress and prosperity to countries and regions. Both national and international economies have become dependent on the financial services industry.

The objective of this book is to acquaint students with the various financial services in India and to give them an insight into financial markets. Thus, the intention behind writing this book is to provide an understanding of the various financial services, financial markets and institutions primarily in an Indian context.

The book would be found useful by a wide section of readers. The teachers and students of finance, management and commerce would find it of special interest and use.

The book has been written strictly according to the syllabus prescribed for the students of BBA. We wanted a textbook that students would find user friendly, a book they would enjoy reading and could learn from on their own.

This book reflects the efforts of many people. First and foremost, we would like to thank Mr. Jignesh Furia. We would also like to thank the entire team at Nirali Prakashan for being instrumental in ensuring the quality and usefulness of the textbook. Finally a special thanks to our family members for their constant encouragement and support.

In spite of the significant effort that has been expended on this book, it would be safe to say that some errors may still exist. In an attempt to create the most error free and useful textbook possible, we strongly encourage both instructors and students to write me or Nirali Prakashan with comments and suggestions for improving the textbook. We welcome and value your input!

Authors

Syllabus ...

1. Indian Financial System : An Overview (9)

1.1 Introduction to Financial System

1.2 Structure of Financial System - Financial Institutions, Financial Markets, Financial Instruments and Financial Services

1.3 Overview of Indian Financial System since 1991

1.4 Financial Intermediaries in Financial System: Merchant Bankers, Underwriters, Depositories, Brokers, Sub brokers, Bankers etc.

2. Introduction to Financial Markets (14)

2.1 Capital Market - Primary Market – Management of IPO, Secondary Market – Stock Exchanges in India – Introduction, NSE, BSE, OTCEI

2.2 Role of SEBI as a regulatory authority

2.3 Introduction to Derivatives, Futures and Options

2.4 Money Market – Introduction, Money Market instruments – Call and Notice money market, Treasury Bill, Commercial Papers, Certificate of Deposits, Money Market Mutual Fund, Inter corporate deposits

2.5 Difference between Money Market and Capital Market

3. Financial Services in India (9)

3.1 Mutual Fund

3.2 Factoring and Forfeiting

3.3 Credit Rating

3.4 Venture Capital

4. Banking and Insurance Sector in India (5)

4.1 Introduction

4.2 Structure of Banking and Insurance Sector in India

4.3 Role of RBI and IRDA as a regulatory authority

5. Recent Trends in Accounting and Finance (11)

5.1 Zero Base Budgeting

5.2 Inflation Accounting

5.3 Human Resource Accounting

5.4 Activity Based Costing

5.5 Mergers and Acquisition

✍ ✍ ✍

Contents ...

✍ ✍ ✍

Chapter **1** ...

Indian Financial System: An Overview

Contents ...

Learning Objectives ...

- To study the Indian Financial System
- To discuss the Structure of the Indian Financial System
- To know the History of the Indian Financial System
- To explain the Role of various Financial Intermediaries in the Financial System

1.1 Introduction

The word money is derived from the Latin word 'Moneta' which was the name of an ancient Roman Goddess of marriage and queen of the Gods. The Roman Goddess 'Juno Moneta' was the protector of funds and money in ancient Rome.

Money is a necessity for mankind. It is required to satisfy the basic needs of food, clothing and shelter. Likewise, it is equally important for a modern economy. Perhaps, the easiest way to think about the importance of money is to consider a situation without money; we would still be stuck with the barter economy, which had its own difficulties and limitations.

Money is something that holds its value over time and can be easily translated into prices and is widely accepted. Oxford Dictionary defines money as 'a medium of exchange in the form of coins and banknotes'. Hence, it is an item or verifiable record that is generally accepted as payment for goods and services and repayment of debts in a particular country or socio-economic context.

"Money is a matter of four functions, a medium, a measure, a standard, a store".

The term **"Finance"** simply put is perceived as equivalent to '**Money**'. In Economics we read about Money and Banking, about Monetary Theory and Practice and about Public Finance. But finance exactly is not money; it is the source of providing funds for a particular activity. It is one of the most useful instruments that man has ever created. One cannot imagine a world without money or finance.

George Christy and **Peter Roden** state that "to finance means to arrange payment for it." They further observe that finance may be generally defined as the study of money, its nature, creation, behaviour, regulation and problems. Hence Finance is the study of money management.

Three aspects of the study of money are relevant in the study of finance –

1. The connection between the total supply of money on the one hand and price levels and business activity on the other.

2. The structure and behaviour of the financial system which is based on money.

3. The role of the financial system as a barometer of business conditions.

All financial activities guide us to believe that finance is management of money. However, the scope of finance is broader which includes arranging for money and making efficient use of the same. A few common objections which are given against the description of finance as money management are –

1. Many activities associated with finance like payment for things, giving or getting credit do not necessarily require the use of money.

2. Money is not what ultimately pays for things.

3. Money, like goods and services, can be bought and sold.

Thus, we can say that finance is a source of funding an activity and proper management of money is called finance. In this respect providing or securing finance by itself is a distinct activity or function, which results in Financial Management, Financial Services and Financial Institutions.

1.2 Financial System

1.2.1 Introduction

The study and understanding of various financial services necessitates knowledge of the financial system prevailing in the country. The financial system plays a very important role in bringing about economic development of any country. It consists of financial institutions and the mechanism which affects the generation, mobilisation and distribution of savings of the community among all those who demand the funds for investment purposes. A healthy and a sound financial system lead to economic development by stimulating the accumulation of capital and efficient allocation of the same. The prime function of a financial system is to establish a bridge between the savers and the investors and to help transformation of savings into investments. The economic development of a nation is reflected by the progress of the various economic units, broadly classified into corporate sector, government and household sector. While performing their activities, these units will be placed in a surplus/deficit/balanced budgetary situation.

1.2.2 Meaning

A system is a set of interrelated parts working together to achieve some purpose. The word "system", in the term "financial system", implies a set of complex and closely connected or interlined institutions, agents, practices, markets, transactions, claims, and liabilities in the economy. The financial system is concerned about money, credit and finance – the three terms are intimately related yet are somewhat different from each other. Indian financial system consists of financial market, financial instruments and financial intermediation. Procedures and practices adopted in the markets and financial interrelationships are also parts of the system. The financial system is concerned with money, credit and finance – the terms are intimately related but somewhat different from each other.

- Money refers to the returned medium of exchange or means of payment.
- Credit or loan is a sum of money to be returned normally with interest. It refers to a debt of an economic unit.
- Finance is monetary resource comprising debt and ownership funds of the state, company or person.

A typical structure of a financial system in any economy is given below.

There are areas or people with surplus funds and there are those with a deficit. A financial system or financial sector functions as an intermediary and facilitates the flow of funds from the areas of surplus to the areas of deficit. A financial system is a composition of various institutions, markets, regulations and laws, practices, money manager, analysts, transactions and claims and liabilities.

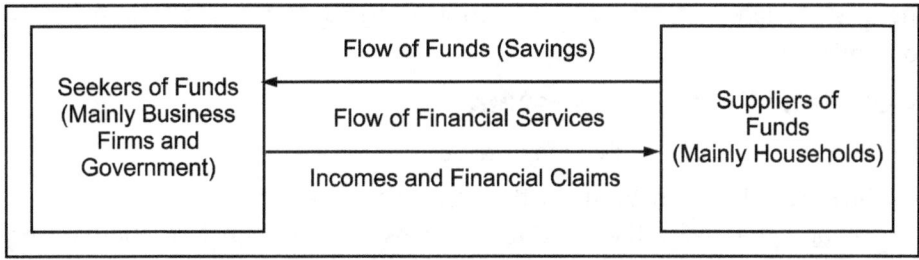

Fig. 1.1: Financial System

1.2.3 Definitions

1. A financial system may be defined as a set of institutions, instruments and markets which foster savings and channel them to their most efficient use.   **H. R. Machiraju.**

2. A system that aims at establishing and providing a regular, smooth, efficient and cost effective linkage between depositors and investors is known as financial system.

3. A set of complex and closely connected instructions, agents, practices, markets, transactions, claims and liabilities relating to financial aspects of an economy may be referred to as a financial system.

Thus, we can say that all the activities related to finance and organised into a system may be called financial system. The financial system plays a very important role in leading the country to economic development. This is achieved by accelerating the accumulation of capital and judicious allocation of the same. A well-developed financial system allows for the transfer of resources from depositors to investors and facilitates smooth functioning of the economy.

1.2.4 Features of Financial System

1. **Important Connecting Link:** The financial system serves as an ideal link between depositors and investors, which leads to acceleration in savings and investments. It tries to establish a bridge between the savers and the investors and helps transform the savings into investments.

2. **Expansion of markets:** It is possible with the help of a sound financial system. The participants in the market are linked by formal trading rules and communication networks for originating and trading financial securities.

3. **Efficient allocation of resources:** A well developed financial system ensures efficient allocation of scarce financial resources. Moreover, allocation is for socially desirable and economically productive purposes.

4. **Leads to economic development:** The economy as a whole is a beneficiary of a well developed financial system. Economic activity and growth are also greatly facilitated. There is efficiency of the market in mobilising savings and allocating them among competing users.

1.2.5 Groups of Financial System

A financial system consists of two major groups namely –

1. **Institutions:** All the institutions that encourage savings among the public, collect, transfer and channelise the same to the investors. These include the banking system, the insurance companies, mutual funds and investment funds.

2. **Investors:** This category includes individual investors, industrial and trading companies, government etc.

1.2.6 Structure of Financial System

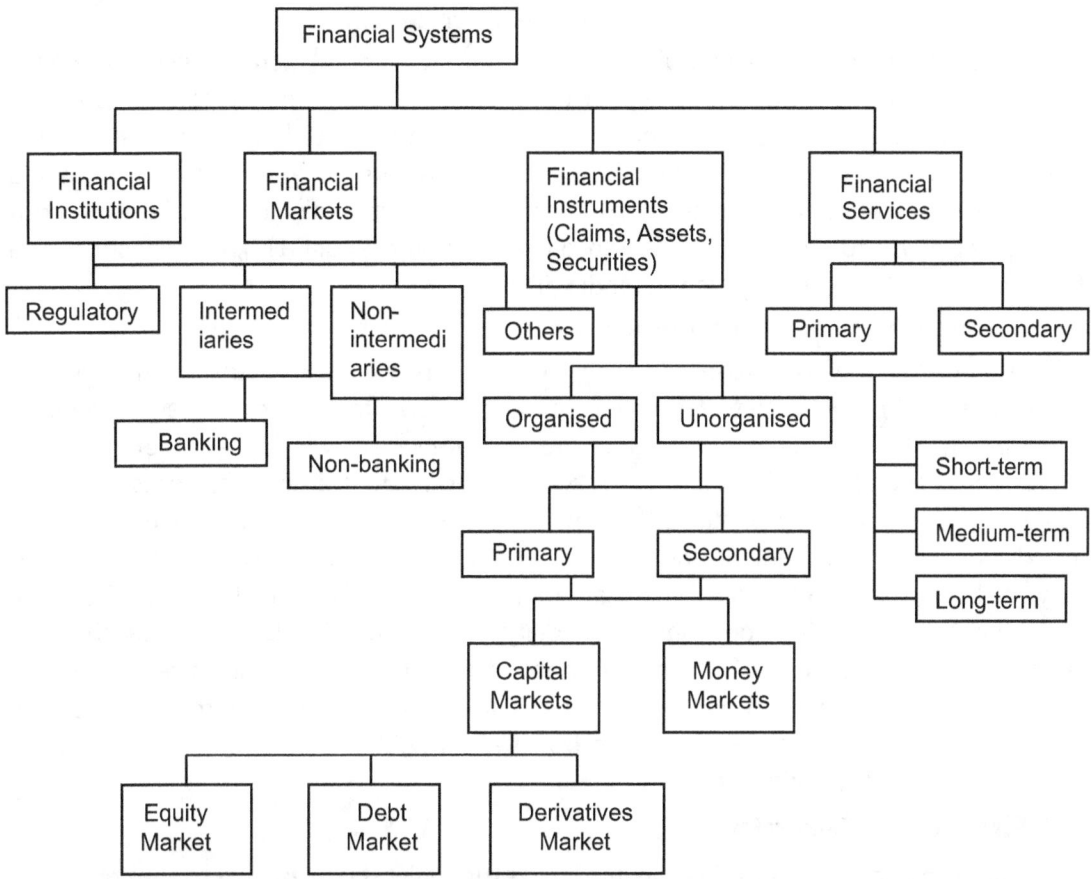

Fig. 1.2: Classification of Financial System into various Parts and Types

1.2.7 Financial Institutions

'Financial Institutions' are business organisations that act as mobilisers and depositories of savings and as purveyors of credit or finance. They also provide various financial services to the community. They differ from 'Non-financial (industrial and commercial) Business Organisations. They deal in financial assets such as deposits, loans, securities and so on and the business organisations deal with real assets such as machinery, equipment, stocks of goods, real estate and so on.

Classification of Financial Institutions

1. Banking and Non-Banking Institutions

According to one classification, financial institutions are divided into banking and non-banking ones. The banking institutions have quite a few things in common with the non-banking ones, but their distinguishing character lies in the fact that, unlike other institutions –

(a) They participate in the economy's payment mechanism, that is, they provide transaction services;

(b) Their deposit liabilities constitute a major part of the national money supply;

(c) They can, as a whole, create deposits or credit, which is money.

Banks subject to legal reserve requirements can advance credit by creating claims against themselves, while other institutions can lend only out of resources put at their disposal by the savers. The distinction between the two has been highlighted by characterising the former as "creators" of credit, and the latter as mere "purveyors" of credit. While the banking system in India comprises commercial banks and co-operative banks, the examples of non-banking financial institutions are Life Insurance Corporation of India (LIC), Unit Trust of India (UTI) and Industrial Development Bank of India (IDBI).

2. Intermediaries and Non-Intermediaries

This is another way of classification of financial institutions. As the term indicates, intermediaries intermediate between savers and investors, they lend money as well as mobilise savings; their liabilities are towards the ultimate savers, while their assets are from the investors or borrowers. Non-intermediary institutions do the loan business but their resources are not directly obtained from the savers. All banking institutions are intermediaries. Many non-banking institutions also act as intermediaries and when they do so they are known as Non-banking Financial Intermediaries (NBFI). The UTI, LIC and GIC are some of the NBFIs in India. The non-intermediary institutions like IDBI, IFC and NABARD came into existence because of the government efforts to provide assistance for specific purposes, sectors and regions. Their creation as a matter of policy has been motivated by the philosophy that the credit needs of certain borrowers might not be otherwise adequately met by the usual private institutions.

1.2.8 Financial Markets

A financial market can be defined as the market in which financial assets are created or transferred. As against a real transaction that involves exchange of money for real goods or services, a financial transaction involves creation or transfer of a financial asset. Financial assets or financial instruments represent a claim to the payment of a sum of money sometime in the future and /or periodic payment in the form of interest or dividend.

1. **Money Market:** The money market is a wholesale debt market for low-risk, highly-liquid, short-term instrument. Funds are available in this market for periods ranging from a single day up to a year. This market is dominated mostly by government, banks and financial institutions.

2. **Capital Market:** The capital market is also called as the Securities Market and is designed to finance the long-term investments. It is the market from where productive capital is raised and made available for industrial purpose. It may be defined as a market for borrowing and lending long-term capital funds required by business enterprises. It is an ideal source of external finance and it is classified into primary and secondary market in India. The transactions taking place in this market will be for periods over a year.

3. **Forex Market:** The forex market deals with the multicurrency requirements, which are met by the exchange of currencies. Depending on the exchange rate that is applicable, the transfer of funds takes place in this market. This is one of the most developed and integrated markets across the globe. It is a market where foreign exchange is bought and sold. The purpose of such a market is to facilitate international trade and investments.

4. **Credit Market:** Credit market is a place where banks, FIs and NBFCs purvey short, medium and long-term loans to corporates and individuals.

1.2.9 Financial Instruments

(A) Money Market Instruments

The money market can be defined as a market for short-term money and financial assets that are near substitutes for money. The term short-term means generally a period up to one year and near substitutes to money is used to denote any financial asset which can be quickly converted into money with minimum transaction cost.

The instruments dealt within the money market are liquid and can be turned over quickly at a low transaction cost and without loss of value.

Some of the important money market instruments are briefly discussed below –

1. Call/Notice Money
2. Treasury Bills
3. Term Money
4. Certificate of Deposits
5. Commercial Papers

1. Call/Notice Money Market

Call/Notice money is the money borrowed or lent on demand for a very short period. When money is borrowed or lent for a day, it is known as Call (Overnight) Money. Intervening holidays and/or Sundays are excluded for this purpose. Thus, money borrowed on a day and repaid on the next working day, (irrespective of the number of intervening holidays) is "Call Money". When money is borrowed or lent for more than a day and up to 14 days, it is "Notice Money". No collateral security is required to cover these transactions.

2. Inter-Bank Term Money

Inter-bank market for deposits of maturity beyond 14 days is referred to as the term money market. The entry restrictions are the same as those for Call/Notice Money except that, as per existing regulations, the specified entities are not allowed to lend beyond 14 days.

3. Treasury Bills

Treasury Bills are short-term (up to one year) borrowing instruments of the union government. It is an IOU of the government. It is a promise by the government to pay a stated sum after expiry of the stated period from the date of issue (14/91/182/364 days, that is, less than one year). They are issued at a discount to the face value, and on maturity the face value is paid to the holder. The rate of discount and the corresponding issue price are determined at each auction.

4. Certificate of Deposits

A marketable document of title to a time deposit for a specified period may be referred to as a 'Certificate of Deposit' (CD). It takes the form of a receipt given by a bank or any other institution for funds deposited with it by the depositor. It is a negotiable money market instrument and issued in dematerialised form or as a Usance Promissory Note, for funds deposited at a bank or other eligible financial institution for a specified time period. They are in the form of negotiable term-deposit certificates issued by commercial banks/financial institutions at a discount to face value at market rates with a maturity period ranging from 15 days to one year.

Guidelines for issue of CDs are presently governed by various directives issued by the Reserve Bank of India, as amended from time to time. CDs can be issued by (i) scheduled commercial banks excluding Regional Rural Banks.(RRBs) and Local Area Banks (LABs); and (ii) select all-India financial institutions that have been permitted by RBI to raise short-term resources within the umbrella limit fixed by RBI. Banks have the freedom to issue CDs depending on their requirements. An FI may issue CDs within the overall umbrella limit fixed by RBI, that is, issue of CDs together with other instruments, namely, term money, term deposits, commercial papers and inter-corporate deposits should not exceed 100 percent of its net owned funds, as per the latest audited balance sheet.

5. Commercial Paper

Debt instruments that are issued by corporate houses for raising short-term financial resources from the money market are called Commercial Papers (CPs). They are unsecured debts of corporates evidencing the debt obligation of the issuer. On issuing commercial paper the debt obligation is transformed into an instrument. CP is thus an unsecured promissory note privately placed with investors at a discount rate to face value determined by market forces. These are redeemable at par on maturity and are freely negotiable by endorsement and delivery.

A company shall be eligible to issue CP provided –

(a) The tangible net worth of the company, as per the latest audited balance sheet, is not less than ₹ 4 crore;

(b) The working capital (fund-based) limit of the company from the banking system is not less than ₹ 4 crore and

(c) The borrowable account of the company is classified as a standard asset by the financing bank/s. The minimum maturity period of CP is 7 days. The minimum credit rating shall be P-2 of CRISIL or such equivalent rating by other agencies.

(B) Capital Market Instruments

The capital market generally consists of the following long-term period, that is, more than one year period, financial instruments; in the equity segment equity shares, preference shares, convertible preference shares, non-convertible preference shares etc. and in the debt segment debentures, zero coupon bonds, deep discount bonds etc.

(C) Hybrid Instruments

Hybrid instruments are so called as they resemble equity as well as debentures, that is, they have both the features of equity and debentures. Examples are convertible debentures, warrants etc.

1.2.10 Financial Services

Services that are offered by finance companies are called as 'financial services'. An orderly functioning of the financial system depends, to a great extent, on the range and the quality of financial services extended by a host of providers.

Financial services serve the needs of individuals, institutions and corporates through the network of elements such as financial institutions, financial markets and financial instruments. They are regarded as the fourth element of the financial system.

Financial systems deal in financial services and claims that are many and varied in character. This is so because of the diversity of motives behind borrowing and lending. The general characteristics of these claims are given in the following sections.

1. Financial Asset

The financial asset represents a claim to the payment of a sum of money sometime in the future (repayment of principal) and/or a periodic (regular or not so regular) payment in the form of interest or dividend. With regard to bank deposits or government bonds or industrial debentures, the holder receives both the regular periodic payments and the repayment of the principal at a fixed date. Whereas, with regard to ordinary shares or periodic bonds, only periodic payments are received (which are regular in the case of perpetual bonds that may be irregular in the case of ordinary shares).

2. Financial Securities

Financial securities are classified as primary (direct) and secondary (indirect) securities. The primary securities are issued by the ultimate investors directly to the ultimate savers as ordinary shares and debentures; while the secondary securities are issued by the financial intermediaries to the ultimate savers as bank deposits, units, insurance policies and so on.

Financial instruments differ from each other in respect of their investment characteristics which, of course, are interdependent and interrelated. Among the investment characteristics of financial assets of financial products, the following are important: (i) liquidity, (ii) marketability, (iii) reversibility, (iv) transferability, (v) transaction costs, (vi) risk of default or the degree of capital and income certainty and a wide array of other risks, (vii) maturity period, (viii) tax status, (ix) options such as, call-back or buy-back, (x) volatility of prices and (xi) the rate of return – nominal, effective and real.

Features of Financial Services

- Financial services are intangible in nature.
- Quality of service provided and innovativeness are the main ingredients for gaining the trust of the clients.
- Financial services are highly customer-oriented. They develop innovative financial strategies that give due regard to costs, liquidity and maturity for various financial products.
- Services have to be performed simultaneously, that is, creating and supplying financial services are joint tasks keeping in mind the resources of the financial services firm and the clients.
- Financial services cannot be stored and they are perishable. They are supplied according to the requirements of the clients.
- Lastly, the financial services must be dynamic. They need constant review and control. They need to be constantly redefined on the basis of socio-economic changes occurring in the economy.

Objectives of Financial Services

- Raising of required funds from a host of investors, individuals, institutions and corporates.
- To ensure an effective deployment of funds raised.
- Provide assistance in decision-making regarding the financing mix.
- Provide specialised services like credit rating, venture capital financing, lease financing, factoring, merchant banking, credit cards etc.
- To contribute to the economic growth and development.

1.2.11 Equilibrium in Financial Markets

The equilibrium in financial markets is usually determined by assuming that there would be perfect competition and by using the well-known tool of supply and demand.

Financial markets are said to be perfect when,

(a) A large number of savers and investors operate in markets;

(b) The savers and investors are rational;

(c) All operators in the market are well-informed and information is freely available to all of them;

(d) There are no transaction costs;

(e) The financial assets are infinitely divisible;

(f) The participants in markets have homogenous expectations and

(g) There are no taxes.

In India money market is regulated by Reserve Bank of India (www.rbi.org.in) and Securities Exchange Board of India (SEBI) [www.sebi.gov.in] regulates capital market. Capital market consists of primary market and secondary market. All Initial Public Offerings (IPO) comes under the primary market and all secondary market transactions deals in secondary market. Secondary market refers to a market where securities are traded after being initially offered to the public in the primary market and/or listed on the Stock Exchange. Secondary market comprises of equity markets and the debt markets. In the secondary market transactions BSE and NSE play a great role in exchange of capital market instruments.

1.2.12 Nature, Role and Characteristics of Financial System

1. The **price** in financial markets is called as "rate of interest". Under perfect competition conditions, the equality between total expected demand for funds and total planned supply of funds determines the equilibrium rate of interest.

2. The **intervention** between authorities in the form of managing interest rates causes an excess demand or supply of funds, which consecutively requires an official policy for direct allocation of financial resources.

3. The **supply of funds** depends on aggregate savings and credit creation by the banking system, while the requirement for funds depends upon demand for investment, consumer durables, housing and so on.

4. The functions of a financial system are created to establish a **bridge** between savers and investors and thus encourage savings and investment, provide finance in expectation of savings, increase markets over space and time and allot financial resources efficiently for productive purposes. The final objective of the financial system is to speed up the rate of economic development.

5. **Deficient financial markets** are characterised by the lack of information-based game, by accurate assessment of assets, by maximisation of convenience and marginal efficiency of capital and minimisation of transaction costs.

6. Actually, the contribution of a financial system to growth is **highly constrained** because it does not work well and capital is not the most significant obstacle to growth. The role of finance in development is considered secondary by many experts.

7. A framework to assess the functioning of any financial sector must consist of **economic, commercial as well as social and ethical criteria.**

8. **Financial innovations** refer to broad-ranging changes in the financial system. The introduction of new financial establishments, markets, instruments, services, technologies, organisations and so on.

9. **Financial engineering** denotes skilful development and use of new financial technology that creates solutions and tools to deal with financial changes. It involves construction, designing, re-construction of inventive financial instruments, institutions and processes to decrease risk and to maximise profits rapidly.

10. **Financial revolution** means that the magnitude, speed and spread of changes in the financial sector are simply extraordinary.

11. The markets which attract funds in large volume and from all types of investors are called as **broad financial markets.**

12. The markets which **provide opportunities** for sufficient orders at fine rates below and above the market price are called **deep financial markets.** The underdeveloped markets because of government regulations and controls are termed as **shallow financial markets.**

13. **Financial repression** exists when the regularity polices of the government distort interest rates, discourage savings, decrease investment and misallocate resources.

14. **Financial reforms** or liberalisation aim at creating market-oriented competitive financial systems by **removing the physical, administrative and direct controls.**

15. **Financial integration** refers to the establishment of close and effective inter-connections between different parts and sub-parts of the financial system so that interest rate differentials in the system are minimised.

16. **Securitisation** refers to fast growth, direct financial instruments and to a collateralised financing through the "sale" of the existing assets of financial establishments.

17. **Disintermediation** refers to the "switch out" of the liabilities of financial intermediaries by the investors.

18. **Internationalisation or globalisation** of financial markets takes place when the national and foreign markets are incorporated.

1.3 Indian Financial System

1.3.1 Introduction

The Indian financial system comprises a set of financial institutions, financial markets and financial infrastructure. The financial institutions mainly consist of commercial and co-operative banks, Regional Rural Banks (RRBs), All-India Financial Institutions (AIFIs) and Non-Banking Financial Companies (NBFCs).

The banking sector which forms the bedrock of the Indian financial system falls under the regulatory ambit of the Reserve Bank of India under the provisions of the Banking Regulation Act, 1949 and the Reserve Bank of India Act, 1934. The Reserve Bank also regulates select AIFIs. Consequent upon amendments to the Reserve Bank of India (Amendment) Act in 1997, a comprehensive regulatory framework in respect of NBFCs was put in place in January 1997.

The financial market in India comprises the money market, the government securities market, the foreign exchange market and the capital market. A holistic approach has been adopted in India towards designing and development of a modern, robust, efficient, secure and integrated payment and settlement system. The Reserve Bank set up the Institute for Development and Research in Banking Technology (IDRBT) in 1996, which is an autonomous centre for technology capacity building for banks and providing core IT services.

1.3.2 Financial Institutions

Scheduled Commercial Banks (SCBs) occupy a predominant position in the financial system accounting for around three fourths of the total assets in the financial system. While the public sector banks (PSBs), consisting of eight banks in the State Bank group and 19 nationalised banks, constitute almost three fourths of the total assets of SCBs, the private sector banks, 30 in number, constitute less than one-fifth of the total assets. The 33 foreign banks operating in India account for about 6-7 percent of the assets of SCBs. The 196 RRBs play a critical role in extending credit to the poorer sections of the rural society. The ownership of RRBs jointly rests with the Central Government, the State Governments and the sponsor banks. The co-operative banking system, with two broad segments of urban and rural co-operatives, forms an integral part of the Indian financial system. While the urban co-operative banking system has a single tier comprising the Primary Co-operative Banks (commonly known as urban co-operative banks – UCBs), the rural co-operative credit system is divided into long-term and short-term co-operative credit institutions which have a multi-tier structure.

The term-lending institutions are mostly government-owned and have been the traditional providers of long-term project loans. Non-Banking Financial Companies (NBFCs) encompass an extremely heterogeneous group of intermediaries and provide a gamut of financial services. Primary Dealers (PDs) in the government securities market constitute a systemically important segment of the NBFCs. At present, there are a total of 17 PDs playing an active role in the government securities market. A majority of them are promoted by banks.

Apart from this, India has a well-established and vibrant insurance sector within the financial system. The Insurance Regulatory and Development Agency (IRDA) has been established to regulate and supervise the insurance sector.

1.3.3 Overview of Indian Financial System Since 1991

1. Pre-reforms Phase

Until the early 1990s, the role of the financial system in India was primarily restricted to the function of channelling resources from the surplus to deficit sectors. Whereas the financial system performed this role reasonably well, its operations came to be marked by some serious deficiencies over the years.

The banking sector suffered from lack of competition, low capital base, low productivity and high intermediation cost. After the nationalisation of large banks in 1969 and 1980, the government-owned banks dominated the banking sector. The role of technology was minimal and the quality of service was not given adequate importance. Banks also did not follow proper risk management systems and the prudential standards were weak. All these resulted in poor asset quality and low profitability. Among non-banking financial intermediaries, development finance institutions (DFIs) operated in an over-protected environment with most of the funding coming from assured sources at concessional terms. In the insurance sector, there was little competition. The mutual fund industry also suffered from lack of competition and was dominated for long by one institution, namely, the Unit Trust of India. Non-banking financial companies (NBFCs) grew rapidly, but there was no regulation of their asset side.

Financial markets were characterised by control over pricing of financial assets, barriers to entry, high transaction costs and restrictions on movement of funds/participants between the market segments. This apart from inhibiting the development of the markets also affected their efficiency.

2. Post-reforms Phase

The organisation of the Indian financial system, since the mid-eighties in general and the launching of the new economic policy in 1991 in particular, has been characterised by profound transformation. The fundamental philosophy of the development process in India shifted to free market economics and the consequent liberalisation, deregulation and globalisation of the economy. Major economic policy changes such as macroeconomic stabilisation, de-licensing of industries, trade liberalisation, currency reforms, reduction in subsidies, financial sector, capital market and banking reforms, privatisation and disinvestments in public sector units, tax reforms and company law reforms in terms of simplifications and de-bureaucratisation were gradually implemented and they have had far-reaching impact on the structure of the corporate industrial sector in India.

In such an emerging scenario, the role of the government in the economic management obviously did shrink and with greater momentum in the process of economic liberalisation and globalisation, the relative importance of the government in this sphere will decline further. The capital market is emerging as the main agency for the allocation of resources and all segments of the Indian economy like the public sector, private sector and state governments are competing to raise resources in the capital market. The essence of these developments is the fact that the Indian financial system is poised for integration with the savings pool in the domestic currency and abroad.

1.3.4 Structure of Indian Financial System

The notable developments in the organisation of the Indian financial system during this phase are outlined below with reference to: (i) privatisation of financial institutions; (ii) reorganisation of institutional structure and (iii) investor protection. The Phase III organisation of the Indian financial system is portrayed in the Fig. 1.3.

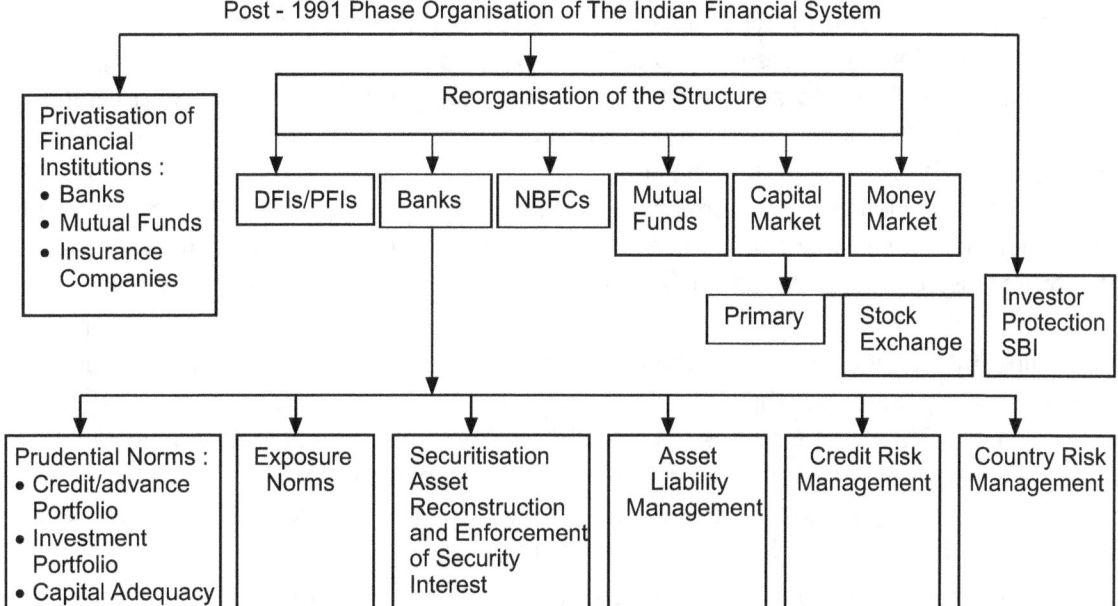

Fig. 1.3: Phase III: Post 1991 Organisation of the Indian Financial System

(A) Privatisation of Financial Institutions:

An outstanding development in this sphere was the conversion of the Industrial Finance Corporation – the pioneer development finance institution in the country into a public company (IFCI Ltd.). The IDBI and IFCI Ltd. offered their equity to private investors. Private mutual funds have been set-up under the guidelines prescribed by SEBI. A number of private banks under the RBI guidelines have also come into existence. With the setting-up of the Insurance Regulatory and Development Authority (IRDA) and the enactment of Insurance Regulatory and Development Authority Act, 1999, private insurance companies sponsored by both domestic and foreign promoters have re-emerged on the Indian financial scene. With the establishment of Pension Fund Regulation and Development Authority (PRDA), private entities are poised to enter the pension business. Thus, the state monopoly over financial institutions in India till the early nineties has been dismantled in a phased manner.

(B) Re-organisation of Institutional Structure:

This is illustrated with reference to the emerging changes in the role, organisation, operating policies, sponsorship of the institutions by development finance institutions/ development banks/term lending institutions, commercial banks, mutual funds, securities/ capital market, money market and so on. The main elements of the reorganisation of the institutional structure are briefly outlined below.

(a) Development/Public Financial Institutions (DFIs/PFIs)

Although the DFIs/PFIs constituted the backbone of the Indian financial system and despite the fact that they still played a dominant role until 2000, their relative significance in the emerging financing scenario had been declining, indicating a shift in corporate financing in India, in terms of greater reliance of industry on non-institutional sources of finance and greater recourse to the capital market.

Secondly, in addition to the financing of industry by these institutions in the traditional form of rupee/foreign currency term loans for project finance, underwriting, direct description, lease financing and so on, they also started providing core working capital to industries. Another pointer to the capital market-orientation in the operations of the term-lending institutions was the growing focus on non-fund based financial activities/services such as merchant banking and project counselling, portfolio management services, credit syndication, new issue management, mergers and acquisition, corporate advisory services, debenture trusteeship, registrar/transfer agents, sponsoring mutual funds and so on.

Further, the pattern of financing of the development banks, which consisted predominantly of funds from the Government and the RBI, was progressively geared to assessing the capital market through issue of capital to the public, issue of innovative floating interest rate bonds and other types of bonds without government guarantee. Similarly, these institutions introduced floating rates of interest on term loans. The bonds issued by the DFIs were no longer eligible as SLR assets for banks. They were meeting almost their entire requirements of funds at market-related interest rates.

Another significant indicator of the change in the structure of the FFIs, in tune with capital markets, was the nature of institutions sponsored by them. The focus shifted from development finance to that of promoting institutional infrastructure, geared to capital market development. These included three credit rating agencies CRISIL, ICRA, CARE and also two stock exchanges, namely, Over-the-Counter Stock Exchange of India (OTCE) Ltd. and National Stock Exchange (NSE) Ltd. The other organisations/institutions sponsored by the government in conformity with the requirement of the growing capital/securities market are the Stockholding Corporation of India (SHCI), Investor Services of India Ltd. (ISIL), ICICI Securities and Finance Ltd. (I-SEC), IFCI Financial Services Ltd., IFCI Investors Services Ltd. and IFCI Custodian Services Ltd. and so on. Thus, the development banks had assumed the character of financial conglomerates/super markets in contrast to their earlier limited role as term-lending institutions.

(b) Commercial Banks

The post-1991 era of Indian banking is characterised by prudential/viable/profitable banking. By the mid-nineties, a geographically wide and functionally diverse banking system had emerged as reflected in the phenomenal branch expansion especially in the rural and semi-urban and un-banked areas, phenomenal growth in deposits and increase in the share of the priority sector in total bank lending. However, serious weaknesses developed in the form of decline in productivity and efficiency of the banking system and consequently a serious erosion of its profitability with implication for its viability itself. Gross profits progressively declined. In case of some banks, the incremental cost of operation per rupee of working funds was more than the incremental income per rupee of the working funds. The factors which had adversely affected the profitability of the banking system were partly external in terms of macro-policy environment and partly internal in terms of organisation, staffing and branch spread.

(c) NBFCs

NBFCs broaden the range of financial services. These are partly fee-based and partly fund-based. The important fund asset activities of NBFCs are equipment leasing, hire purchase, bills discounting, loans/investment, venture capital, housing finance, factoring and forfeiting, stock broking, merchant banking etc. Their fee-based/advisory services include issue management, portfolio management, corporate counselling, loan/lease syndication, merger and acquisition and so on.

NBFC sector in India has recorded a marked growth in the recent years in terms of numbers, deposits and so on. A regulatory framework for their operations has evolved over the years on the basis of a number of committees in the context of the contemporary financial scenario. Based on their recommendations, the main elements of the regulation currently in force are: (i) Chapter III B of the RBI Act amended in 1998; (ii) RBI Acceptance of Deposits Regulations, 1998; (iii) NBFCs Prudential Norms (RBI) Directions, 1998 and (iv) NBFCs Auditor Reports (RBI) Directions, 1998. With a view to giving sharper focus to supervision over the NBFCs, the RBI has set up a separate department of non-banking supervision which undertakes both onsite and offsite surveillance over the institutions. They now operate within the rigorous framework of RBI's directions relating to: (a) acceptance of public deposits; (b) prudential norms and (c) auditors reports.

(d) Mutual Funds

In contrast to the position around the mid-eighties which consisted primarily of the monolithic Unit Trust of India, the structure has been considerably strengthened by the emergence of a broad-based pattern. The present structure consists of domestic mutual funds sponsored by the UTI, bank subsidiaries, insurance organisations, the private sector with foreign collaborations and foreign institutional investors/merchant banks. In addition, there are several off-shore/overseas/country funds sponsored by the Indian financial institutions as well as foreign institutional investors. Between them they offer a wide variety of schemes focusing on income, growth, tax savings, insurance linkage and special categories like children and senior citizens, sector-specific, money market mutual to suit the investment requirements of the heterogeneous category of investors. Mutual funds are emerging as the backbone of the Indian capital market and as the vehicle for institutionalisation of security investments for the relatively small investors.

They are conceived as the preferred route for equity investments in terms of –

(i)   Increase in the threshold/minimum limit in direct primary market investment from Rs. 1,000 to Rs. 5,000.

(ii) Introduction of the scheme of firm allotment to financial institutions including 20 percent of issues of capital to mutual funds.

(iii) Proportional allotment in case of over-subscription to issues of capital.

(iv) The treatment of units of mutual funds as long as long-term capital assets, if held for 12 months, as against 36 months earlier, for purposes of capital gains tax, and

(v) Complete tax exemption to unit-holders on income from mutual funds.

(vi) Reservation of 5 percent share for mutual funds to QIBs under book building.

The reorganisation of UTI recently has added a new dimension to the growing significance of mutual funds as a highly vibrant component of the Indian financial system. UTI is now a fully SEBI-compliant mutual fund.

(e) Securities/Capital Market

Historically, India's capital market was dormant till the mid-1980s. The long-term needs of the corporate sector were by and large met by the DFIs as well as other investment institutions, namely, LIC and UTI. Activities in the capital market were limited mainly due to the administered structure of interest rates and easy availability of credit loans from banks and FIs. From being a marginal institution in the mid-eighties, the securities market has emerged as the most important mechanism for allocating resources in the economy. The structure of both the segments of the market – primary, new and secondary, stock exchange – has witnessed significant changes.

(ii) **Primary Market:** The major reforms that have taken place in the primary market are given below –

- Merit-based regime to disclosure-based regime.
- Mutual funds are encouraged, both in public and private sectors and they have been permitted to invest overseas.
- Disclosure and Investor Protection (DIP) guidelines issued.
- Guidelines for private placements of debt issued.
- Pricing of public issues determined by the market.
- SEBI promoted Self-regulatory Organisation (SROs).
- A system of proportional allotment of shares introduced.
- Allocation to retail investors increased from 25 percent to 35 percent.
- Banks, FIs and PSUs allowed raising funds from the primary market.
- Separate allocation of 5 percent to domestic mutual funds within the QIB category.
- Accounting standards are close to the international standard.
- Freedom to fix face value of shares below Rs. 10 per share only in cases where the issue price is Rs. 50 or more.
- Corporate Governance Guidelines issued.
- Shares allotted on a preferential basis as well as the pre-allotment holdings are subject to a lock-in period of six months to prevent sale of shares.
- Discretionary allotment system to QIBs withdrawn.
- FIIs allowed to invest in primary issues within the sectoral limits (including G-Sec).

(ii) Secondary Market: The secondary market, which represented an institutional mechanism that was inadequate, non-transparent, hardly regulated and rarely geared to investor protection till the early nineties, has also witnessed notable developments.

A few stock exchanges dominated by the Bombay Stock Exchange (now BSE Ltd.) provided the trading platforms for the secondary market transactions. Under an open outcry system major reforms in the secondary markets/stock exchange took place. They are given below –

- Mandatory registration of market intermediaries.
- Capital adequacy norms specified for the brokers, sub-brokers of stock exchanges.
- Guidelines issued on listing agreements between stock exchanges and corporates.
- Shortening of settlement cycle to T+2.
- Regular inspection of stock exchanges and other intermediaries including mutual funds put in place.
- Regulation of Substantial Acquisition of Shares and Takeovers.
- FIIs allowed investing in the Indian capital market since 1992.
- Separate trading platform, namely IndoNext for the SME sector launched.
- Corporatisation and demutualisation of stock exchanges notified.
- Settlement and Trade Guarantee Fund/Investor Protection Fund set up.
- Comprehensive risk management system including capital adequacy, trading and exposure limit margin requirement, index-based market-wide circuit breaker, on-line position monitoring automatic disablement of terminology put in place.
- Comprehensive surveillance system.
- Securities Appellate Tribunal (SAT) set up.
- Mutual funds and FIIs to enter the Unique Client Code (UCC) pertaining to the parent entity as the order entry level and enter the UGCs for the individual schemes/sub-accounts on the post-closing session.
- Introduction of exchange traded derivatives.
- Order driven, fully automatic anonymous screen-based trading introduced.
- Depositories act enacted.
- Guidelines on corporate governance issued.
- SEBI has prohibited fraudulent and unfair trade practices, including insider trading.
- Straight thought processing introduced and made mandatory for institutional trades.
- Margin trading and securities lending and borrowing schemes introduced.

(f) Money Market

In the post 1990 period and particularly in the context of a de-regulated economic environment, a sophisticated and articulate money market emerged in the country. A notable development has been the emergence of specialised institutions, namely Primary Dealers (PDs) and money market mutual funds (MMMFs). Alongside activating the existing instruments through a modification in the procedures, deregulation of interest rates and enlargement of participants, a number of new instruments have been introduced. The organisation of the Indian money market consists of a number of inter-related submarkets, namely, Call/Notice market, Commercial Bills market, T-bills market, Commercial Papers (CPs) market, Certificate of Deposits (CDs) market and Repo market. There are also indications of a trend towards an integration of the forex and the money market. The RBI is now using the open market operations, bank rates, cash reserve ratios and repos as active instruments of monetary policy.

(C) Protection of Investors: Securities and Exchange Board of India (SEBI)

The security market which emerged from the periphery to enter the mainstream of the financial market in India has been one of the significant institutional developments since the mid-eighties, especially since the beginning of the nineties. It has witnessed a spectacular growth, both in terms of its ability to mobilise resources and to allocate it with some efficiency. The corporate sector has come to rely on the securities market increasingly to finance its long-term requirement of funds In contrast to a decade earlier, when the DFIs were the sole purveyors of long-term funds.

Although a fairly comprehensive legislative code had been put in place in the pre-1990 phase, the focus was on control. The framework was fragmented, both in terms of the laws/acts under which the regulatory functions fell and the agencies and Government departments that administered them.

The need of the growing securities market in India was a focused and integrated regulatory framework administrated by an independent autonomous body. The Capital Issues Control Act was repealed in 1992 and the Office of the Controller of Capital Issues (CCIs) was abolished. The Securities and Exchange Board of India (SEBI) was set up in April 1988 by an administrative order and acquired a statutory status in 1992. It has emerged as an autonomous and independent statutory body with a definite mandate which requires it to –

(i)   Protect the interest of the investors in securities;

(ii) Promote the development of the securities market and

(iii) Regulate the securities market. In order to achieve these objectives, SEBI exercises powers under –

    (a) The SEBI Act;

    (b) The Securities Contracts (Regulation) Act;

    (c) The Depositors Act and

    (d) The delegated powers under the Companies Act. The SEBI regulates and supervises the securities markets through: (1) regulations and (2) guidelines and schemes.

SEBI prohibits fraudulent and unfair trade practices, including insider trading. It also regulates substantial acquisition of shares and takeovers. In order to ensure investor protection and to safeguard the integrity of markets, there is a comprehensive surveillance system. Stock exchanges are the frontline regulators for detection of market manipulation, price rigging and other regulatory breaches regarding the capital market functioning. This is accomplished through the surveillance system.

In order to make the surveillance system more effective, the SEBI has signed an agreement with a consortium of HCL Technologies Limited and Securities Markets Automated Research, Training and Surveillance Limited, Australia, to put in place an Integrated Market Surveillance System (IMSS) by March, 2006. The proposed IMSS solution is expected to generate alerts that will help SEBI identify and detect serious market manipulations, insider trading and other types of fraudulent activities.

Enforcement of the regulations is done through investigations and adjudications. After a preliminary investigation, if it is found necessary, the cases are taken up for formal investigation. In case of formal investigation, the SEBI Act provides for the calling of information, compelling production of documents and examination of witnesses and so on. There is an elaborate procedure which is followed for the adjudication and prosecution of persons/agencies responsible for a violation of the regulations. The Chairman and the 'Whole Time Members' of the SEBI are vested with statutory power to impose penalties, issue directions, suspend/cancel a registration and so on. Moreover, a set of adjudicating officers work independently for this purpose and pass orders. These orders are posted on the SEBI website for the purpose of wider dissemination.

There is a Securities Appellate Tribunal (SAT) which functions independently to hear cases that are filed by the parties against the adjudication orders passed by the SEBI. SAT is an integral part of India's judicial system, with power equivalent to that of a High Court and which is designed to hear cases relating to the securities market.

Investors' confidence depends largely on the corporate governance standard which is based on the Narayana Murthy Committee Report, revised Corporate Governance by December 31, 2005 under Clause 49 of the Listing Agreement. Moreover, SEBI has been encouraging the credit rating agencies to evolve suitable corporate governance indeed as a measure of wealth creation by the corporate. A premier credit rating agency, namely CRISIL, has developed a yardstick in the form of "Governance and Value Creation" (GVC) rating for the corporate sector. SEBI would continue its endeavour to further improve corporate governance in India.

Investor education assumes importance in the context of very low level of household participation in the Indian capital market. *"An educated investor is a protected investor".*

In order to segregate the management function from the ownership and trading rights, there is a need for a demutualisation of stock exchanges. Moreover, stock exchanges should function as a body corporate, similar to any other 'for profit' corporate entity. In India the BSE is a corporate entity, while the NSE and the OTCEI are demutualised from their inception. The corporatisation and demutualisation of stock exchanges is a priority item in the SEBI agenda.

1.4 Financial Intermediaries in Financial System

1.4.1 Introduction

Having designed the instrument, the issuer should then ensure that these financial assets reach the ultimate investor in order to garner the requisite amount. When the borrower of funds approaches the financial market to raise funds, mere issue of securities will not suffice. Adequate information of the issue, issuer and the security should be passed on to take place. There should be a proper channel within the financial system to ensure such transfer. To serve this purpose, **financial intermediaries** came into existence.

Financial intermediation in the organised sector is conducted by a wide range of institutions functioning under the overall surveillance of the Reserve Bank of India. In the initial stages, the role of the intermediary was mostly related to ensure transfer of funds from the lender to the borrower. This service was offered by banks, FIs, brokers, and dealers. However, as the financial system widened along with the developments taking place in the financial markets, the scope of its operations also widened. Some of the important intermediaries operating in the financial markets include; investment bankers, underwriters, stock exchanges, registrars, depositories, custodians, portfolio managers, mutual funds, financial advisers financial consultants, primary dealers, satellite dealers, self regulatory organisations, etc. Though the markets are different, there may be a few intermediaries offering their services in more than one market, for example, underwriter. However, the services offered by them vary from one market to another.

Intermediary	Market	Role
Stock Exchange	Capital Market	Secondary market to securities
Merchant Bankers, Investment Bankers	Capital Market, Credit Market	Corporate advisory services, Issue of securities
Underwriters	Capital Market, Money Market	Subscribe to unsubscribed portion of securities
Brokers, Sub-brokers, Bankers	Capital Market, Credit Market	Corporate advisory services, Issue of securities
Registrars, Depositories, Custodians	Capital Market	Issue securities to the investors on behalf of the company and handle share transfer activity
Primary Dealers, Satellite Dealers	Money Market	Market making in government securities
Forex Dealers	Forex Market	Ensure exchange ink currencies

The term **financial intermediary** may refer to an institution, firm or individual who performs intermediation between two or more parties in a financial context. Typically the first party is a provider of a product or service and the second party is a consumer or customer.

Financial Intermediaries (FIs) are banking and non-banking institutions which transfer funds from economic agents with surplus funds (surplus units) to economic agents (deficit units) that would like to utilise those funds. FIs are basically two types: Bank Financial Intermediaries (BFIs – Central banks and Commercial banks) and Non-Bank Financial Intermediaries (NBFIs – insurance companies, mutual trust funds, investment companies, pensions funds, discount houses and bureaux de change).

1.4.2 Services of Financial Intermediaries

Their services include –

(i)   Issue Management

(ii)   Underwriting

(iii)   Portfolio Management

(iv)   Corporate Counselling

(v)   Stock Broking

(vi)   Syndicated Credit

(vii)   Arranging Foreign Collaboration Services

(viii) Mergers and Acquisitions

(ix)   Debenture Trusteeship

(x)   Capital Restructuring

1.4.3 Financial Intermediaries as Markets for Firm's Assets

- Financial intermediaries appear to have an important role in the restructuring and liquidation of companies that are in distress. Particularly, there is a proof that financial intermediaries play an active role in reallocating displaced capital, intended both as the piece-meal reallocation of assets (such as the redeployment of individual plants) and, more generally, as the sale of entire bankrupt companies to healthy ones. An important part of reorganisation under main bank supervision is the execution of a plan of asset sales with proceeds normally used to recover bank loans. In Germany the function of banks during reorganisations is to "use bank contacts to facilitate a merger with another firm as a means of resolving the crisis". Understanding possible synergies among companies, banks can suggest solutions for the efficient reallocation of assets and of corporate control and that in many countries there is extensive anecdotal evidence, on this role of banks. Healthy companies look around for the displaced capital of bankrupt companies but matching is imperfect and companies can end up with machines inappropriate for them.

- Financial intermediaries arise as internal, centralised markets where information on machines and buyers is easily available, enabling displaced capital to migrate towards its most productive uses. Financial intermediaries can perform this role by aggregating the information on companies gathered in the credit market. The function of intermediaries as matchmakers between savers and companies in the credit market can support their function as internal markets for assets. Instinctively, by raising the number of highly productive matches in the credit market, intermediaries increase the share of highly productive second hand users in the decentralised resale market. This improvement in the quality of the decentralised secondary market decreases the incentive of companies to address financial intermediaries for their ability as redeployers. On the other hand, by increasing the number of highly productive matches in the credit market, intermediaries also create wealthy buyers without assets and contribute to reduce the thickness of the decentralised resale market. This makes the decentralised market less attractive and increases the incentive of companies to use intermediaries as resale markets. When the quality improvement in the decentralised market is not too large and the second effect prevails, better matchmaking in the credit market supports the function of intermediaries as internal markets for assets.

1.4.4 Role of Financial Intermediaries in Financial System

The financial system is a key factor when it comes to explaining and understanding the development of the world's economy throughout the years. The creation of money as a means of exchange and the increasing need of people to find an efficient and beneficial way to trade their assets, and more importantly to take advantage of the great monetary value attached to them has caused the appearance of specific institutions, markets and individuals that provide the appropriate environment to perform these activities. The evolution of this system is therefore, the result of lenders and borrowers wishing to make the most out of their situation. With this purpose, funds are to be efficiently transferred between deficit and surplus units that are brought together in order to achieve higher production and efficiency for the economy as a whole. The channelling of funds between the two groups mentioned can only happen accurately in the presence of particular participants and via main routes such as financial intermediaries or through the use of organised financial markets. The difficulty that lenders (savers) and borrowers (spenders) encounter when confronted with finding and dealing directly with each other has provoked the appearance of financial intermediaries.

These financial intermediaries are engaged in bringing the two parties together by borrowing funds from lenders and lending them to borrowers so that both parties find the transaction more favourable than if they traded directly with each other. Financial intermediaries such as banks, investment companies, mutual funds, credit unions and insurance companies pool resources from various small investors so that they can be able to later lend those funds.

It is important to analyse the way not only lenders and savers but also financial intermediaries benefit from this situation. Mishkin and Eakins (2006) discuss that financial intermediaries can substantially reduce transaction costs that can be defined as the time and money spent in performing financial transactions, for instance the exchange of assets, goods or services. Because of their large size and expertise, they are able to take advantage of economies of scale. The low transaction costs allow these institutions to offer liquidity services as it is simpler to sell financial instruments to raise cash. In addition, financial intermediaries are able to greatly reduce the exposure to potential risks by sharing the risks among various investors and consequently achieving significant diversification due to the large and varied volume of resources they deal with. In this way, they virtually turn risky assets into safer ones for the benefit of investors and for theirs, as well as they gain profits on the difference between the returns and the payments they make.

Another important reason why financial intermediaries play such a significant role in the financial system is because of the inequality of information available between parties. Asymmetric information is fundamental to understanding the need for regulation as it affects the sense of balance that any market needs to remain in a stable situation. Its presence makes it difficult to tell whether the terms of the transactions being held between parties are mutually satisfying and therefore, jeopardises the solidity of market conditions. Allegedly, financial intermediaries are able to lessen these problems. The reason is that because of the financial involvement in the intermediation process, they are able to screen out bad risks and monitor the utilisation of the loans provided. Nonetheless, this feature has not always proven to be correct. After recent corporate scandals such as the ones that occurred in Enron, Arthur Andersen, General Motors, WorldCom, and Adelphia, just to name a few, investors' confidence in financial intermediaries has dropped dramatically.

It is evident that financial intermediaries play a key role in improving the performance of the economy and are therefore successful elements of the financial system. Financial markets and institutions embody a mixture of specific elements that are brought together with the sole purpose of controlling and coping with the enormous amount of assets available and the income generated by them. However, it is important to analyse the new trends that are complicating their position and the factors that are needed to return the confidence to the market and avoid instability of the financial system.

1.4.5 Types of Financial Intermediaries

There are several intermediaries who carry out various activities of different nature in the financial system. The legal framework of operations of these intermediaries is prescribed by SEBI. These intermediaries are listed below –

1. Merchant Bankers
2. Underwriters
3. Bankers to an issue
4. Brokers to the issue
5. Sub-brokers
6. Registrars to the issue
7. Share Transfer Agents
8. Debenture Trustees
9. Portfolio Managers
10. Depository Services
11. Depository Participants

1.4.6 Merchant Bankers

Merchant bankers play a significant role in the financial services sector. Merchant banking is a non-banking financial activity which resembles banking function. The intermediaries in the stock market who are responsible for public issue management are known as 'merchant bankers or lead managers'. Merchant bankers require compulsory registration with the SEBI to carry out their activities. They provide financial services like investment banking, counselling, negotiating insurance and a host of other services. In India, public money is playing a very important role in financing a large number of projects both in the public and the private sector. A large amount of money is raised from the capital market to finance industrial projects. In order to raise money from the capital market, promoters have to bank upon merchant bankers who manage the whole show by rendering various services.

Definition of Merchant Banking

1. According to Random House Dictionary, "Merchant bank is an organisation that underwrites securities for corporations, advises such clients on mergers and is involved in the ownership of commercial ventures. These organisations are sometimes banks which are not merchants and sometimes merchants who are not banks and sometimes houses which are neither merchants nor banks."

2. According to SEBI (Merchant Bankers) Rule, 1992, 'A merchant banker is any person who is engaged in the business of issue management either by making arrangement regarding selling, buying or subscribing to securities as manager, consultant, advisor or rendering corporate advisory services in relation to such issue management.'

3. According to Charles P. Kindleberger, "Merchant banking is the development of banking from commerce which frequently encountered a prolonged intermediate stage known in England originally as merchant banking."

4. Merchant Bankers: "A set of financial institutions that are engaged in providing specialist services, which generally include the acceptance of bills of exchange, corporate finance, portfolio management and other banking services".

Role/Functions of Merchant Bankers in the Capital Market

Merchant bankers provide important services to their clients. A merchant banker may specialise in one activity, and take up other activities, which may be complementary or supportive to the specialised activity. Merchant bankers provide a host of services to the clients as listed below –

1. **Pre-issue management activities like –**
   ➢ Obtaining approval for the issue from SEBI
   ➢ Drafting of prospectus
   ➢ Getting the prospectus approved from various agencies
   ➢ Arranging underwriting for the proposed issue

➢ Drafting and finalisation of other documents such as application forms, newspaper advertisements and other statutory requirements

➢ Selection of registrar to the issue, printing press, advertising agencies, brokers and bankers to the issue

➢ Arranging press conferences for brokers' and investors

➢ Deciding the opening and closing dates of issue

➢ Deciding and fixing the branches from where application money should be collected

2. **Post-issue management activities like**

➢ Getting the daily report of application money collected at various collection points

➢ Obtaining subscription to the issue

➢ After the close of issue, getting consent of the stock exchange for deciding the basis of allotment

➢ Sending compliance report to SEBI

➢ Obtaining letter from the regional stock exchange approving the basis of allotment for different categories

➢ Sending copy of the letter of the regional stock exchange to other stock exchanges where the listing permission is sought

➢ Confirm that the listing formalities have been complied with

➢ Obtaining permission for allotment of shares and debentures to NRIs and FIIs

3. **Underwriting:** Merchant bankers act as underwriters for new issues of companies. Underwriting is a process which absorbs the risk of the issue not being fully subscribed. Moreover, SEBI has made underwriting compulsory for new issue of shares.

4. **Corporate Counselling:** These include a whole range of financial services provided with a view to aid corporate financial management. Various services like economic analysis, cost analysis, pricing strategies, financial analysis, project management, legal counselling, feasibility reports, advising on financing mix etc. are provided by the merchant bankers.

5. **Government Consents** like obtaining necessary approvals, licenses, permissions from government for industrial projects, guiding the companies on rules, regulations, capital goods clearance, import clearance etc.

6. **Credit Syndication:** This involves raising finance with the help of consortium of banks and financial institutions. Merchant bankers render syndication services to their clients thereby assisting raising rupee and foreign loans for long-term use.

7. **Portfolio Management:** In this area, merchant bankers provide assistance like advising on investment in government securities, undertaking purchase and sale of securities, management of individual investment portfolio of investors etc.

8. **Mergers and Takeovers:** Merchant bankers also provide advisory services relating to mergers and takeovers, for example, appraisal of the proposals, financial viability, technical feasibility, negotiation with the concerned parties, determination of the purchase consideration, exchange ratio, assistance relating to procedural and legal aspects, obtaining necessary approvals etc.

9. **Arranging Offshore Finance:** This assistance includes arranging for financing of exports and imports, long-term foreign currency loans, joint ventures abroad etc.

10. **Management of Fixed Deposits of Companies:** The merchant bankers help the companies in raising finance by way of public deposits. They provide the required guidance and act as brokers for the mobilisation of public deposits. They manage the procedural and the legal aspects and take care of the collection and subsequent servicing of the deposits.

11. In addition to the above services, the merchant bankers also assist the NRIs regarding identification, selection of securities, purchase and sale of securities and their portfolio management. Besides they also render services to the sick industries as required and assist in the rehabilitation package.

1.4.7 Underwriters

A company contemplating to issue shares and debentures is exposed to the risk of the issue not being fully subscribed. This risk is mitigated by the underwriters. Underwriting is a process which absorbs this risk and ensures the minimum subscription to the company. Underwriter guarantees that the shares underwritten by him will be sold and in case the shares are not taken by the public, the underwriter himself will purchase the remaining shares and thus the company will be able to obtain the subscription for all the shares issued.

According to Gerstenberg, "Underwriting is an agreement entered into before the shares are brought before the public that in the event of the public not taking up the whole of them the underwriter will take an allotment of such part of the shares as the public has not applied for."

SEBI has made underwriting compulsory for the companies going in for public subscription. Underwriters are appointed by the issuing companies in consultation with the merchant bankers to the issues. Merchant bankers also act as underwriters for new issue of companies. Underwriters maintain high standards of integrity and make all efforts to protect the interest of the clients. They also need to obtain a certificate of registration from SEBI in order to act as underwriters.

Types of Underwriting

There are different types of underwriting as given below –

1. **Firm Underwriting:** In this type of underwriting, the underwriter agrees to take up a specified number of securities, irrespective of the number of securities being offered to the public. It is an outright purchase of securities by the underwriter, wherein the underwriter is given a preference to buy securities over the general public. A firm underwriting agreement creates confidence in the minds of the investing public.

2. **Sub-underwriting:** This type of an agreement involves more than one underwriter. When a large number of securities are issued, the securities are contracted by the main underwriter to the sub-underwriter. This type of underwriting helps the main underwriter to minimise the risk of loss of investment in case of an unpopular issue.

3. **Joint Underwriting:** As the name suggests, in this case the issue is underwritten by two or more underwriters jointly. The purpose is to minimise the risk and share the benefit arising from a successful capital issue. This type of underwriting is also helpful for underwriters with limited resources, who can jointly take up the issue.

4. **Syndicate Underwriting:** Syndicate underwriting is a type of underwriting in which a syndicate of underwriters, by means of an agreement, underwrite the issues of securities collectively. This arrangement is followed in case of very risky issues, so that the risk is minimised. There will be two types of agreements in this case namely, one between the issuing company and the underwriters, and the other agreement among the underwriters themselves stating the terms and conditions.

Benefits of Underwriting –

- It enables a company to raise the necessary capital without much difficulty.
- It gives an assurance to the company regarding availability of required funds within a reasonable and agreed time.
- Underwriters also offer expert advice on matters pertaining to the soundness of the proposed plan. They also provide important information regarding investors attitude, market conditions etc.
- The goodwill of the issuing company is enhanced as their issue is supported by the underwriters.
- The investors are assured of low risk and they have more confidence for the company which is underwritten.
- Underwriting ensures better and successful marketing of the securities. This is so as the underwriters have a wide network with other underwriters and brokers at the national and global level.
- The information and the expert advice of underwriters which is published in various newspapers are very helpful for the buyers of securities.
- Underwriters also provide stability to the price of securities by buying and selling the securities.

1.4.8 Bankers to an issue

The bankers to an issue are engaged in activities such as acceptance of applications along with application money from the investors in respect of issues of capital and refund of application money to the applicants to whom securities could not be allotted. They play an important role in the working of the primary market. In order to carry out their activities, the bankers also need to obtain a certificate of registration from the SEBI, which is granted on the application and payment of a registration fee and annual fee.

The issuing company has to enter into a contract with the banker to an issue. This contract includes detailed information regarding the number and addresses of collection centres at which applications and application money will be received, the fees for the services and other terms and conditions of the contract.

A daily statement giving the details regarding the number of applications and the amount of money collected from the investors is generally submitted by the bankers to the issuing company/registrar to an issue. Necessary information regarding issue and collection details also needs to be furnished to SEBI.

Functions of bankers –

➢ Distribution of application forms of issue through their network of branches all over the country.

➢ Collection of money from the applicants on behalf of the company.

➢ Collection of application forms, co-ordination and monitor the same along with the registrars and issue manager.

➢ Refund of application money to non-allottees.

RBI and SEBI's Role –

RBI is empowered to carry out the inspection of the bankers to the issue with a view to protecting the investors' interest and also promoting compliance with SEBI Act, rules and regulations. SEBI may order the suspension of the registration of the banker in such circumstances as the violation of the provisions of SEBI Act, rules and regulations, failure to submit the required information, submission of wrong or false information, failure to resolve investors' complaints or give satisfactory reply to SEBI, guilty of misconduct or unprofessional conduct etc.

1.4.9 Brokers and Sub-brokers to an Issue

Brokers are the persons mainly concerned with the procurement of subscription to the issue from the prospective investors. They are engaged by the companies to find suitable market for the securities but they do not guarantee the sale of securities. Commission or brokerage is paid to them by the issuer only on the amount of applications received with their signatures. The appointment of brokers is not compulsory and the companies are free to appoint any number of brokers.

Thus, a stock broker is a member of a recognised stock exchange who buys, sells or deals in securities. A certificate of registration from SEBI is mandatory to act as a broker.

Features of Brokers –

➢ They are the intermediaries responsible for procuring the subscription to the issue from the prospective investors.

➢ They provide a vital connecting link between the investors and the issuer.

➢ They assist in the speedy subscription of issue by the public.

➢ Broker appointment is not compulsory.

➤ Brokers have expert knowledge, professional competence and a high level of integrity.

➤ Brokers need to obtain consent from the stock exchanges to act in the said capacity.

➤ Company is free to decide the number of brokers for its issue.

➤ The names and addresses of the brokers to the issue are disclosed in the prospectus.

➤ Brokers are paid their fees in the form of brokerage by the issuing company. This brokerage should be according to the provisions of the Companies Act, rules and regulations, the agreement between the broker and the company, and guidelines prescribed by SEBI.

➤ The brokers have to meet all mailing costs, canvassing expenses and all other out-of-pocket expenses relating to the subscription of the issue out of their brokerage.

A sub-broker acts on behalf of a stock broker as an agent for assisting investors in buying, selling or dealing in securities through such brokers, but he is not a member of a stock exchange. Sub-brokers also need registration with SEBI and those sub-brokers wanting to do business with more than one broker need to be separately registered with SEBI for each broker. SEBI grants registration certificate to a sub-broker subject to the following conditions –

➤ that he pays the prescribed fees,

➤ he takes adequate steps for redressal of investor grievances within one month of the receipt of the complaint,

➤ keeps SEBI informed about the number, nature and other particulars of the complaints and

➤ is authorised in writing by a broker for affiliation in buying, selling or dealing in securities.

Sub-brokers are obliged to enter into agreements and maintain the data base of their clients as per the SEBI format.

1.4.10 Registrars to an Issue and Share Transfer Agents

Registrars and Share Transfer Agents are of two categories namely,

Category I – carry out activities of Registrars as well as Share Transfer Agents.

Category II – carry out activities either of a registrar to an issue or as a share transfer agent.

Functions of Registrars

➤ Collecting application from the bankers

➤ Keeping a proper record of applications and money received from investors

➤ Keeping a proper record of applications and money paid to the seller of securities

➤ Assisting companies in determining the basis of allotment of securities as per stock exchange guidelines and in consultation with stock exchanges

➤ Finalising the allotment of securities

> ➢ Dispatching allotment letters, refund order, share certificates, debenture certificates and related documents in respect of issue of capital
> ➢ Sending rejection letters to the rejected applications stating the reasons for rejection
> ➢ Maintain list of allottees and non-allottees
> ➢ Functioning as Depository Participants

Functions of Share Transfer Agents

> ➢ Maintaining records of holders of securities of the company for and on behalf of the company
> ➢ Handling all matters related to transfer and redemption of securities of the company
> ➢ Functioning as Depository Participants

Responsibilities of Registrars and Share Transfer Agents

> ➢ A certificate of registration is to be obtained from SEBI in order to function as registrar and share transfer agents. This certificate is issued on fulfillment of the conditions as laid down by SEBI regarding adequacy of infrastructure, past experience, capital adequacy and payment of the fees as prescribed.
> ➢ Registrars and share transfer agents have to maintain proper records relating to an issue (as listed above in functions) and the books are to be preserved for three years from the date of issue.
> ➢ Registrars and Share Transfer Agents have to observe the code of conduct prescribed by SEBI.
> ➢ They should ensure that enquiries from investors are adequately dealt with and proper steps are taken for allotment of securities and refund of excess application money as per law and without undue delay.

1.4.11 Debenture Trustees

When a company seeks to issue debentures or debenture stock, it is customary to appoint a trustee to protect the interests of the debenture holders. A debenture trustee is a trustee for a trust deed needed for securing any issue of debentures by a company. They are to be appointed before issue of debentures by a company.

A trust deed is a deed which is executed by the company in favour of the trustees named therein for the benefit of the debenture holders. Certificate from SEBI is mandatory in order to act as a debenture trustee.

A scheduled bank carrying on commercial activity, a public financial institution, an insurance company or a body corporate are eligible to be appointed as debenture trustees.

Role and Responsibilities

> ➢ A certificate of registration is to be obtained from SEBI in order to function as debenture trustees. This certificate is issued on fulfillment of the conditions as laid down by SEBI regarding adequacy of infrastructure, past experience, capital adequacy, professional qualification and payment of the fees as prescribed.

➢ Consent in writing must be given to the body corporate to act a debenture trustees before the debenture issue.

➢ The debenture trustees shall carry out the inspection of books of accounts, records, registers of the body corporate and the trust property to the extent necessary for discharging its obligations.

➢ A debenture trustee shall take possession of trust property in accordance with the provisions of the trust deed and enforce security in the interest of the debenture holders.

➢ A debenture trustee shall carry out activities in such a way so as to protect the interests of the debenture holders.

➢ He must also ensure that the debenture certificates and interest warrants have been dispatched to the debenture holders in accordance with the provisions of the Companies Act.

➢ A debenture trustee needs to exercise due diligence to ascertain whether the assets of the body corporate which are offered by way of security are sufficient to discharge the claims of debenture holders as and when they become due.

➢ A debenture trustee shall call for a meeting of the debenture holders whenever it is requisitioned by the debenture holders. This requisition of meeting needs at least one-tenth of the debenture holders' consent and the debenture holders can give requisition in the event of a default by the company which is affecting the interest of the debenture holders.

➢ The debenture trustee shall abide by the prescribed code of conduct.

➢ The debenture trustee needs to maintain proper books of accounts and records relating to trusteeship functions for a period of not less than 5 financial years preceding the current financial year. The place of maintenance of books of accounts needs to be intimated to SEBI.

➢ The debenture trustee needs to furnish periodic information to SEBI regarding –

(i)   Number and nature of grievances of debenture holders received and resolved.

(ii) Copies of trust deed.

(iii) Non-payment/delayed payment of interest to debenture holders, if any, in respect of each issue of debentures of a body corporate.

(iv) Details of dispatch and transfer of debenture certificates giving therein the dates, mode etc.

(v)   Inspection conducted and disciplinary proceedings, if any.

(vi) Any other information that is relevant to the debenture trustees.

1.4.12 Portfolio Managers

Portfolio managers are defined as persons who, in pursuance of a contract with clients, advise/direct/undertake the management/administration of portfolio of securities/funds of clients on behalf of the latter. The term 'portfolio' means the total holdings of securities belonging to any person. It is a collection of assets; physical or financial like shares, bonds, debentures, preference shares etc.

Portfolio manager means any person who pursuant to a contract or arrangement with a client, advises or directs or undertakes on behalf of the client, the management or administration of a portfolio of securities or the funds of the client, as the case may be.

Portfolio managers can be of two types namely –

➢ **Discretionary:** They exercise their discretion with regard to management of the portfolio of the securities/funds.

➢ **Non-discretionary:** They manage funds in accordance with the directions of the clients.

Functions of Portfolio Manager

➢ To frame the investment strategy for the client

➢ To select an investment mix to achieve the desired investment objective of the client

➢ To provide a balanced portfolio which acts as a hedge against inflation, and at the same time generates optimum returns with the associated degree of risk

➢ To make timely buying and selling of securities

➢ To maximise the post-tax returns by investing in various tax saving investment instruments

In short, portfolio managers manage the funds of their clients and they also need to have a certificate of registration from SEBI in order to act as portfolio managers. A certificate/renewal of registration is valid for three years. The portfolio manager has to also give an undertaking to take adequate steps for the redressal of grievances of clients within one month of the receipt of the complaint. He also has to keep the SEBI informed about the number, nature and other particulars of the complaints and abide by its rules and regulations.

1.4.13 Depository Services

The capital market transactions in India are characterised by mounting paper work. There has been a lot of increase in the volume of transactions coupled with inadequacies and delays in the settlement mechanism. The share certificates are physically moved during allotment and transfer, thereof. This movement of share certificates and ownership details needs to be recorded in the company's books. Various problems are faced by investors and the company as given below –

➢ Inordinate delays in transfer of securities

➢ Return of share certificates as bad deliveries on account of forged signatures or signature mismatch or fake certificate
➢ Delay in the receipt of securities after allotment
➢ Delay in receiving the refund orders on non-allotment
➢ Delay in getting duplicate shares/debenture certificates
➢ Inadequate infrastructure in banking and postal segments to handle large volume of applications
➢ Problem of storage of share certificates

To overcome the above problems and to eliminate the physical handling of securities, scripless trading in the dematerialised form was introduced. This also ensured Indian stock markets to be at par with the international markets. A major reform of the Indian stock markets has been the introduction of the depository system and scripless trading mechanism since the year 1996. Scripless trading is a mechanism in which transactions in securities take place by a book entry method, without the physical delivery of securities. Securities are held in a dematerialised form through the depositories.

In scripless trading through depositories, all certificates are surrendered to the issuer company that has issued the securities. On receipt of certificates through the depository participants and on the advice of the depository with whom the company has entered into an agreement, the certificates are cancelled. The depositories' name is recorded in the Register of Members of the company and the names of the beneficial owners are deleted. The depository needs to maintain a register and an index of beneficial owners in the manner as provided by the Companies Act. The statement given by the depository is evidence of ownership of the shares. The depository service is an appreciable capital market reform which shall protect an investor from various problems faced by him.

Benefits of Scripless Trading for Investors
➢ Speedier settlement
➢ Greater liquidity and quick registration
➢ Prompt receipt of dividend
➢ Prompt allotment of rights/bonus shares
➢ Faster transfers at reduced costs
➢ No problems due to loss of share certificates, forgery or mutilation of securities
➢ Immediate transfer after allotment of shares

Benefits of Scripless Trading for Companies
➢ Prompt communication with investors regarding meetings, accounts, dividend etc.
➢ Ready and up-to-date availability of names and addresses of security holders
➢ Reduction in printing and distribution expenses
➢ Better services to investors
➢ Less administration work

The depository system in India operates within the framework of Depositories Act, 1996 and the SEBI Depositories and Participants Regulation, 1996. National Securities Depositories Limited (NSDL) and Central Depositories Services Ltd. (CDSL) are the two main depositories currently operating in India; having 1.39 crores and 98 lakhs demat accounts respectively as on 30/06/2015.

1.4.14 Depository Participants

They are persons dealing directly with depository on their own account or for their clients. The depository participant is an important link between the investor and the depository. The depository participant acts in the capacity of an agent of depository and has to be registered with SEBI.

The relationship between the DPs and the depository is governed by an agreement made between the two under the Depositories Act. In India, commercial banks, public financial institutions, stock exchanges, state financial corporations, registered stock brokers, NBFCs etc. are permitted to be registered as depository participants. In order to become a participant, an application for the grant of certificate of registration has to be made in the prescribed form to SEBI through depository in which the applicant proposes to act as a participant. This form is to be submitted along with registration fees and annual fees.

An investor who wishes to avail of the services will have to open an account with the depository through the depository participant. The investor also needs to enter into an agreement with the depository participant, after which he is issued a client account number.

The role of participant is very important in the entire depository system. The participant needs to fulfill the requirements regarding its net worth and the necessary infrastructural facilities thereof. As of 2012, there were 288 DPs of NSDL and 563 DPs of CDSL registered with SEBI.

Points to Remember

- A financial system may be defined as a set of institutions, instruments and markets which foster savings and channel them to their most efficient use.
- A financial market can be defined as the market in which financial assets are created or transferred.
- The money market is a wholesale debt market for low-risk, highly-liquid, short-term instrument.
- The capital market is also called as the securities market and is designed to finance the long-term investments.
- The Forex market deals with the multicurrency requirements, which are met by the exchange of currencies.
- Credit market is a place where banks, FIs and NBFCs purvey short, medium and long-term loans to corporate and individuals.

- Call/Notice money is the money borrowed or lent on demand for a very short period. When money is borrowed or lent for a day, it is known as Call (Overnight) Money.

- Inter-bank market for deposits of maturity beyond 14 days is referred to as the term money market.

- Treasury bills are short-term (up to one year) borrowing instruments of the union government.

- A marketable document of title to a time deposit for a specified period may be referred to as a 'Certificate of Deposit' (CD).

- Debt instruments that are issued by corporate houses for raising short-term financial resources from the money market are called Commercial Papers (CPs).

- The financial asset represents a claim to the payment of a sum of money sometime in the future (repayment of principal) and/or a periodic (regular or not so regular) payment in the form of interest or dividend.

- The term **financial intermediary** may refer to an institution, firm or individual who performs intermediation between two or more parties in a financial context.

- A merchant banker is any person who is engaged in the business of issue management either by making arrangement regarding selling, buying or subscribing to securities as manager, consultant, advisor or rendering corporate advisory services in relation to such issue management.

Questions for Discussion

1. What is a financial system? Give a brief overview of the Indian financial system.
2. What are financial intermediaries? Discuss their role in the financial system.
3. Explain the financial institutions in the Indian financial system.
4. Define 'financial system'. Explain the structure of the financial system.
5. Write short notes on:
   (a) Structure of financial system
   (b) Financial markets
   (c) Indian financial system since 1991
   (d) Financial intermediaries

✍ ✍ ✍

Chapter 2...

Introduction to Financial Markets

Contents ...

Learning Objectives ...

- To understand the concept of Capital Market: Primary Market and Secondary Market
- To study the management of IPO
- To explain the Stock Exchanges in India: BSE, NSE, OTCEI
- To learn the role of SEBI as a regulatory authority
- To elaborate the Types of Derivatives: Futures and Options
- To study the Money Market in India
- To discuss the various money market instruments including Call and Notice Money Market, Treasury Bill, Commercial Papers, Certificate of Deposits, Money Market Mutual Funds, Inter-Corporate Deposits
- To differentiate between Money Market and Capital Market

2.1 Introduction

The function of the financial market is to facilitate the transfer of funds from surplus sectors (lenders) to deficit sectors (borrowers). Normally, households have investible funds or savings, which they lend to borrowers in the corporate and public sectors whose requirement of funds far exceeds their savings. A financial market consists of investors or buyers of securities, borrowers or sellers of securities, intermediaries and regulatory bodies. A financial market does not refer to a physical location. Formal trading rules, relationships and communication networks for originating and trading financial securities link the participants in the market.

2.2 Capital Market

Capital market is a market dealing in medium and long-term funds. It is an institutional arrangement for borrowing medium and long-term funds and it provides facilities for marketing and trading of various kinds of securities like shares, debentures, bonds etc. It is an organised mechanism meant for the effective and smooth transfer of money capital or financial resources from the investors to the entrepreneurs. Capital market helps to mobilise the financial resources on a nation-wide scale and ensures the most effective utilisation of the mobilised financial resources. It offers an ideal source of external finance and is an important part of a country's financial system. It consists of two different segments namely primary market and secondary market.

2.3 Primary Market

2.3.1 Introduction

The primary market deals with the issue of new instruments by the corporate sector such as equity shares, preference shares and debt instruments. Central and state governments, various Public Sector Industrial Units (PSUs), statutory and other authorities such as State Electricity Boards and Port Trusts also issue bonds/debt instruments.

Companies, governments and other groups obtain financing through debt or equity-based securities. Primary markets are facilitated by underwriting groups, which consist of investment banks that will set a beginning price range for a given security and then oversee its sale directly to investors. A primary market is also known as a "New Issue Market" (NIM).

The primary markets are where investors can get first crack at a new security issuance. The issuing company or group receives cash proceeds from the sale, which is then used to fund operations or expand the business. Exchanges have varying levels of requirements which must be met before a security can be sold.

Once the initial sale is complete, further trading is conducted on the secondary market, which is where the bulk of exchange trading occurs each day. Primary markets can see increased volatility over secondary markets because it is difficult to accurately gauge investor demand for a new security until several days of trading have occurred.

- Market in which a loan is actually made to the borrower, distinguished from the secondary market where securities backed by loan receivables are sold to investors. A bank or thrift institution that holds its loans on its own records, and does not engage in secondary market sales, is known as a portfolio lender.

- Market where government securities are sold to primary dealers who then remarket securities to investors in the secondary market.

- Market in which newly issued securities are offered for sale, futures contracts are offered for sale, and options are purchased.

The primary market is that part of the capital markets that deals with the issue of new securities. Companies, governments or public sector institutions can obtain funding through the sale of a new stock or bond issue. This is typically done through a syndicate of securities dealers. The process of selling new issues to investors is called underwriting. In the case of a new stock issue, this sale is an Initial Public Offering (IPO). Dealers earn a commission that is built into the price of the security offering, though it can be found in the prospectus. Primary markets create long-term instruments through which corporate entities borrow from capital market.

2.3.2 Features of Primary Markets

Features of primary markets are:

1. This is the market for new long-term equity capital. The primary market is the market where the securities are sold for the first time. Therefore it is also called the New Issue Market (NIM).

2. In a primary issue, the securities are issued by the company directly to investors.

3. The company receives the money and issues new security certificates to the investors.

4. Primary issues are used by companies for the purpose of setting up new business or for expanding or modernising the existing business.

5. The primary market performs the crucial function of facilitating capital formation in the economy.

6. The new issue market does not include certain other sources of new long-term external finance, such as loans from financial institutions. Borrowers in the new issue market may be raising capital for converting private capital into public capital; this is known as "going public."

7. The financial assets sold can only be redeemed by the original holder.

Methods of issuing securities in the primary market are:

1. Initial public offering;

2. Rights issue (for existing companies);

3. Preferential issue.

A market where investors purchase securities or assets from other investors, rather than from issuing companies themselves is a secondary market. The national exchanges such as the New York Stock Exchange and the NASDAQ are secondary markets.

A newly issued IPO will be considered a primary market trade when the shares are first purchased by investors directly from the underwriting investment bank; after that any shares traded will be on the secondary market, between investors themselves. In the primary market prices are often set beforehand, whereas in the secondary market only basic forces like supply and demand determine the price of the security.

2.4 IPO (Initial Public Offering)

When companies decide to raise capital, they often do so by going public and selling shares of stock. The initial sale of a company's stock is known in the stock market as an Initial Public Offering or IPO. Many IPOs are the subject of intense investor attention and interest, but the process allows few, if any, opportunities for average individual investors to take part in the initial sale of shares.

An initial public offer, as the name indicates, is the first (initial) instance of a company (called the issuer) offering its commons stock (or shares) to the general public for subscription.

It is a common misconception that only newly formed companies resort to raising money through an IPO. Even long established private companies can access the IPO route to raise capital, and become publicly traded companies as a result. An IPO is considered as a "rite of passage" into the big league of publicly traded stocks. Any company that needs to be listed on a stock exchange has to offer its shares to the public.

In addition to IPO, an already listed and publicly traded company may issue an FPO – a Follow on Public Offer – to raise further capital for the company. At any given time, there are a number of IPO and FPO issues floating around in the market; therefore, it is essential to understand the difference between the two.

Shares issued in an IPO are bought in the primary market, while shares brought from another investor are exchanged in the secondary market. The distinct between primary and secondary market is notional, there is no physical separation between the two. An important distinction between shares purchased during an IPO and shares purchased from the secondary market is that while in case of an IPO, the money goes directly into the company coffers; in case of secondary market, the money is transferred from one investor to another.

Companies offering an IPO are sometimes new, young companies, or sometimes companies which have been around for many years but are finally deciding to go public. IPOs are often risky investments, but often have the potential for significant gains. IPOs are often used as a way for a young company to gain necessary market capital.

- An Initial Public Offering (IPO) thus refers to the first time that an organisation sells stock to the general public.
- An IPO allows an organisation to sell securities in exchange for cash to invest in new projects. These securities provide funds for the organisation to invest but require a rate of return to investors, which will be a future cost to the organisation.
- An IPO allows an organisation to grow financially because it provides immediate funds for the organisation to use for new projects that will produce revenue-generating assets.
- This immediate availability of funds allows the organisation to grow more rapidly than it would be able, limited to its own revenue generating capabilities and limited access to immediate funds necessary to implement new projects.

2.4.1 How does IPO Work?

An IPO or Initial Public Offering occurs when a private company offers up shares of its company for sale to the public, who by purchasing those shares own a piece of the company. Small private companies carry out IPOs to raise capital for growth and expansion, while well-established private companies have IPOs to become publicly traded and even bigger. For example when Rupert Murdoch's News Corporation went public, it sold about a 19% stake of the company to raise almost $3 billion.

Investors who buy a company's shares buy a piece of ownership in the company for a chance to benefit from its future profits. For the owners of a company, it means giving up some control depending on what percentage of the company is sold, opening the company up to public and government scrutiny, and being accountable to shareholders.

Primary and Secondary Markets

The private corporation's board of directors, who are elected by the shareholders, must authorise the number of shares that can be issued. Since issuing shares means opening up the firm to more owners, or sharing it more, only the existing owners have the power to do so. Generally, it authorises more shares than it means to issue, so it has the choice of issuing more as required.

Those authorised shares are then issued through an initial public offering or IPO. Thereupon the firm goes public. The IPO is a primary market transaction, which happens when in the beginning, the stock is sold and the profits go to the firm issuing the stock. Subsequently, the firm is publicly traded; its stock is outstanding, or publicly available.

Then, every time the stock changes hands, it is a secondary market transaction. The owner of the stock may sell shares and realise the proceeds. When individuals think of "the stock market," they are thinking of the secondary markets.

Due to the secondary market's existence the stock becomes a tradable asset, which decreases its risk for both the issuing firm and the investor buying it. The investor gives up the capital in order to get a share of the company's profit, with the risk that there will be no profit to compensate for the opportunity cost of sacrificing the capital. The secondary markets decrease that risk to the shareholder because the stock can be resold, permitting the shareholder to recover at least some of the invested capital and to make new choices with it.

In the meantime, the firm issuing the stock must pay the investor for assuming some of its risk. The less that risk is, due to the liquidity given by the secondary markets, the less the company has to pay. The secondary markets reduce the firm's cost of equity capital.

A firm employs an investment bank to manage its Initial Public Offering of stock. For good organisation, the bank generally sells the IPO stock to institutional investors. Generally, the original owners of the corporation keep large amounts of stock in addition.

What does this mean for individual investors? Some investors believe that after an initial public offering of stock, the share price will increase because the investment bank will have originally underpriced the stock with the intention of selling it. This is not always the case, however. Share price is in general more unstable after an initial public offering than it is after the shares have been outstanding for a while. The longer the firm has been public, the more information is known about the firm and the more predictable its earnings are and thus share price.

When a firm goes public, it may issue a quite small number of shares. Its market capitalisation—the total dollar value of its outstanding shares—may thus be small. The number of individual shareholders, mostly institutional investors and the original owners also may be small. Consequently, the shares may be "thinly traded," infrequently or in small quantities.

Thinly traded shares may add to the volatility of the share price. One large shareholder deciding to sell could result in a decrease in the stock price, for instance, whereas for a firm with several shares and shareholders, the actions of any one shareholder would not be important. As always, diversification—in this case of shareholders—reduces risk. Thinly traded shares are less liquid and more risky than shares that trade more frequently.

Financial capital is one of the most important components of a business. The need for financial capital grows with a growth in the business. At a certain stage, it becomes imperative to raise a large amount of financial capital to expand and sustain the business, and at an affordable cost to the company. An IPO is one of the most popular methods of raising money from the general public and investors.

2.4.2 IPO Lifecycle Stages

The issuance of an IPO is a process with distinct stages. The lifecycle of an IPO is known to be spread over these steps or stages. The different stages in the lifecycle of an Initial Public Offering are as follows.

- **Initialisation:** In this stage, the firm employs different entities that are important in the management of the IPO. These entities include the issue managers or book runners (mostly investment banks) and registrars to the issue.

- **Pre-Issue Activities:** In this stage, the draft offer prospectus is prepared and submitted to SEBI (Securities and Exchange Board of India). The lead manager may perform road shows, which are mostly marketing activities, to generate awareness about the issue.

- **Prospectus Review:** SEBI reviews the prospectus submitted to it, and any changes and revisions suggested by SEBI are incorporated at this stage. Once the draft is approved by SEBI, it is termed as the Offer Prospectus.

- **Submit Prospectus to Stock Exchange:** The offer prospectus is now submitted to appropriate stock exchange for approval. When the date of issue and the price band (and not the exact price) is decided and included into the offer prospectus, it becomes the 'Red Herring Prospectus'.

- **Distribution of Red Herring Prospectus and IPO Forms:** The prospectus and the forms are distributed to retail investors through the syndicate members. A red herring prospectus includes the liabilities the firm may incur with regards to lawsuits filed against it.

- **Public Issue:** In this stage, the issue is thrown open to the public and the bids are collected. The public issue closes at a fixed date. This stage is considered to be the "public face" of the IPO.

- **Price Fixing:** Once all the bids are collected, the lead managers determine the final issue price, and inform the stock exchange and SEBI.

- **Processing of IPO Applications by Registrar:** This is the 'clerical' stage, wherein the forms are collected, checks are processed, share allotment is finished, shares are transferred to the demat accounts and any excess money is refunded.

- **Listing on the Stock Exchange:** Once the date of listing is determined, the shares of the 'issuer' firm are listed on the stock exchange.

2.4.3 Management of IPO

Putting together an IPO is not an easy task. Most experts estimate that it takes at least one year of intense work above and beyond the day-to-day running of your business. Some of the basic steps needed to prepare for an IPO are –

1. **Complete Business Plan:** A detailed (40 to 60 pages) document supporting the corporate profile is the first step. The company should fully disclose all aspects of the business including debt, the use of proceeds, critical processes, and any other factor

that may be important in the success of the business. It is important to show that the company has considered a wide variety of factors and have a plan of how to deal with them.

2. **Corporate Profile:** Two to four-page document describing a company's financials, business, principals, their backgrounds, and a description of the market for their product or service. The corporate profile is presented to potential underwriters (investment bankers) to interest them in participating in the IPO.

3. **Economic Analysis:** Information for potential investors on the economic viability of the business. Absolute necessities are rate of growth and net profit margins. Other financial ratio analysis and market analysis are useful.

4. **Financial Reporting:** Quarterly, audited financial statements for the past three years must be prepared by a professional, accredited accounting firm.

5. **Management Team:** An organisational chart with key players that have strong background and experience that fit with the company's projected plans.

6. **Money:** The IPO process is costly and it can't all be financed by the IPO itself. In addition to internal staff needed to prepare the IPO, there are the external audits, legal and investment banker's fees.

7. **Underwriters:** A good investment banker is critical for the management of IPO. They draft the prospectus, assist with the filing, solicit investors, determine the offering price and sell the stock. Their compensation is usually a percentage of the offering plus options on buying a certain number of shares of stock in the future. The company must conduct due diligence on a number of firms to assess which one is the right one for its particular business. Underwriters usually specialise in different types of businesses or industries and finding the right match makes the whole process smoother and more profitable.

Management of IPO

(a) **Appointment of Bankers:** When the company issues prospectus to the public, it has to make the appointment of bankers to receive the application money, allotment money and the call money on shares on behalf of the company. Under Section 69 (4) of the Companies Act, 1956 all moneys received with applications for shares have to be deposited in a special account to be opened for the purpose with a scheduled bank. The secretary of the company has to secure the consent of the bankers to act as the bankers of the company. The company has to fill up a special application form for opening an account with the bankers. The Board of Directors must pass a resolution to that effect.

The Secretary has to supply following documents to the bankers while opening an account –

(i)   A copy of Memorandum of Association.

(ii) The Certificate of Incorporation of the company.

(iii) A copy of the resolution passed by the Board of Directors

(iv) Specimen signatures of the persons who are authorised to operate the bank account

The company bankers are required to receive, on behalf of the company, the application forms and the application money from the prospective subscribers and to send daily or twice a week, advice of such receipts along with the application forms and the Pass Book at the registered office or head office of the company.

(b) Appointment of Underwriters or Share Brokers: The promoters and the directors of the company have to make necessary arrangement for the underwriting of shares before they are issued to public and listed on the stock exchange. The underwriters agree to purchase all the shares of the company that have not been subscribed for by the public. Thus, underwriters act as insurers against under-subscription of shares by the public. The investment companies, investment trust, state trading corporation, financial institutions, commercial banks, prominent share brokers normally act as underwriters. The names of the underwriters, their commission and the opinion of the directors that the resources of the underwriters are sufficient to discharge their obligations should be disclosed in the prospectus.

(c) Listing of Shares on Stock Exchange: A stock exchange means an association, organisation and/or body of individuals whether incorporated or not, established for the purpose of assisting, regulating and controlling business in buying, selling and dealing in securities. A Stock Exchange is an organised, regulated market where shares and debentures of a company can be easily bought and sold. If the shares of a company are quoted on a stock exchange, they can be easily marketed.

Listing of securities means the entry of shares or debentures of a company in the official list of a Stock Exchange. Only listed securities can be quoted on the Stock Exchange.

(d) Approval and Filing of Prospectus: Under Section 60 of the Companies Act, 1956, a prospectus must not be issued unless a copy of it, signed by every director or proposed director, or by his agent authorised in writing has been delivered to the Registrar for registration before the date of its publication. Every copy of the prospectus must point out at the top an endorsement that a copy of the prospectus has been filed with the Registrar.

(e) Publicity and Issue of Prospectus: The prospectus should be issued within 90 days of the filing of the copy of it either by newspaper advertisement or otherwise and the copies of the prospectus should be made available at company's bankers and its head office. Every application for shares should be accompanied with a copy of prospectus. Where different classes of shares are issued, the application form for each class will have a different colour, and subscribers will be requested to forward a separate remittance for each class. This helps for quick identification, easy sorting and smooth filing of applications.

(f) Receiving of Applications: The prospective subscribers are requested to forward their applications duly filled in and signed by them, directly to the company's bankers or to the authorised share brokers. Section 69 provides that the amount payable on application on each share shall not be less than 5% of the nominal value of the share. On receipt of applications, the bank issues receipts for the moneys to the applicants in the 'Receipt form' appended with each application form and credits the Share Application Account of the

Company with the amount. The details are then entered on separate sheets which are forwarded to the company as per instructions along with the application forms.

The process of collection of share application forms and share application money will continue till the last date for receiving share application forms has been passed.

(g) Scrutiny and Sorting of Applications: As soon as the company receives applications, the irregular and incomplete application forms are rejected. If insufficient money is received, the applicant may be requested to remit balance, failing which he may be given less number of shares.

The applications are sorted out according to different kinds of shares offered. For quick and easy sorting, application forms of different colours are used to distinguish clearly different types of shares and debentures.

The application forms may be sorted –

(i)   In the alphabetical order of the names of the applicants.

(ii) According to the number of shares applied for, e.g. (5 or 10, 15, 20) and its multiples.

(h) Preparation of Application and Allotment Sheets: After the applications are classified as mentioned above, the details of each application are entered in the 'Application and Allotment Lists/Register'. The subscribers to the Memorandum will be entered first. For each class of shares, different colour sheets may be used. Each application is serially numbered. All entries on the sheet must be finally checked with the application forms and with the bank Pass Book or Bankers list. A final summary sheet is also compiled to record the totals of separate sheets.

2.4.4 New IPO in India

New IPO is issued almost daily in the capital markets of India. Initial Public Offering (IPO) in India means to offer shares by a firm that was not listed earlier. New IPO in India is launched through various methods like book building method, fixed price method or a mixture of both. New IPOs in India generally have a registrar and also lead managers.

Initial Public Offering (IPO) in India is defined as the selling of the shares of a company, for the first time, to the public in the country's capital markets. This is done by giving shares to the public, which are either owned by the promoters of the firm or by issuing new shares. The method of book building was introduced in the country in 1999 and it assists the firm in finding out the demand and price of its shares. The firm that is issuing the Initial Public Offering (IPO) determines the number of shares that it will be issued and also sets the price band of the shares.

Throughout the firm's Initial Public Offering (IPO) in India, an electronic book is opened for at least five days. During this time, bidding takes place in which the individuals who are interested in buying the shares of the firm make an offer within the fixed price band. Once the book building is closed then the issuer plus the book runner of the Initial Public Offering (IPO) assess the offers and then decide a fixed price. The major objectives of New Initial Public Offer in India are to use the proceeds from the issue to fund the firm's plans for the expansion of operations and to meet the expenses of the issue.

2.5 Secondary Market

The secondary market provides a trading place for the securities already issued, to be bought and sold. It also provides liquidity to the initial buyers in the primary market to re-offer the securities to any interested buyer at any price, if mutually accepted.

The secondary market or the Stock Exchange is a market for trading and settlement of securities that have already been issued. The investors holding securities sell securities through registered brokers/sub-brokers of the Stock Exchange. Investors, who are desirous of buying securities, purchase securities through registered brokers/sub-brokers of the Stock Exchange. It may have a physical location like a Stock Exchange or a trading floor. Since 1995, trading in securities is screen-based and Internet-based trading has also made an appearance in India.

Secondary Market thus refers to a market where securities are traded after being initially offered to the public in the primary market and/or listed on the Stock Exchange. Majority of the trading is done in the secondary market. Secondary market comprises equity markets and the debt markets.

For the general investor, the secondary market provides an efficient platform for trading of his securities. For the management of the company, secondary equity markets serve as a monitoring and control conduit—by facilitating value-enhancing control activities, enabling implementation of incentive-based management contracts, and aggregating information (via price discovery) that guides management decisions.

2.5.1 Financial Products/Instrument in Secondary Market

The main financial products/instruments dealt in the secondary market –

Equity: The ownership interest in a company of holders of its common and preferred stock. The different kinds of equity shares are as follows –

- **Equity Shares:** An equity share, normally known as ordinary share also represents the form of fractional ownership where a shareholder, as a fractional owner, undertakes the maximum entrepreneurial risk connected to a business venture. The holders of such shares are members of the firm and have voting rights.
- **Rights Issue/Rights Shares:** The issue of new securities to existing shareholders at a ratio to those already held.
- **Bonus Shares:** Shares issued by the firms to their shareholders free of cost by capitalisation of accumulated reserves from the profits earned in the previous years.
- **Preferred Stock/Preference Shares:** Owners of these types of shares are entitled to a fixed dividend or dividend calculated at a fixed rate to be paid frequently before dividend can be paid regarding equity share. They also have the rights over the equity shareholders in payment of surplus. But in case of liquidation, their claims rank below the claims of the firm's creditors, bondholders/debenture holders.
- **Cumulative Preference Shares:** A type of preference shares on which dividend accumulates if remains unpaid. All arrears of preference dividend have to be paid out before paying dividend on equity shares.

- **Cumulative Convertible Preference Shares:** A type of preference shares where the dividend payable on the same accumulates, if not paid. After a particular date, these shares will be converted into equity capital of the firm.

- **Participating Preference Shares:** The right of certain preference shareholders to partake the profits after a particular fixed dividend contracted for is paid. Participation right is connected to the quantum of dividend paid on the equity shares over and above a certain specified level.

- **Security Receipts:** Security receipt means a receipt or other security, issued by a securitisation or reconstruction firm to any qualified institutional buyer pursuant to a scheme, evidencing the purchase or acquisition by the holder thereof, of an undivided right, title or interest in the financial asset involved in securitisation.

- **Government Securities (G-Secs):** These are sovereign (credit risk-free) coupon bearing instruments which are issued by the Reserve Bank of India for Government of India, in place of the Central Government's market borrowing programme. These securities have a fixed coupon that is paid on particular dates on half-yearly basis. These securities are available in extensive range of maturity dates, from short-dated (less than one year) to long-dated (up to twenty years).

- **Debentures:** Bonds issued by a firm bearing a fixed rate of interest generally paid every six months on specific dates and principal amount repayable on particular date on redemption of the debentures. Debentures are generally secured/charged against the asset of the firm in support of the debenture holder.

- **Bond:** A negotiable certificate indicating indebtedness. It is generally unsecured. A debt security is usually issued by a firm, municipality or government agency. A bond investor lends money to the issuer and in return, the issuer promises to repay the loan amount on a specified maturity date. The issuer generally pays the bond holder periodic interest payments over the life of the loan. The different kinds of bonds are as follows –
  - ✓ **Zero Coupon Bond:** It is a bond issued at a lesser rate and repaid at a face value. No periodic interest is paid. The difference between the issue price and redemption price represents the return to the holder. The buyer of these bonds receives only one payment, at the maturity of the bond.
  - ✓ **Convertible Bond:** A bond giving the investor the alternative to change the bond into equity at a fixed conversion price.

- **Commercial Paper:** A short-term promise to repay a fixed amount that is placed on the market either directly or through a specialised intermediary. It is generally issued by firms with a high credit standing in the form of a promissory note redeemable at par to the holder on maturity and thus doesn't require any warranty. The commercial paper is a money market tool issued generally for tenure of 90 days.

- **Treasury Bills:** Short-term (up to 91 days) bearer discount security issued by the Government as a means of financing its cash requirements.

2.5.2 Composition of the Secondary Market

The secondary market consists of 23 Stock Exchanges including the National Stock Exchange, Over-The-Counter Exchange of India (OTCEI) and Inter-Connected Stock Exchange of India Ltd. The secondary market provides a trading place for the securities already issued, which are bought and sold. It also provides liquidity to the initial buyers in the primary market to re-offer the securities to any interested buyer at any price, if mutually accepted. An active secondary market actually promotes the growth of the primary market and capital formation because investors in the primary market are assured of a continuous market and they can liquidate their investments.

2.6 Stock Exchange

2.6.1 Meaning of a Stock Exchange

In simple terms, a stock exchange is a market where stocks and shares are bought and sold. It is a place where an individual wishing to buy or sell particular security can find a ready customer. This is done on behalf of the individual by others who are expert in the line and who make it their profession to buy or sell securities. They are the members of the stock exchange through whom the public can deal in the market.

2.6.2 Functions and Services

The functions of and services provided by the stock exchange are as follows –

1. The security market provides an organised market for securities which ensures efficient marketability and price continuity for shares so necessary for the needs of the investors.

2. It provides for a reasonable measure of safety and fair dealing in the buying and selling of securities.

3. Through the interplay of the demand for and the supply of securities, a properly organised stock exchange assists in reasonably correct evaluation of securities in terms of their real worth.

4. Through such evaluation of securities, the stock exchange helps the orderly flow of the distribution of savings as between the different types of competitive investments.

The provision of a highly liquid and continuous market is one of the most useful functions of the stock exchange. Such a market ensures liquidity of capital, that is, it enables the conversion of a capital asset into cash quickly and with minimum loss. Another function is the evaluation of the securities at their true worth and through it the direction of the flow of savings into the most productive forms of investment.

Another function of the stock exchange is the evaluation of the securities at their true worth and through it the direction of the law of savings into the most productive forms of investment. The existence of a stock exchange enables a constant and accurate formation and registration of prices, as they change in response to the varying forces of demand and supply.

It provides the machinery whereby the price is evolved and registered. In evaluating prices on a stock exchange, the operators take into account all the relevant factors, present and prospective, concerning the particular enterprise and industry.

In view of this, the difference between the prices of shares of one company and another precisely represents the difference between the profitability and prospects or rather the public's collective estimate of this difference. Such price differentials provide valuable guidance to investors as regards the choice of shares and helps in directing the flow of savings into enterprises which are prosperous and are expected to have a bright future. Further, stock exchanges also facilitate direct placing of new capital by industrial enterprises. An organised stock exchange also ensures, through its regulations and byelaws, a reasonable degree of safety and fair dealings to the investors.

2.6.3 Stock Exchanges in India

As explained in the above section stock exchanges are structured marketplaces where affiliates of the union gather to sell firm's shares and other securities. Indian stock exchanges can either be a conglomerate/firm or mutual group. The affiliates act as intermediaries to their patrons or as key players for their own accounts.

Stock exchanges in India also assist the issue and release of securities and other monetary tools incorporating the fortification of revenues and dividends. The bookkeeping of the trade is centralised but the buying and selling is associated to a particular place as advanced marketplaces are mechanised. The buying and selling on an exchange is only open to its affiliates and brokers.

Stock exchanges are organised marketplaces, either corporations or mutual organisations, where members of the organisation gather to trade company stocks and other securities. The members may act either as agents for their customers, or as principals for their own accounts.

Stock exchanges also facilitate for the issue and redemption of securities and other financial instruments including the payment of income and dividends. The recordkeeping is central but trade is linked to such physical place because modern markets are computerised. The trade on an exchange is only by members and stockbrokers do have a seat on the exchange.

Organisation of Stock Exchange (in India)

The first organised stock exchange in India was started in Bombay in 1875 with the formation of the 'Native Share and Stock Brokers Association'. Thus, the Bombay Stock Exchange is the oldest one in the country with the growth of joint stock companies, the stock exchanges also made a steady growth and at present there are 23 recognised stock exchanges (in our country) with about 6,000 stockbrokers.

The organisation structure of stock exchanges varies from place to place; presently they may take any one of the following forms –

(a) Voluntary non-profit making association – 3 stock exchanges.

(b) Public limited company – 14 stock exchanges.

(c) Company limited by guarantee – 6 stock exchanges.

2.6.4 Management of Stock Exchange

The recognised stock exchanges are managed by "Governing Boards". The governing board consists of elected member directors that form stockbroker members. Public representatives and government nominees nominated by SEBI. The Government has also power to nominate the President and Vice President of stock exchange and to approve the appointment of the Chief Executive and public representatives. The major stock exchanges are managed by the Chief Executive Director and the smaller stock exchanges are under the control of security.

The governing boards have wide powers such as –

(a) Election of office bearers and setting up of committees like Listing Committee, Arbitration Committee, Defaulter's Committees etc.

(b) Admission and expulsion of members.

(c) Management of the properties and finance of the exchange.

(d) Framing and interpretation of rules, bye-laws etc. for the regulation of stock exchange.

(e) Adjudication of disputes among members or outsiders.

(f) Management of the affairs of the exchange in the best interest of the investors and public interest.

2.6.5 Rules for Membership of Stock Exchange

To become a member of a recognised stock exchange, a person must possess the following qualifications –

(a) He should be a citizen of India.

(b) He should not be less than 21 years of age.

(c) He should not have been adjudged as bankrupt or insolvent.

(d) He should not have been convicted for an offence involving fraud or dishonesty.

(e) He should not be engaged in any other business except dealing in securities.

(f) He should not have been expelled by any other stock exchange or declared a defaulter by any other stock exchange. Apart from individuals, a company is also eligible to become a member provided it satisfies the conditions imposed by the stock exchange.

2.6.6 Procedure of Trading in Stock Exchange

The procedure of trading (buying and selling of securities) in the stock exchange differs from one stock exchange to another stock exchange. The trading in stock exchanges can be divided into the following steps –

(a) Placing an Order with a Broker: In the stock exchange only the members are allowed to transact the business. Outsiders interested in buying and selling of securities must perform the activities only through a member broker. The client places his order to buy or sell or both at fixed prices or at the cost market prices. There are many types of orders such as 'Fixed Order', 'Limit Order', 'Option Order' etc. Each order has a clear cut meaning and the broker has to execute the order as given by the client. The order should be precise oral orders or orders given on phone should be confirmed immediately.

(b) Execution of the Order: As soon as the order is received, the broker or his authorised clerk approaches that part of the stock exchange in which the particular security is traded. The clerk asks for the quotation or may quote his own price. Short notes are taken down in pencil regarding the deals such as description of security, number of securities, price and name of the party.

(c) Reporting to the Client about the Deal: After the completion of the transaction it is recorded in the books of the broker. The 'Contract Note' is prepared and sent to the client. The 'Contract Note' gives details about the securities purchased or sold. In case of sales, the client has to hand over the share certificates to the broker. The broker gives the receipt of the certificate received from the client.

(d) Settlement of Transaction: Depending upon the nature of transaction, there are two ways of settlement. In case of ready delivery transactions, payment has to be made immediately on the transfer of securities or within a specified short period. The settlement may be made either through the clearing house or directly without the clearing house.

In case of forward delivery transactions, the settlement is made on a fixed day. The stock exchange announces the settlement programme for different group of securities periodically. All forward transactions are settled through the clearing house which simplifies payment for and delivery of securities. If the transactions of two members are equal, they are crossed out if they are not equal the net balance is paid or received. There is system of carry over to the next settlement if agreed upon by both the parties.

2.6.7 Different Stock Exchanges in India

The Indian stock market comprises two major stock exchanges, the Bombay Stock Exchange (BSE) and the National Stock Exchange (NSE), of which the former is more popular. While the BSE is a 30-stock sensitive index, or Sensex, the NSE index (S&P CNX Nifty) comprises 50 companies. Stock market trading and the functioning of the stock exchanges, brokers, investment advisors and portfolio managers are regulated by the Securities and Exchange Board of India (SEBI).

India is second only to the US in terms of the number of companies listed on its stock exchanges. India has become a preferred location for global investment firms after it liberalised its financial policies in the early 1990s. Although the participation of the middle class has increased since 2000, when the market crossed 6,000 points, the contribution of this section of investors is still limited.

2.6.8 National Stock Exchange (NSE) of India

Integrated in November 1992, the National Stock Exchange of India (NSE) was initially a tariff forfeiting association. In 1993, the exchange was certified under Securities Contracts (Regulation) Act, 1956 and in June 1994 it started its business functioning in the Wholesale Debt Market (WDM). The Equities division of NSE began its operations in 1994 while in 2000 the corporation incorporated its derivatives division.

National Stock Exchange of India (NSE) is India's largest stock exchange and World's third largest stock exchange in terms of transactions. Located in Mumbai, NSE was promoted by leading financial institutions at the behest of the Government of India, and was incorporated in November 1992 as a tax-paying company. In April 1993, NSE was recognised as a stock exchange under the Securities Contracts (Regulation) Act, 1956. NSE commenced operations in the Wholesale Debt Market (WDM) segment in June 1994. Capital Market (Equities) segment of the NSE commenced operations in November 1994, while operations in the derivatives segment commenced in June 2000. NSE has played a catalytic role in reforming Indian securities market in terms of microstructure, market practices and trading volumes. NSE has set up its trading system as a nationwide, fully automated screen-based trading system. It has written for itself the mandate to create world-class stock exchange and use it as an instrument of change for the industry as a whole through competitive pressure. NSE is set up on a demutualised model wherein the ownership, management and trading rights are in the hands of three different sets of people. This has completely eliminated any conflict of interest.

Objectives of NSE

NSE was set up with the objectives of –

- Establishing nationwide trading facility for all types of securities.
- Ensuring equal access to investors all over the country through an appropriate telecommunication network.
- Providing fair, efficient and transparent securities market using electronic trading system.
- Enabling shorter settlement cycles and book entry settlements.
- Meeting international benchmarks and standards.

Within a very short span of time, NSE has been able to achieve its objectives for which it was set up. Indian capital markets are a far cry from what they were 12 years back in terms of market practices, infrastructure, technology, risk management, clearing and settlement and investor service. To ensure continuity of business, NSE has built a full-fledged BCP site operational for the last 7 years.

NSE Markets

NSE provides a fully automated screen-based trading system with national reach in the following major market segments –

- Equity or Capital Markets (NSE's market share is over 65%)
- Futures and Options or Derivatives Market (NSE's market share is over 99.5%)
- Wholesale Debt Market (WDM)
- Mutual Funds (MF)
- Initial Public Offerings (IPO)

Some NSE Figures and Facts

- The equities division of NSE covers around 300 Indian cities, while its derivatives section covers 305 cities.
- The number of securities accessible for buying and selling in NSE exchange in its equities and derivatives section are 1,383 and 3,143 respectively.
- The total amount of settlement warranty fund in NSE equities division and derivatives section are `2,085.25 crores and ₹ 6,018.30 crores respectively.
- The daily turnover of NSE equities division is ₹ 10,336.52 crores, for derivatives segment is ₹ 32,809.96 crores and for wholesale debt division is ₹ 13,911.57 crores.
- NSE uses satellite communication expertise to strengthen contribution from around 400 Indian cities.
- The exchange administers around ₹ 1 million of buying and selling on daily basis.
- It is one of the biggest VSAT incorporated stock exchanges across the world.
- Currently more than 8,500 customers are doing online exchange business on NSE application.

The National Stock Exchange was set up as a first step in reforming the securities market through improved technology and introduction of best practices in management. It started with the concept of an independent governing body without any broker representation, thus ensuring that the operators' interests were not allowed to dominate the governance of the exchange.

Before the NSE was set up, trading on the Stock Exchanges in India used to take place through open outcry without the use of information technology for immediate matching or recording of the trades. This was time-consuming and inefficient. The practice of physical trading imposed limits on trading volumes and hence the speed with which new information was incorporated into prices. To obviate this, the NSE introduced Screen Based Trading System (SBTS) where a member can punch into the computer the quantities of shares and the prices at which he wants to transact. The transaction is executed as soon as the quote punched by a trading member finds a matching sale or buy quote from a counter party. SBTS electronically matches the buyer and seller in an order-driven system or finds the customer the best price available in a quote-driven system and hence, cuts down on time, cost and risk of error as well as on the chances of fraud.

SBTS enables distant participants to trade with each other, improving the liquidity of the markets. The high speed with which trades are executed and the large number of participants who can trade simultaneously allows faster incorporation of price sensitive information into prevailing prices. This increases the informational efficiency of markets. With SBTS it becomes possible for the market participants to see the full market, which helps to make the market more transparent, leading to increased investor confidence. The NSE started nation-wide SBTS, which have provided a completely transparent trading mechanism. Regional exchanges lost a lot of business to NSE, forcing them to introduce SBTS. Today, India can boast that almost 100% trading is taking place through electronic order matching. Prior to the setting-up of NSE, trading is on Stock Exchanges in India took place without the use of information technology for immediate matching or recording of trades. The practice of physical trading imposed limits on trading volumes as well as the speed with which the new information was incorporated into prices. The unscrupulous operators used this information asymmetry to manipulate the market.

The information asymmetry helped brokers to perpetrate a manipulative practice known as "gala". Gala is a practice of extracting highest price of the day for "buy" transaction irrespective of the actual price at which the purchase was actually done and give lowest price of the day for "sell" transactions irrespective of the price at which the sale was made. The clients did not have any method of verifying the actual price. The electronic and now fully online trading introduced by the NSE has made such manipulation difficult. It has also improved liquidity and made the entire operation more transparent and efficient. The NSE has set up a clearing corporation to provide legal counterparty guarantee to each trade thereby eliminating counterparty risk.

The National Securities Clearing Corporation Ltd. (NSCCL) commenced operations in April 1996. Counterparty risk is guaranteed through fine-tuned risk management systems and an innovative method of on-line position monitoring and automatic disablement. Principle of "novation" is implemented by the NSE capital market segment. Under this principle, NSCCL is the counterparty for every transaction and therefore, the default risk is minimised. To support the assured settlement, a "settlement guarantee fund" has been created. A large settlement guarantee fund provides a cushion for any residual risk. As a consequence, despite the fact that the daily traded volumes on the NSE run into thousands of crores of rupees, credit risk no longer poses any problem in the market place.

2.6.9 Bombay Stock Exchange (BSE) of India

The oldest stock market in Asia, BSE stands for Bombay Stock Exchange and was initially known as "The Native Share & Stock Brokers Association." Incorporated in the 1875, BSE became the first exchange in India to be certified by the administration. It attained a permanent authorisation from the Indian government in 1956 under Securities Contracts (Regulation) Act, 1956.

Over the year, the exchange company has played an essential part in the expansion of the Indian investment market. At present the association is functioning as a corporatised body integrated under the stipulations of the Companies Act, 1956.

Some BSE Figures and Facts

- BSE exchange was the first in India to launch Equity Derivatives, Free Float Index, USD adaptation of BSE Sensex and Exchange facilitated Internet buying and selling policy.

- BSE exchange was the first in India to acquire the ISO authorisation for supervision, clearance and settlement.

- BSE exchange was the first in India to have launched private service for economic training.

- Its online trading system has been felicitated by the internationally renowned Standard of Information Security Management System.

- In 2009, the average volume of business conducted on the BSE was approximately $40 billion each month.

- The number of shares traded each month on the BSE is in the range of 40 – 50 million.

- The total market capitalisation for the companies traded on the BSE is in the area of $1.1 trillion. All of the above values are stated in USD.

The Bombay Stock Exchange (BSE) is one of the oldest stock exchanges in all of Asia dating back to 1875 when it was known as the Native Share and Stock Brokers Association. The exchange is home to about 4,900 listed companies with a total market capitalisation of around 81 trillion rupees or nearly $1.8 trillion.

The BSE is also one of the busiest stock exchanges in the world, currently ranking around number five in terms of annual transactions. The exchange has experienced explosive growth with a four-fold increase in trading volume over the last 15 years.

The vision of the Bombay Stock Exchange is to "emerge as the premier Indian stock exchange by establishing global benchmarks." That means the exchange is thinking big in terms of customer service and trading activity. That being said, the market has not only experienced explosive growth in terms of trading volume, but also in terms of overall return to investors.

After compensating for inflation, the BSE has averaged a roughly 18% annual return when measured by Sensex, the most popular stock index in India, over the last 15 years. Other important indices originating from the Bombay Exchange include the BSE 100, BSE 500, BSEPSU, BSEMIDCAP, BSESMLCAP, and BSEBANKEX.

Protecting the interests of investors dealing in securities is one of the primary objectives of the exchange. The exchange provides this additional security by ensuring remedy of grievances whether this is against member companies or member/brokers. Overall guidelines for the marketplace are established by the Securities and Exchange Board of India (SEBI).

The Bombay Stock Exchange has a national reach in India, claiming a presence in over 400 towns and cities throughout the country. The exchange is operated through a unique and propriety computer system known as the "BSE Online Trading System" or BOLT. The exchange has also received ISO 9001:2000 certification in the areas of surveillance and clearing/ settlement functions.

As the first stock exchange in India, the Bombay Stock Exchange is considered to have played a very important role in the development of the country's capital markets. The Bombay Stock Exchange is the largest of 22 exchanges in India, with over 6,000 listed companies. It is also the fifth largest exchange in the world, with market capitalisation of $466 billion.

The Bombay Stock Exchange uses the BSE Sensex, an index of 30 large, developed BSE stocks. This index gives a measure of the overall performance of the Bombay Stock Exchange, and is closely followed around the world. Based on the Sensex, the BSE equity market has grown significantly since 1990.

In addition to individual stocks, the BSE also has a market in derivatives, which was the first to be established in India. Listed derivatives on the exchange include stock futures and options, index futures and options, and weekly options.

The Bombay Stock Exchange is also actively involved with the development of the retail debt market. The debt market in India is considered extremely important, as the country continues to develop and depends on this type of investment for growth. Until recently, the debt market in India was limited to a wholesale market, with banks and financial institutions as the only participants. The Bombay Stock Exchange believes that a retail market will bring great opportunities to individual investors through better diversification.

Objectives of BSE

The main aims and objectives of the BSE are as follows –

- To provide a market place for the purchase and sale of security evidencing the ownership of business property or of a public or business debt.
- It aims to promote, develop and maintain a well-regulated market for dealing in securities.
- To safeguard the interest of members and the investing public having dealings on the Exchange.
- It helps industrial development of the country through efficient resource mobilisation.
- To establish and promote honourable and just practices in securities transactions.

Bombay Stock Exchange is thus a capital market regulator, which aims to ensure fair, transparent and safe market, promote and inculcate honourable and just trading practices in securities and to discourage malpractices. BSE is also positioning itself as a major player in providing training and skill enhancement in the capital markets in India and other emerging markets.

Services offered by BSE

BSE offers a wide range of products for trading in the securities market. An investor can choose from 4,687 listed companies. For the easy reference of investors, companies are classified into A, B1, B2, and Z groups. Another feature of equity trading at BSE is the 'Basket Trading' facility.

It also has a wide range of services to empower the investors and facilitate smooth transactions –

- **Investor Services:** Department of Investor Services redresses grievances of investors.

- **IndoNext:** In order to enable Small and Medium Enterprises (SMEs) to raise equity and debt, and facilitate trading in such companies, BSE has launched a single order book national trading platform called BSE IndoNext.

- **BSE Training Institute:** BTI imparts capital market training and certification, in collaboration with reputed management institutes and universities, offers 40 courses on various aspects of the capital market and financial sector.

- **The BSE Online Trading (BOLT):** BSE Online Trading (BOLT) facilitates online screen-based trading in securities. BSE Online Trading is currently operating in 8000 Trader Workstations located across over 409 cities in India.

- **BSEWEBX.com**: In February 2001, the Exchange introduced the world's first centralised exchange-based Internet trading system, BSEWEBX.com. The initiative enables investors anywhere in the world to trade on the BSE platform.

- **Surveillance:** BSE's Online Surveillance (BOSS) monitors on real time basis price movements, volume positions and member position and real time measurement of default risk, market reconstruction and generation of cross market alerts.

2.6.10 Over-the-Counter Exchange in India (OTCEI)

The over-the-counter market is a place where the buyers seek out sellers and sellers seek out buyers and then they attempt to arrange terms and conditions for purchase or sale acceptable to both, which is different from the other stock markets. It is a negotiated marketplace which exists anywhere without a particular auction market place like other stock exchanges.

Over-the-Counter Exchange in India was formed with the objective of solving the problems of small investors and companies. Earlier, small investors faced various problems like difficulty in access, illiquidity, delay in payment, delay in delivery and uncertainty regarding prices at which their shares are bought or sold. Companies faced problems like prohibitive issue costs, restricted access to markets and administered pricing of their shares. Moreover, there was a long-felt need for a second tier market where companies with small paid-up capital could have the advantages of listing. It has been set up to provide a cost effective and convenient platform for raising finance from the capital market.

OTCEI was incorporated in the year October 1990 and started functioning from September 1992. It is based in Mumbai, Maharashtra. It was set up to access high technology enterprising promoters in raising finance for new product development in a cost-effective manner and to provide a transparent and efficient trading system to investors. The Capital of OTCEI is ₹ 8 crores and is promoted by a consortium of all-India financial institutions and the subsidiaries of public sector banks such as UTI, ICICI, IDBI, IFCI, LIC, GIC and its subsidiaries. It is a ring-less, electronic and national stock exchange designed for investor convenience. OTC market represents the triumph of modern communications over the limitations imposed by geography.

Features of OTC Exchange

1. **Elimination of Trading Ring:** There is no trading ring as is present in the other stock exchanges. Trading in OTC exchange takes place through a network of computers located at several places within the same city or even across cities. It is rightly called as a floorless market with no physical location, no stock exchange building and no hustle and bustle scene of conventional stock exchange.

2. **Negotiated Deals:** The transactions are completed through 'negotiations' rather than through 'auction' which is the practice in the stock exchanges.

3. **Nationwide Reach:** The OTC Exchange has a nationwide reach, enabling widely dispersed trading across cities. There is greater liquidity for the investors and the companies get the benefit of nationwide reach by listing at one exchange.

4. **Computerised Trading:** OTCEI lends more transparency and speed as all the trading activities are computerised. Dealers quote, query and transact through a central OTC computer using telecommunication links.

5. **Exclusive Listing:** The OTCEI does not list and trade in the companies which are already listed on any other exchange. It lists an entirely new set of companies, sponsored by members of OTCEI.

6. OTCEI deals in equity shares, preference shares, bonds, debentures and warrants.

Objectives of OTCEI

➢ To provide more liquidity

➢ To have a fixed and a fair price

➢ To develop secondary market through which small growing companies can raise finance and provide liquidity thereof

➢ To make the process of buying and selling securities more simple and convenient

➢ To create public interest in risky but viable ventures

➢ To provide liquidity to a less traded security or a smaller company

➢ To provide for easy and cheaper means of making public sale of new issues

Operators in the OTC Market

The OTC Market in India comprises of companies, investors, members and licensed dealers. It brings together investors and companies which seek to raise funds from such investors.

Members: They are financial institutions, banks, mutual funds, venture capital funds and large financial companies whose net worth is not less than ₹ 2.5 crores. They perform the following functions –

➢ Act as brokers

➢ Create a market in the scrip

➢ Serve as market makers

➢ Act as sponsors

Dealers: They would be a corporate body, partnership firm or individuals and are selected by the OTC committee after an interview. The dealers should have a net worth of ₹ 5 lakhs and in case of corporate bodies, not less than 40% of their share capital should be held by the promoters. They perform the following functions –

➢ Carry out the trading activities

➢ Act as market makers

Advantages of OTCEI

Advantages to Investors

➢ Simple and convenient ring-less trading

➢ Safety and security due to an OTC card which is provided to the investors free of cost

➢ Immediate confirmation of transactions

➢ Better liquidity

➢ Quick allotment

➢ Quick payment and quick delivery of scripts

➢ Quick share transfer process

➢ Greater accessibility due to computerised network

➢ Greater transparency

➢ Display of prices and market information at every dealer's premises

Advantages to Companies

➢ Smaller and less liquid companies get the listing facility

➢ Lower costs of new issues

➢ Lower expenses of servicing to the investors

➢ More liquidity to the shares

➢ Easy access for closely held and family concerns

➢ Larger number of dealer network

➢ Dealers can operate both in the new issue market and the secondary market

Differences between OTCE and Stock Exchange

Basis of Distinction	OTCE	Stock Exchange
1. Year of establishment	1990	BSE-1875 NSE-1992
2. Minimum issued share capital	₹ 30 lakhs	₹ 3 crores
3. Minimum issue size needed	₹ 20 lakhs	₹ 1.80 crores
4. Trading ring	Presence of market makers, hence no trading ring	Trading ring exists, which is a place where the agents of seller and buyer can establish physical contact.
5. Price fixation	Prices are fixed by the market makers	There is direct trading between the buyers and sellers who fix the price.
6. Sponsors and market makers	Every company entering OTCEI will have to appoint a sponsor and at least two market makers for its securities.	No such requirement for entering stock exchange.

2.7 SEBI

The Securities and Exchange Board of India (SEBI) is the regulatory authority in India established under Section 3 of SEBI Act, 1992. SEBI Act, 1992 provides for establishment of Securities and Exchange Board of India (SEBI) with statutory powers for –

(a) Protecting the interests of investors in securities

(b) Promoting the development of the securities market and

(c) Regulating the securities market

2.7.1 The Background

Securities and Exchange Board of India, popularly called SEBI, is a quasi government body that was initially formed in 1988 by an administrative order. The Indian capital market had started developing very fast during the 1980s. The amount of capital raised by companies from the primary market increased from a modest 200 crores in 1980 to a substantial 6500 crores in 1990. This implied a great exposure of public money, which also attracted a number of fly-by-night operators. This necessitated a watchdog that could safeguard the interests of investors.

SEBI was provided a statutory status in the immediate aftermath of infamous securities scam perpetrated by Harshad Mehta. The scam shook up the foundations of the Indian financial framework. The stock market, which was making a frenzied climb upwards, collapsed on its face. Thousands of crores of market equity was destroyed overnight and a number of financial institutions and banks were forced to shut shop. That a single individual could twist and tweak the system, with all its apparent loopholes, for earning tremendous profits became painfully apparent to everyone.

A number of financial institutions and other market players were left high and dry after the scam, but the biggest loser turned out to be the common investor. The economy had just started opening up after the 1991 economic reforms, and the Indian market was just taking its first tottering steps. At this stage, such a huge scam would not only have damaged the market, but would have severely damaged investor confidence. In time, investors could have lost trust in the system, thus adversely affecting the ability of companies to raise money in stock market. This, in turn, would have severely restricted industrial growth at a time when the economy had started improving.

The Securities and Exchange Board of India Act was passed in 1992, thus giving the regulatory teeth to the body. SEBI was entrusted with the primary task of protecting the interests of the investors. In addition, SEBI was also entrusted with the twin objectives of developing and regulating the stock market. In this regard, SEBI has done a decent job, though admittedly, there have been instances when the regulator has been caught napping! But overall, the lot of investors has definitely improved due to the policies and steps taken by the regulator.

2.7.2 Offices and Administration

SEBI has its head office located at Mumbai, the financial capital of India. In addition, SEBI has four regional offices, located at New Delhi, Chennai, Kolkata and Ahmedabad. The regional offices have jurisdiction over the companies and institutions located on their designated areas.

To manage its affairs, SEBI has a five member board, headed by a chairperson. Out of the five members, one member each is taken from the Law and Finance ministries, one member is from RBI, and the remaining two members can be eminent members of the industry.

2.7.3 Organisation of SEBI

SEBI has five departments as follows –

1) **Primary Market Department** which deals with policy matters and regulatory issues of primary market and the market intermediaries, and the redressal of investor grievances.

2) **Issue Management Intermediaries Department** which looks after vetting of offer documents, registration, regulation and monitoring of issues related to intermediaries.

3) **Secondary Market Department** to look after policy matters and regulatory issues of the secondary market such as price monitoring, insider trading, kerb trading and administration of major stock exchanges.

4) **Institutional Investment Department** which frames policies for Foreign Institutional Investors (FIIs) and mutual funds and also looks after mergers and acquisitions.

5) **Advisory Committee** which provides advisory inputs in framing policies and regulations for primary and secondary markets.

2.7.4 Role of SEBI as a Regulatory Authority

SEBI has been entrusted with a wide-ranging role to develop and regulate the financial markets. The primary task of SEBI is to regulate the affairs of the stock markets. In this respect, SEBI has introduced a number of notable reforms such as dematerialisation of shares, online share trading, approval for stock indices trading, derivatives trading. This has made the market broad-based and easily approachable by everyone. Over the years, SEBI has also evolved and enforced a code of conduct for the banks, financial institutions, companies, mutual funds, financial intermediaries/brokers and portfolio managers.

In addition, SEBI deals with following activities related to financial markets –

- Primary market issues
- Secondary market issues
- Mutual funds
- Takeovers and mergers and acquisition
- Collective investment schemes
- Share buy backs
- Delisting of shares from stock exchanges

SEBI is also entrusted with handling investor grievances and complaints related to any of the abovementioned activities. SEBI also undertakes periodical investor education initiatives, workshops and seminars to raise investment and financial awareness.

Its regulatory jurisdiction extends over corporates in the issuance of capital and transfer of securities, in addition to all intermediaries and persons associated with securities market. SEBI has been obligated to perform the aforesaid functions by such measures as it thinks fit. In particular, it has powers for –

- Regulating the business in stock exchanges and any other securities markets
- Registering and regulating the working of stock brokers, sub-brokers etc.
- Promoting and regulating self-regulatory organisations
- Prohibiting fraudulent and unfair trade practices
- Calling for information from, undertaking inspection, conducting inquiries and audits of the stock exchanges, intermediaries, self-regulatory organisations, mutual funds and other persons associated with the securities market

Securities and Exchange Board of India (SEBI) was first established in the year 1988 as a non-statutory body for regulating the securities market. It became an autonomous body in 1992 and more powers were given through an ordinance. Since then it regulates the market through its independent powers.

SEBI is a regulator to control the Indian capital market. Since its establishment in 1992, it is doing hard work for protecting the interests of Indian investors. The role of Security Exchange Board of India (SEBI) in regulating the Indian capital market is very important because the government of India can only open or take decision to open new stock exchange in India after getting advice from SEBI.

If SEBI thinks that it will be against its rules and regulations, SEBI can ban any stock exchange to trade in shares and stocks.

2.7.5 Important Functions of SEBI

The important role/functions of SEBI are as follows –

1. To act as an apex institution for development and regulating of securities market.

2. To register stock exchanges and to regulate trading on them. Co-ordinate, integrate and monitor the working of stock exchange and to establish new stock exchanges.

3. To register, monitor, co-ordinate and regulate the activities pertaining to the issue and trading of securities.

4. To grant permission for issue of securities and to formulate guidelines for issue and listing of securities.

5. To define and enforce disclosure requirements on issue of securities both at the time of issue and at regular intervals after listing either in its own or in consultation with professional bodies like the Institute of Chartered Accountants, Institute of Cost and Works Accountants of India and Institute of Company Secretaries of India.

6. To check insider trading and excessive speculation and to control such practices which are not in the interest of investors.

7. To monitor and regulate the functioning of mutual funds and investment companies.

8. To regulate takeover deals, mergers and amalgamation: Many big companies in India want to create monopoly in capital market. So, these companies buy all other companies or deal of merging. SEBI sees whether this merger or acquisition is for development of business or to harm capital market.

9. To conduct inspection, to order special audit of books of brokers, jobbers, merchant bankers, underwriters, investment advisors, to call for evidence and to institute civil and criminal proceedings were required.

10. To conduct investment research and analysis to build up the data bank in the working of public limited companies and to help in setting of national information system.

11. Power to make rules for controlling stock exchange: SEBI has power to make new rules for controlling stock exchange in India. For example, SEBI fixed the time of trading as 9 AM and 5 PM in stock market.

12. To provide license to dealers and brokers: SEBI has power to provide license to dealers and brokers of capital market. If SEBI sees that any financial product is of capital nature, then SEBI can also control that product and its dealers. One of main example is ULIP's case. SEBI said, "It is just like mutual funds and all banks and financial and insurance companies who want to issue it, must take permission from SEBI."

13. To stop fraud in capital market: SEBI has many powers for stopping fraud in capital market. It can ban the trading of those brokers who are involved in fraudulent and unfair trade practices relating to stock market. It can impose penalties on capital market intermediaries if they get involved in insider trading.

14. To audit the performance of stock market: SEBI uses its powers to audit the performance of different Indian stock exchange for bringing transparency in the working of stock exchanges.

15. To make new rules on carry forward transactions: Share trading transactions carry forward cannot exceed 25% of broker's total transactions; 90-day limit for carry forward.

16. To create relationship with ICAI: ICAI is the authority for making new auditors of companies. SEBI creates good relationships with ICAI for bringing more transparency in the auditing work of company accounts because audited financial statements are a mirror to the real face of the company and after this, investors can decide to invest or not to invest. Moreover, investors of India can easily trust audited financial reports. After the Satyam scam, SEBI is investigating with ICAI, whether CAs are doing their duty in an ethical way or not.

17. Introduction of derivative contracts on volatility index: For reducing the risk of investors, SEBI has now decided to permit stock exchanges to introduce derivative contracts on volatility index, subject to the condition that –

    (a) The underlying Volatility Index has a track record of at least one year.

    (b) The exchange has in place the appropriate risk management framework for such derivative contracts.

    Before introduction of such contracts, the stock exchanges shall submit the following –

    • Contract specifications

    • Position and exercise limits

    • Margins

    • The economic purpose it is intended to serve

    • Likely contribution to market development

    • The safeguards and the risk protection mechanism adopted by the exchange to ensure market integrity, protection of investors and smooth and orderly trading.

- The infrastructure of the exchange and the surveillance system to effectively monitor trading in such contracts, and
- Details of settlement procedures and systems
- Details of back-testing of the margin calculation for a period of one year considering a call and a put option on the underlying with a delta of 0.25 and -0.25 respectively and actual value of the underlying link

18. To require report of portfolio management activities: SEBI has also power to require report of portfolio management to check the capital market performance. Recently, SEBI sent the letter to all registered portfolio managers of India for demanding reports.

19. To educate the investors: Time to time, SEBI arranges scheduled workshops to educate the investors. On 22nd May 2010, SEBI conducted a workshop.

2.7.6 Objectives of SEBI

As an important entity in the market it works with the following objectives –

1. It tries to develop the securities market.
2. Promotes investors' interest.
3. Makes rules and regulations for the securities market.

Since its inception SEBI has been working targeting the securities and is attending to the fulfilment of its objectives with commendable zeal and dexterity. The improvements in the securities markets like capitalisation requirements, margining, establishment of clearing corporations etc. reduced the risk of credit and also reduced the market.

SEBI has introduced the comprehensive regulatory measures, prescribed registration norms, the eligibility criteria, the code of obligations and the code of conduct for different intermediaries like, bankers to issue, merchant bankers, brokers and sub-brokers, registrars, portfolio managers, credit rating agencies, underwriters and others. It has framed bye-laws, risk identification and risk management systems for clearing houses of stock exchanges, surveillance system etc. which has made dealing in securities both safe and transparent to the end investor.

Another significant event is the approval of trading in stock indices (like S&P CNX Nifty and Sensex) in 2000. A market index is a convenient and effective product because of the following reasons –

- It acts as a barometer for market behaviour
- It is used to benchmark portfolio performance
- It is used in derivative instruments like index futures and index options
- It can be used for passive fund management as in case of index funds

Two broad approaches of SEBI is to integrate the securities market at the national level, and also to diversify the trading products, so that there is an increase in number of traders including banks, financial institutions, insurance companies, mutual funds, primary dealers etc. to transact through the exchanges. In this context the introduction of derivatives trading through Indian stock exchanges permitted by SEBI in the year 2000 is a real landmark.

SEBI appointed the L. C. Gupta Committee in 1998 to recommend the regulatory framework for derivatives trading and suggest bye-laws for Regulation and Control of Trading and Settlement of Derivatives Contracts. The Board of SEBI in its meeting held on May 11, 1998 accepted the recommendations of the committee and approved the phased introduction of derivatives trading in India beginning with Stock Index Futures. The Board also approved the "suggestive bye-laws" as recommended by the L. C. Gupta Committee for Regulation and Control of Trading and Settlement of Derivatives Contracts.

SEBI then appointed the J. R. Verma Committee to recommend Risk Containment Measures (RCM) in the Indian Stock Index Futures Market. The report was submitted in November, 1998.

However, the Securities Contracts (Regulation) Act, 1956 (SCRA) required amendment to include "derivatives" in the definition of securities to enable SEBI to introduce trading in derivatives. The necessary amendment was then carried out by the government in 1999. The Securities Laws (Amendment) Bill, 1999 was introduced. In December 1999 the new framework was approved.

Derivatives have been accorded the status of "securities". The ban imposed on trading in derivatives in 1969 under a notification issued by the Central Government was revoked. Thereafter SEBI formulated the necessary regulations/bye-laws and intimated the Stock Exchanges in the year 2000. The derivative trading started in India at NSE in 2000 and BSE started trading in the year 2001.

2.7.7 Powers of SEBI

SEBI has to perform its functions and exercise such powers under the Securities Contracts (Regulation) Act, 1956 as may be delegated to it by the Central Government which are as follows:

1. Call for periodical returns from stock exchanges
2. Grant approval to any recognised stock exchange to make bye-laws for the regulation on control of contracts
3. Make or amend bye-laws of recognised stock exchanges
4. Compel a public company to list its shares in any stock exchange
5. Licensing of dealers in securities in certain areas
6. Appoint any person to make enquiries into the affairs of stock exchange
7. Suspend business of any recognised stock exchange
8. Prohibit contract in certain cases

2.8 Derivatives

2.8.1 Introduction

A derivative can be defined as a financial instrument whose value depends upon (or derives from) the value of other basic underlying variables. Very often, the variables underlying derivatives are the prices of traded assets. For instance, a commodity alternative is a derivative whose value depends on the price of a stock. The underlying variable can be anything. Active trading occurs in credit derivatives, electricity derivatives, weather derivatives, insurance derivatives etc. New types of interest rates, foreign exchange and equity derivative products have been formed. Derivatives are the most modern financial tools in hedging risk.

Against unexpected market conditions, derivatives are not only used as trading products, but also for hedging the position of the producer or trader. Hedging is defined as taking simultaneous but equal and offsetting positions on the cash and futures markets. The basic thought behind hedging is to hold opposing positions in the two markets simultaneously. Each market position provides protection from a bad price change in the other market. The cash market position is an essential part of the producer. This cash market position puts the producer in danger from a decline in grain prices. Taking an offsetting position in the futures market is a 'hedge' against the potential for a risky move in the cash market price. Simultaneously, the cash market position can guard him from losses on the futures market.

The individuals and firms who wish to avoid or reduce risk can deal with the others who are willing to accept the risk for a price. A common place where such transactions take place is called the 'derivative market'.

In recent years, derivative securities have become increasingly important in the field of finance. They are also known as contingent claims. To understand the concept of derivatives, let us take the example of wheat which is a major raw material for a number of products. Generally, the price of wheat decreases during the harvesting season but becomes high before and after the harvest. A wheat farmer, who is exposed to such type of fluctuations, can eliminate the risk of price fluctuations by selling the wheat at a future date by entering into a forward or a futures contract, in the derivatives market. The prices in the derivative market are driven by the spot price of the underlying asset, which is wheat in this case.

Derivatives can be compared to insurance policies. Insurance takes care of specific risks such as fire, floods, accidents, health etc. Derivatives take care of market risks such as fluctuation in interest rates, currency rates, share prices etc.

Following are the important derivative securities:

1. Forward Contracts
2. Futures Contracts
3. Options

2.8.2 Forward Contracts

A forward contract is a simple derivative security which is an agreement to buy or sell an asset at a certain future time for a certain price. The contract is usually between either two financial institutions or a financial institution and one of its corporate clients. It is a private agreement between two parties and it is not traded on a stock exchange.

One of the parties to a forward contract assumes a long position and agrees to buy the underlying security on a certain specified future date for certain specified price. The other party assumes a short position and agrees to sell the asset on the same date for the same price. A forward contract is settled at maturity. The holder of the short position delivers the security to the holder of the long position in return for cash equal to the delivery price.

Thus, a forward contract is a contract to buy or sell a specified quantity of an asset at a future date at a certain specified price agreed upon today.

2.8.3 Futures

A futures contract is a standard contract that is traded on a futures market exchange. The contract specifies the product, place of delivery, and time of delivery. Quality, if the specification is not mentioned in the listed contracts, is an explicit part of each contract. Price is the only important part of the futures contract that is not pre-specified. Price is decided by the communication of buyers and sellers in a location (called the trading pit) designated by the exchange. The exchange establishes the time periods when trading occurs, develops and implements other rules connected to trading, and gives additional services required by traders. The actual buying and selling that takes place in the trading pit is done by people that have purchased the right to trade (called a seat) on the exchange. Therefore, the general public buys or sells futures contracts through a broker who has access to a seat on the exchange.

Although the processes involved in trading futures contracts may look difficult, knowledge of only a few basic marketing concepts is required to understand the concept of hedging. Through the broker, it is possible to sell a futures contract today with the understanding that you must offset the short position at a later date. The idea of selling something before buying something may seem strange, particularly if you have by tradition sold in cash markets. It is significant to remember that the futures contract is a formal agreement, and you can agree to sell something in the future even when you don't have something to sell now. If prices reduce between the time you sell and buy the futures contract, you then buy the contract at a price that is less than your sale price. You receive the gain connected to this sell-high, buy-low transaction. If you initially sell a futures contract and the price increases, you must buy at the higher price. You suffer the loss connected to this sell-low, buy-high transaction.

As a futures trader, it is also possible to buy a futures contract with the understanding that you must offset with a sale at a future date. The effects of price changes from this long position are just the opposite of those discussed for the short (sale) position above.

Specifically, if you take a long position and price reduces, you incur a loss on the buy-high, sell-low transaction. If you take a long position and price rises, you gain from the buy-low, sell-high transaction. Buying or selling futures contracts requires the service of a broker with access to the exchange where futures contracts are traded. Your broker carries out trades on your behalf per your instructions. You pay a fee to the broker for implementing an order to buy or sell a futures contract. Like payment for any service, commissions differ broker to broker. Commissions are generally quoted for entering and closing a futures position (called a round turn).

Since all traders with a futures position can potentially suffer losses, all traders must create a deposit (a margin) to guarantee all losses will be paid. A margin is the money deposited by both the buyer and seller to guarantee performance under the terms of the futures contract. Minimum margins are set by each commodity exchange, but individual brokers may have higher margin needs. This original margin is normally a small part of the total value of the contract, and may not cover a trader's total loss over time. Thus, a margin call is a request for additional money the futures trader must deposit if adverse price moves considerably and devalues the initial margin deposit. If the market moves against your position by an amount such that your initial margin may not cover additional losses (called the maintenance margin), the broker asks for more money. That is, you receive a margin call from your broker and the additional money is required to keep your futures position.

Since the idea of hedging is for losses on one market to be offset by gains in the other market, price changes in the two markets should be connected. This price connection between the cash and futures market is measured by a concept called basis. Basis is the difference between the price at cash market and the futures price (that is, cash price minus the futures price).

This relationship (or basis) is a significant concept in effective hedging. The complete reason behind hedging is for adverse price moves in the cash market to be offset by favourable price moves in the futures market. If the two markets aren't connected in some way, hedging doesn't work. Therefore, measuring and understanding basis is the key to successful hedging.

Basis is usually calculated as local cash price minus the nearby futures price. Basis is frequently quoted as over a positive basis or under a negative basis. 'Over' or 'under' refers to the cash price being above or below the futures price, respectively. Basis relationships change over time. A weakening basis takes place when the cash price declines relative to the futures price. A strengthening basis takes place when the cash price increases in relation to the futures price.

2.8.4 Options

A commodity option is a two-party agreement that gives the buyer the right, but not the obligation, to take a futures position. This prospective position can be either a short or a long position in a designated futures contract (called the underlying futures contract). The futures position will be given at a specified price (called the strike price or exercise price), and the right exists until a pre-established date (called the expiration date). Although expiration dates differ, most options on grain futures expire during the last week of the month before the contract month of the underlying futures contract.

An option is purchased from an option seller (called the writer or grantor). The writer of an option has the obligation to give the option holder the futures position at the agreed-upon strike price. As the buyer, you buy the option at the going market price (called the premium). If cash grain prices move unfavourably, you may use the option to get the protection connected to a futures position. The option seller is duty-bound to give you the futures position at the strike price. On the other hand, you don't want the protection connected to a futures position if cash grain prices move favourably. As the holder of the option, you are not obligated to take a futures position. Therefore, options are like purchasing insurance. You pay the premium, but you may or may not require the protection of the underlying futures position. The basic characteristics of options are limited loss, high leverage potential and limited life.

Types

There are mainly two types of options –

➢ Put Option

➢ Call Option

The purchase of a put option gives the holder the right to a short futures position at the strike price. The seller of the put must provide the holder with the specified short futures position. Thus a put option gives its owner the legal right to sell shares to someone else within certain time and at certain price. Put option is purchased by those who hope to make a profit from a decline in the price of shares.

The purchase of a call option gives the holder the right to a long futures position at the strike price. In this case, the seller of the call option must provide you as the holder with the specified long futures position. In other words, a call option is a choice to buy shares, wherein the holder gets the privilege of purchasing a given number of shares of a given stock from the maker within a certain time and at a certain price. It is purchased by those who hope to profit from a rise in the price of shares.

Purchasing a put option (the right to sell a futures position) protects you as the holder of the put against falling cash prices. If prices fall, you have the right to a short futures position at the higher strike price. A short futures position at a high price means you can offset with a buy at the current lower market price and receive the gain. Purchasing a call option (the right to buy a futures position) protects you as the holder of the call against rising prices. If prices rise, you have the right to a long futures position at the lower strike price. A long futures position at a low price means you can offset with a sale at the current higher market price and receive the gain. A call option can also be used as a fairly low risk strategy to participate in market price gains after your physical commodity has been sold.

There are technical terms used in option contracts. The common words used in an option contract are explained below –

1. **Strike Price:** The "specified price" in the option is referred to as the exercise price or strike price. This is the price at which the underlying commodity can be exchanged and is fixed for any given option, put or call. There are several options with different strike prices traded during any period of time. As a general rule, the more volatile the price is for the underlying commodity, the greater the number of options at different strike prices that will be available for trade. If the price of the underlying commodity changes over time, then additional strike prices may be traded.

2. **Underlying Commodity:** The underlying commodity for the commodity option is not the commodity itself, but rather a futures contract for that commodity. For example, a June chilli option will actually be an option for a June delivery chilli futures contract. In this sense, the options are on futures and not on the physical commodity.

3. **Buyers and Sellers:** In the option market, as in every other market, every transaction requires both a buyer and a seller. The buyer of an option is referred to as an option holder. Holders of options may be either seekers of price insurance or speculators. The seller of an option may also be either a speculator or one who desires partial price protection. Whether one chooses to buy (hold) or sell (write) an option depends primarily upon his/her objectives. The market will contain many insurers and price speculators, each providing a service to the other.

4. **Expiration:** Options on agricultural commodities have futures contracts as the underlying commodity. Futures contracts have a definite predetermined maturity date during the delivery month. So too, options will have a date at which they mature and expire. For example, a ₹ 5,100 June chilli option is an option to buy or sell one June chilli futures contract at ₹ 5,100. The option can be exercised by the holder on any business day until mid-May at which time the option expires. Trading in most options will not be conducted during the futures contract delivery month. Upon expiration, the option becomes worthless.

5. **Option Premiums:** The option (put or call) writer or grantor is willing to incur an obligation in return for some compensation. The writer of an option is an option seller. The compensation is called the option premium. Using the insurance analogy, a premium is paid on an insurance policy to gain the coverage it provides and an option premium is paid to gain the right granted in the option. The premium is determined by public outcry and acceptance in an exchange trading pit, and like all commodity prices, can be expected to change daily.

2.8.5 Distinction between Futures and Options

Futures	Options
1. Futures create obligation to make or take delivery at some future date	1. Options confer rights but not the obligation to do the same
2. No payment is involved for entering into future contract	2. Payment is involved and premium paid on options is non-refundable
3. Futures contracts are usually larger in value	3. Options are smaller in value
4. They establish a price	4. Options set a range within or outside which a position proves profitable
5. The parties of the contract must perform at the settlement date. They are not obligated to perform before the date	5. The buyer can exercise option any time prior to the expiry date

Money Market Futures and Options

Active trading in money market futures and options occurs on number of commodity exchanges. They function in the similar manner like any other futures and options.

2.9 Money Market

The money market is an important part of the financial system as it is the pivot of monetary operations conducted by the central bank in its pursuit of monetary policy goals. The money markets in India have eventually evolved generating new instruments and participants with differing risk profiles that are similar to the changes in the operating processes of monetary policy. Along with the shifts in the operating procedures of monetary policy, the liquidity management operations of the Reserve Bank have also been modified to improve the efficiency of monetary policy signalling. The increasing financial innovations as a result of greater openness of the economy necessitated the shift from monetary targeting to a multiple indicator approach with greater stress on rate channels for monetary policy formulation. As a result, short-term interest rates have appeared as an important tool of monetary policy since the introduction of Liquidity Adjustment Facility (LAF), which has become the main mechanism of modulating liquidity conditions on a daily basis.

Due to different policy initiatives, there has been an important transformation of the money market, with regards to instruments, participants and technological infrastructure. Different reform measures have resulted in a relatively deep, liquid and vibrant money market. The changes in the money market structure and monetary policy operating procedures in India have been largely in step with international experience and best practices.

Despite the significant progress made so far, further development of the money market requires more measures. Direct regulation in the form of prudential limits on borrowing and lending in the call money market would need to graduate to a system, where such limits are taken care of by banks' own internal system of ALM framework. Greater efforts are needed to speed up development of the term money market. Moreover, there is a need to think about broad-basing the pool of underlying collateral securities for repo transactions. This would not only ease liquidity management but also promote the development of underlying debt instruments. The need for rating for issuing CP could potentially be made more flexible. In the end, liquidity forecasting methods are required to be further refined for proper evaluation of liquidity conditions by the Reserve Bank.

The money market is a market for overnight to short-term funds and for short-term money and financial assets that are close substitutes for money. Short-term in the Indian context means a period of up to one year. Close substitute for money means any financial asset, which can be quickly converted into money.

The major participants in this market are the commercial banks, the other financial intermediaries, large corporates and the Reserve Bank of India. The RBI plays a major role and occupies a strategic position in these markets. It influences the availability and cost of credit.

2.9.1 Objectives of Money Market

The basic objectives of these markets are to provide –

1. A mechanism for evening out short-term surpluses and deficiencies.
2. A focal point of central bank intervention for influencing liquidity in the economy.
3. A reasonable access to the users of short-term funds to meet their requirements at realistic costs.

In the money market, the operations are for a short duration as compared to the capital markets. There are a large number of participants in the money market. The depth of this market depends on the number of participants. This is a wholesale market. The volumes here are very large and therefore, there is a need for professionals to operate in these markets. Trading here is conducted mainly on telephones, followed by a written confirmation from both the parties.

2.9.2 Components of Money Market

The money market has two components – the organised and the unorganised.

1. Organised Money Market

The organised market is dominated by the commercial banks. The other major participants are the Reserve Bank of India (RBI), Life Insurance Corporation (LIC), General Insurance Corporation, Unit Trust of India (UTI), Securities Trading Corporation of India Ltd. and Discount and Finance House of India, other primary dealers, commercial banks and mutual funds. The core of the money market is the inter-bank call money market, whereby short-term money borrowing/lending is effected to manage the temporary liquidity mismatches. The Reserve Bank of India occupies a strategic position of managing market liquidity through open market operations of government securities, access to its accommodation, cost (interest rates), availability of credit and other monetary management tools. Normally, monetary assets of a short-term nature, generally less than one year, are dealt with in this market.

2. Unorganised Money Market

Despite the rapid expansion of the organised money market, through a large network of banking institutions that have extended their reach even to the rural areas, there is still an active unorganised market. It consists of indigenous bankers and moneylenders. In the unorganised market, there is no clear demarcation between short-term and long-term finance and even between the purposes of finance. The unorganised sector continues to provide finance for trade as well as personal consumption. The inability of the poor to meet the 'creditworthiness' requirements of the banking sector make them take recourse to the institutions that still remain outside the regulatory framework of banking. But this market is shrinking fast due to the opening up of the economy.

2.9.3 Functions

The money market is a market for short-term funds, that is, up to one year maturity. Thus, it covers money, and financial assets that are close substitutes for money. The money market is generally expected to perform three broad functions –

1. It should provide an equilibrating mechanism to even out demand for and supply of short-term funds.

2. The money market should provide a focal point for central bank intervention for influencing liquidity and general level of interest rates in the economy.

3. It should provide reasonable access to providers and users of short-term funds to fulfil their borrowing and investment requirements at an efficient market-clearing price.

RBI is the most important constituent in the money market. By virtue of the implication for the conduct of monetary policy, money market comes within the direct purview of RBI regulation. The primary aim of the Reserve Bank of India's operations in the money market is to ensure that the liquidity and short-term interest rates are maintained at levels consistent with the monetary policy objectives of maintaining price stability, ensuring adequate flow of credit to productive sectors of the economy and bringing about orderly conditions in the foreign exchange market. The Reserve Bank of India influences liquidity and interest rates through a number of operating instruments, namely, cash reserve requirements of banks, operation of refinance schemes, conduct of open market operations, report transactions, changes in the bank rate, and at times through foreign exchange swap operations.

2.9.4 Evolution of Money Market in India

The Committee to Review the Working of the Monetary System (Chairman: Mr. Sukhamoy Chakravarty) was the first to make several recommendations in 1985 for the development of money market. As a follow-up, the RBI set up a Working Group on Money Market under the Chairmanship of Mr. N. Vaghul, which submitted its report in 1987. Based on the recommendations, RBI initiated a number of measures in the eighties to widen and deepen the money market.

The main initiatives were –

1. In order to impart liquidity to money market instruments and help the development of secondary market in such instruments, the Discount and Finance House of India (DFHI) was set up as a money market institution jointly by the Reserve Bank of India, public sector banks and financial institutions in 1988. RBI has since divested its shareholding and is only a minority shareholder now.

2. To increase the range of money market instruments, Commercial Paper, Certificates of Deposit, and Interbank Participation Certificates were introduced in 1988-89. There is a wide range of instruments now.

3. To enable price discovery, the interest rate ceiling on call money was freed in stages from October 1988. Currently, all the money market interest rates are by and large determined by market forces.

Reform in the Money Market in the Nineties

In line with the deregulation and liberalisation policies of nineties, financial sector reform was undertaken in our country early in the reform cycle.

Naturally, reform in the money market formed a part of the reform process.

Call Money Market

The call/notice money market was predominantly an interbank market until 1990, except for UTI and LIC, which were allowed to operate as lenders since 1971. The RBI's policy relating to entry into the call/notice money market was gradually liberalised to widen and provide more liquidity. In the absence of adequate avenues for deployment of short-term surpluses of non-bank institutions, easier norms were announced by the RBI for increasing the participants in the call and notice money market. Entities that could provide evidence of surplus funds have been permitted to route their lendings through PDs. This was also meant to further help corporates, who had just moved to the term lending discipline from the earlier system of cash credit, with large balances to deploy their funds in the short-term and get some return. Thus, as of now, broadly speaking, banks and PDs are operating as both lenders and borrowers, while a large number of financial institutions and mutual funds are operating only as lenders. The behaviour among banks in the call money market is not uniform. There are some banks, mainly foreign banks and new private sector banks, which are active borrowers and some public sector banks that are major lenders. The RBI has been a major player in the call/notice money market and has been moderating liquidity and volatility in the market through repos and refinance operations and changes in the procedures for maintenance of cash reserve ratio.

Term Money Market

The term money market in India had been somewhat dormant. Statutory pre-emotions on interbank liabilities, regulated interest rate structure, cash credit system of financing, high degree of volatility in the call money rates, availability of sector specific refinance, inadequate Asset Liability Management (ALM) discipline among banks and scarcity of money market instruments of varying maturities were usually cited as factors that inhibited the development of term money market.

2.9.5 Benefits of Money Market

- Money markets exist to facilitate efficient transfer of short-term funds between holders and borrowers of cash assets.
- For the lender/investor, it provides a good return on their funds.
- For the borrower, it enables rapid and relatively inexpensive acquisition of cash to cover short-term liabilities.
- One of the primary functions of money market is to provide focal point for RBI's intervention or influencing liquidity and general levels of interest rates in the economy. RBI being the main constituent in the money market aims at ensuring that liquidity and short-term interest rates are consistent with the monetary policy objectives.

2.10 Indian Money Market

The Indian money market is a monetary system that involves the lending and borrowing of short-term funds. The Indian money market has seen exponential growth just after the globalisation initiative in 1992. It has been observed that financial institutions do employ money market instruments for financing short-term monetary requirements of various sectors such as agriculture, finance and manufacturing. The performance of the Indian money market has been outstanding in the past 20 years.

The central bank of the country, the Reserve Bank of India (RBI) has always been playing a major role in regulating and controlling the Indian money market. The intervention of RBI is varied – curbing crisis situations by reducing the cash reserve ratio (CRR) or infusing more money in the economy.

2.10.1 Structure of Indian Money Market

The Detailed Structure of Indian Money Market

I. Organised Sector

1. Reserve Bank of India
2. DFHI (Discount and Finance House of India)
3. Commercial Banks
   (i) Public Sector Banks
       - SBI with 7 subsidiaries
       - Co-operative banks
       - 20 nationalised banks
   (ii) Private Banks
       - Indian banks
       - Foreign banks
4. Development Banks
   IDBI, IFCI, ICICI, NABARD, EXIM, LIC, GIC, UTI etc.

II. Unorganised Sector

1. Indigenous banks
2. Money lenders
3. Chits
4. Nidhis

III. Co-operative Sector

1. State Co-operatives
   - Central co-operative banks
   - Primary agri credit societies
   - Primary urban banks
2. State land development banks*
   - Central land development banks
   - Primary land development banks

*Now known as Agriculture and Rural Development Banks

As mentioned above the money market is a mechanism that deals with the lending and borrowing of short-term funds. The Indian Money Market has come of age in the past two decades. In order to study the money market of India in detail, we at first need to understand the parameters around which the money market in India revolves.

The performance of the Indian Money Market is heavily dependent on real interest rate, that is, the interest rate that is inflation adjusted. Though the money market is free from interest rate ceilings, structural barriers and other institutional factors can be held responsible for creating distortions in the Indian Money Market. Apart from the call market rates, the other interest rates in the Indian Money Market usually do not change in the short run.

It is due to this disparity between the opposite forces that is prevalent in the money market in India that a well defined income path cannot be traced.

Owing to the deregulation of the interest rate in the early nineties following the economic reforms laid down by the then finance minister, Dr. Manmohan Singh, studies concerning the behaviour of interest rate were restricted. However, the liquidity of the market makes it a good subject for empirical research.

The Indian Money Market involves a wide range of instruments. Here, maturities range from one day to a year, issued by banks and corporate of various sizes. The money market is also closely linked with the Foreign Exchange Market through the process of covered interest arbitrage in which the forward premium acts as a bridge between domestic and foreign interest rates.

It is a centre in which financial institutions join together for the purpose of dealing in financial or monetary assets, which may be of short-term maturity or long-term maturity. The short term means, generally a period up to one year and the term maturity denotes any financial asset which can be quickly converted into money with minimum transaction cost.

2.10.2 Features / Characteristics of Indian Money Market

Money is unique in nature. The money market in developed and developing countries vary clearly from each other in many senses. Indian money market is not an exception to this. Though it is not a developed money market, it is a leading money market among the developing countries.

Indian Money Market has the following major characteristics –

1. **Dichotomic structure:** It is an important feature of the Indian money market. It has a simultaneous existence of both the organised money market and unorganised money markets. The organised money market includes RBI, all scheduled commercial banks and other recognised financial establishments. On the other hand, the unorganised part of the money market includes domestic money lenders, indigenous bankers, traders, etc. The organised money market is in complete control of the RBI. On the other hand, RBI does not have authority over unorganised money market. Therefore, both the organised and unorganised money market exists at the same time.

2. **Seasonality:** The demand for money in Indian money market is of a seasonal nature. India being a major agriculture economy, the demand for money is generated from the agricultural operations. During the busy season, that is, between October and April more agricultural activities take place leading to a higher demand for money.

3. **Multiplicity of interest rates:** In Indian money market, we have several levels of interest rates. They vary from bank to bank from time to time and even from borrower to borrower. Again in both organised and unorganised sectors the interest rate vary. Thus there is a continuation of several rates of interest in the Indian money market.

4. **Lack of organised bill market:** In the Indian money market, the organised bill market is not common. Though the RBI tried to introduce the Bill Market Scheme in 1952 and then the New Bill Market Scheme in 1970, still there is no accurate organised bill market in India.

5. **Absence of Integration:** This is a significant aspect of the Indian money market. Simultaneously it is divided among numerous segments which are loosely associated with each other. There is a lack of synchronisation among these different parts of the money market. RBI has complete control over the components in the organised section but it cannot control the components in the unorganised section.

6. **High Volatility in Call Money Market:** The call money market is a market for very short-term money. Here money is demanded at the call rate. Essentially the demand for call money comes from the commercial banks. Establishments such as the GIC, LIC, etc. suffer huge fluctuations and therefore it has remained highly volatile.

7. **Limited Instruments:** It is actually a fault of the Indian money market. In money market the supply of different instruments such as the Treasury Bills, Commercial Bills, Certificate of Deposits, Commercial Papers, etc. is very limited. In order to meet the different needs of borrowers and lenders, it is necessary to develop many instruments.

2.10.3 Defects or Drawbacks of Indian Money Market

Though the Indian money market is considered as the advanced money market among developing countries, it still suffers from many drawbacks or defects. These defects limit the efficiency of market.

Some of the significant drawbacks of the Indian money market are –

1. **Absence of Integration:** The Indian money market is roughly divided into the Organised and Unorganised Sectors. The former includes the legal financial establishments backed by the RBI. The unorganised statement of it comprises of different establishments such as indigenous bankers, village money lenders, traders, etc. There is a lack of proper integration between these two sections.

2. **Multiple Rate of Interest:** In the Indian money market, particularly the banks, there are many rates of interests. These rates differ for lending, borrowing, government activities, etc. Different rates of interest create confusion among the investors.

3. **Insufficient Funds or Resources:** The Indian economy with its seasonal structure often faces lack of financial recourse. Lower income, lower savings, and lack of banking habits among people are some of the causes for it.

4. **Shortage of Investment Instruments:** In the Indian money market, different investment instruments such as Treasury Bills, Commercial Bills, Certificate of Deposits, Commercial Papers, etc. are used. But considering the size of the population and market these instruments are insufficient.

5. **Shortage of Commercial Bill:** In India, many banks keep huge funds for liquidity reason, the use of the commercial bills is very limited. In the same way since a large number of transactions are preferred in the form of cash, the scope for commercial bills are limited.

6. **Lack of Organised Banking System:** In India even though we have a large network of commercial banks, still the banking system suffers from major failings such as the NPA, huge losses, and poor efficiency. The lack of an organised banking system is the main problem for the Indian money market.

7. **Less number of Dealers:** There are very less dealers in short-term assets who can act as negotiators between the government and the banking system. The less number of dealers leads to the slow contact between the end lender and end borrowers.

These are some of the major drawbacks of the Indian money market; several of these are also the features of our money market.

2.10.4 Recent Reforms in Indian Money Market

Indian Government appointed a committee under the chairmanship of Sukhamoy Chakravarty in 1984 to review the Indian monetary system. Later, Narayanan Vaghul working Group and Narasimhan Committee were also set up. As per the suggestions of these study groups and with the financial sector reforms started in the early 1990s, the government has accepted the following major reforms in the Indian money market.

1. **Deregulation of the Interest Rate:** Recently, the government adopted an interest rate policy that is of moderate nature. It removed the ceiling rates of the call money market, short-term deposits, bills rediscounting, etc. Commercial banks are directed to see the interest rate changes occur within the limit. During the economic reforms, there was an additional deregulation of interest rates. Presently, except for a few regulations, interest rates are decided by the working of market forces.

2. **Money Market Mutual Funds (MMMFs):** In April 1992, in order to give additional short-term investment revenue, the Reserve Bank of India motivated and established the Money Market Mutual Funds (MMMFs). MMMFs are permitted to sell units to different companies and people. The upper limit of 50 crore investments has also been removed. Financial establishments such as the IDBI and the UTI have set up such funds.

3. **Establishment of the DFI:** In April 1988, to impart liquidity in the money market, the Discount and Finance House of India (DFHI) was established. It was established mutually by the Reserve Bank of India, public sector banks and financial establishments. DFHI has played a significant role in stabilising the Indian money market.

4. **Liquidity Adjustment Facility (LAF):,** The Reserve Bank of India, through the LAF remains in the money market on a constant basis through the repo transaction. LAF regulates liquidity in the market through absorbing and injecting the financial resources.

5. **Electronic Transactions:** An electronic dealing system is started to impart transparency and efficiency in the money market transaction. It covers all deals in the money market. In the same way it is of use for the Reserve Bank of India to oversee the money market.

6. **Establishment of the CCIL:** The Clearing Corporation of India limited (CCIL) was established in April 2001. The CCIL clears all transactions in government securities, and reported on the negotiated dealing system.

7. **Development of New Market Instruments:** The government has constantly tried to introduce new short-term investment instruments. Examples: Treasury Bills of various durations, Commercial papers, Certificates of Deposits, MMMFs, etc. have been introduced in the Indian Money Market.

In India, these are the main reforms that are carried out in the money market. Except for these, the stamp duty reforms, floating rate bonds, etc. are some other important reforms in the money market in India. Therefore, finally we can conclude that the Indian money market is developing at a good speed.

2.10.5 Money Market Elements

Money Market refers to the market for short-term requirement and deployment of funds.

- Call Money: Money lent for one day.
- Notice Money: Money lent for a period exceeding one day.
- Term Money: Money lent for 15 days or more in inter-bank market.
- Held till maturity: Securities which are not meant for sale and shall be kept till maturity.
- Held for trading: Securities acquired by the banks with the intention to trade by taking advantage of the short-term price/ interest rate movements will be classified 'under held' for trading.
- Available for sale: The securities which do not fall within the above two categories, that is, HTM or HFT will be classified under available for sale.
- Yield to maturity: Expected rate of return on an existing security purchased from the market.
- Coupon Rate: Specified interest rate on a fixed maturity security fixed at the time of issue.
- Treasury Operations: Trading in government securities in the market. An investor bank can purchase these securities in the primary market. Trading takes place in the secondary market.
- Gilt-edged Security: Government security that is a claim on the government and is a secure financial instrument which guarantees certainty of both capital and interest. These securities are free of default risk or credit risk, which leads to low market risk and high liquidity.

2.11 Money Market Instruments

The money market is a market for short-term financial assets that are close substitutes of money. The most important feature of a money market instrument is that it is liquid and can be turned over quickly at low cost and provides an opportunity for balancing the short-term surplus funds of lenders and the requirements of borrowers. By convention, the term "money market" refers to the market for short-term requirement and deployment of funds. Money market instruments are those instruments, which have a maturity period of less than one year. The most active part of the money market is the market for overnight call and term money between banks and institutions and repo transactions. Call Money/Repo are very short-term money market products. There is a wide range of participants (banks, primary dealers, financial institutions, mutual funds, trusts, provident funds etc.) dealing in money market instruments. Money market instruments and the participants of money market are regulated by RBI and SEBI. As a primary dealer SBI DFHI is an active player in this market and widely deals in short-term money market instruments.

Following are some of the important money market instruments.

2.11.1 Call Money/Notice Money and Term Money

Call Money is essentially a money market instrument wherein funds are borrowed/lent for a tenure ranging from overnight to 14 days and are at call or notice. The borrower or lender must convey his intention to repay/recall with at least a 24-hour notice. However, money can also be borrowed/lent with a specified maturity date that is, repaid/recalled on the date of maturity. It is a short-term, highly liquid and an unsecured loan. Call money market is also referred to as 'overnight funds market'.

Notice money is a transaction where the participants will take time to receive or deliver for more than two days but generally for a maximum of 14 days.

Money lent for a fixed tenure for more than 14 days is called **Term Money.**

- Interest to be calculated on a daily/365 days a year basis.
- The rate of interest is known as call rate, which is generally low and varies from day-to-day.
- Interest to be payable on maturity and rounded-off to the nearest rupee.
- In case of the maturity of Term Money falling on a holiday, the repayment will be made on the next working day at the contracted rate.

The receiver of funds will collect the cheque and give the receipt. The same procedure should be followed on the reversal of the deal.

Call money markets are mainly located in big industrial and commercial cities such as Mumbai, Kolkata, Delhi, Ahmedabad etc. Call money market is the indicator of liquidity position of money market.

Call money is mainly used by the banks to meet their temporary requirements of cash. They borrow and lend money from each other normally on a daily basis. Hence in India, it represents the market for inter-bank lending and borrowing.

To sum up, these transactions reflect temporary mismatch of funds during the short period of 1 to 14 days. The participants, who have surplus, lend their money to shed the mismatch for the relative period. The participants, who are short of funds, would borrow for the relative period.

2.11.2 Treasury Bills

Treasury Bills popularly known as T-bills, are short-term finance bills issued by RBI on behalf of the government. T-Bills are promissory notes issued to meet the short-term requirements of funds of the government. These bills are highly liquid and risk-free as they are backed by a guarantee from the government. Unlike commercial bills, these bills are not backed by trade transactions. But, they are highly secured as they are guaranteed by the government and they have a highly active secondary market.

These bills are issued by the auctions conducted by RBI and they are issued for a period of 14/91/182/364 days. They are normally issued at a price less than their face value; and redeemed at face value. So the difference between the issue price and the face value of the bill represents the interest on the investment.

In India, T-Bills have a narrow market and are underdeveloped.

The RBI as the lender and controller of money market buys and sells these treasury bills. The buying and selling operations are conducted by DFHI on behalf of RBI for stabilising the money market. Banks, financial institutions, corporations, mutual funds, insurance companies etc. normally play a major role in the Treasury Bill market.

2.11.3 Commercial Papers

Commercial Papers (CPs) are short-term usance promissory notes with fixed maturity issued mostly by the leading, nationally reputed, credit-worthy and highly rated large corporations. CPs are also known as Industrial Paper, Finance Paper and Corporate Paper – the names depend upon whose liability the paper is. If it is the liability of the business or industrial or commercial or manufacturing concern, it is known as Industrial or Commercial Paper. If it is the liability of the Financial Company, it can be called a Finance Paper. Corporate is a wider term indicating that it is issued by corporations which may be either financial or non-financial. CPs are issued in domestic as well as international financial markets; in the latter they are known as Euro-commercial Paper.

Features

Strictly speaking, CPs are unsecured; they are backed only by general credit standing of the issuing companies and by the lines of credit that they might be in a position to obtain from banks. They are negotiable by endorsement and delivery. They are regarded as highly safe and liquid instruments; they are believed to be one of the highest quality investment instruments available from the private sector. They are also known to be simple and flexible instruments with respect to the documentation needed and the spread of maturities available.

CPs are like Treasury Bills (TBs), but unlike TB because the latter are secured against self-liquidating goods or trade transactions. Finance papers like TBs, particularly represent a floating debt. CPs are close competitors of TBs, but the latter have an edge over the former because they are less risky and more easily marketable. CPs normally have a buy-back facility; the issuers or the dealers usually buy-back CPs, if needed.

Issue

CPs are normally issued in a bearer form on the discount of face value basis. The issues of CPs are mostly in large denominations and they may be made through banks or dealers or brokers in the open market or they may be sold through direct placement with lenders or investors.

Maturity

The maturity period of CPs can vary from 30 days to six months.

Interest Rate

Interest rates on CPs are market-determined. The cost of CP finance is lower than or comparable to that of bank credit.

Purpose

CPs are mostly issued to finance current transactions and seasonal and interim needs for funds. They are rarely issued to finance fixed assets and permanent working capital.

Strengthening the Process of Securitisation

The rising cost of bank loans and the difficulty in obtaining bank loans in the tight money conditions led large companies to diversify their sources of funds by issuing CPs which they found to be somewhat cheaper, simpler and more flexible sources of funds. The raising of short-term debt through the issue of CPs apparently represents the strengthening of the process of "recognized ion" and the weakening the process of "intermediation". CPs serve as a means of "disintermediation", which brings the large borrowers and large investors (lenders) in direct contact with one another. However, in practice the banks are one of the major buyers of CPs which shows that the transaction does not result in disintermediation to a significant extent.

CPs in India

A company has to satisfy the following conditions for issuing Commercial Papers –

1. The issuing company should have a tangible net worth of not less than ₹ 4 crores as per the latest balance sheet.
2. The company should have a working capital limit of not less than ₹ 4 crores.
3. The current ratio should be minimum 1.33 as per the latest balance sheet.
4. The company should have minimum P2/A2 rating from CRISIL/ICRA/CARE or any other Credit Rating Agency. The rating should not be more than two months old from the date of issue of the commercial paper.
5. The borrowed account of the company is classified as standard asset by the financing, banking company/companies.

No commercial paper can be issued for a period less than 15 days from the date of its issue. There shall be no grace period for the payment of commercial papers. The RBI has increased the maturity period of the commercial papers from a minimum of six months to a maximum of less than one year from the date of the issue. Commercial papers may be issued to any person including individuals, banks, companies and other corporate bodies registered/incorporated in India and unincorporated bodies; they cannot however be issued to NRIs.

A company issuing commercial papers may request the banking company to provide standby facility for an amount not exceeding the amount of issue for meeting the liability of a commercial paper on maturity. The financing, banking company/companies shall correspondingly reduce the working capital limits of every company issuing the commercial paper.

Issue

As per the guidelines issued by RBI, a company will issue CPs through the same bank/consortium of banks from which it has a line of credit. In other words, instead of taking loans and advances, the bank will deal in the issue. Another underlying issue is the time dimension. The companies applying for the issue of CP to RBI have to obtain credit rating which should not be more than two months old. This implies that the company intending to issue CP has to obtain fresh rating if time lapses. Besides, once the RBI approves a company's application, it has to make arrangements within 15 days for placing the CP privately.

Advantages

The advantages of CP lie in its simplicity, involving hardly any documentation between the issuer and the investor and its flexibility with regard to short-term maturity. A well-rated company can diversify its sources of finance from banks to short-term money markets at a somewhat cheaper cost, especially in a situation of an easy money market. The CP provides investors with higher returns than they could obtain from the banking system. They have to pay off their debts semi-annually.

2.11.4 Certificate of Deposit

CDs are marketable receipts in bearer or registered form of funds deposited in banks for a specified period of time at a specified rate of interest. They are transferable, negotiable, short-term, fixed-interest bearing, maturity dated, highly liquid and risk-less money market instruments. Banks issue or sell CDs either directly to the investors or through dealers. They may be issued on the initiative of the secondary market dealers who may persuade banks to issue particular CDs either to hold in their own portfolios or often to meet the requirements of customers who approach them instead of their banks.

Purpose

Banks issue CDs to compete with other financial intermediaries and to counter the process of ecognized ion.

Issue

CDs can be issued to individuals, corporations, companies, trust funds, associations and NRIs.

Period

The maturity period of CDs varies between three months to one year.

Rate of Interest

The rate of interest on CDs is also market-determined and it is more attractive than that on bank deposits.

Primary Market for CPs and CDs

The primary market for CPs and CDs are yet underdeveloped in India. The presence of DFHI should help to develop these markets.

Size of the CDs Market

The size of the CDs market is much bigger than that of the CPs market. The amounts and interest rates on both CPs and CDs have been subject to a high degree of both intra-year and inter-year fluctuations.

Market Disruption/Bank Holidays

Occasionally, unforeseen events mean that market participants will have entered into contracts for a particular maturity date only to find, subsequently, that day is declared a public holiday. There are many instances of outstanding disputes amongst market participants and in settling them, the principle of no undue enrichment should be followed. It is a normal market practice to extend contracts maturing on a non-business day to the next working day.

Unscheduled Holiday

In case of an unscheduled holiday, rollover of call deals may happen if there is a strike, natural calamity etc. The strike could involve either or both the counter-parties. In case of disruption of work, due to which funds cannot be delivered or cannot be received, the deals are necessarily rolled over. It is recommended that the rate be fixed as the previous working day's NSE MIBOR.

2.11.5 Money Market Mutual Fund (MMMF)

Money Market Mutual Fund schemes were introduced by the Reserve Bank of India in the year 1992. The main aim of MMMFs was to provide an additional short-term avenue to individual investors and to bring money market instruments within the reach of individuals. Banks, financial institutions and institutions in private sector are allowed to set up money market mutual funds.

These funds are permitted to issue units to corporate enterprises and other mutual funds. Resources mobilised by MMMFs are required to be invested in call money, CDs, CPs, commercial bills arising out of genuine trade transactions, T-Bills and government dated securities.

Since March 2000, MMMFs have been brought under the purview of SEBI regulations. So far, 3 MMMFs have been set up; one each by IDBI, UTI and one in private sector.

At present, there is no ceiling of raising resources by MMMFs. Individual investors and also NRIs can subscribe to the units of MMMFs. The investors cannot be guaranteed a minimum rate of return.

Advantages of MMMFs

- Individual investor can have access to the money market.
- Investment is highly liquid
- Returns are attractive and yield is high
- Contribution to economic development through productive investment and capital formation
- Short-term surplus funds can be profitably invested

2.11.6 Inter-Corporate Deposits

An Inter-Corporate Deposit (ICD) is an unsecured borrowing by corporates and FIs from other corporate entities registered under the Companies Act 1956. The corporates having surplus funds would lend to another corporate who is in need of funds. This lending would be on an uncollateralised basis and hence a higher rate of interest would be demanded by the lender.

The short-term credit rating of the corporate would determine the rate at which the corporate would be able to borrow funds. It is a source of short-term financing and the tenor of ICD may range from 1 day to 1 year, but the most common tenure of borrowing is for 90 days.

Features

- It is a popular source of short-term finance.
- Procurement procedure is simple and convenient.
- It is an unsecured loan.
- The rate of interest on such deposits is not fixed. It depends upon the amount involved, the tenure of lending and the short-term credit rating of the borrower.
- It is an uncertain source of finance, as the deposit can be withdrawn at any time.
- It is also considered as a risky source of finance.

Types: Such deposits are of three types –

1. **Call Deposit:** Such a type of deposit is withdrawn by the lender by giving a notice of one day. However, in practice, a lender has to wait for at least 3 days.

2. **Three-month Deposit:** As the name suggests, such type of a deposit provides funds for up to three months to meet the short-term cash inadequacy.

3. **Six-month Deposit:** The lending company provides funds to another company for a period of six months.

Advantages

- Surplus funds can be effectively utilised by the lender company.
- Procurement procedure is simple and convenient.
- Funds can be quickly raised at a short notice.
- Investing company can achieve higher growth rates compared to keeping all of its funds in cash.

Disadvantages

- A company cannot lend more than 10% of its net worth to a single company and more than 30% of its net worth in total.
- The market for such source of financing is not structured.

2.12 Difference between Money Market and Capital Market

Money market is a place for short-term lending and borrowing, typically within a year. It deals in short-term debt financing and investments. On the other hand, Capital market refers to stock market, which refers to trading in shares and bonds of companies on recognised stock exchanges. Individual players cannot invest in money market as the value of investments is large, on the other hand, in capital market, anybody can make investments through a broker. Stock market is associated with high risk and high return as against money market which is more secure. Further, in case of money market, deals are transacted on phone or through electronic systems as against capital market where trading is through recognised stock exchanges.

Money market and Capital market exhibit similar characteristics in some ways as listed below –

- Transfer of resources from surplus units to deficit units
- Commercial banks are actively involved in both the markets
- Institutions enter these markets to adjust their liquidity position
- Flow of funds from money market to capital market and vice versa is possible, as lenders and borrowers have access to both these markets
- Various investment avenues available in both the markets to suit the requirement of the investors
- Interest rates in both the markets are inter-dependent

However, a money market differs from capital market in many ways which are given below –

Basis of Distinction	Money Market	Capital Market
Meaning	Money market is a place for short-term lending and borrowing, typically within a year.	Capital market refers to stock market that is, trading in shares and bonds of companies on recognised stock exchanges.
Definition	Money market is the collective name given to the various firms and institutions that deal in the various grades of near money. Near money refers to bank deposits, bills of exchange, money at call and short notice.	A capital market may be defined as an organised mechanism meant for the effective and smooth transfer of money or financial resources from the investors to the entrepreneurs.
Location/Market Place	Money market is not a market in usual sense of the word that is, it does not have a definite place where borrowers and lenders come together. Transactions take place wherever lenders and borrowers come in direct or indirect contact through telephones, telegraphs, mail or any other arrangement.	There are organised market places in which stocks, shares and other securities are traded. Securities are traded in the stock exchanges that provide a central trading place at which groups of brokers and dealers meet regularly and transact business with one another for their customers and their own accounts.

... (Contd.)

Basis of Distinction	Money Market	Capital Market
Lenders	Central bank, commercial banks, discount houses, acceptance houses, brokers etc.	Investing public, household savings, corporate savings, institutional investors, government, foreign capital, bank credit etc.
Borrowers	Commercial banks, stock brokers, financial institutions, business houses, government etc.	Industries, manufacturing companies, that is public sector and private sector
Period of Finance	Short-term, that is, funds are made available for a short period only which may be one day, a week or for three to six months or in exceptional cases for the period of more than six months but less than one year.	Medium and long-term with maturities ranging from 1 to 5 or 10 years.
Main Function	Lending and borrowing to facilitate liquidity adjustment.	Mobilisation and effective utilisation through lending.
Players	Individual players cannot invest in money market as the value of investments is large.	Anybody can make investments through a broker.
Connecting Link	Between depositors and borrowers.	Between investors and entrepreneurs.
Risk	Considered more secure, low credit and market risk.	High credit and market risk is witnessed in the stock market.
Price fluctuations	Not much	High
Liquidity	High	Low
Dealings in Transactions	Deals are transacted on phone or through electronic systems.	Deals are transacted through recognised stock exchanges.
Financial Instruments/Financial Products	Treasury Bills, Bills of Exchange, Commercial Papers, Certificate of Deposit, Banker's Acceptance, Money Market Mutual Funds, Inter-Corporate Deposits etc.	Equity Shares, Preference Shares, Debentures, Bonds, Government Securities, Deep Discount Bonds, Convertible Debentures etc.

... (Contd.)

Basis of Distinction	Money Market	Capital Market
Purpose of Loan	Meeting short-term financial needs of industry, commerce, trade, agriculture, government developmental activities, stock exchange brokers etc.	For industrial and commercial financing, expansion, developmental activities, mergers, acquisitions etc.
Underwriting	Not a primary function.	Is a primary function.
Sub-markets	Stock Market, Bill market, bullion market, call money market, acceptance market, treasury bill market, collateral loans market etc.	Primary Market, Secondary Market, debt market, government securities market etc.
Negotiations	Dealings can take place without any personal contact and negotiations are not formal.	Funds are lent after negotiations between the lending and the financial institutions and the borrowing corporate entity.
Dominant Institutions	Commercial banks	Non-banking financial companies and special financial institutions.
Regulatory Authority	RBI monitors and controls the money market in India.	SEBI is the regulatory authority for controlling the capital market in India.
Reach	Money market has a local, regional or national reach.	The operations of capital market can extend to an international level also.

Points to Remember

- The **primary market** deals with the issue of new instruments by the corporate sector such as equity shares, preference shares and debt instruments.
- An **initial public offer** is the first (initial) instance of a company (called the issuer) offering its commons stock (or shares) to the general public for subscription.
- The **secondary market** provides a trading place for the securities already issued, to be bought and sold.
- An **equity share**, commonly referred to as ordinary share also represents the form of fractional ownership in which a shareholder, as a fractional owner, undertakes the maximum entrepreneurial risk associated with a business venture.
- **Rights Issue/Rights Shares:** The issue of new securities to existing shareholders at a ratio to those already held.

- **Bonus Shares:** Shares issued by the companies to their shareholders free of cost by capitalisation of accumulated reserves from the profits earned in the earlier years.

- **Preferred Stock/Preference Shares:** Owners of these kinds of shares are entitled to a fixed dividend or dividend calculated at a fixed rate to be paid regularly before dividend can be paid in respect of equity share.

- **Cumulative Preference Shares:** A type of preference shares on which dividend accumulates if remains unpaid.

- **Cumulative Convertible Preference Shares:** A type of preference shares where the dividend payable on the same accumulates, if not paid.

- **Participating Preference Share:** The right of certain preference shareholders to participate in profits after a specified fixed dividend contracted for is paid.

- **Government Securities (G-Secs):** These are sovereign (credit risk-free) coupon bearing instruments which are issued by the Reserve Bank of India on behalf of Government of India, in lieu of the Central Government's market borrowing programme.

- **Debentures:** Bonds issued by a company bearing a fixed rate of interest usually payable half yearly on specific dates and principal amount repayable on particular date on redemption of the debentures.

- **Bond:** A negotiable certificate evidencing indebtedness. It is normally unsecured. A debt security is generally issued by a company, municipality or government agency.

- **Commercial Paper:** A short-term promise to repay a fixed amount that is placed on the market either directly or through a specialised intermediary.

- **Treasury Bills:** Short-term (up to 91 days) bearer discount security issued by the Government as a means of financing its cash requirements.

- A **Stock Exchange** is a market where stocks and shares are bought and sold.

- The **Securities and Exchange Board of India (SEBI)** is the regulatory authority in India established under Section 3 of SEBI Act, 1992.

- A **derivative** can be defined as a financial instrument whose value depends upon (or derives from) the value of other basic underlying variables.

- A **forward contract** is a simple derivative security which is an agreement to buy or sell an asset at certain future time for certain price.

- A **futures contract** is a standardised contract that is traded on a futures market exchange.

- A **commodity option** is a two-party agreement that gives the buyer (or holder) the right, but not the obligation, to take a futures position.

- The **money market** is a market for overnight to short-term funds and for short-term money and financial assets that are close substitutes for money.

- **Call Money** is essentially a money market instrument wherein funds are borrowed/lent for a tenure ranging from overnight to 14 days and are at call or notice.

- **Notice money** is a transaction where the participants will take time to receive or deliver for more than two days but generally for a maximum of 14 days.

- **Treasury Bills** popularly known as T-bills, are short-term finance bills issued by RBI on behalf of the government.

- **Commercial Papers** (CPs) are short-term usance promissory notes with fixed maturity issued mostly by the leading, nationally reputed, credit-worthy and highly-rated large corporations.

- **Certificates of Deposit** are marketable receipts in bearer or registered form of funds deposited in banks for a specified period of time at a specified rate of interest.

- An **Inter-Corporate Deposit** (ICD) is an unsecured borrowing by corporates and FIs from other corporate entities registered under the Companies Act, 1956.

Questions for Discussion

1. What is a money market? Discuss its nature and role in the Indian context.

2. Discuss the features and functions of a money market.

3. Explain the structure and composition of the Indian money market.

4. List and explain the popularly used money market instruments.

5. Discuss the advantages and drawbacks of Indian money market.

6. What is Securities and Exchange Board of India (SEBI)? Explain the objectives and Functions of SEBI.

7. Discuss the role and powers of SEBI as a regulatory authority.

8. What is OTC market? Enumerate its features and objectives.

9. Discuss the meaning and features of primary markets and secondary markets.

10. What is National Stock Exchange? Explain its various functions.

11. Write a note on origin, powers and functions of SEBI.

12. What is a stock exchange? Explain the organisation and management of stock exchanges in India.

13. What is a derivative security? Distinguish between futures and options.

14 What are 'options'? Explain the different types of options.

15. Discuss the steps involved in the floatation of new issues in the market.

16. Distinguish between
    - (1) OTCEI and Stock Exchange
    - (2) Money Market and Capital Market

17. Write short notes on –
    - (1) Call and Notice Money Market
    - (2) Treasury Bills
    - (3) Commercial Papers
    - (4) Certificate of Deposits
    - (5) Money Market Mutual Funds
    - (6) Inter-Corporate Deposits
    - (7) Bombay Stock Exchange

✍ ✍ ✍

Chapter 3...

Financial Services in India

Contents ...

Learning Objectives ...

To gain an insight into the following :

➤ Mutual Funds

➤ Factoring Services

➤ Forfeiting Services

➤ Credit Rating

➤ Venture Capital

3.1 Financial Services

3.1.1 Introduction

The financial services sector in India is booming and has become one of the biggest money-spinning areas. This sector has undergone a sea change since 1990. The Indian economy got liberalised during 1991 and the financial sector was kept open for private as well as foreign players. During the late eighties, the financial services industry in India was dominated by commercial banks and other financial institutions governed by the Central Government. Economic liberalisation has brought in a complete transformation in the Indian financial services industry.

Prior to the economic liberalisation, the Indian financial service sector was characterised by various other factors, which were related to the growth of this sector. Some of the factors of significance are as follows –

(a) Too much of control and regulation by the apex bodies in the form of interest rates, money rates etc.

(b) Controller of capital issues used to regulate the prices of securities.

(c) Absence of independent credit rating and credit research agencies.

(d) Strict regulation of the foreign exchange market.

(e) Restrictions on foreign investment and foreign equity.

(f) Non-availability of debt instruments on a large scale.

However, after the economic liberalisation the entire financial sector has undergone a considerable change and now the new financial instruments are entering the capital market on a daily basis. The present scenario in the Indian capital market is characterised by financial innovation and financial creativity.

3.1.2 Defining Financial Services

The term "financial services" in its broader sense refers to "the mobilising and allocation of savings".

It is identified as inclusive of all those activities involved in the process of converting savings into investment. Financial services also include "financial mediators", such as merchant bankers, venture capitalists, commercial banks, insurance companies etc.

In other words, financial services are concerned with individuals, organisations and their finances – that is to say, they are services that are directed specifically at people's intangible assets (that is, their money/wealth).

"Financial services basically mean all those kinds of services provided in financial or monetary terms, where the essential commodity is money. The term is often used broadly to cover a whole range of banking services, insurance (both life and general), stock trading, asset management, credit cards, foreign exchange, trade finance, venture capital and so on".

These different services are designed to meet a range of different needs and take on many different forms. They usually require a formal relationship between the provider and the consumers and they typically require a degree of modification (quite limited in the case of a basic bank account, but quite extensive in the case of venture capital).

The financial services sector is growing in India and it has passed through the following three main stages –

1. Early Period (1960-80)
2. Second Period (1980-90)
3. Third Period (1990-2002)

1. Early Period (1960-80)

In the earlier period, financial services introduced many innovative services like merchant banking, insurance and leasing finance. Until 1960 the word merchant banking was not known. It was originally used as an umbrella function. Its activities began from project appraisal to mobilisation of finance from suppliers. They also underwrote the public issues and assisted in getting the shares listed in the stock exchange. Leasing activities began from the year of 1970. Originally, leasing firms were involved in equipment lease financing. Later, they undertook different types of leasing like financial lease, operating lease and wet leasing. During the early period, LIC, GIC and UTI initiated to enter into this section.

2. Second Period (1980-90)

Financial services entered the second period and it approximately covered the duration of 10 years. In this period it introduced many innovative value added services, for example, over the counter share transfers, depositing of shares, mutual funds, factoring, discounting, venture capital and credit rating. In developed countries, mutual funds provide major fund to the industry anywhere. Credit rating decreases malpractices in the capital market and this rating is only implemented on debt instruments. Now this rating is required for commercial papers and fixed deposits.

3. Third Period (1990-2002)

This period in financial services includes the establishment of new institutions and instruments. This period began after the period of post-liberalisation. The depositories, the stock lending schemes, online trading, paperless trading, dematerialisation and book buildings were the contemporary problems of this stage. This period started popularising book building to help both investors and fund mobilise.

In this period, the government had initiated a few projects to allow foreign institutional investors into the capital market. For delivering effective financial services, the government of India is now renewing the Companies' Act, Income Tax Act, MRTP Act etc.

3.1.3 Nature and Characteristics of Financial Services

It is important to understand the nature and characteristics of financial services, which are as follows –

(1) Financial services involve at least two people or firms, namely, the service provider and the service user.

(2) Financial institutions intermediate the flow of funds between the different economic decision-making units.

(3) Financial services are intangible. They smoothen the functioning of the corporate sector by providing funds within the stipulated period of time.

(4) Financial services must be customer friendly and they should provide the services according to the requirements of the customers.

(5) Financial service is an innovative activity and requires dynamism.

(6) It has to be consistently redefined and refined on the basis of the economic changes that occur in the global market.

3.1.4 Activities of Financial Services

Activities of financial services can be broadly divided into two parts, namely

1. Traditional activities

2. Modern activities

Traditional Activities

Conventionally, financial services were identified under two heads.

(i) Fund-based activities

(ii) Non-fund-based activities.

(i) Fund-based activities

The conventional services which come under fund-based activities are as follows –

(a) Underwriting of shares, debentures etc.

(b) Dealing in foreign exchange market activities.

(c) Equipment leasing, hire purchase, venture capital etc.

(d) Dealing in secondary market activities.

(e) Participating in money market instruments like treasury bills, discounting bills, commercial papers etc.

(ii) Non-fund-based activities

Non-fund-based activities include –

(a) The management of capital issues (pre-issue and post-issue management).

(b) Arrangement for the placement of capital and debt instruments with the investment institutions.

(c) Placement of capital and debt instruments with investment institutions.

(d) Preparation of working capital for the clients.

(e) Assisting in the process of obtaining the government clearance.

(f) Arrangement of funds from financial institutions.

Modern Activities

Modern activities include –

(a) Providing project advisory services, right from the preparation of the project report till the raising of funds for starting the project.

(b) Planning for mergers and acquisitions and assisting for their smooth functioning.

(c) Directing corporate customers in capital restructuring.

(d) Acting as trustees to the debenture holders.

(e) Recommending suitable changes in the management structure and management style envisaging the achievement of better results.

(f) Portfolio management of large public sector undertakings.

(g) Capital market services such as clearing services, registration and transfers, collection of income on securities etc.

3.1.5 Current Trends in Financial Services

(a) **Dynamism**: Presently, the financial system in India is in a process of rapid transformation, after the liberalisation of the financial sector. The main objective of the financial sector reforms is to promote an efficient, competitive and diversified financial system in the country. Currently, the Indian financial services sector is very dynamic and is adopting itself to the changing needs.

(b) **Primary Equity Market:** The primary market in India is now very active. India is now witnessing the emergence of many private sector financial services. Capital market is one of the major places to raise finance. The collective funds raised in the Indian capital market have doubled over a decade.

(c) **Concept of Credit Rating:** The facility of credit rating helps the investors in finding a profitable and safe debt capital. It rates the debt issues and instructs the investors not to invest in the debt capital of the firms that are badly rated. The regulators of the Indian capital market are considering the introduction of equity grading, which helps the investors to cautiously invest their savings.

(d) **Process of Globalisation:** Globalisation has made way for the entry of innovative and advanced financial products in India. The Government of India is very enthusiastic in removing all the barriers in the financial sector. Indian capital market has high potential for the introduction of innovative financial products.

(e) Process of liberalisation: The Finance Act of the Government of India is bringing in various modifications every year to keep the financial sector very flexible. The Government of India has initiated many steps to reform the financial services industry. The interest rates have been deregulated. The private sector has been permitted to participate in banking and mutual fund sectors.

Five Trends in the Financial Sector

D. Murali, THE HINDU

Reforms, crisis, convergence, engineering, and inclusion are the five recent trends in the financial sector, says R. Shanmugham in 'Financial Services' (www.wileyindia.com).

Indian financial reforms started with the Narasimhan Committee recommendations, the author traces. "The committee proposed a wide range of proposals which laid the strong foundation for the strength and the resilience of the financial system today. Reforms were focused on the banking sector, financial institutions (FIs), capital market, and money market."

As a result of the committee's recommendations, SEBI (Securities and Exchange Board of India) was made a statutory body, and the Capital Issues Control Act was repealed to pave the way for an era of free pricing, he reminisces. "SEBI issued guidelines for each of the market intermediaries and made the market micro-structures ready for a more transparent and orderly growth of the market. Global depository receipts (GDRs) were launched in 1992, and investment norms for NRIs (non-resident Indians) and OCBs (overseas corporate bodies) were also prescribed. FIIs (foreign institutional investors) were permitted to invest in the Indian capital market."

Financial crisis, the second trend listed in the book, is a topic that is fresh in the minds of most of us. Through a timeline, therefore, Shanmugham plots the happenings of recent times, beginning with the surfacing of the US sub-prime crisis in mid 2007, followed by the collapse of Bear Stearns, and the avalanche of failures thereafter.

The spill-over to other economies, or the contagion effect, manifested as reverse capital flows and non-availability of credit led to financial turbulence. He rues, "The crisis has affected the real economy. Growth prospects of emerging economies have been affected by the financial crisis."

Under 'financial convergence,' the author discusses 'universal banking,' whereby all financial services are made available to customers under one roof. For example, a bank, apart from its ordinary business of accepting deposits and lending money, may also offer investment banking, credit card services, or sell insurance policies.

"Commercial banks in India also market the mutual fund schemes. India Post sells a whole range of saving schemes, gold coins, etc. in addition to its postal services." Subtle differences in the lines of business of different entities in the system have narrowed down, he notes.

'Financial engineering,' the next trend, is about the development and creative application of financial technology for solving financial problems, exploiting financial opportunities, and for otherwise adding value, as Shanmugham explains. The phrase, however, came under a cloud when derivative securities such as CDS (Credit Default Swap) and CDO (Collateralised Debt Obligation) were behind the excessively speculative positions that caused the downfall of many FIs. Hence the caution sounded by Warren Buffett, that these instruments could be 'financial weapons of mass destruction'!

The fifth and the final trend, 'financial inclusion,' is what have repeatedly been mentioned in policy pronouncements of many nations. "Financial inclusion is the process of ensuring access to financial services and timely and adequate credit where needed by vulnerable groups such as weaker sections and low-income groups at an affordable cost," reads a quote from the report of the Rangarajan Committee (2008).

Another definition cited in the book is from the UN, and it speaks of a financial sector that provides 'access' to credit to all 'bankable' people and firms, insurance to all 'insurable' people and firms, and to savings and payment services for everyone.

3.2 Mutual Funds

3.2.1 Introduction

Mutual fund is a trust that pools money from a group of investors (sharing common financial goals) and invests the money thus collected into asset classes that match the stated investment objectives of the scheme. Since the stated investment objectives of a mutual fund scheme generally form the basis for an investor's decision to contribute money to the pool, a mutual fund cannot deviate from its stated objectives at any point of time.

Every mutual fund is managed by a fund manager, who using his investment management skills and necessary research works ensures much better return than what an investor can manage on his own. The capital appreciation and other incomes earned from these investments are passed on to the investors in proportion of the number of units they own.

3.2.2 Definition of Mutual Funds

A mutual fund is a collection of stocks and/or bonds. A mutual fund works as a company that brings together a group of people and invests their money in stocks, bonds, and other securities. Each investor owns shares, which represent a portion of the holdings of the fund.

Money from a mutual fund is earned in three ways –

1. Income is earned from dividends on stocks and interest on bonds. A fund almost pays out all of the income it obtains over the year to fund owners in the form of a distribution.

2. If the fund sells securities that have increased in price, the fund has a capital gain. Most funds also pass on these gains to investors in a distribution.

3. The fund's shares increase in price if fund holdings rise in price but are not sold by the fund manager.

When an investor subscribes for the units of a mutual fund, he/she becomes part owner of the assets of the fund in the same proportion as his/her contribution amount put up with the total amount of the fund. Mutual fund investor is also known as a *Mutual Fund Shareholder* or a *Unit Holder*. Any change in the value of the investments made into shares, debentures etc. is reflected in the *Net Asset Value* (NAV) of the scheme. NAV is defined as the market value of the Mutual Fund scheme's assets net of its liabilities. NAV of a scheme is calculated by dividing the market value of scheme's assets by the total number of units issued to the investors.

Table of Example
If the market value of the assets of a fund is ₹100,000, the total number of units issued to the investors is equal to 10,000, then the NAV of this scheme would be (A)/(B), that is, 100,000/10,000 or 10.00
Now if an investor 'X' owns 5 units of this scheme, his total contribution to the fund is ₹50 (that is, number of units held multiplied by the NAV of the scheme).

3.2.3 Advantages of Mutual Funds

1. **Choice of Schemes:** Mutual funds give investors different schemes with different investment objectives. Investors have the choice of investing in a scheme having a correlation between its investment objectives and their own financial goals. These schemes additionally have different plans/options.

2. **Professional Management:** The main advantage of funds is the professional management of money. Investors buy funds because they do not have the time to manage their own portfolios. A mutual fund is a cheap way for a small investor to get a permanent manager to create and observe investments.

3. **Diversification:** By owning shares in a mutual fund instead of owning individual stocks or bonds, risk is spread out. The thought behind diversification is to invest in a large number of assets so that a loss in any specific investment is minimised by gains in others.

4. **Economies of Scale:** Because, at a time, a mutual fund buys and sells big amounts of securities, its transaction costs are lesser than what a person would pay for securities transactions.

5. **Liquidity:** Just like an individual stock, a mutual fund allows to request that shares be changed into cash at any time.

6. **Simplicity:** Purchasing a mutual fund is simple. Any bank has its own line of mutual funds, and the minimum investment is small. Most firms also have automatic purchase plans for investment on a monthly basis.

7. **Transparency:** Funds give investors updated information regarding the markets and the schemes. All material facts are revealed to investors as needed by the regulator.

8. **Safety:** Mutual fund industry is part of a well synchronised investment environment where the interests of the investors are guarded by the regulator. All funds are registered with Securities and Exchange Board of India and complete transparency is forced.

9. **Flexibility:** Investors also profit from the convenience and flexibility provided by mutual funds. Investors can switch their holdings from a debt scheme to an equity scheme and from an equity scheme to a debt scheme. In most open end schemes, alternative for systematic investment and withdrawal is also provided to the investors.

3.2.4 Disadvantages of Mutual Funds

1. **Costs Control not in the Hands of an Investor:** The investor has to pay investment management fees and fund distribution costs as a percentage of the value of his investments, regardless of the performance of the fund.

2. **No Customised Portfolios:** The portfolio of securities in which a fund invests is a decision taken by the fund manager. Investors have no right to interfere in the decision-making process of a fund manager, which several investors feel constricted in attaining their financial goals.

3. **Difficulty in Selecting a Suitable Fund Scheme:** Several investors find it hard to choose one alternative from the plethora of funds/schemes/plans available. For this, they may have to take a suggestion from financial planners so as to invest in the right fund to attain their goals.

3.2.5 Types of Mutual Funds

1. **Open-end Funds/Closed-end Funds**

   • **Open-end funds:** Funds that can sell and buy units at any point in time are known as open-end funds. The fund size of an open-end fund is changeable because of constant selling and repurchases by the fund. An open-end fund is not needed to keep selling new units to the investors at all times but is needed to always repurchase, when an investor wants to sell his units. The NAV (net asset value) of an open-end fund is measured daily.

   • **Closed-end funds:** Funds that can sell a fixed number of units only during the New Fund Offer (NFO) period are called as closed-end funds. The quantity of closed-end fund remains the same at all times. After the closure of the offer, purchasing and redemption of units by the investors directly from the funds is not authorised. On the other hand, to guard the interests of the investors, Securities and Exchange Board of India gives investors two avenues to liquidate their positions as follows –

     (1) Closed-end funds are listed on the stock exchanges where investors can buy/sell units from/to each other. The trading is usually done at a discount to the net asset value of the scheme. The net asset value of a closed-end fund is calculated every week.

     (2) Closed-end funds may also offer "buy-back of units" to the unit holders. In this case, the corpus of the fund and its outstanding units do get altered.

2. Load Funds/No-Load Funds

- **Load Funds:** Mutual funds incur different expenses on marketing, distribution, advertising, portfolio churning, fund manager's salary etc. In the form of load, several funds recover these expenses from the investors. These funds are known as load funds. A load fund may impose following types of loads on the investors as follows –

    (i) Entry Load: Also called as front-end load, it refers to the load charged to an investor when he/she enters into a scheme. Entry load is deducted from the investor's contribution amount to the fund.

    (ii) Exit Load: Also called as back-end load, these charges are imposed on an investor when he redeems his units. Exit load is deducted from the redemption proceeds to an outgoing investor.

    (iii) Deferred Load: After a period of time, deferred load is charged to the scheme.

    (iv) Contingent Deferred Sales Charge (CDSC): In some schemes, when an investor stays longer with the fund, the percentage of exit load decreases. This kind of load is called as contingent deferred sales charge.

- **No-load Funds:** All those funds that do not charge any of the above stated loads are called as no-load funds.

3. Tax-exempt Funds/Non-Tax-exempt Funds

- **Tax-exempt Funds:** Funds that invest in securities free from tax are called as tax-exempt funds. All open-end, equity-oriented funds are exempt from distribution tax. Long-term capital gains and dividend income in the hands of investors are tax-free.

- **Non-Tax-exempt Funds:** Funds that invest in taxable securities are called as non-tax-exempt funds. In India, all funds, except open-end, equity-oriented funds are liable to pay tax on distribution income. Profits arising out of sale of units by an investor within twelve months of purchase are grouped as short-term capital gains, which are taxable. Sale of units of an equity-oriented fund is subject to Securities Transaction Tax (STT). STT is deducted from the redemption proceeds to an investor.

3.2.6 Broad Types of Mutual Fund

1. Equity Funds

Equity funds are more risky than other type of funds, but they also give higher returns than other funds. It is advisable that an investor looking to invest in an equity fund should invest for long-term, that is, for 3 years or more. There are different types of equity funds each falling into different risk brackets. In the order of reducing risk level, there are the following types of equity funds –

- **(i) Aggressive Growth Funds:** In aggressive growth funds, fund managers seek maximum capital appreciation and invest in less researched shares of speculative nature. Due to these speculative investments aggressive growth funds become more volatile and therefore, face higher risk than other equity funds.

(ii) **Growth Funds:** Growth funds also invest for capital appreciation but they are different from aggressive growth funds in the sense that they invest in firms that are expected to outperform the market in the future. Without completely adopting speculative strategies, growth funds invest in those firms that are expected to post above average income in the future.

(iii) **Speciality Funds:** Speciality funds have fixed criteria for investments and their portfolio includes only those firms that meet their criteria. Criteria for some speciality funds could be to invest/not to invest in specific areas/firms. Speciality funds are concentrated and therefore are relatively more dangerous than diversified funds. These are the following types of speciality funds.

(a) **Sector Funds:** Equity funds that invest in a specific sector/industry of the market are called as sector funds. The exposure of these funds is limited to a specific sectors like information technology, auto, banking, pharmaceuticals or fast moving consumer goods which is why they are riskier than equity funds that invest in numerous sectors.

(b) **Foreign Securities Funds:** Foreign securities equity funds have the choice to invest in one or more foreign firms. Foreign securities funds attain international diversification and thus they are less risky than sector funds. On the other hand, foreign securities funds are exposed to foreign exchange rate risk and country risk.

(c) **Mid-Cap or Small-Cap Funds:** Funds that invest in firms that have lower market capitalisation than big capitalisation firms are called mid-cap or small-cap funds. Market capitalisation of mid-cap firms is less than that of big, blue chip firms and small-cap firms have market capitalisation of less than ₹500 crores. Market capitalisation of a firm can be measured by increasing the market price of the firm's share by the total number of its outstanding shares in the market. The shares of mid-cap or small-cap firms are not as liquid as of large-cap firms which gives rise to volatility in share prices of these firms and as a result, investment gets risky.

(d) **Option Income Funds:** While not yet available in management, option income funds write options on a big portion of their portfolio. A correct use of options can assist in decreasing volatility, which is otherwise considered as a risky instrument. These funds invest in large, high dividend yielding firms, and then sell options against their stock positions, which produce a steady income for investors.

(iv) **Diversified Equity Funds:** Except for a small part of investment in liquid money market, diversified equity funds mostly invest in equities without any focussing on a specific sector(s). These funds are well-diversified and decrease sector-specific or company-specific risk. On the other hand, like all other funds diversified equity funds too are exposed to equity market risk. One major type of diversified equity fund in management is Equity Linked Savings Schemes (ELSS). As per the order, a minimum of 90 percent of investments by equity linked savings schemes should be in equities at all times. Equity Linked Savings Schemes investors are qualified to claim deduction from taxable income (up to ₹ 1 lakh) when filing the income tax return. Equity linked savings schemes generally has a lock-in period and in case of any redemption by the investor before the expiry of the lock-in period makes him legally responsible to pay income tax on such income(s) for which he may have received any tax exemption(s) in the past.

(v) **Equity Index Funds:** Equity index funds have the objective to match the performance of a specific stock market index. The portfolio of these funds includes the similar firms that form the index and is made up in the same proportion as the index. Equity index funds that follow broad indices (like S&P CNX Nifty, Sensex) are less dangerous than equity index funds that follow narrow sectoral indices (like BSEBANKEX or CNX Bank Index etc). Narrow indices are less diversified and thus, are more risky.

(vi) **Value Funds:** Value funds invest in those firms that have sound fundamentals and whose share prices are under-valued. The portfolio of these funds includes shares that are trading at low price to earnings ratio and a low market to management value (Fundamental Value) ratio. Value funds may choose firms from diversified sectors and are exposed to lower risk level as compared to growth funds or speciality funds. Value stocks are usually from cyclical industries (such as cement, steel, sugar etc.) which make them volatile in the short-term. Thus, it is wise to invest in value funds with a long-term time horizon as risk, significantly in the long term, is reduced.

(vii) **Equity Income or Dividend Yield Funds:** The goal of equity income or dividend yield equity funds is to generate high recurring income and stable capital appreciation for investors by investing in those firms which issue high dividends. Equity income or dividend yield equity funds are usually exposed to the lowest risk level as compared to other equity funds.

2. Debt / Income Funds

Funds that invest in medium to long-term debt instruments issued by private firms, banks, financial institutions, governments and other entities belonging to different sectors are called as Debt / Income Funds. Debt funds are low risk profile funds that aim to generate fixed current income (and not capital appreciation) to investors. In order to guarantee regular income to investors, debt (or income) funds distribute big fraction of their surplus to investors. Even though debt securities are usually less risky than equities, they are subject to credit risk (risk of default) by the issuer at the time of paying the interest. To reduce the risk of default, debt funds usually invest in securities from issuers who are rated by credit rating agencies and are considered to be of "investment grade". Debt funds that target high returns are more risky. On the basis of different investment objectives, there can be following types of debt funds –

(i) **Diversified Debt Funds:** Debt funds that invest in all securities issued by entities belonging to all sectors of the market are called as diversified debt funds. The best characteristic of diversified debt funds is that investments are appropriately diversified into all segments which cause risk reduction. Any loss incurred, due to default by a debt issuer, is shared by all investors which further decreases risk for an individual investor.

(ii) **Focused Debt Funds:** Focused debt funds are narrow focus funds that are restricted to investments in selective debt securities, issued by firms of a particular sector or industry. Some examples of focused debt funds are sector, specialised and offshore debt funds, funds that invest only in tax-free infrastructure or municipal bonds. Due to their narrow orientation, focused debt funds are more risky as compared to diversified debt funds. Although not yet available in management, these funds are conceivable and might be available to investors very soon.

(iii) **High Yield Debt Funds:** As we now understand that risk of default is there in all debt funds, and thus, debt funds usually try to reduce the risk of default by investing in securities issued by only those borrowers who are considered to be of "investment grade". But, high yield debt funds implement a different strategy and prefer securities issued by those issuers who are considered to be of "below investment grade". The intention behind adopting this kind of risky strategy is to earn higher interest returns from these issuers. These funds are more volatile and bear higher default risk, even though sometimes they may earn higher returns for investors.

(iv) **Assured Return Funds:** Although it is not necessary that a fund will meet its goals or give assured returns to investors, but there can be funds that come with a lock-in period and provide guarantee of annual returns to investors during the lock-in period. Any shortfall in returns is suffered by the sponsors or the Asset Management Companies (AMCs). These funds are usually debt funds and give investors a low-risk investment opportunity. On the other hand, the security of investments depends upon the net worth of the guarantor. To protect the interests of investors, SEBI permits only those funds to offer assured return schemes whose sponsors have sufficient net-worth to guarantee returns in the future. Earlier, UTI had offered guaranteed return schemes that guaranteed specified returns to investors in the future. UTI was not capable of fulfilling its promises and encountered large shortfalls in returns. In the end, the government had to intervene and took over UTI's payment obligations on itself. At present, even though it is possible, no asset management companies in management offers guaranteed return schemes to investors.

(v) **Fixed Term Plan Series:** Fixed term plan series generally are closed-end schemes having short-term maturity period that propose a series of plans and issue units to investors at regular intervals. Unlike closed-end funds, fixed term plans are not listed on the exchanges. Fixed term plan series generally invest in debt/income schemes and target short-term investors. The goal of fixed term plan schemes is to satisfy investors by generating some expected returns in a short time.

3. Gilt Funds

Gilt funds also called as Government Securities in management. Gilt funds invest in government papers (named dated securities) having medium to long-term maturity period. Issued by the government of management, these investments have little credit risk (risk of default) and provide safety of principal to the investors. On the other hand, like all debt funds, gilt funds too are exposed to interest rate risk. Interest rates and prices of debt securities are inversely connected and any change in the interest rates causes a change in the net asset value of debt/gilt funds in an opposite direction.

4. Money Market / Liquid Funds

Money market / liquid funds invest in short-term (maturing within one year) interest bearing debt instruments. These securities are highly liquid and provide safety of investment, thus making money market / liquid funds the safest investment option when compared with other mutual fund types. On the other hand, even money market / liquid funds are exposed to the interest rate risk. The distinctive investment alternatives for liquid funds consist of treasury bills, commercial papers and certificates of deposit.

5. Hybrid Funds

As the name implies, hybrid funds are those funds whose portfolio consists of a blend of equities, debts and money market securities. Hybrid funds have an equal proportion of debt and equity in their portfolio. These are the following types of hybrid funds in Management

(i) **Balanced Funds:** The portfolio of balanced funds consists of assets like debt securities, convertible securities, and equity and preference shares held in a comparatively equal proportion. The goals of balanced funds are to reward investors with a regular income, moderate capital appreciation and simultaneously reducing the risk of capital erosion. Balanced funds are suitable for those conservative investors that have a long-term investment horizon.

(ii) **Growth-and-Income Funds:** Funds that join characteristics of growth funds and income funds are called as Growth-and-Income Funds. These funds invest in firms having potential for capital appreciation and those well-known for issuing high dividends. The level of risks involved in these funds is lesser than growth funds and higher than income funds.

(iii) **Asset Allocation Funds:** Mutual funds may invest in financial assets like equity, debt, money market or non-financial assets such as real estate, commodities etc. Asset allocation funds accept a changeable asset allocation strategy that permits fund managers to change from one asset class to another at any time depending upon their attitude for particular markets. In other words, fund managers may change over to equity if they expect equity market to give good returns and change over to debt if they expect debt market to give better returns. It should be noted that changing over from one asset class to another is a decision taken by the fund manager on account of his own judgement and understanding of particular markets, and thus, the success of these funds depends upon the skill of a fund manager in anticipating market trends.

6. Commodity Funds

Those funds that concentrate on investing in different commodities (like metals, food grains, crude oil etc.) or commodity firms or commodity futures contracts are called as commodity funds. A fund that invests in a single commodity or a group of commodities is a specialised commodity fund and a fund that invests in all available commodities is a diversified commodity fund and is less risky than a specialised commodity fund. Precious Metals Fund and Gold Funds are common examples of commodity funds.

7. Real Estate Funds

Funds that invest directly in real estate or give a loan to real estate developers or invest in shares/securitised assets of housing finance firms, are called as specialised real estate funds. The goal of these funds might be to generate regular income for investors or capital appreciation.

8. Exchange Traded Funds (ETF)

Exchange traded funds give investors joint benefits of a closed-end and an open-end mutual fund. Exchange traded funds follow stock market indices and are traded on stock exchanges like a single stock at index related prices. The biggest advantage offered by these funds is that they offer diversification, flexibility of holding a single share simultaneously. Newly introduced in management, these funds are very famous abroad.

9. Fund of Funds

Mutual funds that do not invest in financial or physical assets, but do invest in other mutual fund schemes offered by different annual maintenance contracts are known as Fund of Funds. Fund of funds maintain a portfolio containing units of other mutual fund schemes, just like conservative mutual funds maintain a portfolio containing equity/debt/money market instruments or non-financial assets. Fund of funds give investors an added advantage of expanding into different mutual fund schemes with even little investment, which additionally helps in diversification of risks. On the other hand, the expenses of fund of funds are relatively high because of compounding expenses of investments into different mutual fund schemes.

3.2.7 Other Mutual Fund Schemes

With an increase in interest and awareness about mutual funds amongst investors, there has also been a steady increase in the number of mutual fund schemes offered in management.

Different schemes are introduced to suit different requirements of investors. Mutual funds schemes may have different investment goals which can be to earn recurring income for investors or growth of their invested capital or both. So investors must select a scheme whose investment goal matches their personal goals. To attain the scheme's investment goals, the fund manager, as per his own understanding, invests in a portfolio of asset classes which he thinks may give the best returns to investors in the future. Different assets are exposed to a different level of risk. For instance, it is more risky to invest in equities than in debt and investing in debt is to some extent riskier than investing in money-market instruments. On the other hand, riskier investment alternatives have a higher potential to provide higher returns.

3.2.8 Tax Saving Schemes

Tax saving schemes offer tax rebates to the investors under specific provisions of the Indian Income Tax laws as the Government offers tax incentives for investment in specified avenues. Investments made in Equity Linked Savings Schemes (ELSS) and Pension Schemes are allowed as deduction under Section 88 of the Income Tax Act, 1961.

Special Schemes

- **Industry Specific Schemes:** Industry specific schemes invest only in the industries specified and are limited to specific industries like InfoTech, FMCG and Pharmaceuticals etc.

- **Index Schemes:** These funds attempt to replicate the performance of a particular index such as the BSE Sensex or the NSE 50.

- **Sectoral Schemes:** Under these schemes funds are invested exclusively in a specified industry or a group of industries or various segments such as 'A' Group shares or initial public offerings.

3.2.9 Evaluation of Mutual Fund Schemes

Evaluation between various mutual fund schemes on the basis of their investment objectives, portfolio of investments and the level of risk associated is as follows –

Table 3.1: Equity Funds

Types	Investment Objectives	Portfolio of Investments	Risk Associated
Aggressive Growth Funds	Capital Appreciation	Invest in less researched shares of speculative nature	Highly volatile
Growth Funds	Capital Appreciation	Invest in companies that are expected to outperform the market in the future	Volatile but less than aggressive growth funds
Specialty Funds	Capital Appreciation	They follow stated criteria for investments and their portfolio comprises of only those companies that meet their criteria	Concentrated and hence are riskier than diversified funds
Diversified Equity Funds	Capital Appreciation	A small portion of investment in liquid money market, diversified equity funds invest mainly in equities without concentration on a particular sector	Well diversified and reduce sector-specific or company-specific risk
Equity Index Funds	Capital Appreciation	Portfolio of these funds comprises the same companies that form the index and is constituted in the same proportion as the index	Risk associated is the same as that of the benchmark index. Broader indices (like S&P CNX Nifty or BSE Sensex) are less risky than narrow indices (like BSEBANKEX or CNX Bank Index)
Value Funds	Capital Appreciation	Value funds invest in those companies that have sound fundamentals and whose share prices are currently under-valued.	These funds are exposed to a lower risk level as compared to growth funds or speciality funds
Equity Income or Dividend Yield Funds	To generate high recurring income and steady capital appreciation	Investments are made in those companies which issue high dividends (such as power or utility companies)	These funds are generally exposed to the lowest risk level as compared to other equity funds

Table 3.2: Money Market Funds and Income / Debt Funds

Types	Investment Objectives	Portfolio of Investments	Risk Associated
Diversified Debt Funds	To generate fixed current income	These funds invest in all securities issued by entities belonging to all sectors of the market	Low volatility, default risk remains
High Yield Debt funds	To earn higher interest returns	Invest in securities issued by those issuers who are considered to be of "below investment grade"	More volatile and bear higher default risk than diversified debt funds
Assured Return Funds	To offer assurance of annual returns to investors throughout the stated lock-in period	Predominantly debt securities	A low-risk investment opportunity
Fixed Term Plan Series	To generate some expected returns in a short period	Usually invest in debt / income schemes	Low risk fund
Money-Market Funds	Recurring income and capital safety	Invest in short-term (maturing within one year) interest bearing debt instruments	Safest mutual fund investment option, interest rate risk remains

Table 3.3: Hybrid Funds

Types	Investment Objectives	Portfolio of Investments	Risk Associated
Balanced Funds	To generate regular income, moderate capital appreciation and at the same time minimising the risk of capital erosion	Debt securities, convertible securities, and equity and preference shares held in a relatively equal proportion	Limited risk to principal and moderate long-term growth
Growth-and-Income Funds	Capital growth and some current income	These funds invest in companies having potential for capital appreciation and those known for issuing high dividends	Safer as compared to growth funds and riskier than income funds

Asset Allocation Funds	Capital growth and income generation	These funds invest in financial assets or non-financial (physical) assets	Success of these funds depends upon the skills of a fund manager in anticipating market trends

3.2.10 Risk Factors associated with Investing in Mutual Funds

1. Mutual funds and securities investments are subject to market risks and there is no assurance or guarantee that the objectives of the schemes will be achieved.

2. As with any investment in securities, the NAV of the units issued under the schemes can rise or fall depending on the factors and forces affecting capital markets.

3. Neither the past performance of the mutual funds managed by the sponsors and their affiliates/associates nor the past performance of the sponsors, asset management companies (AMC) or fund is necessarily indicative of the future performance of the schemes.

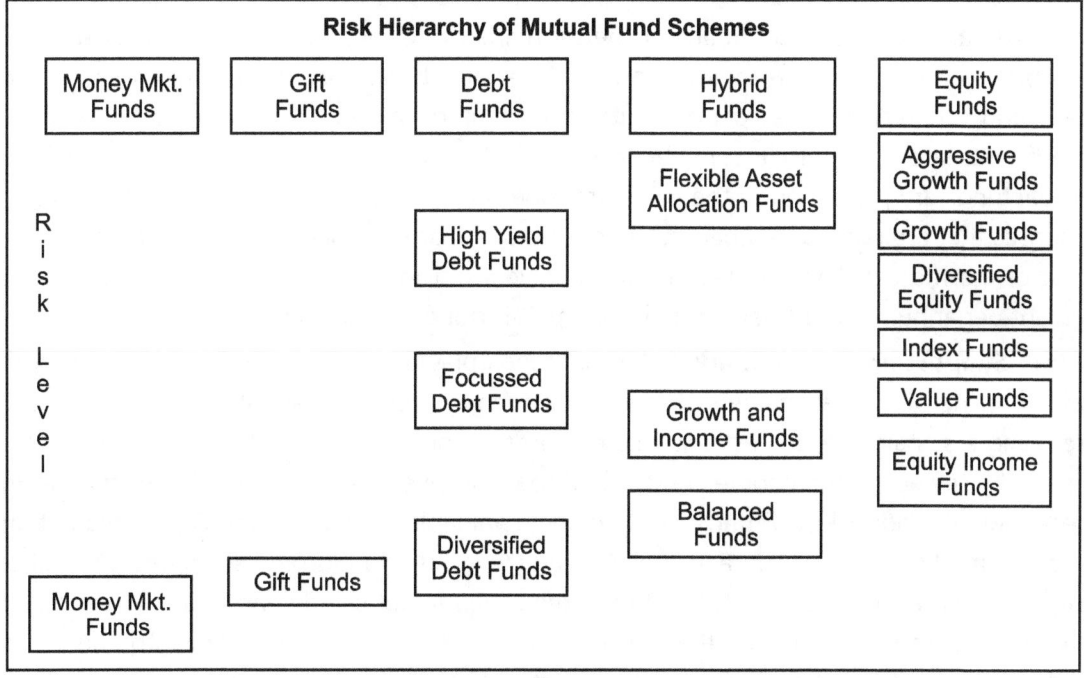

Fig. 3.1: Risk Level of Various Funds

3.2.11 Important/Significant Utility of Mutual Funds

(a) **Channelising Savings for Investment:** Mutual funds act as a vehicle in galvanising the savings of the people by providing different schemes appropriate to different classes of customers for the overall development of the economy. In order to meet the different requirements of the people, several schemes are being offered by mutual funds and thus, savings are directed towards capital investments directly. In the absence of mutual funds, these savings would have remained unused. Thus, the complete economy benefits because of the cost efficient and best use and allotment of scarce financial and real resources in the economy for its quick development.

(b) Offering Wide Portfolio Investment: Small and medium investors used to burn their fingers in a stock market as they are not completely aware of the market risks involved in stock exchange operations. The investors through mutual funds can benefit from the extensive portfolio of the investment. The fund diversifies its risks by investing in a large variety of shares and bonds which cannot be done by small and medium investors. This is in line with the old maxim, 'Not to lay all eggs in one basket'. These funds have big amounts at their disposal and so they carry a clout regarding stock exchange transactions. They are in a position to have a balanced portfolio which is free from risks. Thus, mutual fund provides extensive portfolio diversification.

(c) Providing Better Yields: The pooling of funds from a big number of customers enables the fund to have big funds at their disposal. Because of these big funds, mutual funds are capable of buying cheaper and sell dearer than the small and medium investors. Thus, they are capable of commanding better market rates and lower rates of brokerage. So they provide better yield to their customers. They also benefit from the economies of large scale and can decrease the cost of capital market participation. The transaction costs of big investments are definitely lesser than that of small investments. In fact, all the profits of mutual funds are passed on to the investors by way of dividend and capital appreciation. The expenses that are related to a particular scheme alone are charged to the respective scheme. Most of the mutual funds floated so far has given a dividend at a rate ranging between 12 percent per annum and 17 percent per annum. It is quite a good yield.

(d) Supporting Capital Market: Mutual funds play an important role in supporting the development of capital markets. The mutual fund makes the capital market dynamic by providing a sustainable domestic source of demand for capital market instruments. In other words, the savings of the people are directed towards investments in capital markets through these mutual funds. Mutual funds also provide a valuable liquidity to the capital market and thus, the market is made very active and steady when the foreign investors and speculators exit and re-enter the market. Mutual funds keep the market steady and liquid. In the lack of mutual funds and because of the existence and re-entry of speculators into the capital market, the prices of shares would be subject to extensive price fluctuation. Thus, mutual funds are providing excellent support to the capital market and assisting in the process of institutionalisation of the market.

(e) Promoting Industrial Development: The economic development of any country depends upon its industrial advancement and agricultural development. All the industrial units have to increase their funds by resorting to the capital market by issuing shares and debentures. The mutual fund not only creates a demand for these capital market instruments, but also supplies a big amount of funds to the market and therefore, the industries are guaranteed their capital needs. In truth, the entry of mutual fund has improved the demand for Indian stocks and bonds. Thus, mutual fund gives the necessary financial resources to the industries at market rates.

(f) Keeping the Money Market Active: An individual investor cannot have any access to money market instruments. Then again, mutual funds keep the money market active by investing money in the money market instruments. In fact, the availability of rising money market instruments itself is a good sign for a developed money market which is very important for a Central Bank to operate successfully in a country.

(g) Offering Tax Benefits: Particular mutual funds offer tax benefits to its clients. Thus, apart from dividends, interest and capital appreciation, investors also stand to get the benefit of tax concession.

The mutual fund themselves are completely exempt from tax on all income on their investment. But all the other firms have to pay taxes and they can declare dividends only from the profits after tax. But mutual funds do not deduct tax at source from dividends. This is really beneficial to the investors.

(h) Reducing the Marketing Cost of New Issues: Furthermore, the mutual fund helps to decrease the marketing cost of the new issues. The promoters used to allot a major share of the initial public offerings to the mutual fund and thus, they are saved from the marketing cost of such issues.

3.2.12 Mutual Fund Framework/Structure

The structure of mutual funds in India is governed by SEBI (Mutual Fund) Regulations, 1996. It is mandatory to have a three-tier structure of –

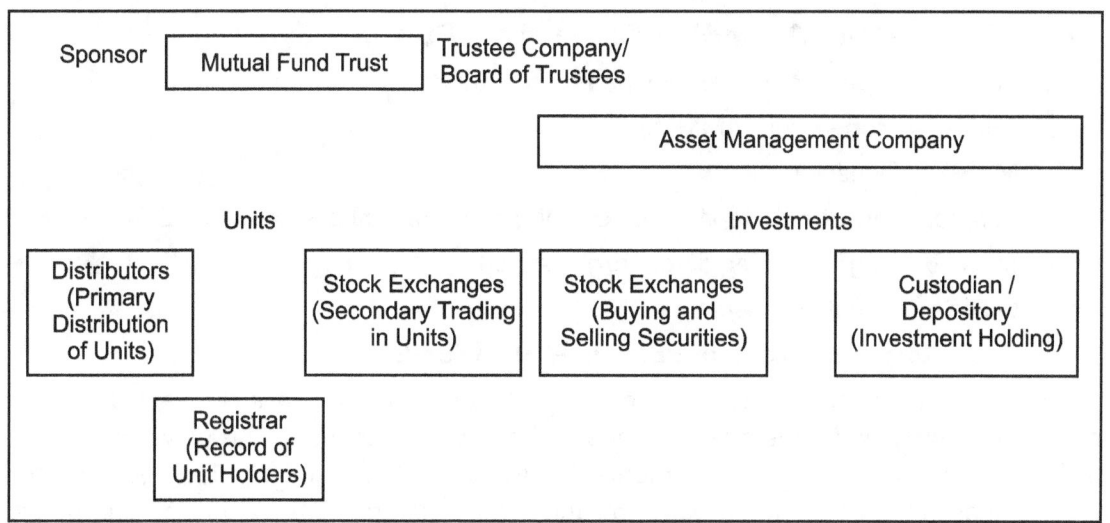

Fig. 3.2: Mutual Fund Framework

Sponsors-Trustee-Asset Management Company

The sponsor is the promoter and he appoints the trustees who are responsible to the investors of the fund. AMC is the business face of the mutual fund as it manages all the affairs of the fund.

1. **Sponsors**
   - 5-year track record
   - 3-year profitability
   - Minimum 40 percent stake in Asset Management Company

2. **Trustee**
   - Indian Trust Act, 1882
     - o Board of Trustees
     - o Trustee Company
   - Trust Deed
   - Minimum 4 trustees
   - Two-thirds "independent trustees"

3. **Asset Management Company**
   - Minimum net worth ₹10 crores
   - One-half "independent directors"
   - Appointment can be terminated by
     - o Majority of Trustees
     - o 75 percent of unit holders

Legal fund structure gives strength to mutual funds as an investment avenue.

3.2.13 Regulating Agencies for Mutual Funds

1. RBI – as a supervisor of bank-owned mutual funds
2. SEBI – as a supervisor of MMMFs
3. Ministry of Finance
4. Company Law Board, Department of Company Affairs and Registrar of Companies
5. Stock Exchanges (self regulatory organisation)
6. Office of the Public Trustee

1. Regulatory Jurisdiction of RBI over Mutual Funds

RBI is the monetary authority and the regulator of the banking system. Bank sponsored mutual funds were under the dual control of RBI and SEBI. Presently RBI is only the regulator of the sponsors of bank sponsored mutual funds. SEBI is the regulator of all mutual funds. Mutual funds are affected by the RBI stipulations on structure, issuance, pricing and trading of government securities.

2. The Role of Ministry of Finance in Mutual Funds

The finance ministry is the supervisor of both the RBI and SEBI. Aggrieved parties can make appeals to the ministry of finance on the SEBI rulings relating to mutual funds.

3. Self Regulatory Organisations

Self Regulatory Organisations are the second-tier regulatory mechanism created by market participants, to regulate the working of a group of persons/organisations. If the self regulatory organisations are registered with the regulatory authority, it obtains certain powers from the regulatory authority. For example though the stock exchanges are regulated by SEBI, they are also registered self regulatory organisations.

4. AMFI and its objectives

With the increase in mutual fund players in India, a need for mutual fund association in India was generated to function as a non-profit organisation. Association of Mutual Funds in India (AMFI) was incorporated on 22nd August, 1995.

AMFI is an apex body of all Asset Management Companies (AMC) which has been registered with SEBI. Till date all the AMCs that have launched mutual fund schemes are its members. It functions under the supervision and guidelines of its Board of Directors.

Association of Mutual Funds India has brought down the Indian Mutual Fund Industry to a professional and healthy market with ethical lines enhancing and maintaining standards. It follows the principle of both protecting and promoting the interests of mutual funds as well as their unit holders.

AMFI can just issue guidelines to members. It cannot enforce regulations. The objectives of AMFI are as follows –

- This mutual fund association of India maintains a high professional and ethical standard in all areas of operation of the industry.
- It also recommends and promotes the top class business practices and code of conduct which is followed by members and related people engaged in the activities of mutual fund and asset management. The agencies that are by any means connected or involved in the field of capital markets and financial services are also involved in this code of conduct of the association.
- AMFI interacts with SEBI and works according to SEBI's guidelines in the mutual fund industry.
- Association of Mutual Fund of India does represent the Government of India, the Reserve Bank of India and other related bodies on matters relating to the Mutual Fund Industry.
- It develops a team of well-qualified and trained agent distributors. It implements a programme of training and certification for all intermediaries and others engaged in the mutual fund industry.
- AMFI undertakes an all-India awareness programme for investors in order to promote proper understanding of the concept and working of mutual funds.

- Last but not the least, the association of mutual fund of India also disseminate information on mutual fund industry and undertake studies and research either directly or in association with other bodies.

3.2.14 Role and Responsibility

1. Asset Management Company

An asset management company is an investment management firm that invests the pooled funds of retail investors in securities in line with the stated investment objectives.

For a fee, the investment company provides more diversification, liquidity, and professional management consulting service than is normally available to individual investors.

The diversification of portfolio is done by investing in such securities which are inversely correlated to each other. They collect money from investors by way of floating various mutual fund schemes.

In typical Indian words, asset management companies called as Asset Reconstruction Company, the global equivalent of which is asset management companies. The word "asset reconstruction" in India owes its origin to Narasimhan who envisaged the setting up of a central Asset Reconstruction Fund with money contributed by the Central Government, which was to be used by banks to shore up their balance sheets to clean up their non-performing loans. This idea never worked, so Narasimhan thought of asset reconstruction companies, the likes of which had already been successful in Malaysia, Korea and several other countries in the world. To keep the tune the same as the original idea of asset reconstruction fund, as also to give an impression that ARCs are not merely concerned with realisation of bad loans but they are going to do "reconstruction", that is, try and resurrect bad loans into good ones. The word ARC has been used in India.

Asset management firms have been established in different countries globally as an answer to the global problem of bad loans.

Bad loans are basically of two types – bad loans produced by the usual banking operations or bad lending, and bad loans which originate out of a systematic banking crisis.

It is in the latter case that banking regulators or governments try to bail out the banking system of a systematic accumulation of bad loans which acts as a drag on their liquidity, balance sheets and generally the health of banking. So, the idea of asset management companies or asset reconstruction companies is not to bail out banks, but to bail out the banking system itself.

There are basically two approaches to taking care of these systematic bail-out efforts. One, leave the banks to manage their own bad loans by giving them incentives, legislative powers, or special accounting or fiscal advantages. The second approach is to do a similar thing, through a centralised agency.

The former approach is known as the decentralised approach and the latter approach is called as the centralised approach. Asset management companies arise out of the second approach, that is, a centralised agency for resolving bad loans created out of a systematic crisis.

Each approach has its own advantages and drawbacks and there is no clear proof of any of the two being better over the other. Different countries have tried either of the two approaches and sometimes have been successful and sometimes have failed in either case.

Advantages of an AMC approach

- Centralisation of bad loans in one or a few hands and therefore obviously has more clout.
- It is possible to give special legislative powers to a few asset management companies rather than to each bank.
- Banks are left with cleaner balance sheets and do not have to deal with problem clients. Regular banking relations with the group are not affected.
- Because it deals with a larger portfolio, it can mix up good assets with bad ones and make a sale which is palatable to buyers.
- It is easier to do a capital-market based funding for an AMC than for the banks themselves.

2. Registrars

"A registrar is an intermediary who performs/arranges the payment of underwriters, brokers and other agents involved in the marketing of new issues and undertake all activities connected with new issue management until the shares are listed on the stock exchange".

The criteria for registrar –

- The competency and expertise
- Adequacy and quality of manpower
- Good track record
- Sufficient infrastructure such as computers, data storage space etc. and
- Capital adequacy for the work

The tenure of authorisation and terms are laid down by the SEBI

According to SEBI guidelines, there are two types of registrars as follow –

1. Security Transfer Agent (STA) and
2. Registrar of Issues (RI)

Role of Registrars

Next to merchant bankers, registrars have a major role, specifically in respect of servicing of investors.

The roles performed by registrars are as follows –

(i) The roles performed by Registrar of Issues (RI)

- Collection of data on applications for new issues

- Prepare table and data classification
- Allotment of shares to applicants
- Dispatch of allotment letters and/or refund orders, etc.
- Arrange for payments to underwriters, brokers and other agents involved in the marketing of new issues
- Undertake all activities connected with new issue management until the shares are listed on the stock exchange

(ii) The roles performed by the Security Transfer Agents (STA)

- Keep the registers of shareholders
- Effect endorsements
- Arrange for splits
- Consolidation of shares
- Transfer of shares, give notices for calls
- Arrange for receipt of call money
- Endorsements of moneys paid, and
- Perform all incidental and consequential acts in both the primary and secondary markets

Responsibility of Registrar

(i) The RTI is responsible for all activities ranging from designing of application forms to processing and dispatch of refunds or allotment letters.

(ii) The STA is responsible to undertake all investor services in the secondary market like

- o Transfers of shares
- o Splits of shares and
- o Consolidation of shares etc.

3. Custodian

"A *custodian is one who keeps the safe custody of the valuables of somebody else, a customer or client or investor*".

The term custodian refers to *"the agent or broker or banker who keeps the safe custody of the client's valuables or investments of the public in securities, which are financial claims"*.

According to investors the valuables are their investments and securities. The safe custody of valuables, in olden days used to be done by commercials, traders, local bankers, shroffs etc. Later on, the safe custody and custodial functions are performed by the commercial and cooperative banks.

- Gold, silver, jeweller, ornaments and a host of other valuables are safely stored in bank lockers for its customers.
- Safe custody is also provided by employers to their employees in respect of some personal effects, these safe custody lockers provides by the Stock Exchange authorities.

- The clubs and social organisations also provide safe lockers, on a temporary basis for its members.
- Railways and Airways provide safe custody of passengers' personal luggage and effects in the clock rooms.

Other roles performed by safe custody are as follows:

- Safe custody and account maintenance
- Preservation from theft, fire, accident, loss etc.,
- Management information services on corporate,
- Trade settlement and clearance,
- Risk avoidance or risk reduction,
- Support services after trade,
- Transfer agent,
- Corporate action, and
- Insurance for preserving the valuables intact in physical form.

The nature of safe custody or custodial services is used in the sense of financial services of non-banking.

Banks sponsored by the nationalised banks are playing the role of custodian for the clients of mutual funds in the form of lockers.

Following are the institutions which are acting as professional custodians –

- Stock Holding Corporation of India (SHCI)
- Citibank and some other foreign banks
- Bank of India holdings for B.S.E.
- Brokers and Industrial Investment Trust Ltd.
- The SHCI has been providing the custodial services to its sponsors, like UTI, IDBI, ICICI, LIC, GIC, etc. But later on it extended its services to many MFs, banks, etc.

Responsibility of Custodian

The responsibilities of the custodian are as follows –

- Receipt and delivery of securities.
- Holding in trust the securities or safekeeping.
- Keeping account of all receipts and deliveries.
- Collecting income/dividend and follow up support like rights, and bonus collection, getting transfers effected before book closure or record dates.
- Corporate actions and services of dividend declaration fees collection etc. and to act as transfer agents.

SEBI Guidelines

- SEBI are taken various aspects into consideration before licensing to custodian such as its organisational strength, its infrastructural facilities, like office staff, computer and telex, fax, communications facilities etc. and then provide license to work as a custodian.

  The details of particulars for SEBI approval are as follows –

  1. Name of the institution, address, fax no. etc.
  2. Name of contact person, address, fax no. etc.
  3. Background information, experience, volume of business handled etc.
  4. Organisational infrastructure and other details on the number of companies, trusts for which it has provided the custodian services.

- As per the SEBI norms custodian has to be an independent organisation which is approved by the RBI as well as SEBI, delinked from the sponsors, the trustee and AMC.

- The approval of the AMC, sponsors, trust board and custodians by the SEBI is a composite exercise and composite authorisation.

- Various public sector mutual funds have set up their own custodian division; SEBI guides to provide their services to other mutual funds not set up by their sponsor.

Other Investments

Table 3.4: Banks vs. Mutual Funds

Comparable Criteria	Banks	Mutual Funds
Returns	Low	Better
Administrative experience	High	Low
Risk	Low	Moderate
Investment options	Less	More
Network	High penetration	Low but improving
Liquidity	At a cost	Better
Quality of assets	Not transparent	Transparent
Interest calculation	Minimum balance between 10th & 30th of every month	Everyday
Guarantee	Maximum ₹1 lakh on deposits	None

3.2.15 Structure of the Indian Mutual Fund Industry

The Indian mutual fund industry is controlled by the Unit Trust of India, which has a total corpus of ₹ 700 billion collected from more than 20 million investors. The UTI has several funds/schemes in all categories, that is, equity, balanced, income etc. with some being open-ended and some being close-ended. The Unit Scheme of 1964 commonly referred to as

US 64, which is a balanced fund, is the largest scheme with a corpus of about ₹ 200 billion. Most of its investors believe that the UTI is owned and controlled by the government, which, while legally wrong, is true for all practical reasons.

The second biggest group of mutual funds is the ones floated by nationalised banks. Asset management floated by Canara Bank and SBI funds management floated by the State Bank of India are the largest of these. GIC AMC floated by General Insurance Corporation and Jeevan Bima Sahayog AMC floated by the LIC are some of the other important ones.

Recent Trends in the Mutual Fund Industry

The most significant trend in the mutual fund industry is the aggressive growth of the foreign owned mutual fund firms and the decline of the firms floated by nationalised banks and smaller private sector players.

In the early 90s, several nationalised banks got into the mutual fund business and got off to a good start because of the stock market boom existing then. These banks did not really know the mutual fund business and they just saw it as another type of banking activity. Few hired specialised staff and usually chose to transfer the employees from the parent organisations. The performance of most of the schemes that floated by these funds was not good. Some schemes had offered guaranteed returns and their parent organisations had to bail out these asset management companies by paying big amounts of money as the difference between the guaranteed and actual returns. The service levels were also terrible. Most of these asset management companies have not been capable of retaining staff, float new schemes etc. and it is uncertain whether, barring a few exceptions, they have serious plans of continuing the activity in a major way.

The experience of some of the asset management companies floated by private sector Indian firms was also very similar. They quickly realised that the AMC business is a business, which makes money in the long term and needs deep-pocketed support in the intermediate years. Some have sold out to firms owned by foreigners, some have combined with others and there is general reorganisation going on.

They can be credited with introducing many new practices such as new product innovation, sharp improvement in service standards and disclosure, usage of technology, broker education and support etc. In truth, they have forced the industry to upgrade itself and service levels of organisations like UTI have radically improved in the last few years in response to the competition given by these.

Performance of Mutual Funds in India

In the year of 1963 the concept of mutual funds took birth in India. Unit Trust of India invited investors or rather to those who believed in savings, to park their money in UTI Mutual Fund. The performance of mutual funds in India in the early stage was not even closer to satisfactory level. People hardly ever understood, and naturally investing was out of question. By the start of liberalisation of the industry in 1992, some 24 million shareholders were used to guarantee high returns. This good record of UTI became a marketing tool for new applicants. In profitability factor, the expectations of investors touched the sky. On the other hand, people were miles away from the preparedness of risks factor after the liberalisation.

By the end of 1987, the assets under management of UTI were ₹67 billion. In March 1993, from ₹67 billion the assets under management rose to ₹ 470 billion and the figure had a three times higher performance by April 2004. It rose as high as ₹1,540 billion. When stock prices started falling in the year 1992, the net asset value (NAV) of mutual funds in India declined. Those days, the market regulations did not allow portfolio shifts into alternative investments. There relatively was no choice apart from holding the cash or to further continue investing in shares. One more thing to be noted, as only closed-end funds were floated in the market, the investors disinvested by selling at a loss in the secondary market.

The performance of mutual funds in India suffered qualitatively. The 1992 stock market scandal, the losses by disinvestments and the absence of transparent rules in the positions rocked confidence among the investors. Due to a very weak stock market performance, mutual funds have not yet recovered, with funds trading at an average discount of 10-20 percent of their net asset value. The measure was taken to make mutual funds the important instrument for long-term saving. The more the variety offered, the quantitative will be investors. In the end, so long as mutual fund firms are performing with lower risks and higher profitability within a short span of time, more people will be inclined to invest until and unless they are completely educated with the dos and don'ts of mutual funds.

3.3 Factoring Services

3.3.1 Introduction

"Factoring is a service involving the purchase by a financial organisation, called a factor, of receivables owned to manufacturer and distributors by their customers, with the factor assuming full credit and collection responsibilities."

In other words, factoring is a financial transaction whereby an exporter sells his accounts receivables (that is, invoices) to a third party (called a factor) at a lesser rate in exchange for instant cash with which to finance continued business. It is a type of financial service given by the specialist organisations. It is one of the oldest forms of business financing. It can be considered as a cash management tool for several firms like garment industry where long receivables are a part of business cycle. Factoring is a service that covers the financing and collection of account receivables in domestic and international trade.

3.3.2 Meaning and Definition

Factoring can be widely defined as the relationship, created by an agreement, between the seller of goods/services and a financial institution called the factor, whereby the latter purchases the receivables of the former and also controls and administers the receivables of the former.

Factoring may also be defined as a continuous relationship between a financial institution (the factor) and a business concern selling goods and/or providing service (the client) to a trade customer on an open account basis, whereby the factor purchases the client's book debts (account receivables) with or without recourse to the client – thereby controlling the credit extended to the customer and also undertaking to administer the sales ledgers relevant to the transaction.

The development of factoring concept in different developed countries of the world has led to some consensus towards defining the term. Factoring can also largely be defined as an arrangement in which receivables arising out of sale of goods/services are sold to the "factor" as a result of which the title to the goods/services represented by the said receivables passes on to the factor. Hence the factor becomes responsible for all credit control, sales accounting and debt collection from the buyer(s).

3.3.3 Glossary of Terminology

The common terminologies used in a factoring transaction are as follows –

   (i) **Client:** He is also called as a supplier. It is a business institution supplying the goods/services on credit and gaining from the factoring arrangements.

  (ii) **Customer:** An individual or business organisation to whom the goods/services have been supplied on credit. He is also known as debtor.

 (iii) **Account receivables:** Any trade debt arising from the sale of goods/services by the client to the customer on credit.

  (iv) **Open account sales:** Wherein by arrangement goods/services are sold/supplied by the client to the customer on credit without raising any bill of exchange or promissory note.

   (v) **Eligible debt:** Debts, which are approved by the factor for making prepayment.

  (vi) **Retention:** Margin maintained by the factor.

 (vii) **Prepayment:** An advance payment made by the factor to the client up to a certain percent of the eligible debts.

3.3.4 Nature of Factoring

Factoring is a tool of receivable management employed to release funds tied up in credit extended to customers.

   1. Factoring is a service of financial nature involving the conversion of credit bills into cash. Accounts receivables, bills recoverable and other credit dues resulting from credit sales appear in the books of account as book credits.

   2. The risk connected to credit are taken over by the factor which buys these credit receivables without recourse and collects them when due.

   3. A factor performs at least two of the following functions –

       i.   Provides finance for the supplier including loans and advance payments.

       ii. Maintains accounts, ledgers relating to receivables.

       iii. Collects receivables.

       iv. Protects risk of default in payments by debtors.

   4. A factor is a financial establishment which provides services relating to management and financing of debts arising out of credit sales. It acts as another financial mediator between the buyer and seller.

5. Unlike a bank, a factor specialises in handling and collecting receivables in a competent way. Payments are received by the factor directly since the invoices are assigned in support of the factor.

6. Factor is accountable for sales accounting, debt collection and credit control protection from bad debts and rendering of advisory services to their clients.

7. Factoring is a instrument of receivables management hired to release funds tied up in credit extended to customers and to solve the problems that are connected to collection, delays and defaults of the receivables.

3.3.5 Characteristics of Factoring

1. Generally the period for factoring is 90 to 150 days. Some factoring firms allow even more than 150 days.

2. Factoring is regarded as an expensive source of finance compared to other sources of short-term borrowings.

3. Factoring receivables is a best financial solution for new and emerging companies with no strong financials. This is because credit value is assessed on the basis of the financial strength of the customer (debtor). Thus, these firms can leverage on the financial strength of their customers.

4. Credit rating is not compulsory. But the factoring firms generally perform credit risk analysis before entering into the agreement.

5. Cost of factoring = Finance cost + Operating cost.

    Factoring cost differs in accordance with the transaction size, financial strength of the customer etc.

    The cost of factoring differs from 1.5 percent to 3 percent per month depending upon the financial strength of the client's customer.

6. For late payments beyond the approved credit time, penal charge of around 1-2 percent per month over and above the normal cost is charged.

3.3.6 Mechanism of Factoring

In the normal course of business, factoring business is generated by credit sales. The major function of factor is realisation of sales. Once the transaction occurs, the role of factor is to intervene to realise the sales/collect receivables. Therefore, factors act as a mediator between the seller and sometimes along with the seller's bank together.

The mechanism of factoring is summed up as below –

(a) An agreement is entered into between the selling company and the company. The agreement provides the basis and the scope of understanding reached between the two for providing factor service.

(b) The sales documents should include the instructions to directly pay to the factor who is allotted the job of collection of receivables.

(c) When the payment is received by the factor, the account of the company is credited by the factor after reducing its fees, charges, interest etc. as agreed.

(d) The factor may give the finance in advance to the selling company and conditions of the agreement so required.

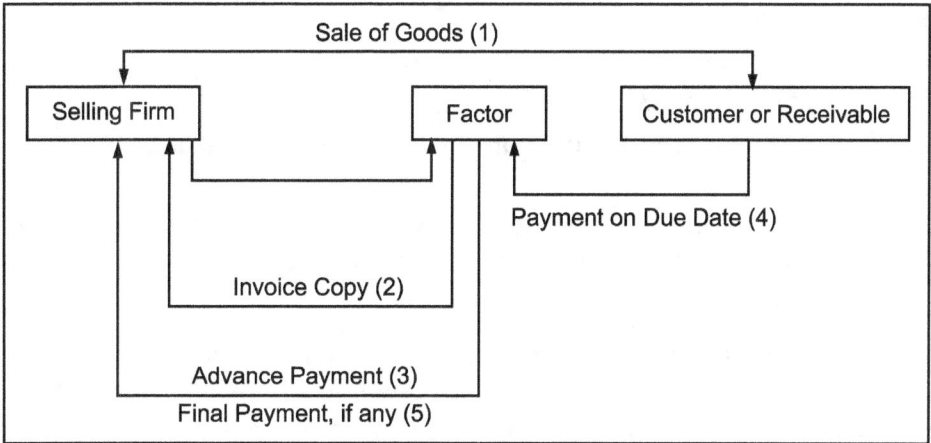

Fig. 3.3: Mechanism of Factoring

3.3.7 Parties to the Factoring

There are basically three parties involved in a factoring transaction.

1. The buyer of the goods
2. The seller of the goods
3. The factor, that is, the financial institution

The three parties communicate with each other during the purchase/sale of goods. The possible process that may be followed is summarised below –

A. The Buyer

1. The buyer enters into a contract with the seller and negotiates the terms and conditions for buying goods on credit.
2. He takes the delivery of goods together with the invoice bill and instructions from the seller to pay the factor on due date.
3. The purchaser pays the factor in time or asks to extend the time. In case of non-payment on due date, he faces lawsuit at the hands of the factor.

B. The Seller

1. The seller enters into an agreement for selling goods on credit as per the purchase order sent by the purchaser stating different terms and conditions.
2. Sells goods to the buyer as per the agreement.
3. Sends copies of invoice, delivery challans along with the goods to the purchaser and gives instructions to the purchaser to pay on due date.

4. The seller sells the receivables received from the purchaser to a factor and receives 80 percent or more payment in advance.

5. After the service charges are paid, the seller receives the balance payment from the factor.

C. The Factor

1. The factor enters into a contract with the seller for providing factor services, that is, collection of receivables/debts.

2. The factor pays 80 percent or more of the amount of receivables copies of sale documents.

3. The factor receives payments from the purchaser on due dates and pays the balance money to the seller after reducing the service charges.

3.3.8 Types of Factoring

Numerous factoring arrangements are possible if an agreement is reached between the selling company and the factor. The most common characteristic of all the factoring transactions is collection of receivables and administration of sale ledger. On the other hand, some of the significant types of factoring arrangements are as follows –

1. Recourse and Non-recourse Factoring

In a recourse factoring arrangement, the factor has recourse to the client (selling firm) if the receivables purchased are bad, the risk of bad debts is to be borne by the client and the factor does not presume credit risks connected to the receivables. Therefore, the factor acts as an agent for collection of bills and does not cover the risk of customer's default in paying the debt or interest on it. The factor has a right to recover the funds from the seller client in case of such defaults as the seller takes the risk of credit and creditworthiness of purchaser. The factor charges the selling company for maintaining the sales ledger and debt collection services and also charges interest on the amount drawn by the client for the period.

But, in case of non-recourse factoring, the risk or loss due to non-payment by the customers of the client is to be borne by the factor and he cannot claim this amount from the selling company. As the factor bears the risk of default, commission or fees charged for the services in case of non-recourse factoring is higher than under the recourse factoring.

The extra fee charged by the factor for bearing the risk of bad debts/non-payment on maturity is called 'del credere' commission.

2. Advance and Maturity Factoring

Under advance factoring agreement, the factor pays only a specific percentage of the receivables beforehand to the client, the balance being paid on the guaranteed payment date. Once the factored receivables are accepted, the advance amount is made available to the client by the factor. The factor charges discount/interest on the advance payment from the date it is to be paid to the date of actual collection of receivables by the factor. The rate of discount/interest is decided based on the creditworthiness of the client, volume of sales and existing short-term rate.

At times, banks also take part in factoring transactions. A bank agrees to give an advance to the client to finance a part say 50 percent of the factored receivables - advance given by the factor.

In case of maturity factoring, no advance payment is given to the client and the client is only paid on the collection of receivables or the guaranteed payment data as the case may be agreed between the parties. Therefore, maturity factoring includes the sale of accounts receivables to a factor with no payment of advance funds at the time of sale.

3. Conventional or Full Factoring

Under this system the factor carries out almost all services of collection of receivables, maintenance of sales ledger, credit collection, credit control and credit insurance. The factor also sets a draw limit on the basis of the bills that are outstanding and takes the corresponding risk of non-payment or credit risk and the factor will have claims on the debtor as also the client creditor.

It is also called as Old Line Factoring. Numerous services such as maturity-wise bills collection, maintenance of accounts, advance granting of limits to a limited discounting of invoices on a selective basis are given. In advanced countries, all these methods are well-known but these methods have just started in India. Factoring agencies like SBI Factors are doing full factoring for good firms with recourse.

4. Domestic and Export Factoring

The basic difference between domestic and export factoring is because of the number of parties involved. In domestic factoring three parties are involved, namely

1. Customer (buyer)
2. Client (seller)
3. Factor (financial intermediary)

All the three parties live in the same country. Export factoring is also called as cross-border/international factoring and is almost the same as domestic factoring except that there are four parties to the factoring transaction, namely, the exporter, the importer or the customer, the export and the import factor. As, two factors are involved in the export factoring, it is also known as two-factor system of factoring.

Two factor system results in two separate but inter-related contracts

1. Between the exporter (client) and the export factor.
2. Export factor and import factor.

The import factor acts as a connection between the export factor and the importer assists in solving the problem of legal formalities and of language. He also assumes customer trade credit risk, and agrees to collect receivables and transfer funds to the export factor in the currency of the invoice. Export/International factoring provides a non-recourse factoring deal. The exporter has 100 percent protection against bad debts loss arising due to credit sales.

5. Limited Factoring

Under limited factoring, the factor reduces only particular invoices on selective basis and changes credit bills into cash in respect of those bills only.

6. Selected Seller-Based Factoring

After invoicing the customers, the seller sells all his accounts receivables to the factor together with the invoice delivery challans, contracts etc. The factor carries out all functions of maintaining the accounts, collecting the debts, sending reminders to the purchasers and does all important and minor functions for the seller. Before entering into a factoring contract, the sellers are generally approved by the factor.

7. Selected Buyer-Based Factoring

Initially, the factor chooses the buyers on the basis of their goodwill and creditworthiness and prepares a list of them. The approved buyers of a firm approach the factor for discounting their purchases of bills receivables drawn in the favour of the company in question. The factor reduces the bills without recourse to the seller and pays the seller.

8. Disclosed and Undisclosed Factoring

In disclosed factoring, the name of the factor is stated in the invoice by the supplier telling the purchaser to pay to the factor on due date. On the other hand, the supplier may carry on bearing the risk of bad debts without passing to the factor. The factor presumes the risk only under non-recourse factoring agreements. Usually, the factor puts down its limitations within which it will work as non-recourse. Beyond this limit the dealings are done on the basis of recourse that is, the seller bears the risk.

Under undisclosed factoring, the name of the factor is not revealed in the invoice. But still the control lies with the factor. The factor maintain sales ledger of the seller of goods, gives short-term finance against the sales invoices but the complete transactions occur in the name of the supplier firm.

3.3.9 Benefits of Factoring

Factoring is nothing but a substitute for in-house management of receivables. Factoring offers a very flexible mode of cash generation against the receivables. Once a line of credit is established, factoring helps in facilitating the availability of cash at an earliest opportunity after sales. Factoring tends to increase the number of rotations by converting the credit sales into cash. Firms availing factoring services may receive the following benefits –

1. **Better Cash Flows:** When the terms are accepted by the factor, the seller can provide credit to the customers and can receive payments on time shortly after it is invoiced. This may not be that expensive than financing and thus, can be availed if the company expects a liquidity problem on a regular basis. In fact, factoring guarantees a definite pattern of cash inflows from the credit sales.

2. **Better Assets Management:** The security for such financial aid is the receivable itself and thus, the other assets will remain available as security for other borrowings.

3. **Better Working Capital Management:** As, finance available from factoring moves directly with the level of the receivables, the necessity of extra working capital to match the sales growth does not come up.

4. **Better Administration:** The debt management services which factors provide relieve the seller of the weight of administration and save on the cost of employees and office space. In other words, factoring allows the seller to focus on developing his/her business.

5. **Better Evaluation:** The debt management service may consist of formal or informal advice on credit standing and factors of information about the trading histories of different companies. This is important to those who are using factoring services and can thus avoid doing business with customers having a poor track record.

6. **Better Risk Management:** In case of non-recourse factoring, the seller will have the advantage of changing the risk position of the customers not paying their due bills. This will be more expensive than recourse factoring and thus allow the seller to avoid the results of customer's default.

3.3.10 Costs of Factoring: Monetary Costs, Non-monetary Costs

However, factoring involves some monetary and non-monetary costs as mentioned below.

1. **Monetary Costs**
    (a) The factor firm usually charges substantial fees and commission for the collection of receivables.
    (b) The advance finance provided by the factor firm would be available at a higher interest cost than the usual rate of interest.

2. **Non-monetary Costs**
    (a) The factor firm doing the evaluation of the creditworthiness of the customer will be primarily concerned with the minimisation of the risk of delays and defaults. In the process, it may tend to ignore a possible sale prospect.
    (b) A factor is a third party to the customer and the latter need not feel comfortable while dealing with it.
    (c) The factoring of receivables may be considered as a symptom of financial weakness. Thus, while evaluating the use of factoring services, the firm must analyse the costs and benefits associated with factoring. It may be noted that though factoring is a costly service, yet some firms may find it to be more economical than to establish their own collection department.

3.3.11 Disadvantages of Factoring

(a) **Cost:** The cash price of the invoices is discounted by the factor company, the upfront cash price being usually 70-90 percent of the face value, depending upon the credit history of the customers and the nature of the adherent's business. The initial price is treated as a cash advance and the adherent typically receives an additional portion of the face value when and if the invoices are collected; the longer the invoice period, the higher the rate. And most factors will not take invoices with longer than 90-day payment periods. The final price is usually between 90-95 percent of the original invoice amount. The adherent's final cost might exceed the amount paid as an interest rate on a short - term commercial loan for an equal amount.

The adherent needs to take into account, before concluding a factoring contract, the size of the annual minimum fee, the length of the commitment period and notice period, and to make sure that factoring is a truly cost-effective decision for the company.

The adherent companies may find that once they rely upon the services of a factor, they may be "locked in" to the relationship even when conditions improve, because of the cash flow implications of any arrangements.

(b) Possible harm to customer relation: The factoring company may be in charge of the invoice collecting; in such circumstances, the adherent should pay attention to the money collection methods the factors employ, so that their personal relationship with their customers will not be impaired.

(c) Company image distortion: In the past, when a company employed the services of a factor, it was considered a sign that the respective company was in financial difficulties. These days, however, the perception has changed, and factoring is considered a normal way to do business and a viable cash management technique.

(d) Factoring may impose constraints on the way you do business: For non-recourse factoring, most factors will want to pre-approve the adherent's customers, which may cause delays in concluding new orders. Also, the factor will apply credit limits to individual customers.

Factoring in India

Factoring service in India is of recent origin. It owes its birth to the recommendations of the Kalyanasundaram Study Group appointed by the Reserve Bank of India in 1989. In accordance with these recommendations, the Reserve Bank of India issued guidelines for factoring services in 1990. The first factoring firm – SBI Factors and Commercial Ltd. (SBI FACS) began functioning in April 1991. This exhibit highlights the significant features of the factoring services in India.

The main recommendations of the Committee/Group are listed as follows –

(1) Considering all the facts, there is sufficient scope for introducing factoring services in India which would be complementary to the services provided by banks.

(2) The introduction of export factoring services would give additional facility to exporters.

(3) While quantification of the demand for factoring services is impossible, it is evaluated that it would grow sufficiently in order to make factoring business a commercially workable proposition within a period of two/three years.

(4) On the export front, there would be a fairly good availment of different services offered by export factors.

(5) With the intention of achieving a balanced dispersal of risks, factors should offer their services to all industries and all sectors in the economy.

---

(6) The pricing of different services by factors would basically depend upon the cost of funds. Factors should try a mix from among the different sources of funds to keep the cost of funds as low as possible, in any case not exceeding 13.5 percent per annum, so that a reasonable spread is available.

(7) The Reserve Bank of India could consider allowing factoring organisations to raise funds from the Discount and Finance House of India Ltd. as also from other approved financial establishments, against their usage of promissory notes covering receivables factored by them, on the lines of revised procedure under bills discounting scheme.

(8) The price for financing services would be around 16 percent per annum and the aggregate price for all other services may not exceed 2.5 percent to 3 percent of the debts services.

(9) At first only select those promoter establishments/groups of people that have a good track record in financial services and competent management should be allowed to enter this new field.

(10) Initially the organisations may be promoted on a zonal basis.

(11) There are different advantages in the banks that are connected to handling of factoring business. The subsidiaries of banks are ideally suited for undertaking this business; at first, it would be desirable to have only four or five organisations which could be promoted either independently by the leading banks or jointly by a few major banks having a big network of branches.

(12) Factoring activities are taken up by the Small Industries Development Bank of India, preferably in association with one or more commercial banks.

(13) The business community should initially be educated through bank branches about the scope of these services and the advantages accruing therefrom.

(14) Without the support of computers, factors cannot extend their services as a fast and dependable means of communication. Simultaneous with consideration of different features relating to the beginning of factoring operations, the promoters should initiate measures for organising network of computers, the branches/agents in different parts of the country for accounting follow-up remittance and other activities involved in factoring business.

(15) The Central Government and the Reserve Bank of India should instantly initiate suitable measures for establishing specialised agencies for credit investigations; until such agencies are completely operational, factors may have to depend on such information about clients/customers as could be gathered through banks or other sources.

(16) Since the suppliers would be capable of acquiring financial services from both banks and factors, it is necessary to provide for proper connection between banks and factoring organisations.

(17) The factoring of Small Scale Industrial (SSI) units could be jointly useful to both factors and small scale industrial units and the factors should work hard to orient their strategy to crystallise, the potential demand for this division.

3.4 Forfeiting

3.4.1 Introduction

The word 'forfeit' is derived from the French word 'forfeit', which means the surrender of rights. Altogether, forfeiting is the non-recourse discounting of export receivables. In a forfeiting transaction, the exporter gives in, without recourse to him, his rights to claim for payment on goods delivered to an importer, in return for instant cash payment from a forfeiter. Consequently, an exporter in India can change a credit sale into a cash sale, with no recourse to the exporter or his banker.

In brief, forfeiting is a mechanism of financing exports which is –

1.   Conducted by discounting export receivables.
2.   Evidenced by bills of exchange or promissory notes.
3.   Without recourse to the seller (namely, the exporter).
4.   Carrying medium-term to long-term maturities.
5.   On a fixed rate basis (discount).
6.   Up to 100 percent of the contract value.

All exports of capital goods and other goods made on medium to long-term credit are eligible to be financed through forfeiting.

Receivables under a deferred payment contract for export of goods, supported by bills of exchange or promissory notes can be forfeited. Bills of exchange or promissory notes, backed by co-acceptance from a bank are supported by the exporter, without recourse, in support of the forfeiting agency in exchange for discounted cash proceeds. The banker's co-acceptance is called as validation. The co-accepting bank should be acceptable to the forfeiting agency. Exim Bank has been given the power by the RBI to facilitate export financing through forfeiting. The Exim Bank acts as a facilitator between the Indian exporter and the overseas forfeiting agency.

On the basis of a request from an exporter for an export transaction which is eligible to be forfeited, Exim Bank will acquire indicative and firm forfeiting quotes – discount rate, commitment and other fees – from overseas agencies. The bank will get avalised bills of exchange or promissory notes, as the case may be and send them to the forfeiter for discounting and will arrange for the discounted proceeds to be dispatched to the Indian exporter. It will issue suitable certificates to allow the Indian exporter to pay the commitment fees and other charges.

To be qualified for forfeiting, the export contract can be implemented in any of the major changeable currencies, for example, US Dollar, Deutsche Mark, Pound Sterling and Japanese Yen. The duration of receivables appropriate for forfeiting is usually between 1 to 5 years. The minimum value of an export contract appropriate for forfeiting and acceptable to a forfeiting agency will usually be equal to US $1,00,000.

Eligibility of an export transaction for forfeiting can be decided when the forfeiting agency is approached for a forfeit quotation. The availability of a forfeiting quote for a specific country depends on the forfeiting agency's insight of risk and the quality of export receivable from that country. The forfeiting agency shows the maximum amount and the time of discount while giving a quotation for forfeiting.

A forfeiting transaction in general has three cost elements: commitment fee; discount fee and documentation fee. Exim Bank charges a service fee for facilitating the forfeiting transaction which can be paid in Indian rupees.

3.4.2 Parties to Forfeiting

There are five parties in a transaction of forfeiting. These are –

(i)   Exporter

(ii) Importer

(iii) Exporter's bank

(iv) Importer's bank

(iv) The forfeiter.

3.4.3 Mechanism

1. The exporter and importer discuss the proposed export sale contract. Then the exporter approaches the forfeiter to determine the terms of forfeiting.

2. The forfeiter gathers details about the importer, supply and credit terms, documentation etc.

3. Forfeiter determines the country risk and credit risk involved.

4. The forfeiter quotes the discount rate.

5. The exporter then quotes a contract price to the foreign purchaser by loading the discount rate, commitment fee etc. on the sale price of the goods to be exported.

6. The exporter and the forfeiter sign a contract.

7. Export takes place against documents guaranteed by the importer's bank.

8. The exporter discounts the bill with the forfeiter and the latter presents the same to the importer for payment on due date or even sell it in secondary market.

3.4.4 Documentation

1. Forfeiting transaction is generally covered either by a promissory note or bills of exchange.

2. Transactions are guaranteed by a bank.

3. Bills of exchange may be 'avalised' by the importer's bank.

'Aval' is an endorsement made on bills of exchange or promissory note by the guaranteeing bank by writing 'per aval' on these documents under right authentication.

3.4.5 The Cost of Forfeiting

1. The Basis for Forfeiting Conditions

The cost of funds, which depends as a rule on the Euromarket interest rates (LIBOR) for the relevant currency and term, provides the foundation on which the conditions of a non-recourse financing transaction are based.

A spread is added to the cost of funds to allow for various factors such as country risk, commercial risk, interest risk, commitment period. Thereby the supply and demand situation on the non-recourse financing market is to be taken into consideration.

It is important to note that the discount rate for non-recourse financing is essentially dependent on the market situation.

2. Cost Components of a Forfeiting Agreement

(a) Commitment fee

Transactions with commitment periods fill the finance house's country limits while it is unable to invest immediately. For this reason, a commitment fee calculated on the financing sum is charged for the period between the conclusion of a financing agreement and the payment of the forfeiting net proceeds to the supplier. As a rule, this commitment fee is payable in advance and amounts to about 1 percent per month for the duration of the commitment period, depending on the specific transaction.

(b) Option fee

If an option is taken out, the commitment fee is replaced by an option fee. This is higher than the commitment fee because the supplier is entitled to withdraw unilaterally from the financing agreement.

The option fee amounts to about 2 percent per month, payable in advance. The normal commitment fee is payable instead of the option fee once the option is exercised.

(c) Special charges/handling fees

Special, non-recurring charges of generally payable in advance, are calculated according to the specific transaction.

(d) Discount rate

Non-recourse financing transactions are always settled at a straight discount, rather than on the basis of a rate of interest, that is, net proceeds are paid over after deduction of the discount for the total term of the financing transaction.

As discounting means deduction in advance, whereas interest is usually payable in arrears, discounting involves a higher charge on the exporter.

(e) Days of grace

Depending on the nature of the claim and where it is payable, several days of grace are allowed, that is, the discount is deducted for some additional days beyond maturity.

Days of grace are calculated because experience has shown that the finance house does not usually have the funds at its disposal until some days after the claim falls due.

(f) Collection costs

In the case of claims in countries where experience has shown that collection costs are debited when the claim matures, the finance house also stipulates this in its offer. Collection costs involve a non-recurring charge of approximately ¼ percent.

(g) Penalty

In the case of forfeiting with a commitment period, a single penalty of about 2 percent is usually charged if the discount documents are not handed over, that is, when the vendor unilaterally fails to execute the contract.

The forfeiting transaction has typically three cost elements –

1. Commitment fee, payable by the exporter to the forfeiter 'for latter's' commitment to execute a specific forfeiting transaction at a firm discount rate within a specified time.

2. Discount fee, interest payable by the exporter for the entire period of credit involved and deducted by the forfeiter from the amount paid to the exporter against the availed promissory notes or bills of exchange.

3. Documentation fee.

3.4.6 Benefits of Forfeiting

There are some major benefits that make forfeiting so convenient and popular. They are –

1. Converts a deferred payment export into a cash transaction, improving liquidity and cash flow.

2. Frees the exporter from cross border political or commercial risks associated with export receivables.

3. Finance up to 100 percent of the export value is possible, as compared to 80–85 per cent financing available from conventional export credit programmes.

4. As forfeiting offers value, without recourse finance to an exporter, it does not affect the exporter's borrowing limits. Thus, forfeiting represents an additional source of funding, contributing to improved liquidity and cash flows.

5. Provides fixed rate finance; hedges against interest and exchange risks arising from deferred export credit.

6. The exporter is freed from credit administration and collection problems.

7. Forfeiting is transaction specific. Consequently, a long-term banking relationship with the forfeiter is not necessary to arrange a forfeiting transaction.

8. Exporter saves on insurance costs as forfeiting obviates the need for export credit insurance.

9. Simplicity of documentation enables rapid conclusion of the forfeiting arrangement.

3.4.7 Forfeiting Compared with Other Means of Financing

Forfeiting combines several banking techniques. It has been described as being roughly halfway between the normal Eurobank lending business and Eurobond business on the one hand, and, between traditional trade financing (by short-term discount of trade drafts) and international factoring on the other. There are elements of these business activities in forfeiting, but by and large, forfeiting is a unique form of trade financing especially suitable for the small business exporter.

Forfeiting shares the following similarities with other classical forms of international finance.

1. Forfeiting is normally done at fixed interest rates, as are Eurobonds.

2. Forfeiting is normally medium-term finance, involving a series of half-yearly maturing notes or bills. This is a term structure similar to normal Eurocurrency credit. In most cases, forfeiting assumes foreign bank or government-related risks, comparable again to the Eurocurrency lending market.

3. Forfeiting is based on discounting trade bills or promissory notes, as is the traditional business of bill discounting.

4. Forfeiting relies on papers associated with most international trade transactions, as does classical trade financing. Financial credits can be non-recourse financing, but require a different procedure.

5. Forfeiting transactions can be of any size covering export deals as large as those seen in the syndicated Eurocurrency banking market.

6. Forfeiting is related to capital goods finance, as are medium-term government export credits.

7. Forfeiting means the purchase of claims from the exporter as does factoring.

8. Forfeiting assumes the risks of international lending from the exporter in a way similar to some governmental export schemes or international insurance.

9. Forfeiting transactions are of investment interest to banks, institutions and individuals, and thus compare with other investments in giving a high yield.

3.4.8 Glossary of Terms Frequently used in Forfeiting Transactions

1. **Forfeiter:** Usually denotes a buyer of forfeiting paper. Forfeiters, however, also will act as sellers of paper from their own portfolios. Usually a bank or other financial institution.

2. **Indicative rate:** A non-binding rate quotation made by the forfeiter to an exporter. Indicative rates are subject to frequent changes in money market conditions and the credit-worthiness of borrowers and guarantors and/or political economic conditions within the borrowers'/guarantors' country.

3. **Firm bid or firm rate quotation:** A binding rate quotation made by the forfeiter to the exporter. Usually the exporter is asked to accept or decline such bids within a 3-day period.

4. **Waiting period:** Period of time which is to elapse between signing of commercial contract and delivery of equipment or services. Forfeiting paper is usually released for payment at the end of the waiting period or upon conclusion of the commercial portion of an export contract.

5. **Option fee:** Some exporters prefer to secure a forfeiting commitment prior to their signing a sales contract. The forfeiter will provide a firm commitment to the exporter against payment of an option fee of 1 percent per annum payable monthly in advance. For large size contracts the option fee may be slightly lower.

6. **Commitment fee:** If an exporter has already signed a commercial contract and thereafter obtains a firm bid from the forfeiter for discounting paper which will be delivered at a pre-determined future date, the exporter will be required to pay the forfeiter a commitment fee during this period at the same rate and basis as the option fee described above. In the event the exporter is faced with a contract cancellation, the forfeiter usually asks that the commitment fee be paid pro-rata until notification by the exporter without any additional penalty fees.

7. **Clean paper:** This refers to all documentation relating to a specific deal being unconditional/irrevocable in conformity with necessary authorisations, licenses and legal jurisdictions of the obligor's (and guarantor's) country, as well as forfeiting market practices and correct verification of all signatures appearing on the paper.

8. **Grace days:** Additional days which are added on to any one note or series of notes to compensate the forfeiter for possible loss of income due to payment transfer delays.

9. **Value date:** The date agreed upon between exporter and forfeiter at which time cash will be paid by the forfeiter to the exporter against presentation of forfeiting paper.

10. **"Straight and Yield":** When providing either indicative or firm discount rates, the forfeiter will indicate whether this is a "straight discount" rate or a "discount-to-yield" rate.

3.4.9 Examples of Forfeiting

Some examples of goods and services which are financed through forfeiting –

(A) Capital Goods

*   Turn-key engineering projects
*   Aircraft parts and accessories
*   Construction equipment
*   Cranes
*   Mining equipment
*   Trucks, buses, special purpose road vehicles
*   Power/Electrical equipment
*   Railroad equipment

- Machine tools and parts
- Tractors and agricultural equipment
- Printing press
- Compressors and motors
- Telecommunication equipment
- Both new and used capital equipment can be furnished through forfeiting

(B) Services

- Engineering studies
- Management consulting
- Computing software

Sample of a Forfeiting Transaction: Commitment Letter

The commitment letter text shown below provides a complete outline of the steps required by an exporter to conclude a forfeiting transaction and has been taken from an actual transaction concluded in 1984.

(FORFEITER LETTERHEAD)

(Exporter)

To the attention of: Mr. _____, Treasurer

Dear Sirs,

Re: Without Recourse Financing - Bills of Exchange accepted by (importer) and avalised by (bank of importer) - our Reference No. ( )

We refer to our recent meeting and are pleased to confirm our agreement to finance the above transaction on a non-recourse basis, subject to all the documentation found to be satisfactory by us when received at our offices and on the following terms and conditions:

Value of Export: U.S. Dollars 638,376.00 FOR

Total Face Value of Bills: U.S. Dollars 638,376 plus interest at 17.31 percent.

Deliveries: In five shipments, each to be evidenced by a series of 10 semi-annual Bills of Exchange. First maturity of each series to be six months from date of shipment.

Documentation: To consist of Bills of Exchange drawn by (exporter) accepted by (importer) and avalised by the (importer's bank).

The bills to be paid at (importer's bank). The bills should have the same wording as the photocopies we have already given you, that is, payment should be in effective U.S. Dollars and without deduction for, and free of any taxes, imposts, levies, or duties present or future of any nature.

All the signatures appearing on the bills should be confirmed to us as valid and legally binding on the parties concerned, that is (importer's bank) should confirm to us that the signatures of the buyer are valid and legally binding. We will confirm (importer's bank) signatures. In addition, we will need a written confirmation from (importer's bank) (either a key-tested telex or side letter) stating that all necessary stamp duties, taxes or other charges have been paid for the

---

issuance of these notes or bills and that once they are released by us to you, such notes/bills will constitute a binding irrevocable and unconditional obligation of the (importer) as well as the (importer's bank) to pay the full face value of the bills or notes to any future bona-fide holder. They should also confirm that no collection or banking charges will be incurred by the bona-fide holder.

Terms: Each series of bills to be discounted to yield on a semi-annual compounded basis of 17.31 percent p.a. plus 7 days of grace to be added on each maturity calculated on a 365/360 day basis.

Option Period: From September 2, 1984 until latest November 2, 1984.

Option Fee: 1/00 (one per million) per month from date of acceptance of our firm bid until conclusion of contract, payable monthly in advance.

Availability: The first series of bills will be available for discounting 4 months from date of signing of the underlying contract. Contract to be signed by latest November 2, 1984. The remaining 4 series of bills will be available for discounting one every month after the first series. Last series to be available for discounting by latest July 2, 1985.

Commitment Fee: 1/00 (one per million) per month from date of conclusion of contract to date of release of drafts, payable monthly in advance. Commitment fee comes into effect as soon as the underlying contract is signed and at that time the option fee will cease to be payable.

We expect that you will require the (importer) to open a letter of credit in your favour to cover the shipment.

We can be your U.S. bank, if you wish. Apart from any particular conditions that you would require under the L/C, we suggest that the exact terms of the deferred payment be clearly stated on the L/C and a condition made that pre-avalised promissory notes (with date of issue, maturity dates and amounts left blank – be lodged with ourselves in trust prior to shipment. As trustee bank we should be instructed by the (importer's bank) to hold the bills or notes, complete them in accordance with their instructions and release them to you for discounting on submission of credit conform documents.

We should be grateful if you would sign and return to us the second copy of this letter signifying that you are in agreement with the foregoing, and ask you to send us your cheque for the first month's option fee based on an approximate total amount of $940,000 including interest. Option fee calculations are as follows –

$$\frac{940{,}000 \times 1.2 \text{ percent p.a.} \times 30 \text{ days}}{360 \times 100}$$

= $940.00

We thank you for the conclusion of this transaction and invite you to contact us if you have any further questions either on this or any new business.

Yours sincerely,

(FORFEITER)

3.5 Credit Rating

3.5.1 Definition

Credit rating is neither a general-purpose evaluation of a corporate entity nor an overall assessment of the credit risk likely to be involved in all the debts contracted or to be contracted by such issues. A rating is specific to a debt/financial instrument and is intended to grade different and specific instruments in terms of the credit risk associated with the particular instrument. Although rating is an opinion expressed by an independent professional organisation, after making a detailed study of all the relevant factors, it does not amount to any recommendation to buy, hold or sell an instrument as it does not take into consideration factors such as market prices, personal risk preferences of an investor and such other considerations, which may influence an investment decision.

A credit rating defines the financial strength of a borrower and helps the investor determine the likelihood that the bond issuer will pay coupon payments in a timely fashion and more importantly the initial investment at maturity.

As a fee-based financial advisory service, credit rating is obviously extremely useful to the investors, the corporates (borrowers), banks and financial institutions. To the investors, it is an indicator expressing the underlying credit quality of a (debt) issue programme. The investor is fully informed about the company, as any effect of the changes in business/economic conditions on the company, is evaluated and published regularly by the rating agencies. The corporate borrowers can raise funds at a cheaper rate with a good rating. This minimises the role of 'name recognition' and less known companies can also approach the market on the basis of their rating. The fund ratings are useful to the banks and other financial institutions, while deciding lending and investment strategies.

The first rating agency, Credit Rating Information Services of India Ltd. (CRISIL), was started in 1988. The first private sector credit rating institution was set up as a joint venture between JM Financials and Alliance Group, and the international rating agency Duffs and Phelps in 1995, known as Duff's and Phelps Credit Rating India Ltd. (DCR).

In recent years, the elimination of strict regulatory framework has caused a surge in the number of firms borrowing directly from the capital markets. In the recent past, there have been numerous cases where the "fly-by-night operators" have cheated unwary investors. In such circumstances, it has become more and more difficult for an ordinary investor to differentiate between 'safe and good investment opportunities' and 'unsafe and bad investments'. Investors find that a borrower's size or name is no longer a sufficient guarantee of timely payment of interest and principal.

Investors see the need for an independent and credible agency, which judges neutrally and in a professional way, the credit quality of different firms and help investors in making their investment decisions. Credit rating agencies, by providing an easy system of gradation of corporate debt instruments, help lenders to form an opinion on the relative capacities of the borrowers to meet their financial and investment obligations. These credit rating agencies, therefore, help and the establishments in India form an important part of a broader programme of financial disintermediation and widening and deepening of the debt market.

Credit rating is used widely for assessing debt instruments. These include long-term instruments, like bonds and debentures plus short-term obligations, like commercial paper. Besides that, future deposits, certificates of deposits, inter-corporate deposits, structured obligations including non-convertible part of Partly Convertible Debentures (PCDs) and preferences shares are also rated.

The Securities and Exchange Board of India (SEBI), the regulator of Indian Capital Market, has now decided to implement mandatory rating of all debt instruments regardless of their maturity.

3.5.2 Meaning

Credit rating agencies rate the debt instruments of different firms. They do not rate the firms, but their individual debt securities. Rating is an opinion concerning the timely repayment of principal and interest thereon; it is communicated by allotting symbols, which have definite meanings.

A rating reflects default risk only, not the price risk connected to the changes in the level or shape of the yield curve. It is significant to highlight that credit ratings are not recommendations to invest. They do not consider many features, which influence an investment decision. They do not, for example, assess the rationality of the issue price, possibilities of earning capital gains or consider the liquidity in the secondary market. Ratings also do not consider the risk of prepayment by the issuer, or interest rate risk or exchange rate risks. Even if these are frequently connected to the credit risk, the rating basically is an opinion on the relative quality of the credit risk. It has to be noted that there is no privity of contract between an investor and a rating agency and the investor is not protected by the opinion of the rating agency. Ratings are not an assurance against loss. They are just opinions, based on analysis of the risk of default. They are useful in making decisions based on specific preference of risk and return.

A company, desirous of rating its debt instrument, is required to approach a credit rating agency and pay a fee for this service. It is not compulsory for the corporate sector to acquire or publicise the credit rating except for particular instruments. The credit rating agencies frequently analyse the financial position of different companies and allot and revise the ratings or their securities. The different rating agencies rarely give different ratings for the same security. If two rating agencies do give the same security for different ratings, it is called split rating; the few differences that occur are rarely more than one rating grade level apart. Every week the accepted ratings are published in the media. According to the industrial practice in India, rating agencies do not publish ratings which are not accepted by issuers.

3.5.3 Importance of Credit Rating

"Credit rating is an assessment, by an independent agency of the capacity of an issuer of debt security to service the debt and repay the principal as per the terms of issue of debt."

A credit rating agency collects the qualitative as well as the quantitative data from a company, which has to be rated, and assesses the relative strengths and capability of the company to honour its obligations contained in the debt instrument throughout the duration of the debt instrument.

(a) Credit rating imposes a financial discipline on the borrowers.

(b) Credit rating helps the financial intermediary in discharging the functions relating to the debt issues.

(c) Credit rating guides the investor regarding the commitment towards a particular debt instrument for better returns.

(d) Credit rating facilitates the formulation of the public guidelines on the institutional investment.

(e) Credit rating may provide adequate funds for the high rated companies at a low rate of interest.

(f) Credit rating lends greater credibility to the financial and other representatives.

(g) Credit rating encourages transparency of information and better accounting standards.

3.5.4 Credit Rating Procedure

(a) The issuing company approaches the credit rating agencies.

(b) To appraise the financial position of the company, the rating agency appoints a team of experts on the basis of client needs.

(c) The team of experts makes a report to the agency appointed to appraise the financial positions.

(d) Credit rating agency submits its observations about the quality of debt instrument through symbols.

3.5.5 Benefits and Criteria of Assessment

Some of the businesses are engaged in a highly capital intensive activity, with long gestation periods; therefore, assessing the quality of the agencies involved assumes great importance in facilitating decisions that may not result in vast unnecessary expenditure of resources causing an undue strain.

With this in mind, the grading of such agencies is designed to benefit the various entities involved in the manner mentioned below.

(a) **Project Owner:** The grading provides a fair assessment of the likelihood of the project being completed as per the terms and the investment yielding the planned returns.

(b) Contractor: The grading facilitates acceptance and highlights the contractor's competence, thus eliminating the need to undercut or resort to unrealistic bidding.

(c) Consultant: The barriers to entry in the consultancy sector are low. The grading enables the consultant to stand out in a crowd.

(d) Project: The grading provides a forewarning on the risk and deficiencies in the enabling infrastructure and financing. The project also benefits from the lower cost of indemnities and the easier access to funds.

Grade Assessment Process

The assessment process for the contractor, the consultant and the project owner commences at the request of the respective entity. Once the mandate letter is received, the rating agency requires, inter alia, the entity's financial statements and details regarding its organisational structure and project experience. Once the information is received, a team of analysts takes up the task of preparing a report on that entity, highlighting its business and financial risks. The support of in-house-research facilities and databases of rating agencies are availed of. A report prepared by the analysts is presented to the Grading Committee for assessing the entity. The whole process is highly interactive and includes inputs from respective sector experts. The rating agency ensures strict confidentiality of all information collected during the assessment process.

Methodology: The Contractor, Consultant and Owner all are graded under two broad risk categories – business risk and financial risk. The indicative criteria, among other factors are mentioned below.

A. Criteria to Assess a Contractor

1. Business Risk Determinants

- Sector of operation
- Project composition
- Market position
- Client category and diversity
- Management quality
- Ability to be an integrator
- Project quality track record
- Project management and design systems for timely completion
- Labour relation track record
- Contract evaluation

2. Financial Risk Determinants

- Leverage
- Financial flexibility and cash flow
- Cost structure
- Working capital management

- Customer advances
- Creditworthiness of clients
- Bank guarantee rates
- Contingent liabilities
- Insurance cover
- Liquidated damages exposure
- Accounting quality

B. Criteria to Assess a Consultant

1. Business Risk Determinants

- Market reputation
- Sector of operation
- Client category and diversity
- Project quality track record
- Engineering, procurement, inspection and planning services
- Human resources quality
- Quality of design system
- Project composition and size

2. Financial Risk Determinants

- Financial flexibility
- Liquidated damages exposure
- Insurance cover

C. Criteria to Assess the Project Owner

1. Business Risk Determinants

- Industry characteristics
- Market position
- Operational efficiency
- New projects
- Management quality

2. Financial Risk Determinants

- Funding policies
- Financial flexibility
- Accounting quality

D. Criteria to Assess Project Risks

The criteria to assess the project risks include an analysis of the following factors, among others –

- Completion risk
- Price risk

- Resource risk
- Technology risk
- Political risk
- Casualty risk
- Environmental risk
- Permitting risk
- Exchange rate risk
- Interest rate risk
- Insolvency risk
- Project development risk
- Site risk
- Financial closure risk

3.5.6 Credit Rating Agencies

There are four credit rating agencies in the country which rate corporates. They are –

(i)   Credit Rating Information Services of India (CRISIL) Ltd.;

(ii) Investment Information and Credit Rating Agency of India (ICRA) Ltd.;

(iii) Credit Analysis and Research (CARE) Ltd.;

(iv) Duffs and Phelps (India) (DCR) Ltd.

In addition, the Onida Individual Credit Rating Agency of India (ONICRA) Ltd. seeks to rate the creditworthiness of non-corporates/individuals. In fact, the rating is not of the individual but of the risk associated with entering into a transaction with an individual at a particular point of time, that is default risk.

(i) CRISIL Ltd.

As the first credit rating agency in India, it was promoted in 1987 jointly by the ICICI and the UTI. Other shareholders include Asian Development Bank, Life Insurance Corporation of India, State Bank of India, Housing Development Finance Corporation Ltd., General Insurance Corporation of India etc. The CRISIL Ltd. commenced operations on January 1, 1998. As a matter of fact, it pioneered the concept of credit rating in the country.

Rating Services: The principal objective of CRISIL is to rate debt obligations of Indian companies. It now rates rupee denominated credit instruments, both long-term and short-term, namely debentures, deposits, structured obligations, preference shares and commercial papers.

Information Services: Although credit rating remains the primary business, CRISIL has diversified into information services as a thrust area for the future. The extensive compilation and analysis of data by the CRISIL for rating business is also used to provide information services to the corporate clients. Till now, its main information product is the CRISIL Card. CRISIL also launched the CRISIL 500 Equity Index, a market value weighted composite index of 500 companies.

Advisory Services: A thrust area in the context of the emerging financial scenario is the provision of advisory services by the CRISIL to the government, banks and other financial institutions and so on. It utilises its information base and expertise in credit rating to provide counselling on aspects such as privatisation of public sector undertakings, debt securitisation and credit evaluation system and so on.

(ii) ICRA Ltd.

The ICRA Ltd. has been promoted by IFCI Ltd. as the main promoter to meet the requirements of the companies based in the north. Apart from the main promoter which holds 26 percent of the share capital, the other shareholders are State Bank of India, Unit Trust of India, Punjab National Bank, and Life Insurance Corporation Bank of India etc. It started operations in 1991. As in the case of the CRISIL, the primary objective of ICRA is to rate credit instruments/debt obligations, to award a grade in consonance with the risk associated with them, to reflect the relative capability of timely servicing of the obligations. ICRA has ventured into Earnings Prospects and Risk Analysis (EPRA). The focus of EPRA popularly referred to as equity rating, is on grading the primary market at the instance of the issuer and assessment of the secondary market at the instance of the investor. The ICRA also undertakes rating of LPG/kerosene firms/dealers and banks. In addition to credit rating, it also provides two services – credit assessment and general assessment.

Credit Assessment: ICRA takes up assignments for credit assessment of companies/undertakings intending to use the same for obtaining a specific line of assistance from commercial banks, financial/investment institutions, factoring companies and financial services, companies.

General Assessment: ICRA provides services of general assessment. At the request of banks or any other potential users, it prepares as per their requirements, a general assessment report. This service is also likely to be useful for other non-banking, non-financial agencies for the purpose of merger, amalgamation, acquisition, joint ventures, collaboration and factoring of debts and so on.

(iii) CARE Ltd.

The Credit Analysis and Research Ltd. (CARE) is a credit rating and information services company promoted by the Industrial Development Bank of India (IDBI) jointly with investment institutions, banks and finance companies. It commenced its credit rating operations in October 1993 and offers a wide range of products and services in the fields of credit information and equity research. The instruments, credit-rated by CARE are debentures, fixed deposits, certificates of deposits, commercial papers and structured obligations. The philosophy of CARE is to focus on growth in the normal rating business.

(iv) Duff and Phelps Credit Rating India Pvt. Ltd. (DCR)

It is the latest entrant in the credit rating business in the country. A joint venture between the international credit rating agency Duffs and Phelps and JM Financial and Alliance Group, it proposes, in addition to debt instruments, rating of companies and countries on their request. It has recently commenced rating of commercial papers. The RBI has included the DCR in the existing list of eligible agencies which can rate CPs from August 1996.

(v) Onida Individual Credit Rating Agency (ONICRA) Ltd.

It is the first rating agency in India which seeks to rate the creditworthiness of non-corporate/individual borrowers. Sponsored by the Onida Finance Ltd. (OFL), its concept of rating is the rating not of the individual but of the risk associated with entering into a transaction with an individual at a particular point of time, that is, default risk. Its benefit is that the user of the rating is able to measure the credit risk involved and consequently assess the default rate. This type of credit rating has applications in credit cards, housing finance, leasing/hire purchase, rental agreements, personal loans and bank finance.

Process: It is the finance firm that insists on its customer obtaining an individual credit rating to reduce its risk exposure.

Rating Symbols

Table 3.5: Long-term Instruments Ratings

	CRISIL	ICRA	CARE
Highest Safety, Timely Payment of the Principal and Interest	AAA	LAAA	CARE AAA
High Safety	AA	LAA	CARE AA
Adequate Safety	A	LA	CARE A
Moderate Safety	BBB	LBBB	CARE BBB
Inadequate Safety	BB	LBB	CARE BB
High Risk	B	LB	CARE B
Substantial Risk	C	LC	CARE C
Likely to Default	D	LD	CARE D

The **suffixes (+) and (–)** indicate the comparative position within the group covered by the symbol. Thus, LAA+ lies notch above LAA. The letter (P) in parenthesis after the rating symbol would indicate that a new company for financing a new project is issuing the debt instrument to raise resources and the rating assumes successful completion of the project.

Table 3.6: Medium-term Instruments Ratings

	CRISIL	ICRA	CARE
Highest safety	FAAA	MAAA	(Are same as for long-term instruments)
High safety	FAA	MAA	
Adequate Safety	FA	MA	
Inadequate Safety	FB	MB	
High Risk	FC	MC	
Default	FD	MD	

The plus(+)/minus(-) signs may be applied for ratings to reflect the comparative standing within the same grade or category.

Table 3.7: Short-term Instruments Ratings

	CRISIL	ICRA	CARE
Highest safety	P1	A1+/A1	PR-1
High safety	P2	A2+/A2	PR-2
Adequate Safety	P3	A3+/A3	PR-3
Inadequate Safety	P4	-	PR-4
High Risk	-	A4+/A4	-
Default	P5	A5	PR-5

Credit rating agency may apply '+' (plus) sign from P1 to P3 to reflect a comparatively higher standing within the category.

The credit rating agencies of India provide credit ratings to the companies that are involved in offering debt obligations like bonds, debentures and many more to the investors.

These products are traded on the secondary securities market and are provided by several companies, as well as the national government. The credit rating agencies of India provide a clear picture of the creditworthiness of a particular financial institution. The creditworthiness of a particular financial institution describes the financial ability of that company of paying back a loan and providing good interest rates for the loans.

Key things to know about credit ratings

- Credit ratings are opinions about relative credit risk.
- Credit ratings are not investment advice, or buy, hold, or sell recommendations. They are just one factor investors may consider in making investment decisions.
- Credit ratings are not indications of the market liquidity of a debt security or its price in the secondary market.
- Credit ratings are not guarantees of credit quality or of future credit risk.

3.6 Venture Capital

3.6.1 Introduction

In India, venture capital came into existence during the pre-independence period when many of the managing agency houses acted as venture capitalists, providing both finance and management to many new and high-risk industries. The first origins of modern venture capital in India can be traced to the setting up of a Technology Development Fund (TDF) in the year 1987-88, through the levy of a cess on all technological payments. TDF was meant to provide financial assistance to innovative and high-risk technological programmes through the Industrial Development Bank of India (IDBI). This measure was followed up in November 1988 by the issue guidelines by the (then) Controller of Capital Issues (CCI).

In January 1988, the IFCI Venture Capital Funds Limited (IVCF) was established by the IFCI by reconstituting the Risk Capital and Technology Finance Corporation Limited, which was earlier known as Risk Capital Foundation (RCF). The objective behind the establishment of IVCF is to focus on supporting projects set up by first generation entrepreneurs involving relatively innovative technologies, products and services through technology finance and venture capital schemes. The IVCF provides assistance in the form of conventional loans or interest-free conditional loans on a profit and risk – sharing basis with the project promoters and subscribes to the equity of projects with suitable buy-back arrangements with the promoters.

Consequently, the ICICI Venture Funds Capital Management Company was established by the ICICI and UTI in July, 1988. Under the Companies Act, 1956, as the country's first venture capital finance company which has became operational in August, 1988 to provide assistance to small and medium industries conceived by technocrat entrepreneurs in the form of project loans, direct subscription to equity and quasi-equity instruments called 'conditional loan', spread across sectors like information technology, health care, light engineering and services etc.

Subsequently, at the state level, Venture Capital Funds were established at Andhra Pradesh and Gujarat by the respective Industrial Development Corporations. In 1992, another venture capital fund was established by the SIDBI with an initial corpus of ₹10 crores to encourage small ventures with innovative features in the small-scale sector.

3.6.2 Concept of Venture Capital

The term consists of two words – 'Venture' and 'Capital'. The dictionary meaning of venture is "undertaking chance or danger" and capital means "the estimated total value of the business". Thus, Venture Capital refers to the estimated total value of a business used for undertaking a chance or danger. According to International Finance Corporation (IFC) "Venture capital is an equity featured capital seeking investment in new ideas, new companies, new production, new process or new services that offer the potential of high returns on investments".

Venture Capital is a form of "risk capital". In other words, capital that is invested in a project (a business) where there is a substantial element of risk relating to the future creation of profits and cash flows. Risk capital is invested as shares (equity) rather than as a loan and the investor requires a higher "rate of return" to compensate him for his risk.

Thus, the investments made by venture capitalists generally involves –

1. Financing new and rapidly growing companies.
2. Purchasing equity securities.
3. Taking higher risk in expectation of higher rewards.
4. Having a long frame of time period, generally of more than 5-6 years.

5. Actively working with the company's management to devise strategies pertaining to the overall functioning of the project.

6. Networking and marketing of the product/service being offered.

Venture capital as explained earlier refers to money that is invested in companies during the early stages of their development. Such funds may come from wealthy individuals, government-backed Small Business Investment Companies (SBICs), or professionally managed venture capital firms. Since investing in an unproven business venture is highly speculative, venture capitalists generally target companies that they believe offer significant potential for growth, and therefore an opportunity to earn a high rate of return in a relatively short period of time.

Like other sources of equity financing, venture capital offers both advantages and disadvantages.

1. The main advantage is that the business is not obligated to repay the money. For a start-up company, this frees up important cash flow that might otherwise be needed to service debt.

2. The involvement of high-profile investors may also help increase the credibility of a new business.

3. The main disadvantage to venture capital financing is that the investors become part owners of the business, and thus gain a say in business decisions. The company's founders face a dilution of their ownership positions and a possible loss of autonomy or control.

4. Even for business owners willing to make the trade-off, venture capital is scarce and often difficult to obtain.

5. Venture capitalists tend to be highly selective in choosing investments. Some will only consider investments in specific technologies, industries, or geographic areas. In fact, the larger venture capital firms typically reject more than 90 percent of the requests for funding that they receive.

6. They evaluate the remaining requests thoroughly, and at considerable expense, before selecting a few that closely match the investors' areas of expertise and offer the best earnings potential. As a result, private equity financing is more likely to be an option for existing businesses with a solid track record and good prospects for future growth than for start-up companies. It is a particularly good choice for fast-growing companies that have few tangible assets to use as collateral for loans.

3.6.3 Procedure for Obtaining Venture Capital

1. For a business owner, the process of obtaining venture capital begins with a formal proposal. The most important element of this proposal is a detailed business plan describing the company's goals and strategies.

2. The proposal should also include recent financial statements, projections of future growth, a brief history of the company, biographies of key managers, the amount of money requested, and a description of how the funds will be used.

3. Experts recommend that companies seeking equity financing evaluate several venture capital firms before entering into a deal. Managers should also hire professionals to help them understand the terms of the agreement to avoid giving away too much control.

4. On receiving a proposal of interest, a venture capital firm usually follows up with a thorough investigation of the company's investment potential.

5. This process might include analysing financial statements, interviewing customers and suppliers, and meeting with the management team.

6. If the venture capital firm remains interested following the evaluation phase, it usually responds with a proposal of its own, known as a term sheet. The term sheet acts as a blueprint for the investment deal, with provisions covering such issues as the valuation of the investment, voting rights, and liquidation options.

7. The final terms are decided through negotiations between the business managers and the venture capital firm. One of the most important factors in the negotiation process is agreeing upon the valuation of the business, which determines the amount of equity that is required in exchange for the venture capital (a business with a low valuation must provide a high percentage of equity, and vice versa).

8. As a general rule, venture capital firms seek to control between 30 and 40 percent of equity in the companies in which they invest. This amount allows the venture capital firm to exercise influence without assuming control or eliminating the management team's incentive to grow the business. The venture capital firm usually hopes to achieve a return of three to five times the original investment within five years, by selling its equity either to the company's management or on the public stock markets.

What is involved in the investment process?

The investment process, from reviewing the business plan to actually investing in a scheme, can take a venture capitalist anything from one month to one year but normally it takes between 3 and 6 months. There are always exceptions to the rule and deals can be completed in very short time frames. A great deal depends on the quality of data given and made available.

The important phase of the investment process is the initial assessment of a business plan. Most approaches to venture capitalists are rejected at this phase. Taking the business plan into consideration, the venture capitalist will consider several principal aspects.

- Is the product or service commercially workable?
- Does the firm have potential for sustained growth?

- Does management have the ability to exploit this potential and control the firm through the growth phases?
- Does the possible reward justify the risk?
- Does the potential financial return on the investment meet their investment criteria?
- In structuring its investment, the venture capitalist may use one or more of the following types of share capital.

Ordinary Shares: These are equity shares that are entitled to all income and capital after the rights of all other classes of capital and creditors have been fulfilled. The ordinary shares have votes. In a venture capital deal, rather than the venture capital company, the shares are held by the management and family shareholders.

Preferred Ordinary Shares: These are equity shares with special rights. For example, they may be entitled to a fixed dividend or share of the profits. Preferred ordinary shares have votes.

Preference Shares: These are non-equity shares. They rank ahead of all groups of ordinary shares for both income and capital. Their income rights are defined and they are generally entitled to a fixed dividend (for example, 10 percent fixed). The shares may be redeemable on fixed dates or they may be irredeemable. Sometimes they may be redeemable at a fixed premium (for example, at 120 percent of cost). They may be changeable into a group of ordinary shares.

Loan Capital: Venture capital loans normally are entitled to interest and are generally, though not necessarily repayable. Loans are secured on the firm's assets or may be unsecured. A secured loan will rank ahead of unsecured loans and certain other creditors of the firm. A loan might be changeable into equity shares. On the other hand, it may have a warrant attached which gives the loan holder the choice to subscribe for new equity shares on terms fixed in the warrant. They normally carry a higher rate of interest than bank term loans and rank behind the bank for payment of interest and repayment of capital.

At the point of investment, venture capital investments are frequently accompanied by additional financing. This is almost always the case where the business in which the investment is being made is comparatively mature or well set up. In this case, it is suitable for a business to have a financing structure that includes both equity and debt.

Other forms of finance provided in addition to venture capitalist equity include –

Clearing Banks: Principally provide overdrafts and short to medium-term loans at fixed or more generally, variable rates of interest.

Merchant Banks: Organise the provision of channel to longer-term loans, generally for larger amounts than clearing banks. Later they can play a significant role in the process of "going public" by advising on the terms and price of public issues and by arranging underwriting when required.

Finance Houses: Provide different forms of instalment credit, ranging from hire purchase to leasing, frequently asset-based and generally for a fixed term and at fixed interest rates.

Factoring Companies: Provide finance by purchasing trade debts at a discount, either on a recourse basis or on a non-recourse basis.

Mezzanine Firms: Provide loan finance that is halfway between equity and secured debt. These facilities need either a second charge on the firm's assets or are unsecured. Because the risk is subsequently higher than senior debt, the interest charged by the mezzanine debt provider is higher than that from the principal lenders and at times a modest equity "upside" will be needed through alternatives or warrants. It is usually most suitable for larger transactions.

Making the Investment – Due Diligence

• To support an initial positive evaluation of a business proposition, the venture capitalist will want to evaluate the technical and financial feasibility in depth.

• External consultants are frequently used to evaluate market prospects and the technical feasibility of the proposition, unless the venture capital company has the qualified people in-house. Chartered accountants are frequently called on to do much of the due diligence, for example, to report on the financial projections and other financial features of the plan. These reports often follow a comprehensive study, or a one or two-day overview may be all that is needed by the venture capital company. They will evaluate and review the following points regarding the firm and its management.

- Management information systems
- Forecasting techniques and accuracy of past forecasting
- Assumptions on which financial assumptions are based
- The latest available management accounts, including the company's cash/debtor positions
- Bank facilities and leasing agreements
- Pensions funding
- Employee contracts, etc.

The due diligence review aspires to support or contradict the venture capital company's own initial impressions of the business plan formed during the early phase. References may also be taken up on the firm.

Overall, venture capital can provide a valuable source of financing for growing businesses. Because of its associated risks, however, experts generally suggest that it be viewed as one of a number of potential sources of financing and be used in combination with debt financing whenever possible. "Private equity isn't for the faint of heart," Klein acknowledged. "But then again, entrepreneurs aren't known for being timid."

The growth of venture capital investment in India, though remarkable by Indian standards has still not been satisfactory as compared to developed and other developing countries. The review of stage-wise investment has highlighted the fact that investment in going by safer route as against taking a risky road. Venture capitalists are playing safe and are investing in companies which are already well established and are moving away from providing seed capital to start-ups.

3.6.4 Objectives of Venture Capital

1. The goal of venture capital is to build companies so that the shares become liquid (through IPO or acquisition) and provide a rate of return to the investors (in the form of cash or shares) that is consistent with the level of risk taken.

2. With venture capital financing, the venture capitalist acquires an agreed proportion of the equity of the company in return for the funding. Equity finance offers the significant advantage of having no interest charges.

3. It is "patient" capital that seeks a return through long-term capital gain rather than immediate and regular interest payments, as in the case of debt financing. Given the nature of equity financing, venture capital investors are therefore exposed to the risk of the company failing. As a result the venture capitalist must look to invest in companies which have the ability to grow very successfully and provide higher than average returns to compensate for the risk.

4. When venture capitalists invest in a business they typically require a seat on the company's board of directors. They tend to take a minority share in the company and usually do not take day-to-day control. Rather, professional venture capitalists act as mentors and aim to provide support and advice on a range of management, sales and technical issues to assist the company to develop its full potential.

3.6.5 Advantages of Venture Capital

Venture capital has a number of advantages over other forms of finance, such as –

1. It injects long-term equity finance which gives a solid capital base for future growth.

2. The venture capitalist is a business partner, sharing both the risks and rewards. Venture capitalists are rewarded by business success and the capital gain.

3. The venture capitalist is capable of giving practical advice and support to the firm based on past experience with other firms which were in similar circumstances.

4. The venture capitalist also has a network of contacts in several areas that can add value to the firm, for example, in recruiting important employees, providing contacts in international markets, introductions to strategic partners, and if required co-investments with other venture capital companies when extra rounds of financing are needed.

5. The venture capitalist may be capable of providing additional rounds of funding should it be required to finance growth.

Venture capital provides long-term, committed share capital, to help unquoted companies grow and succeed. If an entrepreneur is looking to start-up, expand, buy-into a business, buy-out a business in which he works, turnaround or revitalise a company, venture capital could help do this. Obtaining venture capital is substantially different from raising debt or a loan from a lender. Lenders have a legal right to interest on a loan and repayment of the capital, irrespective of the success or failure of a business. Venture capital is invested in exchange for an equity stake in the business. As a shareholder, the venture capitalist's return is dependent on the growth and profitability of the business. This return is generally earned when the venture capitalist "exits" by selling its shareholding when the business is sold to another owner.

What kinds of businesses are attractive to venture capitalists?

Venture capitalists prefer to invest in "entrepreneurial businesses". This does not necessarily mean small or new businesses. Rather, it is more about the investment's aspirations and potential for growth, rather than by current size. Such businesses are aiming to grow rapidly to a significant size. As a rule of thumb, unless a business can offer the prospect of significant turnover growth within five years, it is unlikely to be of interest to a venture capital firm. Venture capital investors are only interested in companies with high growth prospects, which are managed by experienced and ambitious teams who are capable of turning their business plan into reality.

3.6.6 The Evaluation Process

As it is frequently difficult to assess the income potential of new business ideas or very young firms, and investments in such firms are unprotected against business failures, venture capital is a very risky industry. Consequently, venture capital companies establish strict policies and needs for the kinds of proposals they will even consider. Some venture capitalists specialise in specific technologies, industries, or geographic areas, for example, while others need a particular size of investment. The maturity of the firm may also be a factor. While most venture capital companies need their client firms to have some operating history, a small number handle start-up financing for companies that have a well-considered plan and an experienced management group.

On the whole, venture capitalists are most interested in supporting firms with low current assessments, but with good opportunities to attain future profits in the range of 30 percent annually. Most striking are innovative firms in rapidly accelerating industries with few competitors. Ideally, the firm and its product or service will have some unique, marketable feature to differentiate it from imitators. Most venture capital companies search for investment opportunities in the $250,000 to $2 million range, although some are ready to think about smaller or larger projects. As venture capitalists become part owners of the firms in which they invest, they tend to look for companies that can increase sales and generate strong profits with the aid of a capital infusion. Due to the risk involved, within five years, they expect to obtain a return of three to five times their initial investment.

Venture capital organisations normally reject the huge majority, 90 percent or more of proposals quickly because they are considered a poor fit with the company's priorities and policies. They then investigate the remaining 10 percent of the proposals very cautiously and at substantial cost. Whereas banks tend to concentrate on the firms' past performance when assessing them for loans, venture capital companies tend to concentrate instead on their future potential. Consequently, venture capital organisations will inspect the features of a small business's product, the size of its markets, and its projected income.

As part of the in depth investigation, a venture capital organisation may employ consultants to assess highly technical products. They also may contact a firm's customers and suppliers so as to acquire information about the market size and the firm's competitive position. Several venture capitalists will also appoint an auditor to confirm the financial position of the firm and an attorney to check the legal form and registration of the company. Perhaps the most significant factor in a venture capital organisation's assessment of a small company as a potential investment is the environment and capability of the small company's management. **Hosmer** noted that "many venture capital firms really invest in management capability" rather than a small business's product or market potential. As the abilities of management are often hard to evaluate, it is possible that an agent of the venture capital organisation would spend a week or two at the firm. Ideally, venture capitalists like to have experienced and committed management team in the industry. Another plus is a complete management group with clearly defined responsibilities in particular functional areas, such as product design, marketing, and finance.

3.6.7 Different Stages of Financing

The venture capital identifies different stages of financing, namely –

1. **Early Stage Financing:** This is the first stage of financing when the company is undertaking production and require extra funds to sell its products. It involves seed/initial finance for supporting an idea of a businessman. The capital is given for product development, R&D and initial marketing.

2. **Expansion Financing:** This is the second stage of financing for working capital and expansion of a business. It involves development financing so as to facilitate the public issue.

3. **Acquisition/Buyout Financing:** This later stage involves
   - Acquisition financing in order to acquire another company for further expansion.
   - Management buyout financing in order to allow the operating groups/ investors for acquiring an existing product line or company.
   - Turnaround financing so as to revitalise and restore the sick enterprises.

In India, the venture capital funds (VCFs) can be categorised into the following groups –

1. Those promoted by the Central Government controlled development finance establishments, for example

   - ICICI Venture Funds Ltd.
   - IFCI Venture Capital Funds Limited (IVCF)
   - SIDBI Venture Capital Limited (SVCL)

2. Those promoted by State Government controlled development finance establishments, for example

   - Gujarat Venture Finance Limited (GVFL)
   - Kerala Venture Capital Fund Pvt. Ltd.
   - Punjab Infotech Venture Fund
   - Hyderabad Information Technology Venture Enterprises Limited (HITVEL)

3. Those promoted by public banks, for example

   - Canbank Venture Capital Fund
   - SBI Capital Markets Limited

4. Those promoted by private sector firms, for example

   - IL&FS Trust Company Limited
   - Infinity Venture India Fund

5. Those established as an overseas venture capital fund, for example

   - Walden International Investment Group
   - SEAF India Investment & Growth Fund
   - BTS India Private Equity Fund Limited

All these venture capital funds are governed by the Securities and Exchange Board of India (SEBI). SEBI is the nodal agency for registration and regulation of both domestic and overseas venture capital funds. In view of that, it has made the following regulations, namely, Securities and Exchange Board of India (Venture Capital Funds) Regulations 1996 and Securities and Exchange Board of India (Foreign Venture Capital Investors) Regulations 2000. These regulations provide extensive guidelines and processes for establishing venture capital funds both within India and outside it; their management structure and set-up; as well as size and investment criteria of the funds.

Points To Remember

- The financial services sector in India is booming and has become one of the biggest money-spinning areas. This sector has undergone a sea change since 1990.
- The term "financial services" in its broader sense refers to *"the mobilising and allocation of savings"*.
- It is identified as inclusive of all those activities involved in the process of converting savings into investment. Financial services also include "financial mediators", such as merchant bankers, venture capitalists, commercial banks, insurance companies etc.

- A mutual fund is a collection of stocks and/or bonds. A mutual fund works as a company that brings together a group of people and invests their money in stocks, bonds, and other securities. Each investor owns shares, which represent a portion of the holdings of the fund.

- Factoring is a service involving the purchase by a financial organisation, called a factor, of receivables owned to manufacturer and distributors by their customers, with the factor assuming full credit and collection responsibilities.

- The word 'forfeit' is derived from the French word 'forfait', which means the surrender of rights. Simply put, forfeiting is the non-recourse discounting of export receivables. In a forfeiting transaction, the exporter surrenders, without recourse to him, his rights to claim for payment on goods delivered to an importer, in return for immediate cash payment from a forfeiter.

- Credit rating is an assessment, by an independent agency of the capacity of an issuer of debt security to service the debt and repay the principal as per the terms of issue of debt.

- A credit rating agency collects the qualitative as well as the quantitative data from a company, which has to be rated, and assesses the relative strengths and capability of the company to honour its obligations contained in the debt instrument throughout the duration of the debt instrument.

- Venture capital refers to money that is invested in companies during the early stages of their development. Such funds may come from wealthy individuals, government-backed Small Business Investment Companies (SBICs), or professionally managed venture capital firms.

- Since investing in an unproven business venture is highly speculative, venture capitalists generally target companies that they believe offer significant potential for growth, and therefore an opportunity to earn a high rate of return in a relatively short period of time.

KEY WORDS

Mutual Funds: Mutual fund is a trust that pools money from a group of investors (sharing common financial goals) and invests the money thus collected into asset classes that match the stated investment objectives of the scheme.

Factoring: Factoring is a service provided by a financial organisation, involving a purchase (Factor) of receivables owned to manufacturer and distributors by their customers, with the factor assuming full credit and collection responsibilities.

Forfeiting: Forfeiting is the non-recourse discounting of export receivables.

Credit Rating: Credit rating is neither a general-purpose evaluation of a corporate entity nor an overall assessment of the credit risk likely to be involved in all the debts contracted or to be contracted by such issues.

Questions for Discussion

1. What are financial services? Explain the various current trends in financial services in India.

2. What are mutual funds? What are the major advantages of investment through mutual funds?

3. Define the different types of schemes floated by mutual funds and explain them briefly.

4. Comment on "The role of factors has increased significantly in India."

5. What do you mean by credit rating? Analyse the important features of credit rating business in India.

6. What is the concept and mechanism of factoring? What are recourse and non-recourse factoring?

7. Explain the origin, meaning and characteristics of factoring.

8. Explain the types and advantages of factoring.

9. Critically analyse the role of factoring as a source of financing.

10. Distinguish between 'factoring' and 'forfeiting' and explain their respective scope in India.

11. Explain the term credit rating. What are its advantages?

12. What is the concept of venture capital?

✍ ✍ ✍

Chapter **4**...

Banking and Insurance Sector in India

Contents ...

Learning Objectives ...

- To explain the structure of the banking system prevalent in India
- To give a brief outline of the structure of the insurance sector in India
- To trace the evolution of the banking system in India
- To discuss the progress made in the insurance sector in the last two decades
- To illustrate and explain the major functions of RBI
- To explain the history of IRDAI
- To elaborate the powers and functions of the Insurance Regulatory and Development Authority
- To discuss the role of RBI and IRDA as regulatory authorities

4.1 Introduction

4.1.1 Banking Sector

The earliest record of the activities of money changing, lending and other banking functions date back to as early as 2000 BC, in ancient Babylon, where Babylonian temples were in the banking business. These temples lent gold and silver which had been left with them for safe keeping at high rates of interest.

The basic functions of banks are to accept deposits, lend money and act as collecting and paying agents. Any organised institution which performs these functions can be called a bank. The present day banker has three ancestors namely, the merchant, the money lender and the goldsmith. The merchant was able to collect deposits from his customers because of good reputation. He accepted deposits for the purpose of financing his trading business. The second ancestor, the money lender, usually conducted business with his own money. But, he also accepted spare money for the purpose of investment. The third ancestor, that is, the goldsmith, originated in England. This was the time when gold and silver were used as money. The London merchants deposited their surplus gold and silver in the Tower of London.

The present day banker combines all these functions of his three predecessors. Like the merchant banker, he accepts deposits from his customers; like the money lender, he lends money to the needy from funds entrusted to him; and like the goldsmith, he accepts valuables and money for safe custody.

In India, banking originated long ago. There are evidences of giving loans to others even during the Vedic period. In ancient times, banking was synonymous with money lending. The private money lenders and indigenous bankers played an important part in the Indian society. While money lenders provided loans to people in times of need mainly for consumption purposes; indigenous bankers extended credit for financing trade and industry. However, during the seventeenth century, their importance reduced due to the establishment of agency houses and presidency banks patronised by the English East India Company. This was considered to be the birth of the modern banking in India.

It originated during the latter part of the 19th century and the early 20th century. Currently, banking is a result of a slow and gradual development.

The RBI was originally a shareholders' bank. But it was nationalised by the Reserve Bank (Amendment) Act 1948, consequent to the nationalisation of the Bank of England in 1946. A major historical event in the history of banking in India after the Independence is the nationalisation of 14 major banks on 19th July 1969 and six more private sector banks in 1980.

Another very important development in the Indian banking system is the establishment of new private sector banks. The Narasimhan Committee recommended that there should be no barriers to new banks being set up in the private sector. The banking system was liberalised during the early '90s which led to greater competition and higher productivity and efficiency in the banking system. Accordingly, RBI issued a set of guidelines in January 1993 for the entry of new private sector banks.

The banking sector is the most important part of the financial system and it promotes economic development of a country. Banking sector is very crucial and it is considered as the life and blood of the economic system. Banks function as important financial intermediaries which mobilise savings and divert them to productive investments in the economy. Banks help in capital formation and are regarded as facilitators for economic development. Moreover, they also help in equitable distribution of funds and development of backward regions.

The journey of Indian banking system can be classified into three distinct phases –

Phase I	Early phase from 1786 to 1969	• Setting up of General Bank of India, Bank of Hindustan, Bengal Bank, Bank of Bombay Presidency Bank etc.
		• Growth was very slow
		• Banks also experienced failures
		• Low public confidence
		• Slow deposit mobilisation
		• About 1100 small banks
		• Enactment of Banking Regulation At, 1949
		• Constitution of RBI
Phase II	1969 to 1991	• Nationalisation of Imperial Bank of India
		• Formation of SBI as the principal agent of RBI
		• Extensive banking facilities on a large scale
		• Nationalisation of 14 major private commercial banks; thereby raising deposits by 800 percent and advances by 11000 percent
Phase III	1991 onwards	• Continuation of the banking sector reforms
		• Narasimhan Committee appointed in 1991 to suggest measures for enhancing the efficiency, productivity and profitability of the financial services system
		• Country flooded with foreign banks and ATMs
		• Phone banking, net banking services introduced
		• System more convenient and swift

4.1.2 Insurance Sector

The insurance industry has economic significance and social purpose. It provides social security and promotes individual welfare. It helps to raise productivity by reducing the risk. Insurance organisations typically invest the savings of their policyholders and in exchange promise them and/or their beneficiaries a specified sum either at a later stage or upon the happening of a certain event. Insurance companies may be organised either as corporations or mutual associations. The insurance companies are financial intermediaries that collect and invest large amounts of premiums. Their business consists of spreading risks over time and sharing them between persons and organisations.

The life insurance services have been in existence in India since 1818. The first life insurance company namely, Oriental Life Insurance Company was established in Kolkata in 1818. The general insurance service has shown its presence since 1850 when the first Tritan Insurance Company was established in Kolkata. Since then, the insurance industry in India has grown in terms of the number of companies providing those services, the volume of premium, investible resources and so on.

The history of the existence and working of insurance organisations in India can be presented in the following three phases –

Phase I	Structure
Life Insurance (From 1818 to 1956)	Private sector companies only, competitive market
General Insurance (From 1850 to 1972)	Private sector companies only, competitive market
Phase II	
Life Insurance (From 1956 to 2000)	Nationalisation, public sector or state monopoly, only one company (Life Insurance Corporation of India)
General Insurance (From 1972 to 2000)	Nationalisation, public sector monopoly, one company (General Insurance Corporation of India with its 4 subsidiaries)
Phase III	
Life Insurance and General Insurance (After 2000)	Insurance sector opened to the entry of private domestic and foreign companies, co-existence of public and private sector units, competitive market and higher efficiency.

After the introduction of New Economic Policy in 1991, the government appointed the Malhotra Committee in 1993 to suggest insurance sector reforms in tune with other financial and economic reforms. The insurance sector in India has gone through the process of reforms following the recommendations of the Malhotra Committee. This would lead to improvement in the quality of insurance services in the country. The Insurance Regulatory and Development Authority (IRDA) Bill was passed by the Indian Parliament in December 1999. The IRDA assumed the status of a statutory body in the year April 2000 and has been framing regulations and registering the private sector companies.

It can be said that over a period of about 200 years, the insurance services sector in India has gone through a full circle from being an open competitive market to the nationalised market, and back to a liberalised market again. Even though this is true, still the differences between then and now are noteworthy. Earlier, the number of insurance companies was truly large, and the market was very competitive with no presence of state in the insurance market as an owner. Now, the number of companies is small, the market is oligopolistic in which one operator is a dominant leader and there is heavy concentration of business in the hands of one or two companies. Also the state is present in the sector as an owner. It can be said that the earlier competitive private market has been replaced by the present mixed-ownership and a very weak competitive market.

4.2 Structure of Banking & Insurance Sector in India

4.2.1 Structure of Banking Sector

The banking system in India is performing a key role in accelerating the rate of economic growth in the Indian economy. It is one of the most important pillars of the economy which helps in creation of wealth for the country. The banking sector reforms introduced in the early '90s were mainly aimed at a viable and efficient banking system.

The banking system is a set of complex and closely intermixes of banking institutions, instruments, services, practices, procedures etc. There are organised and unorganised sectors of banking systems operating in India.

Organised banking system comprises of those institutions which come under Banking Regulation Act or work under the control and supervision of RBI. In the organised sector, India has developed a banking system which consists of a commercial banking network of more than 63,000 branches and RBI as a central bank. Public sector banks dominate India's banking and industry and they are accompanied by several private and foreign banks. There are co-operative sector banks, regional rural banks and developmental banks to promote the growth of particular sectors of the economy and to support the banking system. The structure of the banking system prevalent in India is given below.

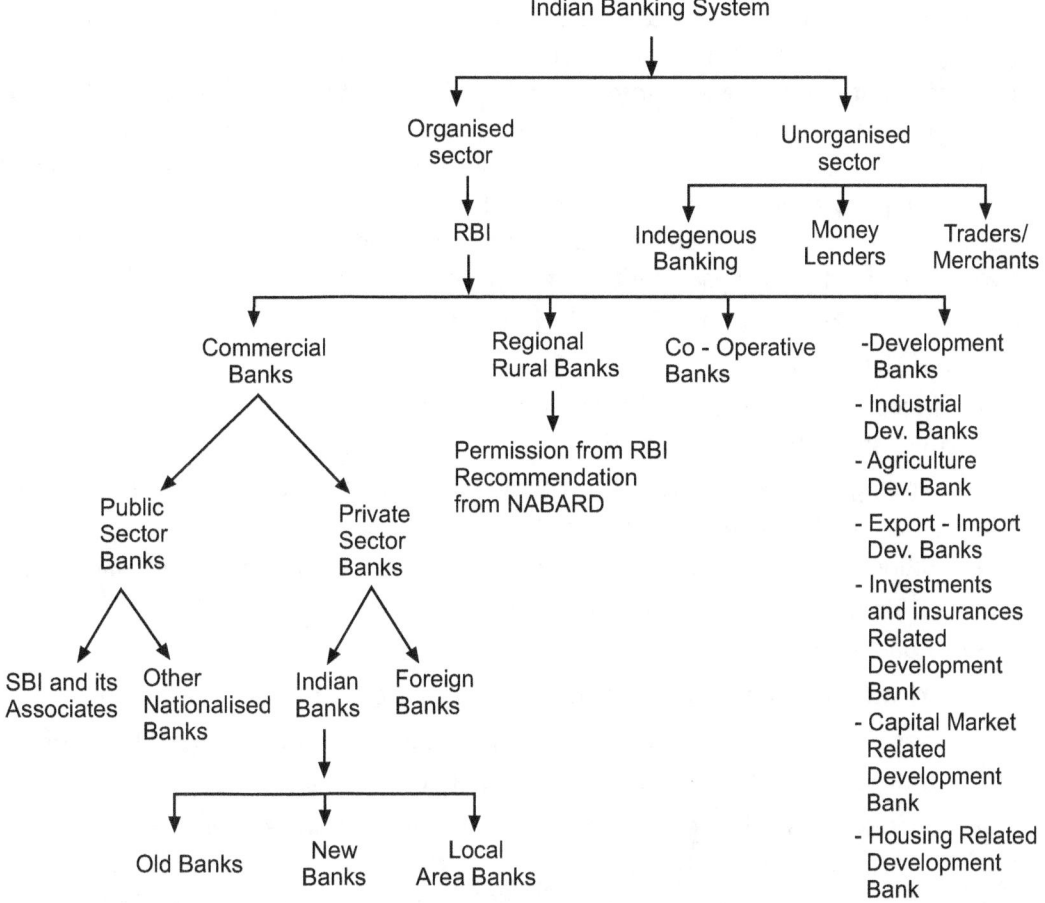

Fig. 4.1: Structure of Banking System in India

The unorganised system consists of a number of moneylenders, indigenous bankers, traders, landlords, and merchants etc. who lend money to the public and the indigenous banks who also accept deposits from them. There are also private finance companies, chit funds and host of other unincorporated bodies whose activities like deposit trading activities, the maturity and interest rates on their deposits etc. are controlled by the RBI and the government. There is no uniformity in operations and working of these institutions.

After independence efforts were made by RBI to regulate and improve working of unorganised sector and improve its working in order to align them with modern organised banking sector.

1. Commercial Banks

Commercial banks play a very important role in our economy. Our economic system would not function efficiently in the absence of commercial banks. They are considered as the heart of our financial structure that makes the complete utilisation of the resources of the nation. They are regarded as instruments of economic growth and social justice. They are the oldest institutions having a wide network of branches, commanding utmost public confidence and having the lion's share in the total banking operations.

The commercial banks are those financial institutions which accept deposits from the public repayable on demand and lend them for short periods. They borrow money in the form of deposits at a lower rate of interest and lend it at a higher rate and thereby make a profit. They have the capacity to create money in the form of demand deposits. They are mainly oriented towards fulfilling short-term credit requirements of trade and industry. The most pertinent feature of commercial banks is that it is the only institution which accepts deposits from the public repayable on demand and withdrawable by cheque. Their main objective is to earn and maximise profit from banking activities.

Commercial banks perform the following functions –

1. Primary Functions
   ➢ Accepting deposits in the form of demand deposits, savings deposits, fixed deposits or time deposits
   ➢ Lending money in the form of overdraft, cash credits, loans and advances, discounting of bills of exchange etc.
   ➢ Acting as intermediaries between the depositors and the borrowers thereby creating additional purchasing power.

2. Secondary Functions
   ➢ Collection of cheques, drafts and bills for their customers
   ➢ Execution of standing orders, for example, payment of commercial bills, collection of dividend warrant and interest coupons etc.
   ➢ Conduct of stock exchange transactions, that is, purchase and sale of securities for the customers
   ➢ Providing income tax services
   ➢ Acting as executors and trustees
   ➢ Conduct of foreign exchange business
   ➢ Safe keeping of valuables
   ➢ Issue of commercial letters of credit, bank guarantees and travellers' cheques.
   ➢ Providing investment advice

The modern commercial banking system in India originated during the 19th and the early 20th centuries. This was due to the development of foreign trade and the emergence of the organised commercial and industrial sector. The commercial banking system in India consists of –

1. Scheduled Banks
2. Unscheduled Banks

The scheduled banks constitute those banks which have been included in the Second Schedule of the Reserve Bank of India (RBI) Act, 1934. This inclusion of the banks in the schedule depends upon the satisfaction of criteria as laid down vide section 42(6)(a) of the

Act. The scheduled commercial banks comprise the State Bank of India and its associates, the nationalised banks, private sector banks, foreign banks, co-operative banks and regional rural banks.

The unscheduled banks are those banks as defined in Clause (c) of Section 5 of the Banking Regulation Act, 1949, which are not included in the Second Schedule of RBI Act 1934. Non-scheduled banks can function in all banking sectors. They are also known as local area banks. Examples of unscheduled banks are Coastal Local Area Bank Ltd., Vijayawada; Capital Local Area Bank Ltd., Phagwara; South Gujarat Local Area Bank Ltd., Navsari; Krishna Bhima Samruddhi Local Area Bank Ltd., Mehboob Nagar; and Subhadra Local Area Bank, Kolhapur.

2. Public Sector Banks

These are the banks where the majority of stake is held by the Government of India or RBI. These banks are owned and controlled by the government. In India, the State Bank of India and its associate banks, nationalised banks, and the regional rural banks come under these categories.

The public sector banks in India developed in four stages as given below –

➢ Nationalisation of the Imperial Bank, organisation of the State Bank of India on 1st July 1955 and reconstitution of the subsidiaries of the SBI

➢ Nationalisation of 14 major Indian commercial banks on 19th July 1969

➢ Establishment of RRBs in 1974

➢ Nationalisation of 6 more Indian banks on 4th September, 1993

The Allahabad Bank, Bank of Baroda, Canara Bank, Indian Bank, Viyaya Bank, State Bank of India, Punjab & Sind Bank are some of the examples of public sector banks.

3. Private Sector Banks

With a view to infusing more competition in the banking sector, private sector banks were permitted to be set up as per the recommendations of the Narasimhan Committee. According to RBI, the new private sector banks must complement the overall financial sector reforms with a view to providing a financially viable, technologically up-to-date and efficiently competitive system that would make possible low cost financial intermediation. The first private sector commercial bank, the UTI Bank Ltd., (now Axis Bank) with its head office in Ahmedabad was inaugurated on 2nd April 1994.

In private sector banks, the majority of their share capital is held by private individuals or corporations and not by the government or cooperative societies. These banks are registered as companies with limited liability.

The private sector banks in India consist of the old generation, the new generation private sector banks and the foreign banks.

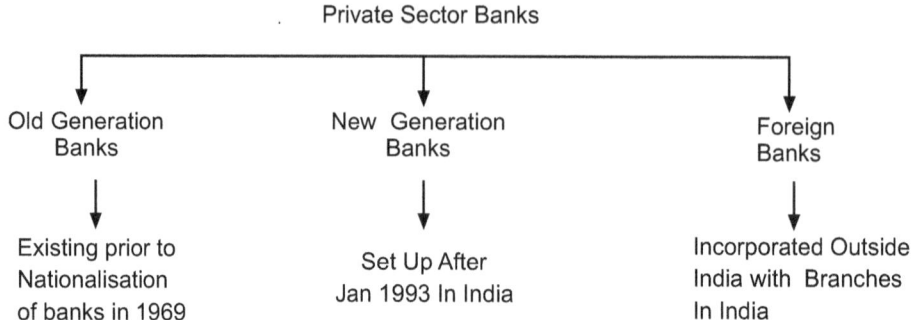

Fig. 4.2: Private Sector Banks

The old generation private banks have a strong regional presence, better knowledge of economic activities of the region and the ability to offer personalised services to customers. These are the banks which were not nationalised, mainly because of their small size and regional focus. ING Vysya Bank Ltd., Federal Bank Ltd., South Indian Bank Ltd., Bank of Rajasthan Ltd., Dhanalakshmi Bank Ltd., Karur Vysya Bank Ltd. are some of the examples of old private sector banks.

The new generation private sector banks have been established on the basis of the recommendations of the Narasimhan Committee Report that "there should be no barriers to new banks being set up in the private sector." The new private sector banks are permitted to do all the functions, a commercial bank is permitted to do. An entry precondition was that they should commence their banking operations in the country on a fully computerised platform. This entry precondition gave a competitive advantage to these new generation banks that have gained a major market share from public sector banks. HDFC Bank Ltd., ICICI Bank Ltd., Kotak Mahindra Bank Ltd., Axis Bank, Indus Ind Bank Ltd. are some of the examples of new private sector banks.

4. Foreign Banks

Foreign banks are those banks which are incorporated outside India with their head office also situated outside India but they have set up their branches in India. These banks were established in India during the late 19th and the early 20th centuries. Foreign banks were established mainly due to the development of trade with other countries during that period. They form an important segment of commercial banking system in India.

These banks are involved with financing of foreign trade and associated activities. They collect credit information regarding importers and exporters, accept and discount foreign bills, issue letter of credit, finance transportation of goods from ports to inland centres and from interior parts to ports etc. Thus, the functions of foreign banks are –

➢ Financing foreign trade both imports and exports
➢ Financing of movement of goods from and to Indian ports
➢ Financing of movement of goods to and from distributing or collecting centres in the interior parts of the country
➢ Discounting of foreign bills

➢ Financing inland trade

➢ Rendering agency services

➢ Merchant banking services

➢ Banking business, namely, accepting deposits, granting loans, providing remittance facilities etc.

Foreign banks are advantageous than Indian banks mainly due to their early beginning coupled with vast resources and superior management.

Foreign banks have branches in important parts of the world. They have made the Indian banking sector more competitive and efficient. They have also brought the latest technology and world class banking practices in India. Bank of Tokyo, Mitsui Bank, Bank of America, Banque Nationale de Paris, HSBC, Citibank N.A. are some of the oldest foreign banks functioning in India.

5. Regional Rural Banks

Regional rural banks evolved during the year 1975 with the aim of increasing the flow of credit and availability of banking facilities to rural areas and to the poorer sections of the rural population. Their main purpose was to facilitate the promotion of rural business in India. These banks concentrate their activities in one or two districts and were set up in accordance with the recommendations of the Banking Commission, 1972. This working group was under the chairmanship of Mr. M. Narasimhan, Additional Secretary, Ministry of Finance and its task was to review the flow of institutional credit especially to the weaker sections of the community. The group felt that the regional and functional gaps in rural credit could be met with a new type of institution suitable to the needs of rural areas. Thus, it recommended the formation of state-sponsored, regionally-based and rural-oriented regional rural banks. The first 5 regional rural banks were formed on 2nd October, 1975. It was clearly emphasised that the role of these banks would be to supplement and not supplant the other institutional agencies in the field. They are spread across the country and have been playing an important role in the development and growth of the rural business and economy.

The RBI has instructed that these banks will have to give more importance to the rural-oriented financing and the lending and deposit rates will be governed by provisions applicable to the RRBs.

RRBs are similar to commercial banks in their methods of operation and organisational setup, but their area of activity is limited to specified district/s and their loaning operations are restricted to specified target groups and purposes. They provide credit to the weaker sections in the rural areas and they are the major investors in different types of operations in the rural areas. As India is an agrarian economy, the growth of the rural sector and the promotion of agricultural sector would give the economy a boost.

Functions of RRBs

> ➢ Granting loans and advances, particularly to small and marginal farmers, agricultural labourers, artisans, small entrepreneurs etc.

> ➢ Granting loans and advances to cooperative societies, agricultural marketing societies, primary agricultural credit societies, service societies for agricultural purposes etc.

> ➢ Granting loans and advances to artisans, small entrepreneurs, persons of small means engaged in trade, commerce or industry or other productive activities, within the notified are in relation to them.

> ➢ The lending rates of RRBs shall not be higher than the rates charged by cooperative societies.

> ➢ RRBs are allowed to pay interest on deposits at half percent more than the rate paid by the commercial banks.

6. Cooperative Banks

The cooperative organisation is one of the forms of business organisation. People who come together to jointly serve common interest often form a cooperative society under the Cooperative Societies Act. When a cooperative society engages itself in banking business, it is called a cooperative bank. This cooperative functions under the overall supervision of the Registrar of Cooperative Societies of the State and as regards its banking business, the society has to obtain a license from RBI before starting banking business and it must follow the guidelines set and issued by RBI.

The basic idea of cooperative movement is that poor people should come together and develop banking habits within small means.

Presently, the cooperative banking system plays a very important role in the development of Indian economy. The cooperative movement was started in India with the passing of the Cooperative Credit Societies Act, 1904. The cooperative banking system is smaller as compared to the commercial banking system and its main objective is to provide finance at low rates of interest to agriculturists.

Although commercial banks and RRBs have established a large network of rural branches to cater to the credit needs of the rural poor, the cooperative banks continue to enjoy a place of crucial importance in the rural credit scenario. Cooperative credit institutions in India comprise both rural and urban cooperative credit institutions. Rural cooperatives play a very important role in the rural credit delivery system and urban cooperatives aim at mobilisation of savings from urban population and provide credit to the weaker sections.

The structure of the cooperative banking system in India is given below.

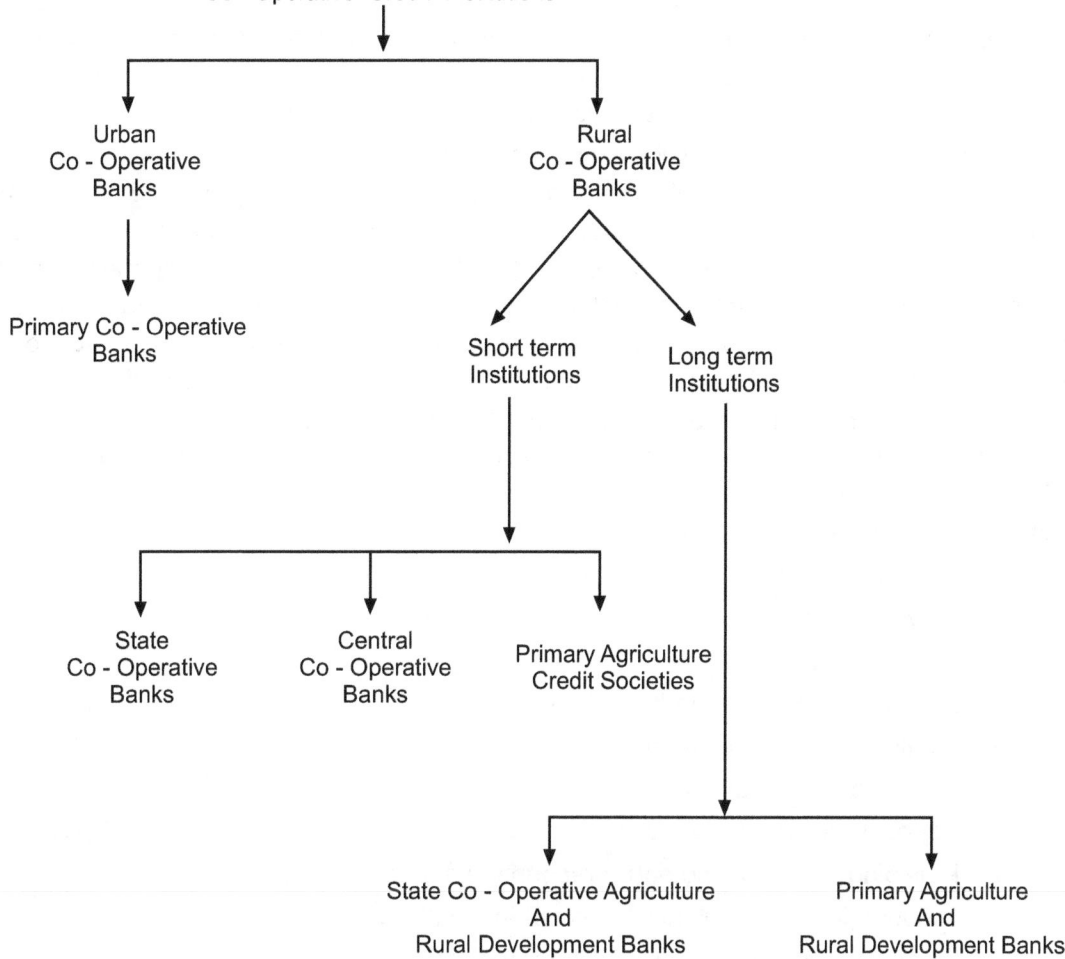

Fig. 4.3: Structure of Co-operative Banking System

The need and importance of agricultural credit is due to the following reasons –

➢ Credit requirements of agriculturists are peculiar in nature

➢ Commercial banks are reluctant to enter into the field of agriculture

➢ Agriculturists cannot provide good securities

➢ Land is the only security available with them and it not acceptable as a primary security for commercial bank advances.

➢ Repayment of loan depends on the crop.

➢ Agriculture is said to be a gamble in the monsoon season

➢ Failure of agriculture may affect the repaying capacity of the borrower

➢ The need for finance is constant irrespective of the productivity

7. Development Banks

In India, the emergence of development banking is a post-independence phenomenon. The Government of India, in order to provide adequate supply of credit to various sectors of the economy, has evolved a well-developed structure of financial institutions in the country. They are called as Development Banks/Development Financial Institutions.

Development banks are specialised financial institutions/banks established by RBI or government to promote the development of a particular sector or providing finance for development of economy. These institutions speed up the pace of economic development. They are able to increase the rate of employment and they also help in development of small scale and medium scale entrepreneurship. They also provide medium and long-term industrial finance and as these banks play an important role in development of an economy, they are called development banks. Fundamentally, they are term leading institutions.

These development banks are unique financial institutions that perform the special task of fostering the development of a nation. They act as catalytic agents in promoting balanced development of the country.

Functions of Development Banks

1. Financial Functions
   - ➢ Providing loans
   - ➢ Underwriting
   - ➢ Equity subscription in industrial concerns
   - ➢ Providing guarantees to industries
2. Promotional Functions
   - ➢ Conducting industrial survey
   - ➢ Providing technical and entrepreneurial guidance
   - ➢ Encouraging the industries to accept innovative ideas
   - ➢ Formulating proposals for new enterprise etc.
   - ➢ Preparation of project reports
   - ➢ Giving advice and guidance to entrepreneurs and professional managers
   - ➢ Encourage self employment
   - ➢ Provision of consultancy services

Various development banks in India are given below –

1. Industry related development banks
   (a) IDBI
   (b) IFCI
   (c) ICICI
   (d) IIBI
   (e) SIDBI
   (f) SFCs

   2. Agriculture related development banks
       (a) NABARD
       (b) KVIB
   3. Investment and Insurance related development banks
       (a) DICGC
       (b) LIC
       (c) GIC
       (d) UTI
   4. Export-Import related development banks
       (a) EXIM
       (b) ECGC
   5. Capital market related development banks
       (a) DFHI
       (b) OTCEI
       (c) NSE
       (d) SEBI
       (e) CRISIL
   6. Housing related development banks
       (a) NHB
       (b) HDFC

The Development Financial Institutions are the source of funding for the growth of industrial and infrastructure sectors in India. The Industrial Finance Corporation of India (IFCI) was the first development bank to be set up in the year 1948. Gradually, many other financial institutions were set up. Development banks in India may be classified into three groups namely –

   (a) Industrial Development Banks
   (b) Agricultural Development Banks
   (c) Export-Import Development Banks

Industrial development banks may further be divided into two groups, namely, all India institutions and some state level institutions. IDBI, IFCI are examples of all India institutions and State Finance Corporations (SFCs), The State Industrial Development Corporation (SIDCs) are examples of state level institutions.

4.2.2 Structure of Insurance Sector

A contract whereby one party, called the 'the insurer or the insurance company', undertakes to compensate the other party called the 'insured', for any loss or damage suffered by the latter, in consideration of payment of 'premium' for a certain period of time, is known as 'insurance'. Insurance means indemnity or protection against risk of loss by spreading the risk over a number of persons, who are exposed to it and who agree to insure themselves against the risk.

The working mechanism of insurance is depicted in the figure below.

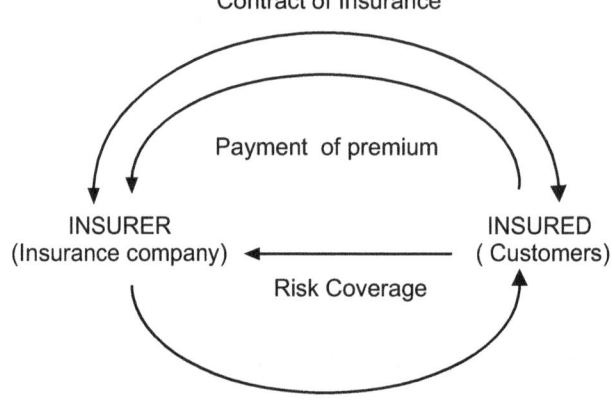

Fig. 4.4: Working Mechanism of Insurance Services

Features of Insurance

> ➢ It is a contract between the insurer and the insured
> ➢ It is a contract of 'indemnity'
> ➢ It is a device for sharing of risk and protecting against loss
> ➢ The contract is embodied in a document which is called as a policy
> ➢ The amount paid by the insured to the insurer is known as 'premium'
> ➢ It is called as insurance by choice and not insurance by chance
> ➢ The quantum of compensation depends upon the extent of loss suffered and the sum insured/assured

Types of Insurance

Insurance can be broadly classified into Life Insurance and General Insurance

1. Life Insurance: This is a contract where the insurance company agrees to pay a particular sum of money to the insured on expiry of certain time or on the death of the person whose life is assured. Life insurance contracts are subject to the principle of utmost good faith and principle of insurable interest. Life insurance serves the purpose of protection as well as investment. It is an investment contract as well, as it gives the assured the advantage of regaining the money with interest and bonus at the end of the policy.

2. General Insurance: This is a contract of indemnity whereby the insurer undertakes to pay compensation to the insured for the actual loss or damage suffered only. If there is no actual loss, the amount is not paid. This type of insurance serves as a protection contract not as an investment contract. This means that the money paid as premium will come back to the insured by way of claims only on the occurrence of some specified events resulting in loss or damage to the insured.

Further sub-division is explained in the table given below.

Major Categories	Types	Brief Explanation
Life Insurance	(a) Whole Life Policy	This policy covers the whole life of the insured and the sum is payable only on the death of the insured person. Premium is to be paid by the insured throughout the life of the policy at regular intervals.
	(b) Endowment Policy	The sum assured is paid on the death of the insured or on expiry of fixed period of time whichever is earlier. Premium is to be paid by the insured for a fixed period of time as per the contract. Thus, this policy runs for a period as specified in the policy document.
	(c) Annuity Policy	Under this policy, a certain amount is paid to the assured regularly up to a certain period or up to his death as per the terms and conditions of the policy.
	(d) With or Without Profit Policy	The assured is entitled to get a share in the profits of the corporation in the form of bonus under With Profit Policy, and in the case of Without Profit Policy, the policy holder is not entitled to get bonus.
	(e) Joint Life Policy	This is taken by two or more persons together on their joint lives. It is payable to either of the surviving persons on the death of any of the joint-policy holders.
	(f) Group Insurance Policy	This is taken on the lives of the members of the family, or the employees of a business concern.

... (Contd.)

Major Categories	Types	Brief Explanation
	(g) Keyman Insurance Policy	This is taken by the business firms on the life of the key employee(s) in order to protect the firms against any financial loss which may occur due to the premature demise of the Keyman.
	(h) Market Policy	This is a kind of policy that gives a person to choose a plan with or without risk. It is a unit linked pension policy ideal for investment for retirement purpose.
General Insurance	(a) Fire Insurance	It is a contract to make good the loss suffered on account of fire. Such loss is possible in case of shops, offices, factories, buildings, warehouses etc. There are various types of fire insurance policies like Valued Policy, Average Policy, Specific Policy, Floating Policy, Blanket Policy, Comprehensive Policy etc.
	(b) Marine Insurance	It is a contract to make good any loss due to marine adventure, transport and marine losses. There are various types of marine insurance policies like Voyage Policy, Time Policy, Mixed Policy, Valued Policy, Floating Policy, Open Policy etc.
	(c) Accident Insurance	It is a contract to make good the loss due to physical injury or damage of property due to any accident.
	(d) Health Insurance	This is designed to give protection against various health related issues.
	(e) Travel Insurance	This covers loss/damage to luggage, money, passport, tickets, flight delays, medical expenses etc. during travel from the date of origin to the date of return.

... (Contd.)

Major Categories	Types	Brief Explanation
	(f) Motor Car Insurance	In this type of contract, the cars are covered for theft, damage, earthquake, fire, flood, landslide etc.
	(g) Credit Insurance	This covers the risk of non-payment of bank loan due to certain events like unemployment, disability, death etc.
	(h) Public Liability Insurance	This covers any damage caused by the insured to a third party's property or health due to the insured's fault.
	(i) Property Insurance	Provides protection for properties, home, office, car and house-hold possessions.
	(j) Fidelity Insurance	This is a special type of insurance for special business mainly financial business.
	(k) Burglary Insurance	Here the loss is made good for burglary.
	(l) Workmen Compensation Insurance	This is a type of insurance for the workmen wherein the insurance company pays to the workmen/employees for any loss of life, limb or any part of the body during the course of employment.
	(m) Unemployment Insurance	This is a contract for paying a certain sum of money to the insured during his period of unemployment, to sustain the basic minimum of expenses.
	(n) Cash Transit Insurance	This insurance covers theft of cash when in transit from one place to another.

Structure of the Indian Insurance Industry

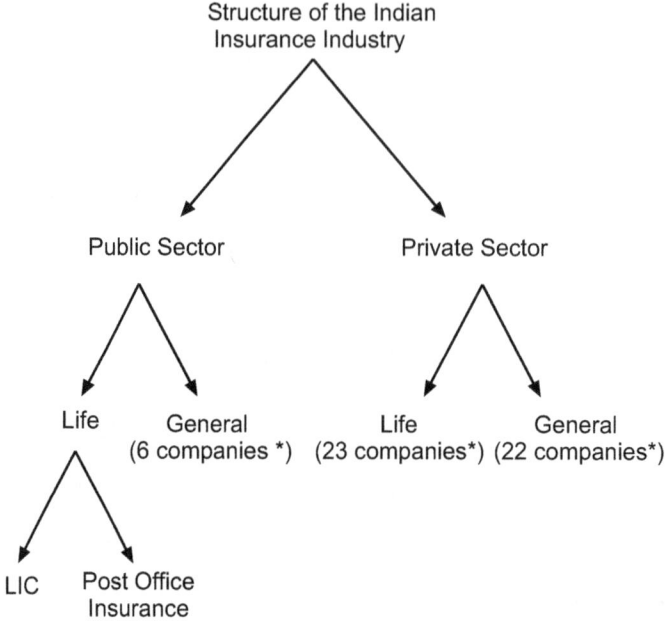

* Status as on 4/2/14

Fig. 4.5: Structure of Indian Insurance Industry

Insurance in India refers to the market which covers both the public and the private sector organisations. It is listed in the Constitution of India in the Seventh Schedule as a Union List subject, meaning it can only be legislated by the Central Government.

The insurance sector has gone through a number of phases by allowing private companies to solicit insurance and also allowing foreign direct investment. The largest life-insurance company in India, Life Insurance Corporation of India is owned by the government and carries a sovereign guarantee for all insurance policies issued by it. Till late 1990, LIC had the monopoly to provide life insurance services. This scenario changed due to entry being granted to the private sector in the insurance industry.

In case of General Insurance, the General Insurance Corporation of India (GIC) was the main operator which had four subsidiaries. However, in December 2000, these subsidiaries were de-linked from the parent company and were set up as independent insurance companies namely, Oriental Insurance Company Ltd., New India Assurance Company Ltd., National Insurance Company Ltd., and United India Insurance Company Ltd.

The insurance industry of India consists of 52 insurance companies of which 24 are in life insurance business and 28 are non-life insurers.

Among the life insurers, Life Insurance Corporation (LIC) is the sole public sector company.

Out of 28 non-life insurance companies, there are six public sector insurers, which include two specialised insurers namely Agriculture Insurance Company of India Ltd. for crop insurance and Export Credit Guarantee Corporation of India for credit insurance. Moreover, there are 5 private sector insurers which are registered to underwrite policies exclusively in health, personal accident and travel insurance segments. They are Star Health and Allied Insurance Company Ltd., Apollo Munich Health Insurance Company Ltd., Max Bupa Health Insurance Company Ltd., Religare Health Insurance Company Ltd. and Cigna TTK Health Insurance Company Ltd.

In addition to 52 insurance companies, there is sole national re-insurer, namely, General Insurance Corporation of India. Other stakeholders in Indian insurance market include licensed agents (individual and corporate), brokers, common service centres, web-aggregators, surveyors and third party administrators servicing health insurance claims.

Profiles of few Insurance Service Providers

1. Life Insurance Corporation of India (LIC)

The LIC was established on 1st September 1956, by nationalising all the life insurance companies in India. Prior to this nationalisation, 245 private insurance companies of different ages, sizes and patterns of organisations operated from 97 centres. LIC took over business of these private insurers on 1st Sept 1956. It is a wholly owned government corporation and it is the largest insurance company in India with an estimated asset value of ₹ 15,60,482 crores. Its affairs are managed by the Board of Directors comprising of 15 directors who are appointed by the Government of India and its central office is located in Mumbai with 8 zonal offices, 113 divisional offices, fully computerised 2048 branch offices and 11,72,983 agents all over India as on 31st March 2013 (as per available company information).

Thus, LIC attained monopoly in the life insurance business. This scenario has witnessed a complete change in this modern era. The erstwhile, sole provider of life insurance in India is today competing with private sector insurers which have been growing in number since the year 2000.

According to company sources, LIC is still the dominant life insurer even in the liberalised state of Indian insurance and is moving fast on a new growth trajectory exceeding its own past records. LIC has issued over one crore policies during the present year. It has crossed the goal of issuing 1,01,32,955 new policies by 15th Oct, 2005, posting a healthy growth rate of 16.67 percent over the equivalent time of the previous year.

From then to now, LIC has achieved many goals and has established extraordinary performance records in different aspects of life insurance business. The same motives which motivated our forefathers to bring insurance into existence in this country motivate LIC to take this message of protection and provide security in as many homes as possible and to assist individuals in giving security to their families.

Objectives of Life Insurance Corporation of India

LIC was established with objectives as listed below –

- Spread life insurance extensively to the rural areas and to the socially and economically backward classes with the intention of reaching all insurable individuals in the country and giving them sufficient financial cover against death at a reasonable cost.
- Maximise mobilisation of people's savings by making insurance-linked savings sufficiently attractive.
- Remember, in the investment of funds, the main obligation to its policyholders, whose money it holds in trust, without losing sight of the interest of the community altogether; the funds to be deployed to the best advantage of the investors plus the community altogether, considering the national priorities and obligations of attractive return.
- Conduct business with utmost economy and with the complete realisation that the money belongs to the policyholders.
- Act as trustees of the insured public in their individual and collective capacities.
- Meet the different life insurance requirements of the community that would take place in the changing social and economic environment.
- Engage all people working in the company to the best of their capability in promoting the interests of the insured public by providing efficient service with courtesy.
- Promote amongst all agents and employees of the company a sense of participation, pride and job satisfaction through discharge of their duties with devotion towards attaining the company's objective.

2. General Insurance Corporation of India (GIC)

The General Insurance Corporation of India is a wholly government owned company. It was incorporated on 22nd November, 1972 under the Companies Act, 1956 as a private company limited by shares and it was formed for the purpose of superintending, controlling and carrying on the business of general insurance in India. Its board of directors consists of 10 members appointed by the Central Government. The head office is situated in Mumbai.

GIC does not transact any direct business except the aviation insurance business of public sector companies and crop insurance. Its main business is that of a reinsurer. As a sole reinsurer in the domestic reinsurance market, GIC provides reinsurance to the direct general insurance companies in the Indian market. GIC receives statutory cession of 5 percent on each and every policy subject to certain limits.

3. Other Public Sector Undertakings

(a) National Insurance Company Ltd.

(b) Oriental Insurance Company Ltd.

(c) The New India Assurance Co. Ltd.

(d) United India Insurance Co. Ltd.

4. Private Insurance Companies

There are 45 private insurance companies in India and some of them are listed below –

(a) Birla Sun Life Insurance Company Ltd.

(b) Bajaj Allianz Life Insurance Co. Ltd.

(c) HDFC Standard Life Insurance Co. Ltd.

(d) Max Life Insurance Co. Ltd.

(e) Aviva Life Insurance Co. India Ltd.

(f) IDBI Federal Life Insurance

(g) Star Health and Allied Insurance Co. Ltd.

(h) Reliance General Insurance Ltd.

4.3 Role of RBI and IRDA as a Regulatory Authority

4.3.1 Introduction

A study of financial services cannot be complete without discussing the regulatory framework of the country. As the financial markets are characterised by different degrees of imperfections, the need for regulation or a liberalised framework cannot be denied.

The financial system deals in other people's money and, thus, their confidence, trust and faith in it is significant for its smooth functioning. Financial regulation is required to generate, maintain and promote this trust. The reason people lose their trust is because the savers or investors or intermediaries take too much risk, which could engender defaults, bankruptcies, and insolvencies. Therefore, a regulation is required to monitor imprudence in the system.

The task of efficient regulation is made difficult by the very nature of financial assets, which are mobile, easily movable or negotiable; and also by the nature of financial markets which are prone to a systemic risk. The modern trading technology and the possibility of high leveraging allow market participants to take big stakes, which are inconsistent with their own investments.

Often, there are instances of dishonest, unfair, fraudulent, and unethical practices or activities of the market intermediaries or agencies such as brokers, merchant bankers, custodians, trustees, etc. The regulation is required to guarantee that the investors are safeguarded; that disclosure and access to information are sufficient, timely, and equal; that the participants' meet the standards of the rules of the market place; and that the markets are both fair and well-organised. In this context, it is said that fairness and efficiency are two sides of the same coin; if the market is unfair, ultimately, it is also inefficient.

The regulatory framework for the financial sector in India widely includes the Ministry of Finance of the Government of India which administers the Companies Act, 1956, and the Securities Contracts (Regulation) Act, 1956; the Reserve Bank of India and the Board of Financial Supervision (BFS) under its guidance; the Securities and Exchange Board of India (SEBI), Insurance Regulatory Authority; the Governing Boards of different stock exchanges and the apex financial establishments such as the IDBI, SIDBI, NHB and NCB. Among these, the RBI and SEBI have special role and responsibility.

We shall for the sake of this book discuss the functioning of the RBI and IRDA only.

4.3.2 RBI as Regulatory Authority of Banking Industry

Reserve Bank of India (RBI) is the apex monetary institution of India. It is also called as the central bank of the country. The bank was established on April 1, 1935 according to the Reserve Bank of India Act, 1934. It acts as the apex monetary authority/institution of the country that regulates the supply, availability and cost of money in the interest of the general public.

The preamble of the reserve bank of India is as follows:

"...to regulate the issue of bank notes and keeping of reserves with a view to securing monetary stability in India and generally to operate the currency and credit system of the country to its advantage."

- ➢ RBI is the apex institution of country's monetary system and the financial system
- ➢ It plays a key role in organising, running, supervising, regulating and developing the monetary and the financial system
- ➢ It's main responsibility is to design and ensure orderly conduct of the monetary and credit policy
- ➢ It was established on 1st April, 1935
- ➢ It was nationalised on 1st January, 1949
- ➢ It's head office is situated in Mumbai
- ➢ It has the sole authority and monopoly for issue of currency notes
- ➢ It acts as the banker, agent and the financial adviser to the state
- ➢ It controls and directs other banking institutions and renders services to them
- ➢ It does not deal directly with public

As the central bank of the country, the RBI performs both the traditional functions of a central bank and a variety of supervisory, developmental and promotional functions.

Objectives of RBI

To elaborate, the main objectives of the RBI are –

- • To **maintain monetary stability** so that the company and economic life can deliver welfare gains of a correct working mixed economy.
- • To **maintain financial stability** and guarantee sound financial establishment so that monetary stability can be safely pursued and economic units can carry out their business with confidence.
- • To **maintain stable payments** system so that financial transactions can be implemented efficiently.
- • To **promote the development of financial infrastructure** of markets and systems and to enable it to function efficiently, that is, to play a leading role in developing a sound financial system so that it can discharge its regulatory function efficiently.
- • To **ensure that credit allocation** by the financial system widely reflects the national economic priorities and societal concerns.
- • To **regulate the overall volume of money** and credit in the economy with the intention of guaranteeing a reasonable degree of price stability.

- The main functions of the bank are to act as **the note-issuing authority**, banker's bank, banker to the government and to promote the growth of the economy within the framework of the general economic policy of the government, consistent with the need to maintain price stability.

- The bank also performs a wide range of **promotional functions** to support the pace of economic development.

- The Reserve Bank is the **controller of foreign exchange**.

- It is the **watchdog** of the entire financial system.

- The bank is the **sponsor bank** of a wide variety of top-ranking banks and institutions such as SBI, IDBI, NABARD and NHB.

- The bank sits on the **board of all banks** and it **counsels** the Central and State Government and all public sector institutions on monetary and money matters.

- The Reserve Bank of India, as the **central bank of the country**, is the centre of the Indian Financial and Monetary System. As the apex establishment, it has been directing, observing, regulating, controlling, and promoting the destiny of the IFS since its inception. It is relatively young in comparison to such central banks as the Bank of England, Riksbanken of Sweden, and the Federal Reserve Board of the US. On the other hand, it is possibly the oldest among the central banks in the developing countries.

- It **was a private shareholders' institution till January 1949**, after which it became a state-owned institution under the Reserve Bank of India Act, 1948. This act allows the central government to issue directions after consulting the governor of the bank, as they might be required in the public interest. In additional, the governor and all the deputy governors of the bank are appointed by the central government.

The bank is managed by a central board of directors, four local boards of directors, and a committee of the central board of directors. The functions of the local boards are to counsel the central board on issues referred to them; they are also need to carry out duties that are delegated to them. The final control of the bank is in the hands of the central board, which includes the governor, four deputy governors, and fifteen directors nominated by the central government.

The **committee of the central board** includes the governor, the deputy governors, and such other directors, perhaps present at a given meeting. The internal organisational unit of the bank is altered and expanded every now and then so as to manage the increasing volume and range of the bank's activities. The underlying principle of the internal organisation is functional specialisation with sufficient coordination.

In order to perform its various functions, the bank has been divided and sub-divided into a large **number of departments**. The pattern of central banking in India was initially based on the Bank of England. England had a highly developed banking system in which the functioning of the central bank as a banker's bank and their regulation of money supply set the pattern. The central bank's function as 'a lender of last resort' was on the condition that the banks maintain stable cash ratios as prescribed from time to time. The effective functioning of the British model depends on an active securities market where open market operations can be conducted at the discount rate. The effectiveness of open market operations however depends on the member banks' dependence on the central bank and the influence it wields on interest rates. Later models, especially those in developing countries showed that central banks play an advisory role and render technical services in the field of foreign exchange, foster the growth of a sound financial system and act as a banker to the government.

The RBI functions within the framework of a mixed economic system. With regard to framing various policies, it is necessary to maintain close and continuous collaboration between the government and the RBI. In the event of a difference of opinion or conflict, the government view or position can always be expected to prevail.

The preamble of the RBI Act, 1934 states that "Whereas it is expedient to constitute a Reserve Bank for India to regulate the issue of bank notes and the keeping of reserves with a view to securing monetary stability in (India) and generally to operate the currency and credit system of the country to its advantage".

Role of the Bank

- In view of the bank's close contacts and intimate knowledge of the financial markets, it is in a position to advise the central and state governments on the quantum, timing and terms of issue of new loans. While formulating the borrowing programme for the year, the government and the bank take into account a number of considerations such as the amount of central and state loans maturing for redemption during the year, the estimate of available resources (based on the estimated growth in deposits with the banks, premium income of insurance companies and accretions to provident funds) and the absorptive capacity of the market.

- In India, banks, insurance companies and provident funds are statutorily required to invest a portion of their liabilities, premium income or accretions, as the case may be, in government and other approved securities, which ensures a captive market for these securities, facilitating the easy absorption of new issues.

- The bank tries to ensure that over a reasonably long period it will be neither a net purchaser of securities from the market nor a net seller so that the loans raised are absorbed by the market outside the bank to the maximum extent.

- The bank actively operates in the gilt-edged market to ensure the success of government loan operations. For instance, the bank grooms the market by acquiring securities nearing maturity to facilitate redemption. If maturing stocks are held by investors to the last, conditions in the money market are likely to be disturbed as most of the cash paid out seeks avenues of reinvestment, but, in practice, all the investors are not equally eager to wait for cash repayment on the redemption date and then undertake reinvestment, as they can reinvest the proceeds at times of their own choosing if these were realised earlier, the bank, therefore, stands ready as the stock approaches maturity to buy all the stocks offered for sale at these terms.

- Thus, in carrying out the loan operations of the government the bank endeavours on the one hand to minimise the effects of such operations on the money market and government securities market, and on the other to obtain the best possible terms for the government concerned.
- The close involvement in the market by its continuous presence and the willingness to deal in the securities at process determined by it give the bank a good degree of flexibility when it is seeking occasions for implementing a shift in policy on prices.
- The timing of the issue of new loans is normally left to the Reserve Bank. The central government and the state governments float market loans separately, but through the Reserve Bank. For the management of the public debt of the government, the bank charges a commission. In addition, the Reserve Bank also charges for all new issues both by central and state government loans, besides recovering brokerage and expenses incurred by the bank on account of printing of loan.

Functions of Reserve Bank of India

The Reserve Bank of India Act of 1934 entrust all the significant functions of a central bank on the Reserve Bank of India.

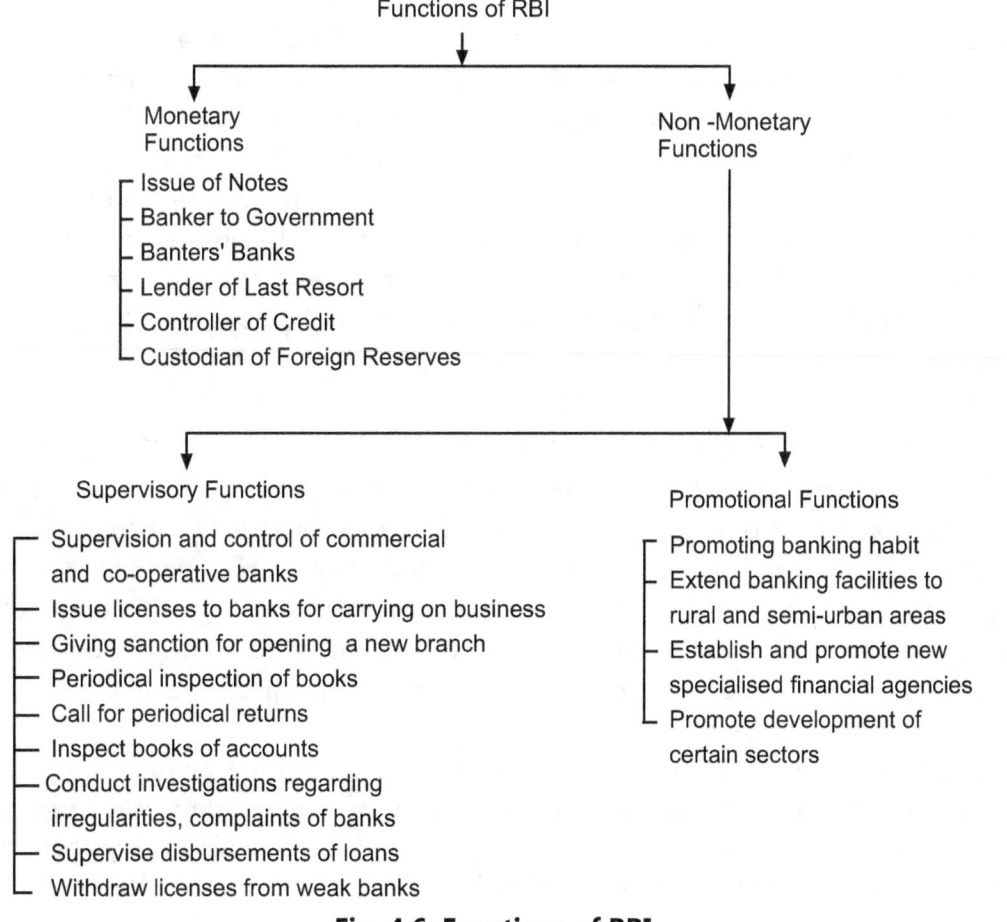

Fig. 4.6: Functions of RBI

1. Issue of notes

Under Section 22 of the Reserve Bank of India Act, it is the only bank that has the right to issue bank notes of all denominations. As the agent of the government the Reserve Bank carries out the distribution of one rupee notes and small coins all over the country. The Reserve Bank has a different issue department which is entrusted with the issue of currency notes. The assets and liabilities of the issue department are kept separate from those of the banking department. At first, the assets of the issue department were to include not less than two-fifths of gold coin, gold bullion or sterling securities given the amount of gold was not less than ₹ 40 crores in value. The remaining three-fifths of the assets are held in rupee coins, government of India rupee securities, eligible bills of exchange and promissory notes payable in India. Because of the exigencies of the Second World War and the post-war period, these terms were significantly altered. Since 1957, the Reserve Bank of India maintains gold and foreign exchange reserves of ₹ 200 crores, of which at least ₹ 115 crores is in gold. The system as it exists today is called as the minimum reserve system.

2. Banker to Government

The second significant function of the Reserve Bank of India is to act as a government banker, agent and adviser. The Reserve Bank is the agent of central government and of all state governments in India except the state of Jammu and Kashmir. The Reserve Bank is obligated to transact government business, to keep the cash balances as deposits free of interest, to receive and to make payments on behalf of the government and to undertake their exchange remittances and other banking operations. The Reserve Bank of India assists the government – both the union and the states to float new loans and to manage public debt. The bank has ways and means to make advances to the government for 90 days. It makes loans and advances to the states and local authorities and acts as a consultant to the government on all monetary and banking matters.

3. Bankers' Bank and Lender of the Last Resort

The Reserve Bank of India acts as the bankers' bank. According to the provisions of the Banking Companies Act of 1949, it was necessary for every scheduled bank to maintain with the Reserve Bank a cash balance that was equal to 5 percent of its demand liabilities and 2 percent of its time liabilities in India. By an amendment of 1962, the difference between demand and time liabilities was abolished and banks are asked to keep cash reserves equal to 3 percent of their aggregate deposit liabilities. The minimum cash requirements can be changed by the Reserve Bank of India.

The scheduled banks can borrow from the Reserve Bank of India based on the eligible securities or get financial assistance in times of need by rediscounting bills of exchange. Since commercial banks can always expect the Reserve Bank of India to help them during crisis, the Reserve Bank becomes not only the banker's bank but also the lender of the last resort.

4. Controller of Credit

The Reserve Bank of India is the controller of credit, that is, it has the power to influence the volume of credit created by banks in India. It can do so through changing the bank rate or through open market operations. According to the Banking Regulation Act of 1949, the Reserve Bank of India can ask any bank not to lend to certain groups or individuals, based on the types of securities. Since 1956, selective controls of credit are increasingly being used by the Reserve Bank.

The Reserve Bank of India has several powers to control the Indian money market. Every bank has to get a licence from the Reserve Bank of India to do banking business within India, the licence can be cancelled by the Reserve Bank if particular conditions are not satisfied. Every bank has to get the consent of the Reserve Bank before it can open a new branch. Each scheduled bank must send a weekly return to the Reserve Bank, giving in-depth information of its assets and liabilities. This authority of the bank to demand information is also meant to give it effective control of the credit system. The Reserve Bank has also the authority to check the accounts of any commercial bank.

As the only banking power in the country, the Reserve Bank of India, thus, has the following powers –

(a) It holds the cash reserves of all the scheduled banks.

(b) It controls the credit operations of banks through quantitative and qualitative controls.

(c) It controls the banking system through the system of licensing, inspection and information.

(d) It acts as the lender of the last resort by providing rediscount facilities to scheduled banks.

5. Custodian of Foreign Reserves

The Reserve Bank of India has the duty to maintain the official rate of exchange. According to the Reserve Bank of India Act of 1934, the bank needs to buy and sell at fixed rates any amount of sterling, not less than ₹ 10,000. The rate of exchange fixed was ₹ 1 = sh. (dollars) 6d. Since 1935 the Bank was capable of maintaining the exchange rate fixed at sh. (dollars) 6d. However, there was a time when there was extreme pressure in support of or against the rupee. After India became a member of the International Monetary Fund in 1946, the Reserve Bank has the responsibility of maintaining fixed exchange rates with all other member countries of the I.M.F.

In addition to maintaining the rate of exchange of the rupee, the Reserve Bank has to act as the guardian of India's reserve of international currencies. The huge sterling balances were obtained and managed by the bank. In addition, the RBI has the responsibility of managing the exchange controls of the country.

6. Supervisory functions

Besides its conventional central banking functions, the Reserve Bank has a specific non-monetary function which requires supervision of banks and promotion of sound banking in India. The Reserve Bank Act, 1934, and the Banking Regulation Act, 1949 have given the Reserve Bank of India extensive powers of supervision and control over commercial and cooperative banks, which is connected to licensing and establishments, branch expansion, liquidity of their assets, management and methods of working, amalgamation, reconstruction, and liquidation. The Reserve Bank of India is authorised to conduct monthly inspections of the banks and to demand returns and required information from them. Due to the nationalisation of 14 major Indian scheduled banks in July 1969, the Reserve Bank of India has been inflicted with new duties for directing the growth of banking and credit policies towards quick development of the economy and realisation of specific social objectives. The supervisory functions of the Reserve Bank of India have helped significantly in enhancing the standard of banking in India and improve the techniques of their operation.

7. Promotional Functions

Since Independence and with economic growth, the range of the Reserve Bank's functions has gradually broadened. The bank now performs several developmental and promotional functions, which, once, was outside the normal capacity of central banking. The Reserve Bank was asked to promote banking habits, extend banking facilities to rural and semi-urban areas, and set up and promote new specialised financing agencies. Accordingly, the Reserve Bank has assisted in establishing the IFCI and the SFC; it set up the Deposit Insurance Corporation in 1962, the Unit Trust of India in 1964, the Industrial Development Bank of India also in 1964, the Agricultural Refinance Corporation of India in 1963 and the Industrial Reconstruction Corporation of India in 1972. These organisations were established by the Reserve Bank to promote saving habits and to mobilise savings, and to give industrial and agricultural finance. In 1935, the Reserve Bank of India established the Agricultural Credit Department to give agricultural credit. But only since 1951 the bank's role in this field has become very significant. The bank has developed the co-operative credit movement to encourage saving, to remove moneylenders from the villages and to direct its short-term credit to agriculture. The Reserve Bank of India has established the Agricultural Refinance and Development Corporation to provide long-term finance to farmers.

Classification of RBI's Functions

The monetary functions also called as the central banking functions of the Reserve Bank of India are connected to control and regulation of money and credit, that is, issue of currency, control of bank credit, control of foreign exchange operations, banker to the government and to the money market. The monetary functions of the Reserve Bank of India are significant as they control and regulate the volume of money and credit in the country.

Similarly significant, are the non-monetary functions of Reserve Bank of India in the context of India's economic backwardness. The supervisory function of Reserve Bank of India may be considered as a non-monetary function. The significant goal of Reserve Bank of India is to promote sound banking in India. The Reserve Bank of India has been given extensive powers, under the Banking Regulation Act of 1949 – these powers relate to licensing of banks, branch expansion, liquidity of their assets, management and methods of working, inspection, amalgamation, reconstruction and liquidation. Under the Reserve Bank of India's supervision and inspection, the working of banks has significantly improved. Commercial banks have developed into financially sound and workable units. The Reserve Bank of India's powers of supervision has now been extended to non-banking financial mediators. Since independence, especially after its nationalisation in 1949, the Reserve Bank of India has followed the promotional functions dynamically and has been accountable for a strong financial support to industrial and agricultural development in the country.

The major powers of the bank in different roles as a regulator and supervisor can be summed up as under –

➢ Power to license

➢ Power of appointment and removal of banking boards/personnel

➢ Power to regulate the business of the banks

➢ Power to give directions

➢ Power to inspect and supervise the banks

➢ Power regarding audit of banks

➢ Power to collect and furnish credit information

➢ Power relating to moratorium, amalgamation and winding up

➢ Power to impose penalties

4.3.3 IRDA as Regulatory Authority of Insurance Industry

The insurance sector is an infrastructural pillar of the financial services sector and the economy as a whole. It plays a key role in economic development. Several empirical studies suggest a strong correlation between the development of financial intermediaries and economic growth.

Insurance Regulatory and Development Authority (IRDA) is regulatory and development authority under Government of India in order to protect the interests of the policy holders and to regulate, promote and ensure orderly growth of the insurance industry. It is basically a ten member team comprising a chairman, five full-time members and four part-time members, all appointed by Government of India. This organisation came into being in the year 1999 after passing of IRDA bill in the Indian parliament. It was the recommendation of the Malhotra Committee Report (1994) that an independent body be established for the insurance sector in India. The agency operates from its headquarters at Hyderabad, Telangana where it shifted from Delhi in 2001.

The IRDA Act, 1999 has also allowed private players to enter the insurance sector in India and has also granted permission to foreign equity participation up to a certain limit. It battled for a hike in the FDI limit to 49 percent in the insurance sector from the erstwhile 26 percent. The FDI limit in insurance sector was raised to 49 percent in July 2014. This will enable the foreign companies to buy up to 49 percent stake in domestic insurance companies.

Duties of IRDA

Under Section 14 of the IRDA Act, the authority's duty is to regulate, promote and to ensure an orderly growth of the insurance and the re-insurance business.

Powers and Functions of IRDA

- It **issues the applicants** in insurance arena, a certificate of registration as well as renewal, modification, withdrawal, suspension or cancellation of such registrations.

- It **protects the interests of the policy holders** in any insurance company in the matters connected to the assignment of policy, nomination by policy holders, insurable interest, and resolution of insurance claim, submission value of policy and other terms and proposals in the contract.

- It also **specifies obligatory credentials**, code of conduct and practical instructions for mediator plus the insurance company. Apart from this, it also defines the code of conduct for the surveyors and loss evaluators engaged in the insurance business.

- One of the major functions of IRDA includes **endorsing competence** in the insurance business. Apart from this, upholding and regulating professional companies in insurance and re-insurance business is also a main duty of IRDA.

- IRDA is also entitled for **asking information, undertaking inspection** and investigating the audit of the insurers, mediators, insurance intermediaries and other organisations associated with the insurance sector.

- It is also concerned with the **regulation of the rates, profits**, provisions and conditions that may be offered by insurers regarding general insurance business if it is not controlled or regulated by the Tariff Advisory Committee.

- It is also entitled **to supervise the functioning** of the Tariff Advisory Committee.

- IRDA specifies **the terms and pattern in which books of accounts are to be maintained** and statement of accounts are given by insurers and other insurance mediators.

- It also **regulates investment of funds by insurance companies** plus the maintenance of margin of solvency.

- It also has the power to engage in the **arbitration of disagreements** between insurers and intermediaries or insurance intermediaries.

- It is intended to specify the **proportion of premium income** of the insurer that will go into finance policies/schemes.

- IRDA also specifies the **share of life insurance business and general insurance business** to be accepted by the insurer in the rural or social sector.

- Exercising other powers as may be prescribed.

Constitution

The IRDA was constituted as a body corporate, having perpetual succession and a common seal with powers, subject to the provisions of the Act. The authority shall acquire, hold and dispose property, can contract and can sue or be sued in its own name.

Impact of IRDA on the Indian Insurance Sector

IRDA's role is to protect rights of policy holders and it provides registration certification to life insurance companies and is responsible for renewal, modification, cancellation and suspension of the registered certificate

The creation of IRDA has brought revolutionary changes in the insurance sector. In more than 10 years of its establishment the insurance sector has seen tremendous growth. When IRDA came into being the only players in the insurance industry were Life Insurance Corporation of India (LIC) and General Insurance Corporation of India (GIC). However in last decade 23 new players have emerged in the field of insurance. The IRDA also successfully deals with any discrepancy in the insurance sector.

Recently the Finance Minister of India announced the setting of insurance repository system. An insurance repository is a facility to help policy holders to buy and keep insurance policies in electronic form, rather than as a paper document. The system was launched on 16th September, 2013. Insurance repositories like share depositories or mutual fund transfer agencies will hold electronic records of insurance policies issued to individuals and such policies are called "electronic policies" or "e-policies", for example, CDSL Insurance Repository Limited (CDSL IR).

The **Insurance Repository in India** is a database of insurance policies. It allows policy holders to make revisions to a policy. It is the world's first of its kind. India's IRDA has issued licenses to five entities to act as insurance repositories –

1) CDSL Insurance Repository Ltd. (CDSL IR)
2) SHCIL Projects Ltd.
3) Karvy Insurance Repository Ltd.
4) National Insurance-policy Repository by NSDL Database Management Ltd.
5) CAMS Repository Services Ltd.

The insurance policies including the existing ones can be converted in an electronic form and held with an 'insurance repository'. The objective of creating an insurance repository is to provide policyholders a facility to keep insurance policies in electronic form and to undertake changes, modifications and revisions in the insurance policy with speed and accuracy. In addition, the repository acts as a single stop for several policy service requirements. The insurance repository system also brings about efficiency and transparency in the issuance and maintenance of insurance policies.

Conclusion: IRDA has taken various initiatives for protecting the interests of policyholders by bringing out regulations, guidelines, circulars etc. applicable to insurers and intermediaries covering the various stages in the lifecycle of an insurance product, commencing from solicitation, sale, policy servicing, to claims servicing and grievance re-dressal.

Further, keeping in view the need for efficient functioning of the insurance sector for protecting the interests of policyholders, it is necessary to have reliable, timely and accurate data relating to insurance. In order to ensure that proper data is collected, processed and disseminated in the manner required, IRDA has set up an independent body, namely the Insurance Information Bureau (IIB). The IIB has started functioning and has already made good progress.

Points to Remember

- The banking system is a set of complex and closely intermixes of banking institutions, instruments, services, practices, procedures etc.
- Organised banking system comprises of those institutions which come under Banking Regulation Act or work under the control and supervision of RBI.
- The unorganised system consists of a number of moneylenders, indigenous bankers, traders, landlords, and merchants etc. who lend money to the public and the indigenous banks who also accept deposits from them.
- The commercial banks are those financial institutions which accept deposits from the public repayable on demand and lend them for short periods.
- Public sector banks are the banks where the majority of stake is held by the Government of India or RBI. These banks are owned and controlled by the government.
- In private sector banks, the majority of their share capital is held by private individuals or corporations and not by the government or cooperative societies.
- Foreign banks are those banks which are incorporated outside India with their head office also situated outside India but they have set up their branches in India.
- Regional Rural Banks are similar to commercial banks in their methods of operation and organisational set-up, but their area of activity is limited to specified district/s and its loaning operations are restricted to specified target groups and purposes.
- The cooperative organisation is one of the forms of business organisation. People who come together to jointly serve common interest often form a cooperative society under the Cooperative Societies Act.
- Development banks are specialised financial institutions/banks established by RBI or the government to promote development of particular sector or providing finance for development of economy.

- Insurance means indemnity or protection against risk of loss by spreading the risk over a number of persons, who are exposed to it and who agree to insure themselves against the risk.
- Reserve Bank of India (RBI) is the apex monetary institution of India. It is also called as the central bank of the country.
- Insurance Regulatory and Development Authority (IRDA) is a regulatory and development authority under Government of India in order to protect the interests of the policy holders and to regulate, promote and ensure orderly growth of the insurance industry.

Questions for Discussion

1. Explain the structure of the banking system prevalent in India.
2. Give a brief outline of the structure of the insurance sector in India.
3. Trace the evolution of the banking system in India.
4. Discuss the progress made in the insurance sector in the last two decades.
5. Illustrate and explain the major functions of RBI.
6. Explain the history of IRDAI.
7. What does Insurance Regulatory and Development Authority mean? Explain its powers and functions.
8. Discuss the role of RBI and IRDA as regulatory authorities.

Chapter **5**...

Recent Trends in Accounting and Finance

Contents ...

Learning Objectives ...

- To understand zero-based budgeting
- To know inflation accounting
- To study human resource accounting
- To explain activity-based accounting
- To define mergers and acquisitions

5.1 Introduction

Accounting as a discipline is believed to be one of the most important elements in the business world where money is almost everything. It is termed as a process in which finances of an organisation are recorded for further assessment. By employing the process of accounting and financial management, the businesses are able to determine as to whether they are earning profits or incurring losses. Contrary to popular misconception, the practice of accountancy was carried out even in the early ages. It is only with new types of accounting ably complemented by Information Technology (IT) that it has advanced to a higher level. The principles of accounting form the basis of carrying out the accounting process.

This chapter covers the recent trends in Accounting and Finance.

5.2 Zero-based Budgeting

The expenditure incurred every year in an organisation is usually continued, taking the previous year's expenditure as the basis for justifying the success of the year's expenditure with incremental adjustments made in the following years. The new items of expenditure that is undertaken each year is required to be justified independently and approved depending upon the availability of resources. The new proposals are not made to compete with the ongoing expenditures, but on the basis of merit are made to claim share of limited resources.

Zero-based Budgeting (ZBB) requires that organisations while preparing their budgets should not take the earlier year's expenditure for granted and, therefore, should start on a clean slate. It implies that while framing a budget for the ensuing year, the organisation concerned should start from ground zero instead of treating the current budget as the starting point or the base.

The concept of zero-based budgeting requires that activities of the given organisation be viewed afresh and priorities among competing claims of allocation of funds settled on the basis of justifications developed by the use of evaluative techniques, like cost-benefit analysis, cost-effectiveness analysis, etc., and on other desirable considerations. It means that a complete re-examination of the ongoing programmes and activities should be carried out by taking a comprehensive or holistic look on these instead of following the incremental approach to budgeting. It further implies that new expenditure proposals should compete on the same footing with the ongoing expenditures based on their respective merits to claim share of the available resources.

5.2.1 The Conceptual Framework

- In a system of zero-based budgeting, the examination of existing programmes and activities has to be done in the same detailed manner as would apply to newly proposed ones. The scientific evaluative techniques used in the process for analysing cost-benefit relationship of proposed expenditures provide a systematic way of evaluating the ongoing and new programmes, activities, operations, and tasks to enable shifting and redeployment of resources from those which have become either redundant or those which have emerged as desirable and, therefore, need to be assigned priority.

- Zero-based budgeting requires eliminating redundant expenditure that no longer serves any clearly defined purpose. The resources thus saved may be reallocated to other desirable demands claiming priority. It has been observed in many organisations that an item of expenditure once started continues to exist even after the need for it is no more there. At the beginning, there is generally sufficient justification for the expenditure. But, over time, it has been observed that due to changes in circumstances, new developments in technology, change in the environment, etc., the expenditure no more serves the purpose for which it was allocated in the first place or, in other words, has become wasteful. A thorough review therefore needs to be conducted for not only finding it out but also for taking appropriate action.

- The second approach in the application of Zero-based Budgeting (ZBB) is to identify and remove duplication or multiplication expenditure. It happens over time that the same activity is carried out by a number of agencies of the same organisation. For instance, fertilisers may be procured, warehoused and distributed in the same rural area by a number of agencies like Cooperatives, Agriculture Department, Rural Development Department, Sugar Factories, etc. Each agency engaged in distribution of fertilisers would be maintaining its infrastructure for procurement, storage, and distribution thereby multiplying expenditure among them for carrying out the same activity. A comprehensive review of the ongoing expenditures would reveal a number of cases of wherein duplication or multiplication of expenditure occurs. If it is rationalised, and the specific activity is assigned to one agency which can perform it more effectively instead of other agencies, then, a lot of money can be saved.

- A third approach involves looking out for a better alternative of incurring expenditure which continues to serve a desired purpose or an established objective. If solar equipment is invented as an alternative to an electric gadget, it should be analysed to find out which of the two would serve the specified objective better, considering cost-benefit relationship of each alternative. The selection of the best alternative amongst the various choices available should be made by using the relevant evaluative techniques.

After proper review and analysis of expenditure, if it is found to be necessary, then, it should be employed in an efficient and economical way.

- A fourth approach in the application of zero-based budgeting, therefore, is to optimise expenditure by making it productive and efficient. This requires application of performance budgeting to establish its interface with zero-based budgeting. Performance budgeting would require establishing a correlation between expenditure to be incurred and physical accomplishments of a programme, scheme, project, operation or task to be achieved. Such a relationship between financial resources and the corresponding targets to be achieved needs to be worked out by using scientific and realistic norms, standards, yardsticks, units of measurement, etc.

The relationship between proposed expenditure and the corresponding target, thus established, is used as a guiding framework for comparing and evaluating the actual achievement. A scheme of performance budgeting, therefore, needs to be supported by a sound system of monitoring and performance review. Performance budgeting as an essential adjunct of a system of zero-based budgeting would thus ensure productivity and efficiency of expenditure control.

The four approaches in the application of zero-based budgeting, as explained above, are translated through a methodology evolved to suit the needs of the organisation concerned. Before, however, entering into a discussion on methodology, it may be of interest to know the historical background of zero-based budgeting.

5.2.2 The Historical Background

A system of zero-based budgeting was first introduced formally in the United States Department of Agriculture in preparing its 1964 fiscal year budget. This meant that all programmes of the department were to be reviewed afresh from the base zero and not merely in terms of incremental changes proposed for the budget year. This experiment of the Department of Agriculture in implementing zero-based budgeting, however, proved unsuccessful. There were a number of reasons responsible for the failure of ZBB in the Agriculture Department. The various agencies of the department, involved in formulating zero-based budgets, proceeded on the assumption that their programmes were necessary and formulated these accordingly. Also, the time for introduction of such a system of budgeting was not ripe as the appropriation bill was behind schedule in the Congress and those preparing the budgets felt more concerned with the level of their appropriations than the need for getting the appropriation at all. Further, the volume of paperwork created in the process of implementation of zero-based budgeting was so much that it could not be managed properly by the agencies concerned.

Later, in 1969, at Texas Instruments, Peter A. Pyhrr developed a system of zero-based budgeting as a tool for planning, budgeting and control. He first applied it to the Research and Development Division of the Company. Encouraged by its success, he extended it to other divisions of Texas Instruments. Based on his experience, he published an article which caught the attention of Jimmy Carter, the then Governor of Georgia State.

Zero-based budgeting was introduced for the first time in a governmental system by Jimmy Carter, who, as the then Governor of Georgia State adopted it in formulation of the budget for the fiscal year 1973. Highly impressed with the success of zero-based budgeting during his tenure as Governor of Georgia State, Mr. Carter, made it a point to include it as a part of his election manifesto for his presidential campaign stating that, if elected, he would introduce ZBB in federal government. Zero-based budgeting received a further boost when as President of U.S.A. Mr. Carter employed it for the preparation of budget of the U.S. Federal Government for the fiscal year 1979. The system, however, did not continue for long and its formal application was stopped within a couple of years. However, periodical review of expenditures on programmes has been retained as a feature of fiscal management, which may be called a legacy of zero-based budgeting.

Back home, the Department of Science and Technology, Government of India, was the first to introduce ZBB. It did so, through its Memorandum of December, 1983, by conveying its acceptance in principle to the Government of India that the budgets of all S&T Departments/Agencies/Institutions shall be formulated each year on the principles of zero-based budgeting.

5.2.3 Methodology

The methodology employed in applying zero-based budgeting involves –

(i)   Identification of Decision Units.

(ii) Formulation and Development of Decision Packages.

(iii) Evaluating and ranking Decision Packages in order of priority, and

(iv) Preparation of budget by allocating resources to activities or decision packages by utilising hierarchical funding cut-off levels.

5.2.4 Decision Unit

A decision unit is a distinct segment of an organisation for which budget is prepared. It can also be a programme, scheme, project, or an operation. However, it has to be kept in view that a decision unit is neither too big nor too small. If it is too big, it would not submit to a meaningful evaluation of its expenditure. In the case of too small decision unit, the paperwork involved and the cost of carrying out analytical studies would become unjustifiably high. The Government of India, keeping in view the prevailing authority structure and the need to keep paperwork within manageable limits, may have the initial decision unit at the level of Head of Department or similar levels. Necessary modification to this approach may, however, be made to suit the needs of a specific organisation. There can, of course, be a hierarchy of decision units above this level, depending upon the way an organisation is structured. It is at the decision unit levels, that discretion and options become available for applying the various approaches implicit in ZBB. At lower management levels, what is given is delegation of powers related to performance of specific functions, activities, or tasks. The lower management levels would, of course, be intimately involved in carrying out analytical studies and an assisting review of expenditures by decision units.

5.2.5 Formulation and Development of Decision Packages

A decision package includes comprehensive justification for budget estimates of an activity. Such a justification is built up by answering a number of questions. The first question to be answered is in regard to the need for the proposed expenditure as to what specific purpose does it intend to serve. This would necessitate the sharpening of the objectives of expenditure so that it could be evaluated by using the relevant active techniques or measures of performance. In case, the proposed expenditure is justified in the context of its objectives, a further question may be asked in order to know whether an alternative way that is better for achieving the specified objectives vis-à-vis its costs in doing so is available.

A decision package is a budget request which should contain the following –

- A description of the function or activity of the decision unit

- The goals and objectives of the various functions/activities of the unit
- Benefits to be derived from financing the activity/programme
- Relevance of the activity/programme to the overall objectives of the organisation /department in the present context
- The consequences of its non-funding
- The projected/estimated cost of the package
- The yearly phasing of the proposed expenditure/project cost
- Alternative ways of performing the same activity or achieving the same objectives

For each activity, different levels of funding need to be analysed for later use as inputs with the resulting output for each level of funding. Consequently, between three to ten levels of funding may be analysed. However, the analysis of too many levels of funding would involve a lot of paperwork. Therefore, the Ministry of Finance, Government of India, has rightly mentioned in their letter to other departments that only three levels of funding, that is, minimum level, current level, and enhanced level (up to 258) of funding may be analysed. The minimum level is the level of funding below which it is not feasible to continue the activity. In some cases, it may not be feasible to operate below the current level, and therefore, current level in such cases corresponds to the minimum level. Zero-based budgeting even permits enhancements that more than commensurate benefits would result from such a higher level of funding, one that fits in with other considerations which are crucial to the decision unit. It is at the decision unit level, that an acceptable level of funding has to be worked out.

5.2.6 Working of Decision Packages

ZBB requires that the Administrator/Manager in-charge of the decision unit should through a joint and participative exercise with his subordinates, rank the decision packages in order of their priority. There are various methods followed in ranking decision packages, such as committee system, a standardised formula, etc. However, the method adopted for ranking of decision packages should be such as would suit the administrative needs and culture of the organisation concerned. The available resources are allocated according to the prioritisation established among the decision packages in terms of their ranking. A cut-off level gets determined in the ranking of decision packages, above which the decision packages are funded, and below which resources are not available for financing these low priority decision packages.

Expenditure of a fixed nature or that which is necessary in order to maintain certain inter-linkages is shown as top priority decision package in the ranking list. The other way to achieve the same purpose would be to segregate from the total available resources that much amount which is required to finance fixed or essential expenditure and reallocate the rest amongst the decision packages in order of their ranking.

The relevance of zero-based budgeting gets emphasised whenever there is a resource crunch and, therefore, the need for allocating scarce resources among competing demands. Here, the ranking process enables the available resources to be allocated according to consciously decided prioritisation amongst decision packages, that is, financing high priority decision packages at the cost of low priority decision packages.

In those cases where there is a hierarchy of decision units in an organisation, the ranking of decision packages has first to be established at the lowest decision unit. This process is rated at each higher decision unit till the decision packages are combined and re-ranked at the level of the highest decision unit.

Problem or Implementation

A main factor contributing to the failure of zero-based budgeting has been due to too much of paperwork involved in the procedure, which was not managed well by the organisations concerned. Also, the reviews and analyses needed to be conducted could not be managed within the normal cycle of the budget process spread over a few months. The approach implemented by the government of India shows that they have taken the required precautions to safeguard against the hazards inherent in this system. They have evidently stated that no separate zero-based budgeting documents are needed to be prepared. To a certain extent, the results of zero-based budgeting exercises are to be reflected in the existing performance budget of the given organisation.

"It is not intended that as a result of this exercise, a separate set of documents will be presented to Parliament. The preparation and presentation or Performance Budgets to the Parliament along with Demands for Grants of the respective Departments will continue as heretofore. As you will readily agree, with the adoption of ZBB approach, performance budget document can be further defined as to increase its usefulness."

Another measure taken by the Government of India to facilitate application of zero-based budgeting is to make review and analysis of expenditures as a continuing process and not tied to the limited period of the budget cycle. It has also been stipulated by the government that to start with, the departments concerned may review one-third of their budget in the year 1987-88, another one-third in the subsequent year, and the remaining one-third in the year following. Once, all items of expenditure have been reviewed, then, further review of the same item of expenditure should be conducted as a periodical exercise. It is evident that the Ministry of Finance, Government of India has adopted a practical approach to keep the work involved in the application of ABB manageable.

The other important problem in the implementation of ZBB is the availability of trained personnel fully aware of the concept, and who can carry out analysis of expenditure by applying the evaluative techniques, like, cost-benefit analysis, cost-effectiveness analysis, etc. The analysis would need to be provided with the necessary aids of electro-magnetic devices, computers, etc., to handle and process the mass of data to generate the required information. It is also imperative that the data collected is reliable. Designing, therefore, a sound information system would be a necessary adjunct of a system of zero-based budgeting.

It is necessary to re-deploy resources like, manpower, material, machinery and equipment, which have become surplus, when a scheme or an activity is found outmoded, it has to be removed. The re-deploying of materials, machinery and equipment is possible by taking the required measures and adjusting with other organisations. But, re-deploying manpower is a complex and delicate issue, especially, in the context of situation existing in India. This could thus pose a real challenge to management. The government of India has rightly decided that no one would be laid-off while applying zero-based budgeting. Those found surplus, would be absorbed in new programmes and schemes.

Re-deploying manpower is a hard task for management but by adopting proper strategy coupled with advance planning, it should be possible to arrange placements for the surplus personnel. The identification of needs for retraining of surplus manpower and providing the necessary facilities for retraining may be a part of the strategy which would also include persuading the Employees' Unions as also the personnel to be re-deployed, that their career prospects would not be hurt.

Another important issue involved in the application of ZBB is the distinction being followed in India between planned and non-planned expenditure. Ideally, prioritisation should be done among all items of expenditure whether ongoing or new, planned or non-planned. But the system in which planned and non-planned expenditure are treated differently and assigned varying priorities, ZBB would have to be applied separately to planned and non-planned expenditures.

The need for zero-based budgeting can hardly be over-emphasised in a situation of resource crunch when demands for desirable expenditures are far outstripping the available resources. In such a circumstance, it is imperative that resources should be saved by –

(i)   Eliminating redundant expenditure,

(ii) Removing duplication or multiplication of expenditure,

(iii) Finding out better alternative ways of spending money to achieve the objectives or the expenditure, and

(iv) Optimising expenditure by making it productive and efficient.

The resources thus saved can be reallocated to other desirable demands by establishing priorities amongst them. These approaches which are implicit in the application of zero-based budgeting assume great significance when the government is facing a severe resource constraint and there is a great need for making all out efforts to find resources which could be reallocated to other desirable demands. This would, however, require the whole-hearted support and involvement of managerial levels below them.

Zero-based budgeting is an approach to budgeting that begins from the principle that no costs or activities should be factored into the plans for the coming budget period just because they figured in the costs or activities for the existing or earlier periods.

To a certain extent, everything that is to be incorporated in the budget should be taken into consideration and justified. This originally looks like a resource-hungry approach, and if applied in this basic form, would rapidly violate the law of diminishing returns. On the other hand, the application of practical common sense to the zero-based budgeting concept rapidly identifies potential gains, and it will be seen that zero-based budgeting also closely aligns to existing initiatives, including, the efficiency agenda, and performance measurement.

Zero-based budgeting first came out in the 1960s and it is not surprising that dissatisfaction with an incremental approach to budgeting has been one of the main drivers in trying to uncover budgeting models that actually serve the purposes and goals of the given organisation.

In its pure form, zero-based budgeting involves the preparation of operating budgets on the supposition that the organisation is starting out afresh in the new planning period – it is as if the life of the organisation exists as a series of fixed term contracts. On the other hand, it is generally used most efficiently where the activities involved are completely discretionary in nature. But it is very easy to fall into the trap of assuming that something is non-discretionary, for no other reason than the activity has been continuing at the same level for several years.

Zero-based budgeting can be usefully applied to budget heads, such as, repairs, maintenance or equipment costs. The traditional incremental approach often pays little attention to these heads, perhaps at best looking at trends of over two or three years, and very often, simply taking 'last year plus x%.' But, it is often possible for service priorities to be proposed, discussed and established without reference to previous years. If proposals for resource allocations are presented with options for service level and predicted outcome, funds can then be allocated on the basis of best value for money. ZBB is there to question set assumptions, and to provide a tool for systematically reviewing, reprioritising, and perhaps withdrawing from long term activities that no longer align properly with an organisation's current objectives.

The successful use of ZBB relies upon the effective involvement of all executive managers. Like all good budgeting processes, it requires that the organisation's objectives are determined and clearly stated. Where it differs from the traditional route, and adds value to the budget process is in the next stage, where different ways of achieving those objectives are explored and assessed, so that the resources associated with the preferred option can be actively justified.

5.2.7 Milestones in the Introduction and Implementation of ZBB

(A) Developing Decision Packages

The 'decision package' is a term associated with ZBB, and refers to an analysis of each discrete activity, according to cost and purpose. The analysis should also extend to considering the benefits of the activity, alternative courses of action, how to measure performance, and the consequences of not performing the activity.

Decision packages should relate to activities that are standalone; a good test is whether a decision could be made to sub-contract, or to abandon the activity altogether, without materially affecting the deliverability of another activity. This is a 'could it be done' question rather than 'should it be done.' If such a decision could not be made, the activity is likely to be part of a larger decision package.

This milestone can be broken down further into –

Stage 1: Defining the scope of ZBB

One has to decide which parts of the organisation are to be assessed using ZBB. For complex, multi-function organisations, it may be helpful to pilot the approach in a few areas where activities are closely aligned to organisational structure.

It is essential that the activities to be assessed have clearly defined objectives, and wherever possible, measurable outputs and outcomes.

Stage 2: Identify the resources

This stage falls into two parts –

* The identification of the schedule of input resources that will be required in order to deliver the outputs.
* The identification of the individuals who will take responsibility for assessing the various options.

Stage 3: Objective matching stage

It is possible that objectives may be deliverable at different service levels, and in these cases, the review should identify, as a minimum, the -

* Basic level of service (usually, in a public sector context, that which is required to meet statutory duties)
* Current level of service
* Any step changes in service
* The options for delivering each level may differ and, will therefore, need to be identified
* Clearly, it is essential to be able to analyse costs between fixed and variable elements

(B) Ranking the Decision Packages

The decision packages should be evaluated and ranked in order of their importance. Performance measurement tools including cost/benefit analysis is a very significant part, but it is also suitable to apply a level of subjectivity. This is because few activities are able to reduce to a manageable number of measures, while some measures might not be practical due to difficulties in implementing in the real world or, just because of the costs involved in such data collection. For instance, the managers may believe that there would be a 'feel good' factor in taking a specific course of action. This could never be exactly quantified.

(C) Allocating resources

The ranking list then results in a priority order for allocating the resources. The most significant activities are funded, irrespective of whether they are existing ones or new. The final budget will comprise the decision packages that have been approved for funding, reallocated into the suitable operational units.

5.2.8 The Pros and Cons of ZBB

ZBB can offer a number of advantages when it is applied intelligently. As mentioned above, it is a potentially very useful tool in terms of the current Efficiency Agenda, and parallels much of the thinking that underlies this initiative, and the approach to the spending review process. The top management can thus have the detailed information – one that will not only enable decision-making but also that which highlights redundant activities or duplication of efforts within its organisation.

The key benefit is that zero-based budgeting serves to concentrate attention on the actual resources that are needed in order to generate an output, rather than the percentage increase or decrease compared to the previous year. It is a practice which, in fact, should be more user-friendly to operational managers than the traditional incremental budget model.

It moves the process away from the bookkeeper's number-crunching spreadsheets, and promotes a balanced partnership between the finance professionals and the budget-holders in the analytical and decision-making processes.

The advantages and disadvantages of ZBB can be summarised quite concisely.

In practice, the balance can be optimised through –

- A phased introduction of ZBB, concentrating initially on less complex areas, in order to build up a foundation of skills and experience.
- Containing the use of ZBB to activities that are truly discretionary.
- Adapting the approach, so that it becomes a consideration of the impact on service delivery of step changes up or down in resource provision.
- Questions accepted beliefs, adds to the time and effort involved in budgeting.
- Focuses on value for money; may have difficulties in identifying suitable performance measures and decision criteria.
- Clear links between budgets and objectives; questioning current practice can be seen as threatening – careful management of the 'people' element is essential.
- Involves operational managers actively, and can lead to uncertainty about costs and resources of options.
- Better communication and consensus other than current practice.
- Has an adaptive approach to changing circumstances.
- Can lead to better resource allocation.

The basic process of zero-based budgeting is to justify budget requests for every budgeting cycle, regardless of prior period budgets. The following sections address the specifics including the history, implementation, drawbacks and solutions, and behavioural impacts of zero-based budgeting.

5.2.9 Implementation of Zero-based Budgeting

The zero-based budgeting system puts the burden of the evidence on the manager, and needs each manager to justify the whole budget comprehensively and prove why he or she should spend the organisation's money in the manner projected. For every project or activity, a 'decision package' should be developed by each manager, which includes an analysis of cost, purpose, alternative courses of action, measures of performance, consequences of not performing the activity, and the profits.

This approach is different than conventional budgeting methods because of the analysis of alternatives. The managers must identify another technique of performing each activity first, like, assessing the costs and benefits of making a project or outsourcing it, or, centralising versus decentralising operations. Besides that, they must recognise different levels for performing each alternative technique of the proposed activity. This means establishing a minimum level of spending, often 75 percent of the current operating level, and then, developing different decision packages that include the costs and benefits of additional levels of spending for that specific activity. The different levels allow managers to take into consideration and asses a level of spending lower than the existing operating level, giving decision-makers the option of removing an activity or the ability to choose from a selection of levels of effort including trade-offs and shifts in expenditure levels among organisational units.

Once they have been formed, the decision packages should be ranked according to their significance. This allows each manager to identify priorities, combine decision packages for old and new projects into one ranking, and permits top management to assess and compare the requirements of individual units or divisions to make funding allocations. In this respect, zero-based budgeting is very different from the conventional rolling budgets. Rolling budgets frequently attract people who prepare budgets because they make budget development much simple. Over here, an inflation factor can be added to the previous year's budget, and then, incorporate any adjustments for major changes. Every year, the rolling budgets also give management a concrete number to assist in making comparisons. On the other hand, traditional rolling budgets tend to create conflict; in order to justify the next year's budget they create an incentive to spend money carelessly. They can also create inefficient operations because of the fact that individual departments or units do not have to justify expenditures on the basis of the operations, but only on the prior year's expenditures.

Zero-based budgeting addresses such problems that can take place with conventional rolling budgets. In zero-based budgeting, each dollar spent by the management must be justified with a full description of what will be purchased, how many labour hours are required, what problems will be encountered, so on and so forth. This gives the management a chance to review operations in detail and make suggestions for changes, if required. The zero-based budgeting process assists managers in identifying redundancies and duplications amongst different departments, focussing on the money required for proposed programmes as opposed to percentage increases or decreases from the previous year. In zero-based budgeting, specific priorities of departments and divisions are recognised more easily. The process also allows comparing different departments as to the respective priorities funded. Zero-based budgeting thus allows a performance audit to determine whether each project or activity has been performed as efficiently as planned.

5.2.10 Zero-Based Budgeting – Drawbacks and Solutions

One main drawback of zero-based budgeting is that the cost in terms of managerial time. It takes a large amount of time to go through the process of reviewing operations thoroughly to justify the costs of each budget cycle without depending on past expenditures. One solution to this problem is to create a rolling budget every year and perform a zero-based budget every three to five years, or when a major change takes place within the operation. This enables an organisation to profit from the advantages of zero-based budgeting without too much work. Similarly, the traditional rolling budgets should never depend on a prior-year budget as well as a percentage; as an aggregate past numbers should always be considered. In some cases, a zero-based budget may depend on some prior numbers where it is very hard to create a budget from scratch. Finally, the process gives top management the chance to judge the performance of managers with regards to allocating resources efficiently and, consecutively, also gives managers more responsibility in developing their budgets.

An organisation must not feel that all budgets should be developed completely in the same way. Some departments can utilise an in-depth study of a zero-based budget; while others can use a rolling budget. This is a way to spread the extensive work over several years rather than focussing on one specific year. Several organisations have implemented the system in some form or another and found that it did not work. If correctly executed, the process could have a substantial improvement over conventional rolling budgets. The number and nature of decision packages differs from company to company; it is not very common for big organisations to identify many packages. Moreover, it is often difficult or even impossible for top executives to have the required information or time to develop rank priorities for thousands of packages.

To overcome this problem, the managers rank their own packages and then have their top executives rank the packages of all the managers that report to them. This approach is used by one of zero-based budgeting's pioneers, Texas Instruments. Another solution is to rank a certain percentage of packages within its own area of responsibility. Under this solution, the first level of management may rank 40 percent of the proposed packages; the next level may rank the next 40 percent of packages, while top management may focus on the remaining budget.

5.2.11 Advantages/Benefits of Zero-Based Budgeting Process
- Efficient allocation of resources, as it is based on needs and benefits
- Drives managers to find cost effective ways to improve operations
- Detects inflated budgets

- Municipal planning departments are exempt from this budgeting practice
- Useful for service departments where the output is difficult to identify
- Increases staff motivation by providing greater initiative and responsibility in decision-making
- Increases communication and co-ordination within the organisation
- Identifies and eliminates wasteful and obsolete operations
- Identifies opportunities for outsourcing
- Forces cost centres to identify their mission and their relationship to overall goals

5.2.12 Disadvantages/Limitations of Zero-Based Budgeting Method

- Difficult to define decision units and decision packages, as it is exhaustive and, therefore, time-consuming
- Forced to justify every detail related to expenditure; the Research and Development (R&D) department is threatened whereas the production department benefits
- Necessary to train managers at various levels, since zero-based budgeting must be clearly understood by them for its successful implementation; difficult to administer and communicate the budgeting because more managers are involved in the process
- In a large organisation, the volume of forms may be so large that no one person could read all; compressing the information down to a usable size might remove critically important details
- Honesty of the managers must be consistent, since exaggeration by even one of them might skew the results

5.3 Inflation Accounting

Inflation accounting is a financial reporting process which records the results of inflation on the financial statements that a firm prepares and publishes at the end of the financial year. It is on the basis of this assumption that the currency is stable. But, in certain nations, this assumption is not valid, particularly for those which are experiencing hyperinflation and where the adjustments are done in accordance with the changes in the purchasing power of the masses.

Inflation accounting is therefore a method of accounting that includes inflation. In inflation accounting, one records price changes that have an effect on the purchasing power of existing assets and the value of the firm's long-term assets and liabilities. This can give an exact picture of a firm's value. It is used to supplement a firm's ordinary financial statements. It is less commonly known as general price level accounting.

5.3.1 History of Inflation Accounting

For over fifty years inflation accounting was practised in the USA by the American Institute of Certified Public Accountants. Throughout the period of Great Depression, several firms reconstructed their financial reports, recording the inflation in them. During those fifty years, several firms were motivated to record the price-level adjusted statements instead of cost-based financial statements. The FSAB or the Financial Accounting Standards Board raised a proposal of publishing the price-level adjustment statements which was withdrawn by them later because of particular problems.

5.3.2 Basic Principle of Inflation Accounting

One of the most significant and basic principles of the accounting process is called as 'The Measuring Unit Principle'. The standard of measurement is the currency which is most related to the economy. The changes in the purchasing power are not considered to be significant. The assumption is that the value of the currency is fixed. On the other hand, the use of the principle actually led to misleading reports. The modifications in the price level were not always considered while preparing the reports. As the price level is considered to be more or less fixed, it may lead to different kinds of distortions. The influence of price change is not clear, the profits are frequently misquoted, the asset values do not reflect the economic value of the business, future earnings and future capital requirements cannot be forecasted correctly. The misconception of real economic performance has extensive effects like, tampering the whole socio-political system of a country.

5.3.3 Models of Inflation Accounting

Inflation accounting as already stated is also called as the Price Level Accounting. In particular inflation accounting models, the price level costs were attained by using certain indices. The second model is the Constant Dollar Accounting. This is another model of accounting, which assists one in changing the non-monetary assets and equities into current dollars using a general price index. The monetary assets are not considered during such conversion.

5.3.4 Inflation Accounting and its Significance

The impact of inflation comes in the form of rising prices of output and assets. As the financial accounts are kept on historical cost basis, they do not consider the impact of an increase in the prices of assets and output. This might sometimes lead to overstated profits, under-priced assets and misleading picture of business etc.

Thus, the financial statements prepared under historical accounting usually prove to be statements of historical facts and do not reflect the existing value of business. This deprives the users of accounts like management, shareholders, and creditors etc., from having a right picture of business to make suitable decisions.

Therefore, it indicates the need for having a system of inflation accounting in place. Inflation accounting is a word that includes various accounting systems designed to correct problems that arise from historical cost accounting in the presence of inflation.

The importance of inflation accounting appears from the inherent restrictions of the historical cost accounting system. The following are the limitations of historical accounting –

1. Historical accounts do not consider the unrealised holding gains arising from the rise in the monetary value of the assets because of inflation.

2. The goal of charging depreciation is to spread the cost of the asset over its useful life and reserve its replacement in the future. But it does not consider the effect of inflation over the replacement cost which may cause an inadequate charge of depreciation.

3. Under historical accounting, inventories obtained at old prices are matched against revenues expressed at existing prices. In the time of inflation, this may lead to the overstatement of profits because of mixing up of holding gains and operating gains.

4. Future earnings are not easily projected from historical earnings.

To measure the impact of inflation on financial statements, the following techniques are used –

1. Current Purchasing Power (CPP) Method

Under this method of adjusting accounts to price changes, all items in the financial statements are restated in terms of a constant unit of money, that is, with regards to general purchasing power. For measuring changes in the price level and incorporating the changes in the financial statements, we use General Price Index (GPI), which might be taken into account as a barometer meant for the purpose. The index is used to change the values of different items in the balance sheet and profit and loss account. This method considers the changes in the general purchasing power of money and overlooks the actual increase or decrease in the price of the given item. Current purchasing power method refurnishes the historical figures at current purchasing power. For this reason, at the end of the period, historical figures are changed into value of purchasing power. Two index numbers are needed – one showing the general price level at the end of the period and, the other, reflecting the same at the date of the transaction.

Under this method, profit is an increase in the value of the net asset over a period, all valuations being made in terms of current purchasing power. Moreover, the value of all assets is adjusted with current price index, and then, it is shown in inflated balance sheet.

Suppose total assets of a business is ₹10,000 in 2000 and now in 2009, and if the said enterprise wants to show its financial statement according to inflation accounting system, then, it can adopt or follow this method. Under this method, 2000 year's price index = 100; 2009's index price = 150

And also, adjust the value of depreciation.

Income statement general price-level adjustment example

On the income statement, depreciation is adjusted for changes in general price levels based on a general price index

	2001	2002	2003	Total
Revenue	33,000	36,302	39,931	1,09,233
Depreciation	30,000	31,500 (a)	33,000 (b)	94,500
Operating Income	3,000	4,802	6,931	14,733
Purchasing Power Loss	–	1,500 (c)	3,000 (d)	4,500
Net Income	3,000	3,302	3,931	10,233

(a) $30,000 \times 105/100 = 31,500$

(b) $30,000 \times 110/100 = 33,000$

(c) $(30,000 \times 105/100) - 30,000 = 1,500$

(d) $(63,000 \times 110/105) - 63,000 = 3,000$

2. Current Cost Accounting (CCA) Method

The current cost accounting is another option to the current purchasing power method. The current cost accounting method matches existing revenues with the current cost of the resources which are used in earning them.

This method is suggested for dealing with the issue of showing the effects of inflation on business profits. Rather than showing assets at their historical cost, less depreciation where suitable, the assets are shown at their current cost at the time of producing the accounts. When inflation was high, this method of accounting was extensively used in the UK in the late 1970s and early 1980s. However, it was not famous, and as inflation began to subside, it has been mostly abandoned.

In this method, the changes in the general price level are calculated by index numbers. If price of a specific asset changes without any general price change then specific price change takes place. Here, the assets are valued at current cost which is the cost at which asset can be replaced as on date.

While the current purchasing power (CPP) method is known as the general price level approach, the current cost accounting (CCA) method is known as specific price level approach or replacement cost accounting.

5.3.5 Benefits of Inflation Accounting

1. Because of inflation, inflation accounting gives an accurate data of net profit because depreciation value is on current market value which will be more than historical cost method. It will reduce the value of profit and therefore shareholders get the present amount of dividend.

2. Replacement is so easy: Since depreciation is charged on fixed assets' current market value, it will obviously reduce the value of net profit and the given firm can simply create a fund out of profit for buying new assets. In the case of historical accounting system, it is very hard to buy new fixed asset at new market value, because depreciation is on historical cost and because depreciation is charged less, it is possible that the firm concerned may have less money at its disposal for buying new fixed asset. But, in inflation accounting, such a scenario will not come up.

3. Correct information to interested parties: All economists believe that inflation reduces the level of new investment because customers start hoarding material goods fearing hyperinflation. At such a time, if a firm makes its accounts on current purchase price and cost price basis, then all parties that are interested can get accurate information about its financial and revenue position.

(a) They can also get information about inflation loss of a firm.

(b) They can also get information of gearing adjustments – meaning what benefits are for shareholders insofar as increasing price index in company.

4. Useful for managerial decision: A manager studies financial statements before taking any decision. If the given firm provides financial statement on the basis of the price level changing or inflation accounting system, it comes in handy for the managers to not only make plans for new investments but also estimate the new sale prices of their products easily.

5.3.6 Limitations of Inflation Accounting

Though inflation accounting is a more practical approach designed to depict the true status of the financial health of the given company, there are certain limitations which come in the way of it becoming a widely accepted and popular system of accounting. The same is as follows –

1. Change in the price level is a continuous process.
2. This system makes calculations a tedious task because of too many conversions and calculations.
3. This system has not been given preference by tax authorities.

Despite being a right method of presenting financial statements, inflation accounting is still not widely prevalent due to the aforesaid limitations. But, with more research and development of accounting software in this field, there is no doubt that inflation adjusted accounting is the future of financial accounting.

5.4 Human Resource Accounting

The company's success purely depends upon the quality of its human resources. It is accentuated by the fact that the human factor is by far the most significant input in any corporate venture. The investments directed to raise information, skills, and aptitudes of the personnel of the organisation are the investments in human resource. In this context, it is useful to study human resource accounting practices in the corporate sector in India.

Human resource accounting emerged recently and is struggling for acceptance. It is clearly said that, human resources accounting is an accounting measurement system, on which a big body of literature outlining the different processes for measurement has been published in the last ten years. Simultaneously, the theory and underlying concepts of accounting measurement has gathered a lot of attention from academicians and a significant body of literature has developed. The conventional accountings of human resources are not identified as physical or financial assets.

The past few decades have seen a global change from manufacturing to service-based economies. The fundamental difference between the two lies in the very nature of their assets. In the former, the physical assets like, plant, machinery, material etc. are of greatest importance. On the contrary, in the latter, knowledge and attitudes of the employees assume greater importance. For example, in the case of an IT company, the value of its physical assets is insignificant when compared with the value of the knowledge and skills of its employees. So is the case with hospitals, academic institutions, consulting companies etc. in which the total value of the given organisation depends mostly on the skills of its employees and the services they offer. Thus, the success of these organisations is dependent on the quality of their human resources – its knowledge, skills, competence, motivation and understanding of the organisational culture. Thus, in knowledge-driven economies, it is essential that the humans be recognised as an important part of the organisation. On the other hand, in order to estimate and project the importance of the human capital, it is necessary that some method of calculating the importance of knowledge, motivation, skills, and contribution of the human element plus the organisational processes like recruitment, selection, training etc. which are used to build and support these human aspects, is developed. In brief, Human Resource Accounting (HRA) denotes just this process of quantification/measurement of the human resource.

5.4.1 Definition

Human resources accounting, also known as 'human asset accounting' involves identifying, measuring, capturing, tracking and analysing the potential of the human resources of a company and communicating the resultant information to the stakeholders of the company. It was a method by which a cost was assigned to every employee when recruited, and the value that the employee would generate in the future. Human resource accounting reflected the potential of the human resources of an organisation in monetary terms, in its financial statements.

- HRA has been defined by American Accounting Association's committee, thus –"HRA is the process of identifying and measuring data about human resources and communicating this information to interested parties."
- Stephen Knauf has defined HRA as "The measurement and quantification of human organisational inputs, such as recruiting, training, experience and commitment."
- According to Eric. G Flamholtz, HRA represents "Accounting for people as an organisational resource. It is the measurement of the cost and value of people for the organisation".

In a nutshell, it can be said that it is the process of developing financial assessment for people within an organisation and society and monitoring of these assessment through the time it deals with.

Even though prevailing situations differ from country to country and sector to sector, yet, a growing trend towards the measurement and reporting of human resources, particularly, in public sector is noticeable during the past few years. BHEL, Cement Corporation of India, ONGC, Engineers India Ltd., National Thermal Corporation, Minerals and Metals Trading Corporation, Madras Refineries, Oil India Ltd., Associated Cement Companies, SPIC, Metallurgical and Engineering Consultants India Limited, Cochin Refineries Ltd. etc. are some of the organisations, which have started disclosing some valuable information regarding human resources in their financial statements.

- Assigning, budgeting, and reporting the cost of human resources incurred in an organisation, including wages and salaries and training expenses.
- It is "the process of identifying and measuring data about human resources and communicating this information to interested parties." HRA, not only involves measurement of all the costs/investments associated with the recruitment, placement, training and development of employees, but also the quantification of the economic value of the people in an organisation.
- It furnishes cost/value information for making management decisions about acquiring, allocating, developing and maintaining human resources in order to attain cost effectiveness. It allows management personnel to monitor effectively the use of human resources. It provides a sound and effective basis for human asset control, that is, whether the asset is appreciated, depleted or conserved.
- It helps in the development of management principles by classifying the financial consequences of various practices.

5.4.2 HRA Approaches

The process of assigning money values to different dimensions of HR costs, investments and the worth of employees is the biggest challenge that the HRA is facing.

HR Accounting basically has two approaches

1. **The Cost Approach** involves methods based on the costs incurred by the firm regarding an employee. Two types of costs are of special importance in HRA – original cost and replacement cost.

   An original/historical cost of human resources is the sacrifice that was made to obtain and develop the resource. These consist of the costs of recruiting, selection, hiring, placement, orientation and on-the-job training.

   The replacement cost of human resources is the cost that would have to be incurred if current employees are to be substituted.

Other cost methods that might be used are the standard cost method and the competitive method. In the standard cost method, the standard costs connected to recruitment, hiring, training and developing per grade of employees are determined annually.

2. **The Economic Value Approach** which includes methods on the basis of the economic value of the human resources and their contribution for the benefit of the firm. The methods for calculating the economic value of individuals are of two types – monetary and non-monetary methods.

The above-mentioned are explained in detail as below –

5.4.3 Methods of Valuing and Accounting of Human Resources

The methods to value and account for human resources can be classified into the following categories –

1. Methods based on costs which consist of costs incurred by the firm to recruit, hire, and train and develop human resources.

2. Methods based on economic value of human resources and the capitalisation of company's earnings.

(A) Methods Based on Costs

- **Historical Cost Method:** Under this method, the cost of acquisition, that is, selection, hiring, training costs of employees are capitalised and written off over the expected useful life of the employees. In case, the employees leave the firm before the anticipated period of service, then, the unamortised portion of costs remaining in the firm's books is written off against the profit and loss account in that year. If the time of service goes beyond the anticipated time, then, amortisation of costs is rescheduled.

- **Replacement Cost Method:** Under this method, the human resources are valued at their replacement cost, that is, the monetary implications of substituting current employees. Replacement costs could be positional, that is, substituting employees for specific positions or replacing specific talent or ability of specific individuals.

- **Competitive Bidding Method:** This approach recommends competitive bidding for insufficient employees in a company, that is, opportunity cost of employees connected to scarcity. The approach suggests the capitalising of additional earning potential of each human resource within the firm.

- **Standard Cost Method**: Under this method, the standard costs of recruiting, hiring, training, and developing per grade of employees are decided yearly. The total standard cost for all employees of the firm is the value of human resources.

(B) Methods Based on Value

- **Jaggi and Lau Method:** This method estimates the importance of human resources on a group basis, as human resource groups justify productivity and performance in organisations.

- **Economic Value Method:** Under this method, the current net value of incremental cash flows attributed to human resources is taken as the asset value.

5.4.4 Need for HR Accounting

- Human resource accounting is required to provide effective management within the organisation concerned.
- If there is any change in the structure of manpower, it is human resource accounting which gives information on it to the management.
- Human resource accounting gives qualitative information plus evaluates the costs incurred on the employees.
- It gives a platform to the management by providing factors for better decision-making for future investment.
- The return on investment on human capital is best assessed through human resource accounting. Human resource accounting interacts with the given organisation and public not only about the importance of human resources but also its correct allocation within the organisation concerned.
- Human resource accounting helps the management in developing principles by classifying the financial results of the different practices.

The basic reason for developing human resource accounting is to overcome problems arising from the assessment of intangible assets. We know that several companies do not give sufficient information to investors in traditional balance sheet and herein human resource accounting proves to be a handy device to overcome it. Human resource accounting provides an insight on employees as assets. Human resource accounting provides a profile to the enterprise, and therefore, improves its image. Human resource accounting investigates to retain intelligent human capital. It goes without saying that, the significance of human resources in business organisation as productive resources was generally overlooked by the accountants until twenty years ago.

During the early and mid-1980s, the behavioural scientists attacked the traditional accounting system because it failed to give importance to human resources of the given organisation along with its other material resources. In this changing viewpoint, the accountants were also called upon to play their role by allotting monetary value to the human resources deployed in a company. Human resource accounting involves the dimension of costs incurred by a company for all its personnel function. Thus, the issue to be addressed is how to calculate the economic value of the people to the given organisation and different cost-based measures to be taken for human resources. The two main constituents of human resources accounting were investments related to the employees and the value generated by them. Investment in human capital consists of all costs incurred in upgrading the employees' skill sets and knowledge of human resources. The output that an organisation generated from human resources was considered as the value of its human resources. Human resources accounting is used to measure the performance of all the individuals in the given organisation, and when this was made available to the stakeholders in the form of a report, it assisted them in taking important investment decisions. All the models emphasised that human capital was regarded as an investment for future earnings, and not expenditure.

For valuing human resources, different models have been developed. Some of them are opportunity cost approach, standard cost approach, and current purchasing power approach. Lev and Schwartz present the value of future earnings as Flamholtz's scholastic rewards valuation models etc. Of these, the model recommended by Lev and Schwartz has become famous. Under this method, the future earnings of the human resources of the given organisation until their retirement is aggregated and discounted at the cost of capital to reach the present value.

What is required is measurement of abilities of all employees in a firm, at every level, to generate value from their knowledge and capability. *"Human Resource Accounting (HRA) is basically an information system that tells management what changes are occurring over time to the human resources of the business. HRA also involves accounting for investment in people and their replacement costs, and also the economic value of people in an organisation,"* says **P. K. Gupta**, the director of strategic development – intercontinental operations, of Legato Systems, India. The current accounting system is not capable of providing the actual value of employee capabilities and knowledge. This ultimately has an effect on the future investments of a firm, as each year the cost on human resource development and recruitment increases.

Different experts show that the information generated by human resource accounting systems can be put to use for taking several managerial decisions like, recruitment planning, turnover analysis, personnel advancement analysis and capital budgeting, which can assist firms concerned save a great deal of trouble in the future.

5.4.5 Part of the Balance Sheet

The organisations concerned can actually discover how much they can earn from an individual, as the intellectual assets of a firm are worth three or four times the tangible book value. Human capital also provides expert services like consulting, financial planning and assurance services, which are important and very much in demand.

Realising this, several firms in the world are making human resource accounting a necessary part on their balance sheets. One of the best examples is of the Denmark Government. The Danish Ministry of Business and Industry has issued a directive that with effect from the trading year 2005, all firms registered in Denmark will need to include information on customers, processes and human capital in their annual reports. A minimum of five measures for each is needed, and comparison with the previous two years must be indicated. Figures for investment in intellectual capital must be indicated and compared with the previous two years. A narrative should match each set of figures. Information for investors about intellectual capital, both current and future, should occupy at least one-third of the report. Where related, information must also be given concerning the environment.

In India, there are only a small number of firms like BHEL, Infosys and Reliance Industries, which have executed human resource accounting and some are working on it. Infosys, which began to show human resource as an asset in its balance sheet, has been reaping high market valuations. NIIT has been following the same method called Economic Value Addition (EVA), which also assists in evaluating the real value that an employee can fetch for the firm.

There were numerous advantages of adopting human resource accounting. It assisted an organisation in taking managerial decisions on the basis of the availability and the necessity of human resources. When human resources were quantified, it gave the investors and other customers, a true insight into an organisation and its future potential. That apart, a correct assessment of human resources helped organisations to remove the negative effects of redundant labour.

This, in turn, helped them to channelise the available skills, talents, knowledge and experience of their employees more efficiently. By adopting and implementing HRA in an organisation, the following important information could be obtained –

- Cost per employee
- Human capital investment ratio
- The amount of wealth created by each employee
- The profit created by each employee
- The ratio of salary paid to the total revenue generated
- Average salary of each employee
- Employee absenteeism rates
- Employee turnover rate and retention rate

Case Study: Infosys Technologies

Valuing Human Resources

In the financial year 1995-96, Infosys Technologies (Infosys) became the first software company to value its human resources in India. The company used the Lev and Schwartz Model and valued its human resources assets at ₹1.86 billion. Infosys had always given utmost importance to the role of employees in contributing to the company's success. Analysts felt that Human Resources Accounting (HRA) was a step further in Infosys' focus on its employees. Mr. Narayana Murthy, the then chairman and managing director of Infosys, said: "Comparing this figure over the years will tell us whether the value of our human resources is appreciating or not. For a knowledge-intensive company like ours, that is vital information."

The concept of HRA was not new in India. HRA was pioneered by public sector companies like Bharat Heavy Electronics Ltd. (BHEL) and Steel Authority of India Ltd. (SAIL) way back in the 1970s. However, the concept did not gain much popularity and acceptance during that time.

It was only in the mid-1990s, after Infosys started valuing its employees, that the concept gained popularity in India. By 2002, HR accounting had been introduced by leading software companies like Satyam Computers and DSQ Software, as well as by leading manufacturing firms like Reliance Industries.

HR managers were quick to respond on the above developments by stating that more and more organisations had now started to realise the importance of skilled workforce. They felt that to be successful in highly competitive markets, the companies concerned require to continuously improve the level of performance of their workforce.

HRA enabled companies to understand whether the skill sets of their human capital was appreciating or not. R. Krishnaswamy, an actuarial accountant, said, "The value can be used internally by an organisation to make comparisons from unit to unit, from year to year, as well as within its industry." Stock market analysts felt that the 'comprehensive disclosure policy' was becoming a differentiating factor among companies in various industries. Yezdi Hirji Malegam, managing director, S. B. Billimoria & Company commented, "In the last few years, people are realising that their intangible assets are worth much more than their tangible ones. Now an attempt is being made to put a value to these intangibles, and to bring these hidden values to book." Analysts felt that HRA was an investor-friendly disclosure, and assured stakeholders that the company had the right human capital to meet its future business requirements.

Background Note

The assets of an organisation could be broadly classified into tangible and intangible assets. Tangible assets referred to all the physical assets which could be presented in the balance sheet including plant and machinery, investments in securities, inventories, cash, cash equivalents and bank balance, marketable securities, accounts and notes receivables, finance receivables, equipment on operating leases etc.

Intangible assets included the goodwill, brand value and human assets of a company; whereas the human assets involved the capabilities, knowledge, skills and talents of employees in an organisation.

In the past, less importance was given by organisations to value their human assets. Moreover, it was also considered difficult to value them since there were no defined parameters of valuation. The companies concerned did not value their human resources as these were never treated as an asset in the past. All investments related to employees, including, salary as well as recruitment and training costs were considered as expenditures.

In addition, the accountants also felt that the stakeholders of a company may not accept the concept of placing a monetary value on human resources.

The importance and value of human assets started to be recognised in the early 1990s when there was a major increase in employment in firms in service, technology and other knowledge-based sectors. In these sector firms, the intangible assets, especially human resources, contributed significantly to the building of shareholder value. The critical success factor for any knowledge-based company was its skilled and intellectual workforce.

HRA in Practice at Infosys

Infosys' HRA model was based on the present value of the employees' future earnings with the following assumptions –

- An employee's salary package included all benefits, whether direct or otherwise, earned both in India and in a foreign nation.

- The additional earnings on the basis of age and group were also taken into account.

To calculate the value of its human assets in 1995-96, all the 1,172 employees of Infosys were divided into five groups, based on their average age. Each group's average compensation was calculated. Infosys also calculated the compensation of each employee at retirement by using an average rate of increment.

5.4.6 Aspects of Human Resources Accounting

Human resources accounting system consists of the following two aspects. They are namely –

(a) The investment made in human resources

(b) The value human resource

The measurement of the investments in human resources will help evaluate the changes in human resource investment over a period of time. The information generated by the analysis of investment in human resources has many applications for managerial purposes. The organisational human performance can be evaluated with the help of such an analysis. It also helps in guiding the management to frame appropriate policies for human resource management. The present performance result will act as an input for future planning and the present planning will have its impact on future result. The same relationship is also applicable to the areas of managerial applications in relation to the human resource planning and control.

Investment in human resources can be highlighted under two heads namely –

A. Investment Pattern

The human resource investment usually consists of the following items –

1. Expenditure on advertisement for recruitment
2. Cost of selection
3. Training costs
4. On-the-job training costs
5. Subsistence allowances
6. Contribution to Provident Fund
7. Educational tour expenses
8. Medical expenses

9. Ex-gratia payments

10. Employee's Welfare Fund

All these items influence directly or indirectly the human resources and the productivity of the organisation concerned.

B. Investment in Current Costs

After analysing the investment pattern in the human resources of an organisation, the current cost of human resources can be ascertained. For this purpose 'current cost' is defined as the cost incurred with which derives benefit of current nature. These are the costs, which have little bearing on future costs. Thus, the expenses incurred for the maintenance of human resources are termed as current costs. Current cost consists of salary and wages, dearness allowance, overtime wages, bonus, house rent allowance, special pay and personal pay.

Amidst this background, it is significant to mention here that the importance and value of human assets were recognised in the early 1990s when there was a major increase in employment in firms in service, technology and other knowledge-based sectors. In the firms of these sectors, the intangible assets, especially, human resources, contributed significantly to the building of shareholder value. The critical success factor for any knowledge-based company was its highly skilled and intellectual workforce. Soon after, the manufacturing industry also seemed to realise the importance of people and started perceiving its employees as strategic assets. For instance, if two manufacturing companies had similar capital and used similar technology, then, it was only their employees who were the major differentiating factor. Due to the above development, the need for valuing human assets besides traditional accounting of tangible assets was increasingly experienced.

From the above discussions, it is felt that human resource accounting provides quantitative information about the value of human asset, which helps the top management to take decisions regarding the adequacy of human resources. Hence, it is concluded that human resources are an indispensable but often neglected element and, is therefore, to be foregrounded into the industrial area for the betterment of the economy.

5.4.7 Objectives of HR Accounting

- It furnishes cost/value information for making management decisions about acquiring, allocating, developing and maintaining human resources in order to attain cost effectiveness.

- It allows management personnel to monitor effectively the use of human resources.

- It provides a sound and effective basis for human asset control, that is, whether the asset is appreciated, depleted or conserved.

- It helps in the development of management principles by classifying the financial consequences of various practices.

The basic reason for developing HRA is to overcome the problems arising from the valuation of intangible assets. We know that many organisations do not provide sufficient information to investors in the traditional balance sheet and herein HRA comes across a useful device to overcome the same. HRA provides an insight on employees as assets. HRA provides a profile to the given enterprise, and thus, improves its image. HRA probes into ways to retain intelligent human capital.

The very importance of HRA in developing countries like India can be best judged through government reports which show that in India, approximately 73% of national income is utilised to compensate employees.

To conclude, the HRA system tries to evaluate the worth of human resources of an organisation in a systematic manner and record them in the financial statement to communicate their worth with changes in time and result obtained from their utilisation to the users of the financial statement. Hence, looking at the importance of HRA, now it is required under law and government guidelines, for undertakings to maintain a separate item in their balance sheet about such HR activities undertaken by them.

5.4.8 Recent Trends in HRA

Providing adequate and valid information on human resources in statistical terms and within traditional balance sheets has proved extremely difficult. Consequently, new approaches introduce financial as well as non-financial information in human resource accounting.

There are still immense problems to overcome before a coherent and reliable measuring technique is established. Part of the dilemma originates from basic questions, such as –

- Is HRA only for internal use in enterprises?
- Should HRA have a standard format for comparability purposes?
- Should HRA be included in traditional financial statements?

These basic questions are followed by methodological and technical ones –

- Is it possible to obtain data on human resources which are reliable and comparable across enterprises?
- Will the costs of gathering and processing this information exceed the benefits of doing so?
- How to establish a coherent terminology?
- How to link reporting on human resources with improved human resource management?

Yet, despite the many problems and unanswered questions, the reasons for developing HRA methods can be summarised in the following six points –

- Inadequacy of traditional balance sheets in providing sufficient information on enterprise performance
- Measuring problems deriving from the valuation of human resources
- Redistribution of social responsibilities between the public and private sectors

- Security versus flexibility in employment
- Improved human resource management
- Formal learning versus in-firm competency acquirement

The focus on HRA in enterprises has lead to a growing interest by stakeholders who have started to identify and formulate their positions. The main stakeholders, such as the enterprises, investors, employees, trade unions and governments are therefore gradually becoming aware of the potential of HRA, albeit from different perspectives.

5.5 Activity-Based Costing

Activity-based costing (or activity-based accounting or activity accounting) is a system that focuses on activities as the fundamental cost objects and uses the costs of these activities as building blocks for compiling the costs of other cost objects. It should be noted that activity-based accounting is generic, that is, it can be part of job-order product costing system or a process product costing system.

Activity-based costing systems presume that activities cause costs and those products and customers create the demands for activities. Costs are assigned to products on the basis of individual products consumption or demand for each activity. Activity-based costing systems recognise that the company must know the factors that drive each activity, the cost of activities and how activities are relevant to the products.

5.5.1 Process of Activity-based Costing

An outline of an activity-based costing system is given below –

1. Identify the major activities that take place in the given organisation.

   ↓

2. Determine the cost driver for each major activity.

   ↓

3. Create a cost centre/cost pool for each major activity.

   ↓

4. Trace the cost of activities to products, according to a product's demand for activities.

The **First Stage** is to recognise the major activities in the organisation. Examples of activities include, machine-related activities, direct labour-related activities and different support activities like ordering, receiving, materials handling, parts administration, production scheduling, packing and despatching.

The **Second Stage** is to recognise factors that influence the cost of a specific activity. The term 'cost driver' is used to describe the events or forms that are the important determinants of the cost of the activities. For instance, if production scheduling cost is generated by the number of production runs that each product produces, then, the number of set-ups would determine the cost driver for production scheduling. Activity-based costing recognises that cost behaviour is dictated by cost drivers, and thus, the tracing of overhead costs to products needs that cost behaviour should be understood so that suitable cost drivers can be recognised. Examples of some of the cost drivers used by the activity-based costing systems include the number of receiving orders for the receiving department, the number of production runs carried out for scheduling and set-up costs, the number of purchase orders for the cost of operating the purchase department and the number of despatch orders for the despatch department. These costs are changeable with output in the short-term. Activity-based costing systems use volume-related cost drivers like direct labour hours or machine hours. For instance, power costs can be traced to products using machine hours as the cost driver, since machine hours drive the consumption of power.

The **Third Stage** requires that a cost centre be created for each activity. For instance, the total cost of all set-ups might form one cost centre for all set-up related costs.

The **Final Stage** is to trace the cost of the activities to products, in accordance with the product demands for these activities during the production process. A product's demand for the activities is calculated by the number of transactions it generates for the cost driver. Suppose, the total cost traced to the cost centre for set-up related costs was ₹1,00,000 and there were 100 set-ups during the period. The charging-out rate would be ₹1,000 per set-up. To determine the set-up costs for a particular product, the number of set-ups for the product will be multiplied by ₹1,000. The same way the cost of other activities can be traced to the products.

5.5.2 Comparison between Traditional vs. Activity-based Cost Allocation

It has been seen that in the first stage, overheads are assigned to cost centres. In the second stage, the costs accumulated in the cost centres are allocated to cost objects (products, services, customers) using selected allocation bases. Traditional costing systems tend to use a small number of second stage allocation bases, typically, direct labour hours or machine hours. Other allocation bases used to a lesser extent by traditional costing systems are – direct labour cost, direct material cost and units of output. Traditional systems assume that direct labour or machine hours have a significant influence in the long-term on the level of overhead expenditure.

A major distinguishing feature of ABC is that overheads are assigned to each major activity rather than departments, which normally represent cost centres with traditional systems. Activities consist of the aggregation of many different tasks associated with objects. Typical support activities include schedule production, set up machines, movement of materials, purchase materials and inspect items and process supplier records. When costs are accumulated by activities, they are known as 'activity cost centres'. Production process activities include machine products and assembly products. Thus, within the production process, activity cost centres are often identical to cost centres used by traditional cost systems.

A further distinguishing feature is that traditional systems normally assign service/ support costs by relocating their costs to production cost centres so that they are assigned to products within the production centre at cost driver rates. In contrast, ABC systems tend to establish cost driver rates for support centres and assign the cost of support activities directly to cost objects without any reallocation to production centres.

(a) Traditional Costing System

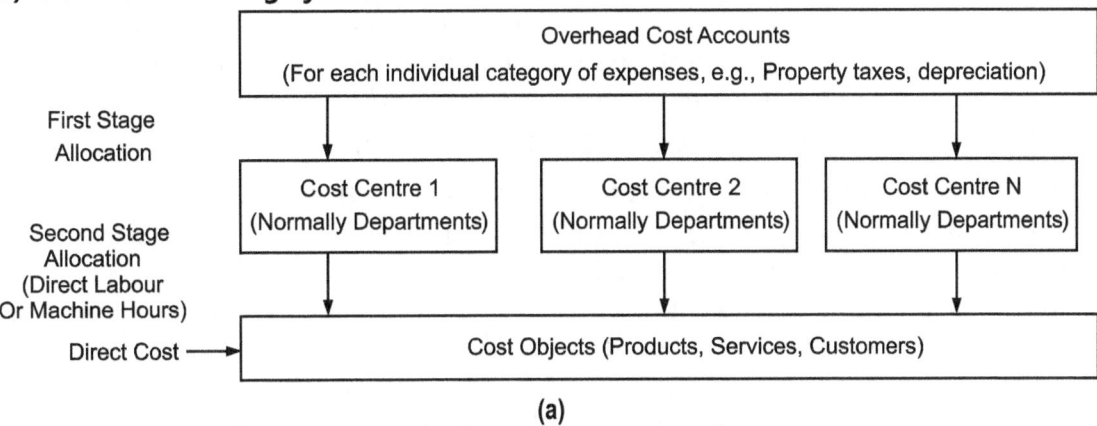

(a)

(b) Activity-based Costing System

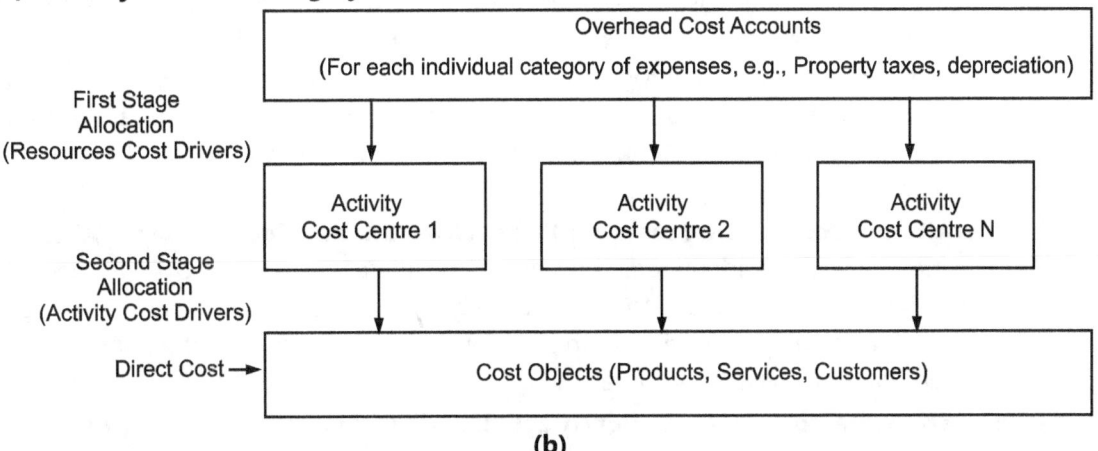

(b)

Fig. 4.1: Two-Stage Allocation Process for Traditional and Activity-based Costing System

5.5.3 Levels of Activities

Normally, there are four levels of activities. These are as follows –

(i) **Unit-level Activities:** These are those activities for which the consumption of resources can be identified with the number of units produced. Examples include direct material, direct labour hour, machine hour.

(ii) **Batch-level Activities:** Activities such as setting up a machine or processing a purchase order are performed each time a batch of goods is produced. The cost of batch-related activities varies with number of batches made, but is common (or fixed) for all units within the batch.

(iii) Product-level Activities: These are the activities which are performed to support different products in the product line. Examples include parts administration, product specification or purchasing may be related to the existence of a particular product line.

(iv) Facility-level Activities: These are the activities which cannot be directly attributed to individual products. These activities are necessary to sustain the manufacturing process and are common and joint to all products manufactured. Examples include ground maintenance, plant security and property taxes. These expenses are allocated in terms of rupees per product value added.

5.5.4 Steps for Activity-based Cost Allocation

Activity-based cost allocation involves various steps. These steps are as follows –

(1) Identifying the activities: Activities consisting of units of work or tasks, for example, and purchase of materials may be identified as separate activities. Each activity consists of different tasks such as receiving a purchase request, identifying suppliers, preparing purchase orders, making purchase orders and performing follow-up. The final choice of activities depends on two factors namely –

(i)   Total cost of activity must be significant to justify separate treatment.

(ii) Ability of a single cost driver to provide satisfactory determinant of the cost of activity, for example, selecting a number of purchase orders as a cost driver, may provide correct information for purchasing cost but does not provide information relating to receiving and using. Therefore, it will be appropriate that material procurement, receiving and issuing are considered as separate activities.

(2) Identify the cost centre (cost pool) of each of the activities in Step I: After the activities have been identified, the cost of resources consumed over a specified period must be assigned to each activity. Many resources may be directly attributable to specific activity centres but others such as lighting and heating costs may be shared by several activities.

(3) Selecting the cost driver for each activity identified in Step I: The cost driver explains why resources are consumed by a particular activity, and therefore, why such activity incurs costs, for example, setting up a machine (activity). The number of set-ups (batch size) is the cost driver. Cost drivers should be significant determinants of the cost of activities.

(4) A cost driver rate for each activity cost centre (cost pool) should be calculated in the same way as overhead rate is calculated in traditional systems –

$$\text{Cost driver rate} = \frac{\text{Activity centre cost}}{\text{Activity driver}} \text{ (cost pool)}$$

$$\text{For example, Rate per set-up} = \frac{\text{Machine set-up cost}}{\text{Total set-up}}$$

(5) **Applying the activity cost driver rates to products (cost units) to arrive at activity-based overhead costs:** The last stage involves applying cost driver rates to products. Therefore, the cost drivers must be measured in a way that will enable it to be identified with the individual products.

5.5.5 Benefits of ABC

Activity-based costing leads to the identification of activities that are required to be cut in order to decrease costs. These activities include set-ups, materials handling and transportation. The advantages of activity-based costing are as follows –

1. Set-up overheads may be decreased by decreasing the time to set up, by producing bigger batches with less resultant set-ups and by using factory workers instead of costlier indirect labour to perform set-ups. Material handling costs may be decreased by making fewer deliveries to and from the factory.

2. An activity-based costing study might convince the management that they must take a few steps to become more competitive. Consequently, they could try to increase quality even while at the same time concentrating on decreasing costs. The cost analysis could emphasise just how costly the manufacturing process is. This, consecutively, could spur activities to reorganise the process, improve quality and decrease costs.

3. With the improved cost analysis, the management could carry out a correct analysis of the volume needed to break-even on low volume products.

4. The management concerned will be in a position to make more competitive bids.

5. Through an analysis of cost information and resource consumption patterns, the given management can start to re-engineer the manufacturing process to attain more efficient and higher quality output patterns.

6. Since the activity-based costing system contains numerous activity cost centres and second stage drivers, the budgeted costs that are used to conduct an activity-based costing study should be expected to be far nearer to actual costs than under traditional systems.

   This advantage decreases the necessity to conduct variance analysis between the budget and actual costing. The role of variance analysis under activity-based costing will probably diminish in importance.

7. The activity-based costing system divides the overheads into four categories, namely, unit level, batch level, product level and facility sustaining level, and thus, improves the given management's capability to make informed decisions. Traditional cost systems do not divide the overheads into those that are connected to production batches of products from those that are product sustaining, for example set-ups and material handling activities. Batch and product sustaining cost reduces only if the number of batches or products is decreased by a prospective decision. These costs are not affected if only the number of units of production is expected to reduce due to the decision.

5.5.6 Use of ABC Information for Decision-making

The process of decision-making is a significant contributor towards organisational effectiveness. Incidentally, as an aid in the decision-making process, activity-based costing can be used effectively by any organisation.

1. **Pricing**: With accurate costs in hand, the management concerned can select its strategy and pricing policy intelligently.

2. **Market Segments and Distribution Channels:** Marketing segments consist of customer groups, region's product lines and order size. Distribution channels consist of retail, wholesale and direct mail. The managers are required to understand the true costs of serving different market segments and distribution channels in order to set prices and allocate resources properly. Several costs of marketing and distribution are buried in 'selling and administrative expenses' and are required to be traced or allocated to segments and channels in order to reach accurate costs.

3. **Make-or-Buy Decisions and Outsourcing:** A good decision concerning the selection with regard to making or buying a product or to concentrate on core competencies and purchase orders requires a correct analysis of costs under each option. If overheads are assigned arbitrarily, the decision as to whether the products should be made in-house or may be bought from elsewhere cannot be correctly arrived at.

4. **Transfer Pricing:** Decentralising requires internal pricing. In all these cases in which cost-based transfer pricing is suitable, cost estimates must be given. It is significant for these prices to reflect true incremental short-run and long-run costs if correct indicators are to be given to managers.

5. **Plant Closings:** Low-cost foreign competition causes management to assess offshore production. In these cases, it is significant for the management concerned to correctly evaluate the costs under each option, including, a proper allocation of overheads and selling and administrative expenses under each option.

6. **Capital Investment:** Investment in new technology depends upon a proper assessment of costs and benefits. New technology frequently improves cycle time, increases productivity and decreases costs. Capturing the full impact of capital investment needs a correct evaluation of the impact of new technology upon overhead costs and upon quality and its costs.

Today, most companies are using ABC not only to make better-informed decisions about pricing, but also as to what type of customers to pursue, and what type of products or services to offer. Activity-based costing determines the true cost and profitability of customers, products and/or services. While traditional accounting may provide one's business with an accurate sense of the direct costs of one's products or services, indirect costs are often less accurately applied. Overheads, such as customer support or marketing costs tend to be allocated based on arbitrary factors.

Activity-based costing measures the costs and profits of an organisation based on the activities performed within that organisation. By focusing on processes that contribute to revenues and business operations, ABC can accurately determine how each process relates back to specific products, customers, or services. This can make a big difference after considering warehouse, sales, customer service, administration and other costs that are often applied at a standard rate, if required. With ABC, one can drill into profitability and performance by almost any factor one can think of.

5.6 Mergers and Acquisitions

The practice of mergers and acquisitions has attained considerable significance in the contemporary corporate scenario which is broadly used for reorganising business entities. Indian industries were exposed to a plethora of challenges both nationally and internationally, since the introduction of Indian economic reform in 1991. The cut-throat competition in international markets compelled the Indian firms to opt for mergers and acquisitions strategies, making it a vital premeditated option.

A **merger or amalgamation** is said to occur when two or more companies combine into one company. One or more companies may merge with an existing company or they may merge to form a new company. In legal terms, the term 'amalgamation' is used to denote merger. Section 2(1A) of the Income Tax Act, 1961, defines 'amalgamation' as the merger of one or more companies with another company or the merger of two or more companies (called amalgamating companies) to form a new company (called amalgamated company) in such a way that all assets and liabilities of the amalgamating company or companies become assets and liabilities of the amalgamated company and shareholders holding not less than nine-tenth in value of the shares in the amalgamating company or companies become shareholders of the amalgamated company.

Mergers or amalgamation may take two forms –

1. Merger through absorption
2. Merger through consolidation

Absorption is a combination of two or more companies into an existing company. All companies, except one, lose their identity in a merger through absorption.

Example: Absorption of Tata Fertilisers Ltd. by Tata Chemicals Ltd.

A consolidation is a combination of two or more companies into a new company. In this form of merger all companies are legally dissolved and a new entity is created. In a consolidation, the acquired company transfers its assets, liabilities and shares to the acquiring company for cash or exchange of shares. In a narrow sense, the terms 'amalgamation' and 'consolidation' are used interchangeably. An example of consolidation is the merger or amalgamation of Hindustan Computers Ltd., Hindustan Instruments Ltd., Indian Software Company Ltd. and Indian Reprographics in 1986 into an entirely new company called HCL Ltd.

Acquisition: A fundamental characteristic of merger (either through absorption or consolidation) is that the acquiring company (existing or new) takes over the ownership of other companies and continues their operation with its own operations. An 'acquisition' may be defined "as an act of acquiring effective control by one company over assets or management of another company without any combination of companies." Thus, in acquisition, two or more companies may remain independent, separate legal entity, but there may be a change in the control of companies.

Takeover: A 'takeover' may also be defined as "obtaining of control over management of a company by another." An acquisition or takeover does not necessarily entail full legal control. A company can have effective control over another company by holding minority ownership. Under the MRTP Act (Monopolies and Restrictive Trade Practices Act) 'takeover' means acquisition of not less than 25 percent of the voting power in a company. Section 372-A of the Companies Act lays down the procedure for company's investment in the shares of another company including loans and guarantees given, provided it does not exceed 60 percent of the share capital and free reserves. If a company wants to invest beyond the overall limit, it would require the prior approval of the Central Government. That apart, it would require the approval through a special resolution passed by the shareholders of the company concerned in their EOGM.

Takeover is Acquisition: Sometimes, the distinction between 'takeover' and 'acquisition' connotes forced or unwilling or hostile acquisition (called takeover) and friendly acquisition (called acquisition). In an unwilling acquisition, the management of the 'target company' would oppose a move of being taken over. When the management of acquiring and target companies mutually and willingly agrees for the takeover, it is called acquisition or friendly takeover. An example of 'acquisition' is the acquisition of the controlling interest (45 percent shares) of Universal Luggage Mfg. Company Ltd. by Blow Plast Ltd. In recent years, due to the liberalisation of the financial sector as well as of the opening up of the window for foreign investors, a number of hostile takeovers were witnessed in India. Examples include the 'takeover' of Shaw Wallace, Dunlop, Mather & Platt and Hindustan Dorr Oliver by the Chhabrias, and Ashok Leyland by the Hindujas.

Holding Company: A company can obtain the status of a holding company by acquiring shares of other companies. A holding company is a company which holds more than half of the nominal value of the equity capital of another company, called a subsidiary company or controls the composition of its Board of Directors. Both holding and subsidiary companies retain their separate legal entities and maintain their separate books of accounts. Like other countries, in USA and UK, and India, it is legally required to consolidate account of holding and subsidiary companies (AS-21 of the Indian Accounting Standards).

5.6.1 Forms of Merger

The following are the three types of mergers. They are –

1. **Horizontal Merger:** It happens when two or more companies dealing in the same lines of activity merge together. Removal or decrease in competition putting an end to price

cutting, economies of scale in production, research and development, marketing and management are the oft-cited motives underlying such mergers.

2. **Vertical Merger:** It is a combination of two or more companies, involved in different stages of production or distribution. Examples comprise the joining of a TV manufacturing (assembly) firm with a TV marketing firm or a group of a spinning company with a weaving company. Vertical merger may take the form of forward or backward merger. When a firm continues with the supplies of raw material, it is known as backward merger and, when it combines with the customer, it is called as forward merger.

3. **Conglomerate Merger:** It is a combination of companies involved in unrelated business activity. A classic example is merging of different businesses like manufacturing of cement products, fertiliser products, electronics products, insurance investments and advertising agencies. L&T and Voltas are examples of conglomerate firms.

5.6.2 Motives and Benefits of Mergers

Mergers and acquisitions are strategic decisions that maximise a company's growth by improving its production and marketing capabilities. It has accelerated because of improved competition, breaking of trade barriers, free flow of capital across countries and globalisation of business as numerous economies are being deregulated and incorporated with other economies. Several reasons are attributed to mergers and acquisitions –

- To limit competition.
- To utilise underutilised market power.
- To overcome the problem of slow growth and profitability in one industry.
- To achieve diversification.
- Gain economies of scale and increase income with proportionately less investment.
- Establish a transitional bridgehead without excessive start-up costs to gain access to a foreign market.
- Utilise under-utilised resources – human and physical and managerial skills.
- Displace existing management.
- Circumvent government regulations.
- Reap speculative gains attendant upon new security issues or change in price/earnings rates.
- Create an image of aggressiveness and strategic opportunism, empire building and to amass vast economic power for the company concerned.

Several benefits of mergers are claimed. On the basis of the empirical evidence and experience of specific firms, the most common motives and advantages of mergers and acquisition are given below –

1. Maintaining or accelerating a firm's growth, especially, when the internal growth is constrained because of insufficient resources.

2. Improving profitability through cost reductions resulting from economies of scale, operating efficiency and synergy.

Economies of scale arise because of expansion of volume of production without corresponding increase in fixed costs. Therefore, fixed costs are distributed over a larger volume of production causing the unit of production to decline. Economies of scale may also arise from other indivisibilities, for example, production facilities, management functions and management resources and system when they are utilised for a big scale of operation.

A combined company may avoid or decrease overlapping functions and facilities. It can consolidate its management functions, for example, manufacturing, marketing, R&D and thus decrease operating costs.

Synergy implies a situation where the continued company is more important than the sum of the individual combining.

1. Diversifying the risk of the firm, especially, when it acquires business whose income streams are not correlated.

2. Reducing tax liability because of the provision of setting off accumulated losses and unabsorbed depreciation of one company against the profits of another.

3. Resulting financial synergy and benefits. A merger may help in –
   - Eliminating the financial constraint.
   - Deploying surplus cash.
   - Enhancing debt capacity.
   - Lowering the financing costs.

4. Limiting the severity of competition by increasing the given company's market power.

5.6.3 Merger and Acquisition Strategies

Mergers and acquisitions are much-used strategic alternatives. They are particularly suited for circumstances in which alliances and partnerships do not go far enough in giving a company access to the much required resources and capabilities. Ownership ties are more permanent than partnership ties, enabling the operations of the merger/ acquisition participants to be tightly incorporated thereby creating more in-house control and autonomy. The difference between a 'merger' and an 'acquisition' is more connected to the details of ownership, management control and financial arrangements than to strategy and competitive advantage. The resources, competencies, and competitive capabilities of the newly created enterprise end up similarly whether the combination is the result of acquisition or merger.

Several mergers and acquisitions are driven by strategies to attain one of the following strategic objectives –

1. To pave the way for the acquiring firm to gain more market share and further create a more efficient operation out of the combined firms by closing high-cost plants and removing surplus capacity industry-wide. The merger that formed Daimler Chrysler was encouraged largely by the fact that the motor vehicle industry globally had far more production capacity than was required; the management at both Daimler Benz and Chrysler believed that the efficiency of the two firms could be considerably improved by shutting some plants and laying off employees, realigning which models were produced at which plants, and squeezing out inefficiencies by combining supply chain activities, product design and administration.

2. To expand a company's geographic coverage.

3. To extend the firm's business into new product categories or international markets. Pepsi company acquired Quaker Oats chiefly to bring Gatorade into the Pepsi family of beverages, and Pepsi company's Frito Lays division has made a series of acquisitions of foreign-based snack foods firms in order to set up a stronger presence in international markets. Firms like Nestle, Kraft, Unilever, and Proctor and Gamble, all racing for global market leadership have made acquisitions an important part of their strategies to broaden their geographic reach and broaden the number of product categories in which they compete.

4. To gain quick access to new technologies and avoid the need for a time-consuming R&D effort. For example, Cisco Systems purchased over 75 technology firms to give it more technological reach and product breadth, thereby supporting its stand as the world's largest supplier of systems for building the infrastructure of the internet. Intel has made over 300 acquisitions since 1997 to widen its technological base, and be a chief supplier of Internet technology and make it less dependent on supplying microprocessor for personal computers.

5. To try to create a new industry that would lead the way for merging industries, whose boundaries are being blurred by changing technologies and new market opportunities.

6. Acquisitions are encouraged by a firm's desire to fill resource gaps, thus, enabling the new firm to do things it could not do before. For example, Clear Channel Worldwide has used mergers and acquisitions to create a leading global position both in outdoor advertising and radio and TV broadcasting.

All mergers and acquisitions do not generate the expected results. Combining the operations of two firms, particularly the big and complex ones, often entails formidable resistance from rank-and-file organisation members, hard-to-resolve conflicts in management styles and corporate cultures, and tough problems of integration. Cost savings, expertise sharing and improved competitive capabilities may take considerably longer than expected or may never materialise at all.

5.6.4 Value created by Merger

A merger makes economic sense to the acquiring company if its shareholders benefit, that is, combined present value of the merged companies is larger than the sum of their individual values as separate entities. For example, if company 'P' and 'Q' merge and they work separately, presume the work is V_p and V_q, respectively, and work V_{pq} in combination, then, the economic advantage of merger will happen, if

$$V_{pq} > (V_p + V_q)$$

If 'P' has to pay price, say, 'Q' for acquiring V_q, then, in that case, Net Economic Advantage = $[V_{pq} - V_p - V_q]$ – [Cash paid – V_q]

Example: Company 'P' has a total market value of ₹ 18 crores (12 lakh shares of ₹ 150 market value per share). Company 'Q' has a total market value of ₹ 3 crores (5 lakh shares of ₹60 market value per share). Company 'P' is considering the acquisition of company 'Q'. The value of 'P' after merger is expected to be ₹ 25 crores. Because of operating efficiencies, company 'P' is required to pay ₹ 4.5 crores to acquire company 'Q'.

The Net Economic Advantage of Merger = [25 – 18 – 37] – [4.5-3] = ₹ 2.5 crores.

The benefit of merger ₹ 4 crores is divided between the target firm ₹ 1.5 crores and acquiring firm ₹ 2.5 crores.

The process of determining the firm's value is on several quantitative variables such as value of the assets and the earnings of the firm.

1. **Book Value:** The book value of a company is based on the balance sheet value of the owner's equity. It is determined by dividing the net worth by the number of outstanding equity shares. The book value is based on historical costs of the assets of the company concerned and do not bear any relationship either to the value of the company or to its ability to generate income.

2. **Appraisal Value:** This is a value acquired from an independent appraisal agency and is generally based on the replacement cost of assets. The technique by itself is not sufficient. Since the value of individual assets may not have much connection to the given company's overall ability to generate income, and thus, the going concern value of the company.

3. **Market Value:** Market value as reflected in the stock market quotations includes another approach for estimating the value of a business. In actual practice, a certain percentage premium above the market price is frequently suggested as an inducement for the present owners to sell their shares.

4. **Earnings per Share:** According to this approach, the value of a prospective acquisition is considered to be a function of the impact of the merger on the earnings per share. In other words, the analysis would concentrate on whether the acquisition will have a positive effect on earnings per share after merger or will it have the effect of diluting it. The future earnings per share will have an effect on the given company's share prices which is a function of price earnings (P/E) ratio and EPS.

Example: XYZ Ltd. is considering a merger with ABC Ltd. XYZ Ltd. shares are currently traded at ₹ 25. It has 200,000 shares outstanding and its Earnings after Taxes (EAT) amount to ₹ 400,000. ABC Ltd. has 100,000 shares outstanding; its current market price is ₹ 12.50 and earnings after taxes are ₹ 100,000. The merger will be effected by means of stock swap (exchange). ABC Ltd. has agreed to a plan under which XYZ Ltd. will offer the current market value of ABC Ltd. shares.

1. What are the pre-merger earnings per share (EPS) and P/E ratios of both the firms?
2. If ABC Ltd. P/E ratio is 8, what is its current market price? What is the exchange ratio? What would be the XYZ Ltd. post-merger EPS be?
3. What must the exchange ratio be for XYZ Ltd. pre-merger and post-merger EPS to be the same?

Solution: Merger and EPS

	XYZ	ABC
Market Price of equity shares	₹ 25	₹ 12.50
No. of equity shares outstanding	200,000	100,000
Earnings after Tax	₹ 400,000	₹ 100,000
EPS	₹ 2.00	₹ 1.00
P/E Ratio	₹ 12.50	₹ 12.50

If ABC Ltd. P/E ratio is 8, its current market price will be 8 × ₹ 1 = ₹ 8, then, the exchange ratio will be 8/25, that is, 32/100. For every 100 shares of ABC, 32 shares of XYZ will be issued (100,000 × 32/100), that is, 32,000 to its shareholders.

$$\text{Post-merger EPS of XYZ Ltd.} = \frac{\text{Total Earnings}}{\text{Total Shares}} = \frac{5,00,000}{2,32,000}$$

Equity shares = ₹ 2.16 per share

Next part, after merger EPS = 2, Total Earnings = ₹ 5,00,000

Hence, ₹ 500,000 ÷ ₹ 2 = 2,50,000 equity shares, that is, 50,000 shares of XYZ will have to be issued to the shareholders of ABC, that is, one share of XYZ will be issued for every two shares held by ABC shareholders.

The Biggest Mergers and Acquisitions deals in India

- Tata Steel acquired 100% stake in Corus Group on January 30, 2007. It was an all cash deal which cumulatively amounted to $12.2 billion.

- Vodafone purchased administering interest of 67% owned by Hutch-Essar for a total worth of $11.1 billion on February 11, 2007.

- India Aluminium and copper giant Hindalco Industries purchased Canada-based firm Novelis Inc. in February, 2007. The total worth of the deal was $6 billion.

- The Oil and Natural Gas Corporation purchased Imperial Energy Plc. in January, 2009. The deal amounted to $2.8 billion and was considered as one of the biggest takeovers after 96.8% of London-based company's shareholders acknowledged the buyout proposal.

- In November, 2008 NTT DoCoMo, the Japan-based telecom firm acquired 26% stake in Tata Teleservices for $2.7 billion.

- India's financial industry saw the merging of two prominent banks - HDFC Bank and Centurion Bank of Punjab. The deal took place in February, 2008 for $2.4 billion.

- Tata Motors acquired Jaguar and Land Rover brands from Ford Motors in March, 2008. The deal amounted to $2.3 billion.

- 2009 saw the acquisition of Asarco LLC by Sterlite Industries Ltd., for $1.8 billion making it the ninth biggest ever M&A agreement involving an Indian company.

- In May 2007, Suzlon Energy obtained the Germany-based wind turbine producer Repower. The 10th largest in India, the M&A deal amounted to $1.7 billion.

5.6.5 Distinction between Mergers and Acquisitions

Even if they are frequently uttered in a similar breath and used as though they were synonymous, the terms 'merger' and 'acquisition' mean slightly different things.

When one firm takes over another and clearly establishes itself as the new owner, the purchase is known as an 'acquisition'. From a legal viewpoint, the target firm ceases to exist, the buyer acquires the business and the buyer's stock continues to be traded.

A 'merger' occurs when two companies, often of about the similar size, agree to go forward as a single new firm instead of separately owning and operating a firm. This kind of action is more accurately referred to as a 'merger of equals.' Both firms' stocks are surrendered and a new company stock is issued in its place. For instance, both Daimler-Benz and Chrysler ceased to exist when the two firms merged, and a new firm, DaimlerChrysler was formed.

In practice, though, actual mergers of equals do not occur frequently. Generally, one firm buys another and as part of the deal's terms, simply allow the acquired company to declare that the action is a merger of equals, even if it is technically an 'acquisition'. Being bought out frequently carries negative connotations, and thus, by describing the deal as a 'merger', the deal-makers and top managers try to make the 'takeover' sound more pleasant.

A purchase deal will also be called a 'merger' when both CEOs agree to merge both companies. But when the deal is unfriendly, that is, when the target firm does not want to be purchased, it is always considered as an 'acquisition'.

Whether a purchase is considered a 'merger' or an 'acquisition' really depends on whether the purchase is friendly or unfriendly and how it is proclaimed. In other words, the real difference lies in how the purchase is expressed and received by the target firm's board of directors, employees and shareholders.

5.6.6 Synergy

Synergy is the magic force that allows for enhanced cost efficiencies of the new business. Synergy takes the form of revenue enhancement and cost savings. By merging, the firms concerned hope to take the advantage from the following –

- **Staff Reductions**: As every employee knows, mergers tend to mean job losses. Consider all the money saved from decreasing the number of staff members from accounting, marketing and other departments. Job cuts will also include the former CEO, who normally leaves with a compensation package.

- **Economies of Scale:** Size matters, whether it is buying stationery or a new corporate IT system, a larger firm placing the orders can save more on costs. Mergers also translate into improved purchasing power to buy tools or office supplies – when placing bigger orders, the firms concerned have a greater ability to negotiate prices with their suppliers.

- **Acquiring New Technology**: To stay competitive, firms need to be ahead in technological developments and their business applications. By purchasing a smaller firm with unique technologies, a big firm can maintain or develop a competitive edge.

- **Improved Market Reach and Industry Visibility**: Firms buy firms to reach new markets and grow revenues and earnings. A 'merger' may expand two firms' marketing and distribution, giving them new sales opportunities. A merger can also improve a firm's standing in the investment community; larger companies frequently have an easier time raising capital than smaller ones.

That said, attaining synergy is not easy – it is not automatically realised once two firms merge. Sure, there must be economies of scale when two companies are merged, but at times, a merger does just the opposite. In several cases, one and one add up to less than two.

Synergy opportunities may exist only in the minds of the corporate leaders and the deal-makers. Where there is no value to be created, the CEO and investment bankers – who have much to gain from a successful M&A deal – will attempt to form an image of improved value. The market, on the other hand, ultimately sees through this and penalises the firm concerned by assigning it a discounted share price.

5.6.7 Varieties of Mergers

From the viewpoint of business structures, there is a host of different mergers. Here are a few types, differentiated by the connection between the two firms that are merging.

- **Horizontal Merger**: Two firms that are in direct competition and share the same product lines and markets.
- **Vertical Merger**: A customer and company or, a supplier and company. Think of a cone supplier merging with an ice cream maker.
- **Market-extension Merger**: Two firms that sell similar products in different markets.
- **Product-extension Merger**: Two firms that sell different but related products in the same market.
- **Conglomeration:** Two firms that have no common business areas.

There are two kinds of mergers that are differentiated by how the merger is financed. Each has specific implications for the firms involved and for investors.

- **Purchase Mergers**: As the name implies, this type of merger happens when one firm purchases another. The purchase is made with cash or through the issue of some kind of debt instrument; the sale is taxable.

  Acquiring firms often prefer this kind of merger because it can give them a tax benefit. Acquired assets can be written-up to the actual purchase price, and the dissimilarity between the book value and the purchase price of the assets can depreciate annually, decreasing taxes payable by the acquiring firm.
- **Consolidation Mergers:** With this merger, a brand new firm is created and both firms are bought and merged under the new entity. The tax terms are the same as those of a purchase merger.

5.6.8 Acquisitions

There is not a lot of difference between an acquisition and merger except for its name. Like mergers, acquisitions are actions through which firms seek economies of scale, efficiencies and enhanced market visibility. Unlike all mergers, all acquisitions involve one company buying another – there is no exchange of stock or consolidation as a new firm. Acquisitions are frequently congenial, and all parties concerned feel happy with the deal; but, sometimes, acquisitions are more hostile.

In an acquisition, a firm can buy another firm with cash, stock or a combination of the two. Another possibility, which is common in smaller deals, is for one firm to acquire all the assets of another firm. Company X buys all of company Y's assets for cash, which means that company Y will have only cash. Of course, company Y becomes only a shell and will in the end liquidate or enter another area of business.

Another kind of acquisition is a reverse merger which is a deal that allows a private firm to get publicly-listed, in a short period of time. A reverse merger takes place when a private firm that has strong prospects and is ready to increase financing, buys a publicly-listed shell firm, generally one with no business and limited assets. The private firm reverse merges into the public firm, and together they become a complete new public company with tradable shares.

Irrespective of their group or structure, all mergers and acquisitions have one common goal; they intend to create synergy that makes the value of the combined firms bigger than the total of the two parts. The success of a merger or acquisition depends on whether this synergy is attained.

Points to Remember

- Zero-based Budgeting (ZBB) requires that organisations while preparing their budgets should not take earlier year's expenditure for granted, and therefore, should start on a clean slate. It implies that while framing a budget for the ensuing year, the given organisation should start from ground zero instead of treating the current budget as the starting point or the base.

- This approach is different than traditional budgeting techniques – the difference here lies in the analysis of alternatives. The managers concerned must identify alternative methods of performing each activity first such as evaluating the costs and benefits of making a project or outsourcing it or centralising versus decentralising operations. In addition, they must identify different levels for performing each alternative method of the proposed activity.

- Inflation accounting is a financial reporting procedure which records the consequences of inflation on the financial statements that a company prepares and publishes at the end of the financial year. It is based on the assumption that the currency is stable.

- Human Resources Accounting, also known as Human Asset Accounting involve the identifying, measuring, capturing, tracking and analysing the potential of the human resources of a company and communicating the resultant information to the stakeholders of the given company.

- The basic reason for developing HR Accounting is to overcome problems arising from the valuation of intangible assets. As organisations do not provide sufficient information to investors in the traditional balance sheet, HRA comes in handy as a device to plug this gap. In short, HRA provides an insight on employees as assets.

- HRA provides a profile to the given enterprise and thus improves its image. HRA probes ways and means for retaining intelligent human capital.

- Activity-based costing (also, activity-based accounting or activity accounting) is a system that focuses on activities as the fundamental cost objects and uses the costs of these activities as the building blocks for compiling the costs of other cost objects. It should be noted that activity-based accounting is generic, that is, it can be part of job-order product costing system or a process product costing system.

- A merger or amalgamation is said to occur when two or more companies combine to form one entity or company. One or more companies may merge with an existing company or they may merge to form an altogether new company.

- Although they are often uttered in the same breath and used as though they were synonymous, the terms 'merger' and 'acquisition' mean slightly different things.

KEY WORDS

Inflation Accounting: Inflation accounting is a financial reporting procedure which records the consequences of inflation on the financial statements that a company prepares and publishes at the end of the financial year.

Activity-based Costing: Activity-based costing (or activity-based accounting or activity accounting) is a system that focuses on activities as the fundamental costs objects and uses the costs of these activities as building blocks for compiling the costs of other cost objects.

Merger: A **merger or amalgamation** is said to occur when two or more companies combine into one company.

Questions to Discussion

1. Explain the concept of zero-base budgeting. State its merits and demerits.
2. What is inflation accounting? State its various characteristics. Also state the advantages and disadvantages of inflation accounting.
3. Write a note on 'methods for accounting of inflation'.
4. What is activity-based costing? Explain the process of activity-based costing. Explain the various benefits of activity-based costing.
5. What are 'mergers'? State the various types of mergers.
6. What are 'acquisitions'? State the meaning of 'takeover'.
7. Explain the importance of mergers and acquisitions.
8. What is human resource accounting? State its objectives and advantages.